Marcello's Promise

Marcello's Promise

Jane Coletti Perry

FIVE STAR
A part of Gale, a Cengage Company

Farmington Hills, Mich • San Francisco • New York • Waterville, Maine
Meriden, Conn • Mason, Ohio • Chicago

LIBRARY OF CONGRESS CATALOGING-IN-PUBLICATION DATA

Names: Perry, Jane Coletti, author.
Title: Marcello's promise / Jane Coletti Perry.
Description: First edition. | Farmington Hills, Mich. : Five Star, 2019. | Identifiers: LCCN 2019012400 (print) | ISBN 9781432858254 (hardcover : alk. paper)
Classification: LCC PS3616.E792964 M37 2019 (print) | DDC 813/.6—dc23
LC record available at https://lccn.loc.gov/2019012400

First Edition. First Printing: December 2019
Find us on Facebook—https://www.facebook.com/FiveStarCengage
Visit our website—http://www.gale.cengage.com/fivestar
Contact Five Star Publishing at FiveStar@cengage.com

Printed in Mexico
1 2 3 4 5 6 7 23 22 21 20 19

In memory of my grandparents and my father.

ACKNOWLEDGMENTS

In 1912 my grandmother arrived in America with her three-year-old son—my father—and joined my grandfather in Cumberland, Wyoming. They lived in this Union Pacific Coal Company town, where my grandfather was a miner, with their growing family until 1927. As a youngster, I was intrigued by stories of life in this immigrant, frontier mining town. Inspired by their experiences, I created a fictional story to honor my family before the memories disappeared forever.

I began to write when my neighbor, Carole Carter, invited me to join a group of friends at her church called Writers in the Spirit. They wrote in many genres—life stories, poetry, fiction. I remember my unease the first time I read my writing aloud to these ladies, but it was a beginning. Continuing education classes led me to join two invaluable groups: Writers' Bloc and Kansas City Writers, which were both weekly gatherings of congenial, like-minded writers who wanted to share and improve their writing skills. They read multiple drafts of *Marcello's Promise* and offered critique, support, and friendship. Larry Hightower, Judy Swofford, Greg Larson, and Aline Zimmer were early readers of the manuscript. My friend Nancy Moser, who makes writing look easy with thirty published novels to her credit, solved formatting puzzles, offered writing suggestions, answered endless questions, and gave encouragement I held dear. And I am indebted to Janie Paul, who spent hours critiquing every word of the manuscript and was perhaps my harshest critic, for making me a better writer.

I am deeply grateful to everyone at Five Star/Cengage who had a part in bringing this book to fruition, especially Tiffany Schofield and Alice Duncan. You have made Marcello and Luisa's journey into the wider world possible. I am forever in your debt.

I am grateful to Lee Smithyman for his legal advice.

I thank my husband, Dick, for his patience and support as I plugged away on my project for days, months, and years. I also thank our children, Stephen and Janet; our son-in-law, Mick; and our grandchildren, Elizabeth, Rachel, Audrey, Isabella, and Alexander, who are my inspiration for recording these stories. Remember where your family came from. I'm much appreciative of my niece, Anna, who was always a keystroke away, translating Italian for me. And to my sister, Karen, and our cousins, descendants of Italy and Cumberland, may the light of our hardworking grandparents never dim. May their big dreams live on in us and our children.

★ ★ ★ ★ ★

PART ONE: 1915–1918

★ ★ ★ ★ ★

Throw off the bowlines. Sail away from the safe harbor.
Catch the trade winds in your sail.
Explore. Dream. Discover.

—H. Jackson Brown Jr.

Chapter 1

Monastero, Northern Italy
July

"Get more water! Hurry!"

Marcello ran down the hillside to the well beside the church, his mother's words ringing in his ears. His hands shook as he lowered the bucket deep into the well, then pulled hard on the rope, raising the brimming bucket back to the surface. He hurried back up the hill to his parents' house, splashing water over the edge of the bucket as he lengthened his stride up the dirt path. When he reached the door, his legs burned, and he bent over to catch his breath.

"Mama," he asked, panting, "how is she? Is she all right?"

His mother emptied warm water from the fireplace kettle into a basin. "Shouldn't be much longer." She walked quickly to the bedroom at the back of the house, closing the door behind her. No sooner had she disappeared than the door opened again, and Marcello's mother-in-law emerged.

"Is there anything I can do?"

She took no notice of him, gathered cloths and towels from the cupboard, and hurried back to the bedroom. He stared after her as the bedroom door closed once again.

Marcello felt sweat clinging to his forehead. He ran trembling fingers through his damp hair, then emptied the bucket of water into the kettle to heat before stepping outside. The yard was deserted. Marcello's two younger brothers were gone for the day, tending the family's cows grazing in the summer pasture farther up into the hills. If this were an ordinary day, he would be with them.

But this wasn't an ordinary day.

A breeze off the mountains stirred the thick July air. He thrust his hands deep into his pockets and paced in front of the house. *Please be all right. Please be all right.* Back and forth he traveled on the dusty path, repeating his incantation. He stopped short and stared vacantly at the family home where he and his siblings had been born and raised. The whitewashed cement walls and timber roof were typical of the houses clinging to the mountains. Crumbling around the edges, the three stories leaned into the rocky hillside as though born of the earth.

How long has it been? Marcello tossed his head back and gauged the sun. *Three hours? Is that too long? Should the baby be here by now?* A sense of dread sent him back inside.

Through the bedroom door he heard his mother's voice rise. "Luisa, push now!" His stomach knotted. *Please, Holy Mother, take care of Luisa and the baby.*

His legs weak, he sank into a chair and leaned forward, elbows on his knees. He wanted a boy, a son to carry on the family name. Luisa had predicted they would have a son who would grow up to look just like him—lean and muscular with a sunny smile that would make his brown eyes sparkle beneath an unruly mop of dark hair. But more than that, she wanted him to have Marcello's optimism and penchant for hard work, his way of looking people in the eye when he spoke, humble and earnest, his easy smile. Her opinion of him was flattering and kind, but that was like her. Luisa saw the best in everyone.

A shriek split the silence, sending a jolt through Marcello's body. He sucked in the sultry air and held it, afraid to breathe, his body rigid.

Silence.

Marcello's chest tightened. He forgot all about his selfish desire for a son and pleaded for the lives of Luisa and their baby. *Please be all right. Holy Mother, let her and the baby be all right.*

The bedroom door opened.

"Come see your son." His mother nodded, and a smile spread across her face. Marcello leaped to his feet and strode to the bedroom. His mother-in-law bent over Luisa and gently wiped perspiration from her daughter's forehead. Marcello knelt beside Luisa and clasped her hand. Her unbraided raven hair spilled across the white pillow in dark ribbons. She opened her eyes with a weary smile. His gaze went from her eyes to the tiny baby wrapped in a white cloth snuggling in the crook of her arm.

He marveled at the miracle. "Our baby," he whispered. He brought Luisa's hand to his lips and kissed it, pained with the knowledge that all too soon, he would be leaving them.

Supper was over, the dishes cleared, and Marcello sat at the plank table in front of the fireplace. The two months since Tony's birth had passed quickly. Next week he and his best friend, Dominic, would buy tickets for passage to America. Marcello's parents lingered beside him in front of the dying fire. His mother leaned across the table and clutched his hand, her face taut with emotion. "Marcello, don't go. The baby's so young. We need you here."

Marcello was stunned. "I can't believe you're saying this. Mama, we've talked about this ever since Luciano left. And Luisa and I planned this before we got married. Why are you bringing it up now? What's changed?"

"We've changed." His father eyed him with an intensity Marcello hadn't seen before. "I need help taking care of the cows and harvesting the hay. Each year it gets harder for me."

"But Batista and Alfonso are here," Marcello said. "They'll help you."

"Too many in this family have gone to America," his mother replied flatly. "We lost Luciano and Angelo—"

"And they're doing well, working in the mines and sending me money so I can go, too. It was always the plan."

"And then Giovanni left." His mother continued with a sense of urgency, counting them off on her fingers. "And Michele, Giacomo, your sisters and their husbands. Thirteen children I had, and now there's just you, Batista, and Alfonso left. I know you have a wife and baby now, but don't turn your back on us. We're your family, too." She reached for the handkerchief in her apron pocket and wiped tears from her eyes.

Marcello was speechless. For as long as he could remember, he'd felt a connection with America. It began with the first letter from his oldest brother, Luciano, after he emigrated eight years ago. Only ten years old at the time, Marcello was fascinated by the curious stamps on the envelope and the news from far-off America, sent to his home in the mountains. After his older sister read the letter to the family, Mama cried, and Papa patted her hand and said, "He's young and strong. He doesn't give up easily. He'll be successful." Over the next two years, Luciano sent money until there was enough for Angelo, the next in line, to emigrate. They called it chain migration, but young Marcello knew it as the unspoken promise of America and the expectation he would be in line someday, too.

"Mama, please don't ask me to stay. After all this time, I finally have enough money to go. I can't change my plans now. I can't." Marcello's face flushed hot. He leaned forward in his chair and blurted, "I'm going. That's all there is to it."

"Don't raise your voice to your mother."

Marcello lowered his eyes at his father's rebuke and stared at the table.

"Reconsider, Marcello. We want you and your younger brothers to hold what's left of our family together," his father continued. "Someone has to care for us when we're old. Our sons and their families should do that."

Marcello raised his eyes, his brow knitted in a frown. "Papa, I thought you wanted me to make the best life for myself and my own family. The best life I can offer them is in America."

His father looked away and cleared his throat. "We hoped after Tony was born you would change your mind and stay here."

"Papa, my son is another reason to *go* to America, not stay here."

"I forbid you to go!" Mama slammed her hand on the table and stood, her eyes fierce, her lips quivering. She held her son in her gaze, then left the room.

Marcello stared after her, his mouth open. There were no words he could say to make the situation better.

"Her heart is breaking." Papa's voice trembled. "She wants to hold on to her children, but they keep slipping away. Try to understand what it's like, saying goodbye to your children and never seeing them again. Remember when Luciano left? She said it was like putting him into his coffin."

Marcello slumped in his chair. In six days he was going to buy passage to America. He would become another lost son to his mother.

Above the kitchen in the cramped loft he and Luisa shared with Tony, Marcello tried to sleep. He lay on one side for a while, rolled over, then lay on his back and stared into the darkness. When he rolled onto his side again, Luisa stirred. "What's the matter," she whispered.

"It's Mama and Papa."

"You argued with them."

"You heard us? I thought you were asleep."

"I heard some of it. They want you to stay."

"Yes."

"What did you say?"

"That I was going anyway. You should have seen their faces. Mama left in tears."

"But it's too late. Don't they understand how much you want this, not just for yourself but for me and Tony?"

"I thought they understood. I think, deep down, they do."

"What are we going to do? If you don't go now, you'll have to wait till next spring."

"I can't put it off till next year, and I won't even think about staying here permanently." Marcello considered the small plot of land his family owned, the rows of beans and onions in the garden beside the house, brown and wilted from the summer heat, the tangled vines of squash and tomatoes that spread toward the grape arbor at the back of the property. He shook his head in the darkness. Feeding a family of fifteen was a lot to ask of such a small piece of land. He admired how his parents toiled. Backbreaking work and a sufficient supply of cow manure coaxed a living from the land.

He ran his finger down the profile of Luisa's nose. "We've been over this so many times. If we stay here, our children's future is the same as ours—a few cows and a plot of ground."

Luisa slid closer to Marcello and settled into the crook of his arm. "Going to America is right for us. We both know that."

"I think they know I'm going, even after what was said tonight. It was their last try to keep me here." Marcella stroked Luisa's hair. "Tomorrow I'll do my best to make it clear this is best for me. They've always wanted the best for their children."

He held her close, nuzzling her hair. As Luisa fell asleep, Marcello's mind drifted back to that perfect autumn day three years ago when he met her. He and his family never missed the

Ferragosto harvest festival each September in Coassolo, the village across the valley. Marcello had just turned seventeen and decided he wouldn't attend the festival that year.

"I'm too old for this," he had told his mother.

"It's a holy day of obligation, Marcello."

"But Mama."

"The whole family is going, and you're not too old to come with us. Besides, for a boy who likes to eat as much as you, remember there's always lots of food.

Marcello couldn't argue with that.

After Mass the day of the festival, Marcello walked from the cool confines of the Coassolo stucco church into the brilliant afternoon and stood on the steps. Brightly colored harvest banners hung from a wire across the front of the church. Three men wearing white tunics and green sashes began playing folk songs on their accordions to the delight of the crowd. The lively cadence of a tarantella floated through the air and drew young and old onto the cobblestone piazza, transforming it into a dance floor. Tables and chairs sat scattered in the shade of the church where villagers ate plates piled with food and clapped in time to the music.

"Hey, Marcello, come dance!" His friend Dominic hollered from the crowd of dancers as he whirled by with his girlfriend.

"No thanks." Marcello raised his voice above the laughter and music. "I came to eat." He grinned and patted his stomach. Dominic, bright-eyed and energetic, paused momentarily and cupped his hand to his ear. "I came to eat," Marcello hollered and was about to tease his friend about not hearing, given that he had such prominent ears, but thought better of it. That would give Dominic an opening to tease him about being a clumsy dancer.

He wove his way through the crowd to a long wooden table laden with platters of prosciutto, salami, and cheese. Bowls brimmed with sliced zucchini and tomatoes marinated with olive oil, vinegar, and basil. Freshly harvested plums and grapes spilled out of baskets. The villagers had worked hard, saving the best of their harvest to make the festival successful.

He grabbed a thick slice of bread, drizzled it with olive oil, and piled on slices of salami and cheese. After adding prosciutto and fruit to his plate, he walked to a table and sat down.

And then he saw her.

She stood talking with a group of girls. He guessed she was about his age. Thick black hair framed her round face and hung loose at her shoulders. She wore a simple white blouse tucked into a blue skirt that fell into folds from her waist to just above her bare feet. The summer sun had tanned her face and arms. Marcello couldn't take his eyes off her. There was something about her, something he felt all the way across the piazza. The girls broke into laughter, and she tossed her head back, joining in. Suddenly she turned in Marcello's direction and caught his gaze with wide dark eyes. She brushed her hair from her face and gave him a shy smile, then looked away.

In that moment, Marcello felt as though he had known her all his life. He left his food untouched, got up from the table, and walked across the piazza to ask Luisa to dance.

That weekend, Marcello hiked across the valley to Luisa's village. He helped her walk their cows to pasture that morning and milk them in the evening. He returned the next weekend and the next. He adored everything about her—her devotion to her widowed mother, how she cared for her siblings when they were sick, her enjoyment in preparing even simple meals of polenta, the care she took growing flowers by her mother's front step. They walked along the Tesso River, which zigzagged through the mountains near the village. Sitting on the river bank they skipped rocks across the shallow waters, talking, teasing, laughing. When Luisa spoke, the lightness of music in her voice reflected the kindness Marcello found in her heart.

One evening in early spring, when the earth smelled damp and stars scattered across the velvet sky, Marcello and Luisa sat together on the hillside by her house. He took both her hands in his.

"I've wanted to go to America ever since I can remember, but it was just for me. You've changed my dream. It's so much bigger now—it's for both of us. I don't want you to be just my sweetheart—I want you to be my wife. I love you, Luisa. Come to America with me. I'll work hard—harder than anyone's ever worked—and I'll take care of you. I'll make a good life for us, I promise."

Luisa leaned into his arms as he wrapped them around her. "Yes, oh, yes," she whispered.

He continued to share his dream, the words tumbling from his mouth. "I'll be a miner, like my brothers. I'll save my money and build a house for us."

"What will our house be like?" Luisa rested her cheek against his chest and listened to the deep resonance of his voice.

"Big enough for all our children," Marcello teased.

Luisa looked up at him and blushed with a smile. "A house for our family . . . and what about a school for our children?"

"They'll get a good education." Marcello grew serious. "And not stop after the fourth year, like we did."

"Our families didn't have a choice. They didn't have money to pay beyond that."

"In America we'll have enough money so our children will finish all the grades, and if they want to go to college, I'll find a way. They'll become teachers or shop owners."

"Or farmers who own land with hay fields that go on forever," Luisa finished. She looked down at her feet and wiggled her toes. "What about shoes?"

"Shoes?" Marcello laughed. "As many pairs as you like. You can wear shoes every day if you want. Even in the summer."

Marcello pulled Luisa close and sealed his promise with a kiss. They would live their lives surrounded by their children with a contentment that comes from accomplishing their goals through opportunity and hard work. With his success, the wolf would no longer be at the door. In America, he would banish the wolf from their lives forever.

Marcello burst through the front door after his day in Lanzo. "I got my tickets. Everything's taken care of." He pulled papers from his shirt pocket and unfolded them, holding them out for Luisa to see. "This one's for the train from Lanzo to Le Havre."

"Le Havre is the port?"

"The same one Luciano and Giovanni sailed from. And here's the ticket for the ship to New York." He kissed the precious paper and waved it in the air. "New York, Luisa, can you believe it? This makes it real—I'm really going!" With a whoop, he grabbed her around the waist and spun her in a circle, a wide grin on his face.

"My gracious, you *are* excited, Mr. Corsi," Luisa caught her breath with a smile and smoothed her apron. She turned to the task at hand and dumped her garden basket of squash and tomatoes on the kitchen table. "What ship are you on?"

His eyes scanned the ticket. "*La Provence.*"

"And the date?" Luisa sliced the squash, her knife thumping against the battered table.

"October fifteenth—that's the day we leave from Lanzo."

Luisa was silent as she scooped squash into a pot. "That's only four weeks away." She turned to Marcello with a forced smile, but he saw the tears in her eyes.

"Don't cry. I can't stand it if you cry." The thrill of claiming his long-awaited prize vanished in an instant. Marcello drew her into his arms. "The thought of leaving you and Tony . . ." His throat tightened, choking off his words. He drew back and held her face in his hands. "I'll get work right away and start saving money so you can join me as soon as possible. I don't think it will take long. We'll be together again before we know it."

"Oh, Marcello, I—" A cry came from their bedroom. "Let me get him." Luisa climbed the wooden stairs to the loft and returned with a squirming bundle in her arms. She sat in a chair beside the fireplace and held Tony close, rocking from side to side, humming softly.

Marcello looked down at the papers in his hand and then at Luisa as she soothed Tony. Caught in the glow of the fire, she had never looked more beautiful, her gentle song wrapping their baby in peace. Marcello etched the moment in his heart. "It will be worth it, Luisa, I promise."

Luisa stopped rocking and gently laid Tony across her lap. She studied his face and traced her finger over his pink cheek. "Don't worry. We'll be all right, Tony and me."

Marcello pulled a stool next to Luisa's chair and sat. She reached for his hand. "Your parents love me like one of their own. They'll take care of us, and we'll take care of them." The traces of tears were gone from her eyes. "It's me who will worry about you. You're taking a chance going to the mine in Kansas and not to Wyoming like your other brothers. You're sure Giovanni knows what he's talking about?"

"I'm sure. Giovanni's always been the brother to go off on his own, but he knows what he's doing. He says there are lots of jobs at his mine. They aren't hiring at the Wyoming mine right now, and I'll get to Kansas sooner anyway. I'll have three or four months' work finished in no time."

Marcello looked down at their son. He slipped his index finger into Tony's hand, and the tiny fingers latched on. "Life's going to be better for you, my son," he whispered. "Better for all of us."

What Marcello couldn't say, what he couldn't tell Luisa, were his own fears buried so deep he refused to acknowledge them: leaving his parents without their blessing; being separated from Luisa and Tony for what would probably be years, not months; and the greatest fear—failing to provide Luisa the kind of life he had promised her.

It was time to put his dream in motion.

Chapter 2

October

The sun crept into the valley, spreading brilliant rays across the treetops in Monastero. Marcello had watched the day begin from his loft window every morning since he could remember. Most mornings he gave it only a brief glance before going downstairs for breakfast and chores. Today he lingered as the sky transformed from gray to blush pink to bright gold.

He felt a sad longing, knowing he was losing this part of his life forever. He loved this place. The river wandering between towering hills and the white-capped mountains to the north would forever be a part of him. He would miss his home but knew it was part of his past, not his future.

His cardboard suitcase lay open on the bed. Two shirts, a pair of trousers, and a sweater Luisa had knitted for him lay folded inside. That was enough, he figured, until he got a job and could afford to buy more clothes. He had lira equal to twenty-five American dollars in the wallet he placed with the tickets in the pocket of his new shirt. He folded his cap, stuffed it into the back pocket of his trousers, and pulled on his jacket.

"You have your tickets?" Luisa asked for the third time.

With a faint smile on his lips Marcello patted his pocket. "Right here." Luisa wrapped a shawl around her shoulders and lifted Tony from his crib. Marcello picked up his suitcase and followed Luisa down the creaking wooden stairs.

The aroma of coffee and fried eggs lingered in the kitchen.

The Corsis had found it difficult to eat this last meal together, so they ate in silence, barely looking at one another. Marcello's stomach roiled with nervous anticipation at leaving home and beginning his long journey, but he forced himself to eat to please his mama.

Luisa cradled Tony in her arms. "We'll wait outside, Marcello, so you can say goodbye to Mama and Papa." Marcello's brothers shifted uneasily by the front door and followed Luisa out into the early autumn morning.

His father stood by the fireplace and stared at the floor, his arm around Marcello's mother. She leaned against him as she wiped away tears that would not stop. In front of her on the table sat his satchel bulging with food. Of course, this is how she would say goodbye, Marcello thought. Nurturing through food had always been her way. She performed baking miracles, making loaves of bread magically appear so her family always had enough to eat. The Corsi children didn't have much—thin coats in the winter, no shoes in summer—but there was always bread. In late winter when rations dwindled, their mother's bread was manna straight from heaven, hearty with a golden, crunchy crust. She got up before dawn the day before his departure to bake bread for his journey.

It took every bit of Marcello's self-control to keep his emotions in check as he went to his mother. His heart ached. Her gray hair was pulled back in a bun; the beauty of her youth lingered, though her face was lined and weathered. She was usually strong and cheerful, but today her head bent down, her shoulders sagged. He leaned over and hugged her as she wept.

She drew in a jagged breath. "You must take care of yourself . . . there're so many dangers out there . . . you must be careful." Her tiny frame shook.

"I will, Mama. I'll take care of myself."

She continued to cry, and Marcello held her until her shaking stopped. She leaned back and reached up to smooth the lock of hair falling over his forehead, just as she had done when he was a child. Her fingers traced the scar just above his right eyebrow, memorizing the details of his face. Marcello didn't remember the fall he'd taken on the rocks beside the front door, only that his mother said he bled more than any little boy should have.

"My dear boy, Marcello. You leave, like all the others, but I'm not angry. It's the way it will be." Her eyes filled with fresh tears. "I hope you find work soon."

"I will, Mama. I'll make you and Papa proud." Marcello hugged her again. "I love you, Mama."

"I love you, son." She grabbed her handkerchief and covered her face.

Marcello turned to his father and extended his hand. "Papa . . ."

His father ignored the outstretched hand and embraced Marcello. "We pray for you, Marcello. For safe travel and good health." His voice faltered. "I love you, my son."

Marcello caught his breath. "I love you, Papa." They clapped each other on the back, and Marcello stepped back for one more look at his father. He saw his stooped posture, gnarled hands, and face creased with sadness beyond tears.

His father reached into his shirt pocket and pulled out a coin that he pressed into Marcello's hand. "This is for you. It's not much, but I hope it will help."

"Papa, I can't . . ."

His father shook his head. "Take it, son."

Marcello stared at the silver lira in his hand. It reminded him of his autumn job as a youngster, to gather chestnuts and sell them in the village. He'd run home with his pay, a coin like this one, and proudly give it to his father, as a contribution to the family. Marcello understood in his father's eyes, the coin he'd just received had greater value as a gift from father to son than as income for the family.

Marcello's resolve fell apart and his eyes flooded. "Thank you, Papa," and he embraced his father again. He slipped the coin into his shirt pocket, wiped his eyes, and picked up his bags. He forced a smile for his parents, looked at them one last time, and summoned the courage to turn away and walk out the door.

Marcello stared at the path as Luisa and his brothers walked down the hill with him in silence. When they reached the village, the sunrise spilled across the piazza, bathing the stucco buildings in a golden glow. It was deserted except for Dominic and his parents, who waited beside a horse-drawn cart in front of the church.

Dominic waved to Marcello. "Ready?" He forced a smile.

Marcello shook his head. "My mama and papa . . ." His voice trailed off.

"I know," Dominic whispered. "I've never seen my papa cry, never. Until this morning." Dominic stole a quick glance at his father. "I suppose we should be going."

Marcello took a deep breath. "I suppose." He put his bags in the back of the cart, and Dominic's parents climbed onto the seat in the front. Marcello hugged each of his brothers. They wiped their eyes and stepped aside, their heads down. Luisa gently placed Tony in Marcello's arms. He looked into his son's sleeping face and whispered, "Papa's going on a long trip. I'm going to miss you very much." He laid his cheek on Tony's head, memorizing the feel of his downy hair and the tiny sounds of his breathing. "Be a good boy for Mama, and do what she tells you." Tony wriggled but continued to sleep peacefully. Marcello kissed him.

He reluctantly gave the baby to Luisa and wrapped both of

them in his arms. Luisa buried her face in his shoulder. "Be safe, Marcello." She choked back a sob. "Be careful . . . take care of yourself." Her lips trembled as they brushed his cheek.

"I'll write you the first chance I get. Promise me you'll write often, and tell me how you and Tony are getting along."

"I will."

"I'll let you know as soon as I find work."

"Please be careful. It's such a long way."

Marcello lifted her chin and kissed her lips. "I love you so much."

"I love you." Luisa's cheeks were wet with tears.

Dominic cleared his throat. "Time to go."

Marcello embraced Luisa one last time and climbed into the back of the cart beside Dominic. The horse leaned forward and clopped away from the church, the sound of his hooves bouncing off the cobblestones in the silent morning.

Luisa took a few hurried steps following the cart. "You still have your tickets?"

"Still here," Marcello patted his pocket and managed a smile.

"Remember, write us as soon as you can, so we know you're all right." Luisa stopped following the cart as it pulled farther away.

"I will. I promise."

The cart turned onto the road that led down the hill to Lanzo. Marcello's eyes never left Luisa. He continued to wave as the distance grew between them, until the road curved under the canopy of trees and she disappeared from view, all the while praying he was worthy of what awaited him on the other side of the ocean.

Chapter 3

The steam engine hissed before its afternoon departure from the Lanzo train station. Marcello and Dominic boarded the train, found two empty seats in the last car, and stowed their bags in the overhead rack. Marcello slid into the seat next to the window and carefully returned his tickets to his shirt pocket. The jumble of passengers already on board leaned out open windows, waving to the crowd on the platform.

Dominic jumped up and released their window latch to lower the pane of glass so they could join in the rush of farewells. They leaned out the window and Dominic waved to the unfamiliar faces gathered beside the train. "Goodbye, Lanzo," he hollered.

Marcello whispered into the wind, "Goodbye, Luisa."

A shrill whistle drowned out the last goodbyes, and the train suddenly lurched forward. It crawled away from the station, the engine gaining momentum, spewing smoke and noise. Each chug of the engine pulled at Marcello, the power resonating deep inside him, replacing his sadness with anticipation.

The train gathered speed, its power overwhelming. The wind caught him full in the face, making his eyes water and his hair stand on end. Faster and faster it sped, feeding Marcello's hunger for adventure. They crested a hill, and Marcello erupted in a whoop of excitement. "Whoo-eee! We're really on our way!"

Dominic gulped the blasts of air. "How fast do you think

we're going?" They looked at each other, unable to stop grinning.

In the exhilaration of the moment, Marcello flashed back to a childhood memory of his father telling stories at night by the fire, stories of ghosts and magical beasts. Marcello imagined he was riding one of those magical beasts now, charging through the countryside, past villages and farms, fields and orchards. The beast gathered speed, all-powerful and unstoppable, as it wound through the valleys. When it approached the mountains in the north, the beast strained and bellowed. Smoke poured from its belly and sparks flew by the window, smacking Marcello's face. When the beast labored through the mountains, smoke and cinders forced Marcello to close the window. His face was cold from the chill mountain air. He raked his fingers through his tousled hair and leaned back in his seat.

Dominic dug through his bag. "We haven't eaten since breakfast. You hungry?" He pulled out grapes, a wedge of cheese, and a canteen of water.

"I'm starving." Marcello reached for his satchel and brought out salami and bread. He sliced the salami with his pocketknife and broke off a chunk of bread, sharing them with Dominic. They ate their supper while the train chugged through the frosty mountain passes into France.

"Do you think we'll have trouble finding a place to stay in Le Havre?" Dominic finished his salami and licked his fingers.

"The ticket agent said there are lots of boardinghouses near the docks. We'll have to see when we get there." Marcello stared out the window at the fading light and found himself frowning. Would they have any trouble being understood when they got to Le Havre? It wasn't Italy, after all. Would the boardinghouses be overcrowded? Would it be safe to sleep among strangers? He had heard tales of thieves who preyed on travelers and stole their money in the night while they slept. He and Dominic planned to sleep with their lira in their shirt pockets.

He slid down into his seat. Everyone he knew who had emigrated from Italy had sailed from Le Havre. Surely, he and Dominic wouldn't have any trouble, either. The chatter of passengers faded to a quiet hum, and his eyes grew heavy as he watched the landscape slip into darkness. Finally, he surrendered to the swaying motion of the train and closed his eyes.

They arrived in Le Havre the next afternoon and found a rundown boardinghouse a block from the shipyards. The room was Spartan—bare floor, double bed, and a nightstand. It was clean enough, but with a cold rain falling by nightfall, it wasn't much warmer in their room than it was outside in the damp October night.

"I can't sleep. It's freezing in here." Dominic pulled the thin blanket away from Marcello.

"I told you to put on more clothes," chided Marcello. He had pulled his heavy sweater over his jacket before climbing into bed. "And stay on your side of the bed," he added, yanking the blanket back to his side.

"Does this mean you're not keeping my side warm if I get out of bed?"

"Don't start. I'm in no mood for jokes."

Dominic leaped out of bed and threw on his jacket. He blew on his hands as he rubbed them together. "I swear, I can see my breath in here." He scrambled back into bed and slid under the blanket.

Marcello rolled over and faced the wall. "Think you can sleep now? Tomorrow's a big day." A slow roll of thunder rumbled in the distance.

"Biggest day of my life . . ." Dominic yawned. "I can get to sleep. Just don't snore."

★ ★ ★ ★ ★

Their coat collars turned up and caps pulled down, Marcello and Dominic walked briskly through a cold drizzle, bags in hand, to the shipyard the next morning. Fog enveloped the dock. Odors of fish and dampness permeated the salty air. They joined the horde of steerage passengers crammed in the third-class boarding area and waited. Finally, burly dockworkers opened a clanking metal gate, and the crowd spilled onto the gangway. As they inched their way up the ramp, Marcello could just make out the hulking shape of *La Provence.* He stopped short and grabbed Dominic's arm.

"Look at that. It's huge." He tipped his head back and followed the ship's outline upward until the smokestacks disappeared into the fog.

"I'm glad it's big," said Dominic. "I don't want to go to America on some cheap little boat."

They followed the stream of steerage passengers, damp from the rain, lugging their baggage down three flights of metal stairs into the dark bowels of *La Provence.*

"Where do we go now?" Dominic asked when they reached the bottom. Marcello shrugged. Two young men in uniform stood beside the stairs and handed each passenger a tin plate, bowl, cup, and utensils. They pointed Marcello and Dominic toward a large open compartment crammed with metal bunks stacked three high.

Passengers pushed past them toward the bunks to claim beds. "Better grab a bed while we can," said Marcello. They tossed their satchels on neighboring top bunks and stowed their other bags on the floor underneath. Marcello raised his head and sniffed the air. "What's that smell?"

Dominic inhaled. "It's sour. Like bad milk."

"Why would it smell bad already? We haven't even left the port."

Marcello and Dominic went up on deck to watch their departure from Le Havre, but the sky opened and forced them below. Rain battered the ship the rest of the day. Marcello peered through the slats of the vents in the dormitory, hoping to catch a glimpse of the sea, but when the fog lifted, all he saw was a canvas of gray—gray water, gray sky, gray rain. By evening the gentle pitch of the ship changed noticeably to sharp jerks.

At suppertime, four crew members brought kettles of meat and boiled turnips into the dormitory and set up to serve the long line of hungry passengers. With plates in one hand and bowls in the other, Marcello and Dominic received their rations and sat at one of the plank tables.

Dominic picked up his fork and poked at the mushy turnips on his plate. "Guess it's better than nothing."

Marcello inspected the meat and turned up his nose. "This looks awful. Maybe I'll eat Mama's bread instead."

"Eat the meat, or whatever this is, and save the bread. We might have food worse than this before we get there."

After supper Marcello and Dominic rinsed their dishes in the lavatory, understanding they were responsible for returning their table service on the last day of the crossing. They returned to their bunks and stretched out on the narrow mattresses, trying to get comfortable. The man in the bunk on the other side of Marcello appeared to be asleep. He began to toss in his bed and muttered something Marcello didn't understand. The muttering turned to a moan as the man clutched his stomach. Marcello looked at Dominic and rolled his eyes, nodding his head toward the annoying passenger. Suddenly the man leaned over the side of his bunk and retched.

"No!" shouted Marcello. He leaped to the floor, but not before vomit splattered his bunk and left a slippery mess underfoot.

The man rolled back onto his bed and covered his face with

his hands. Marcello stood as far away from the stinking mess as possible and eyed his soiled bunk with disgust. "Tell me again, how many days till we get there?"

Chapter 4

Marcello and Dominic climbed the dark stairwell and stepped out into fresh air and sunshine. After eleven days, they'd gained their sea legs; they strode across the rolling deck to their usual place along the rail. They leaned their backs against it and tilted their faces toward the brilliant morning sun, a cheering antidote to the gloom of the dormitory. The wind was crisp. It whipped around them as they pulled their collars tight. Marcello thanked God for the respite from the stench in steerage and filled his lungs with deep breaths. The fresh air cleansed from the inside out.

Marcello looked at his friend. "It's horrible down there. I never imagined how awful a ship could smell. Someone sicked-up in the latrine last night, and it's still not cleaned up."

"I can't get the smell out of my nose. Or my clothes. Mama put a bar of lye soap in my bag. I'll need a scrubbing bath when we get out of here."

"You say that like you take lots of baths." Marcello punched Dominic. "Let's walk."

They fell in pace with the passengers circling the deck who had escaped the heavy air of the hold. Marcello tipped his head side to side to relieve the stiffness in his neck. Dominic swung his arms as they lengthened their stride to go around a heavily bearded man arm in arm with an elderly woman. They passed a tall, olive-skinned girl with three small children in tow and a plumpish woman, a headscarf over her blond hair, chattering to a companion.

"Tomorrow we arrive in America," Marcello announced, as though he and Dominic hadn't counted every day of the crossing. "I remember how excited I was after I bought my ticket and saw 'New York' stamped across the top. It still doesn't seem real, does it, that tomorrow we'll stand on the solid ground of New York."

"This time tomorrow, it will be very real, and none too soon for me. I'm so tired of that vile place," said Dominic. They slowed and eased next to the rail on the opposite side of the promenade.

Marcello leaned his elbows on the cold metal and watched the ocean swells. "I can't wait for the first sight of the Statue of Liberty." He adjusted his balance as the ship dipped into the troughs, then turned to Dominic. "What do you want to do first?"

"Find some decent food."

"That's not what I meant."

"Take a bath?"

Marcello gave Dominic an annoyed look. "The most important thing to do is—"

"Get a job, of course."

"A job in the mine. But I don't want to be just *any* miner. I want to be really good at my job."

"*And* earn lots of money," nodded Dominic. "So, what else?"

"Learn English so I can become a citizen."

"So do I. What does it take to become a citizen?"

The ship dipped into the surging waves and sprayed their jackets. They jumped back from the railing and shook off the cold water. "You could say this puts a damper on you and your big plans," chuckled Dominic.

Marcello rolled his eyes. "Dampen my plans—very funny," Marcello said. A second spray doused their faces. "We'd better go below before we drown." When they reached the stairwell, Marcello stared at the dark hole. "Some choice. Get drenched up here or go below to a place not fit for beasts."

Dominic clapped Marcello on the back. "Only one more day," he said, and together they descended the iron stairs into the gloomy hold.

Marcello and Dominic woke early and washed up quickly, using Dominic's soap. They put on their cleanest shirts and combed their hair. With bags in hand they joined the migration of steerage passengers laden with suitcases, bundled clothes, baskets, and satchels and climbed the stairwell for the last time.

A blast of cold air hit Marcello when he stepped onto the deck, and he turned up his collar as he looked around. "Let's find a good place before they're all taken." They bumped their way through the growing crowd to the railing, where they set down their bags. "We should have a good view from here."

Sun broke through the high clouds and sparkled a path on the ocean surface. Dominic squinted toward the horizon. "I don't see anything yet. How long before we see land?"

"The old man from Naples told me we're near land when we see birds overhead."

Dominic frowned. "How does he know?"

"Said his brother made the trip before. He seems to know everything."

"What does he know about the doctor's exam at Ellis Island?"

"He said most everybody passes the exam, and only a few are turned away." Marcello spoke with authority.

"We shouldn't have any trouble. We're both healthy." The concern on Dominic's face belied his confident tone.

"Strong as a couple of horses, you and me. We'll be fine." Marcello looked away and watched the ship cut through the waves. He remembered the stories he had heard about immigrants who were refused entrance at Ellis Island. It was difficult not to be worried. Trachoma, a contagious eye disease that could lead to blindness, was the immigrants' great fear. Those found to have it were sent back to their port of departure. He could think of nothing worse. After waiting so many years, after coming this far, he and Dominic had to make it through Ellis Island.

Marcello jerked his head back. "There they are, Dominic." High overhead, seagulls floated on air currents, squawked, and dipped toward the ocean, then circled upward.

Moments later shouts erupted. *"Terra!" "Ziema!"* "Land!"

Marcello caught his breath. "Where? I don't see it." Passengers pressed against his back as they crowded the rail, searching the horizon for their first glimpse of America. Marcello kept his eyes on the horizon. What looked like a smudge of clouds slowly revealed itself as sails from a cluster of ships. He blinked in the glare. The ships grew larger as buildings rose behind them like creatures from the sea.

A cheer went up through the crowd. "America!"

"We're almost there." Dominic embraced Marcello in a bear hug.

The man beside Dominic lifted his young daughter onto his shoulders. An old woman in a tattered coat and headscarf stood next to Marcello. Stooped with age, she clutched her companion's hand and wiped tears from her eyes. As he looked at her weathered face, Marcello saw his mama and realized hope for the future knew no age. It belonged to everyone. The old woman glanced his way, and Marcello nodded respectfully. She acknowledged their shared joy with a small smile.

The chant continued. "America! America!"

Another hour passed before they entered the busy harbor. Marcello stared in amazement at the spectacle. Tugboats sped up and down the wide river blasting their horns. Ships anchored at docks ringed the sprawling harbor. In the distance, more buildings than he had ever seen towered into the sky. The sun reflected off their windows and cast a glittering display for their arrival. As the ship neared the port, they heard distant shouts from workmen on the docks and the clang of metal.

La Provence approached Liberty Island, and the passengers suddenly became silent. Marcello held his breath and pulled off his cap as the ship glided past the Statue of Liberty. Her exquisitely chiseled face sent shivers down his back. He looked up at the spires in her crown and her torch thrust into the sky and felt his heart hammer in his chest. How beautiful! He couldn't wait for Luisa to see her, too.

The clapping began quietly, then rose in volume as the crowd cheered until it reached a thunderous level and drowned out all other sound. Marcello clapped and clapped, then raised both fists in the air.

"Uraa, l'America!"

"Why are they leaving, and we aren't?" Marcello frowned, puzzled at the process. He and Dominic stood with the steerage passengers behind a metal barricade on deck and watched a large group of passengers disembark at the Port of New York. He turned to an attendant standing nearby, pointed to the barricade, and raised his arms in a question. When Marcello couldn't understand the reply, he flopped his arms to his sides and shook his head.

"They're first and second class," a man behind him said. "We have to go to Ellis Island."

Marcello ached to get off the ship, to plant his feet on America, but could only watch in envy. Confused and restless, the steerage class waited until a ship official finally arrived with a ledger under his arm. As he read their names, the passengers came forward and collected a numbered tag to pin to their clothing. The man's accent sounded so odd, Marcello and Dominic strained to recognize their own names.

"Mar-kello Cresi," the ship official barked. "Mar-kello Cresi."

"Questosonoio," Marcello shouted and hurried forward to get his tag. *"Mar-chello Corsi, non Cresi. Il mionome e Mar-chello Corsi."*

The official made no response, simply thrust a tag in Marcello's hand and called the next name. "Dominic Me-kina."

"Si," Dominic signaled with a wave of his arm and collected his tag.

Their initial excitement faded as the official droned through the passenger list. Marcello drummed his fingers on the railing, frustrated at the painfully slow progress. With hundreds of passengers to tag, he was certain he'd be an old man before he got off *La Provence.* Disheartened, he sat down on the deck beside Dominic and dug through his satchel for the remnants of his loaf of bread. He found two crusty heels and gave one to Dominic.

"Here. It's going to be a long morning."

"Thanks." Dominic reached into his bag. "I have a few figs," and he gave Marcello a handful.

Marcello took a bite of bread. "The last from home." Now stale and dry, the bread no longer had the taste or texture of Mama's fresh loaves, but in his heart that was what he tasted. It hit him like a physical blow that he would never taste his mother's bread again. He savored the last swallow.

His heart so filled with eagerness to begin life in America suddenly ached for his family, for Luisa and Tony. He stared past the strangers around him, and his eyes flooded with unwelcome tears. He stood and turned away from Dominic into the wind to use it as the excuse for his watery eyes, for if he spoke the truth, he would surely break down and cry.

The ship attendant continued to read names, but Marcello heard nothing. He was in the kitchen with Mama and Papa, embracing them one last time. He was holding Tony, smelling the sweetness of his head. He was watching Luisa wave as the cart carried him from the village. The weight of his loss and the uncertainty of the future made his knees weak, and he swayed against the railing.

When the roll call finally concluded, the barricade came down, and the crowd sprang to life, spilling onto the gangway like water over a dam. Caught in the tangle of passengers and baggage, Marcello and Dominic were swept toward the waiting barge, the sharp edges of suitcases propelling them forward. With every inch of the barge crammed with bodies and baggage, a whistle shrieked, and the craft jerked away.

"We're like chickens going to market," Dominic hollered over the roar of the motor.

"What?" Marcello cupped his ear and leaned toward Dominic.

"Chickens to market."

"What chickens?" Marcello yelled.

"Forget it!"

There was nothing to protect them from the November wind. Marcello hunched his shoulders against the cold with a shiver and thrust his hands deep into his pockets. As the barge cut through the choppy water, he braced his legs to keep his balance.

"Hey, Marcello, look there!" Dominic pointed to a massive red brick building so large it looked like two or three joined as one. Thick white stone edged every window on its three stories. A canopy covered the long walk from the dock to the double-door entrance flanked by imposing white stone arches. Square spires topped with copper domes rose over the blue slate roof from each of the four corners like a cathedral.

They had reached Ellis Island.

Chapter 5

It wasn't what Marcello expected.

Ellis Island, the place where your dream could begin or end, the place of joy or profound sadness, didn't look like the fearsome port of entry Marcello imagined. To him, it looked like a palace.

The barge eased into a slip. Dockhands hollered as they secured the craft with ropes and slammed the metal gangway into place. The first thing Marcello noticed was officials in dark uniforms who directed the passengers toward the walkway to the front door.

"Are they American police?" Dominic whispered. Although their village back home was not large enough to require policing, the residents of Monastero were suspicious of police, fearful of their reputation for overreaching authority.

"Police?" Marcello suppressed a shudder, his fascination with the majesty of Ellis Island suddenly over. "I don't know . . . maybe. Don't look at them. Just keep walking." They had been advised aboard ship to cooperate at Ellis Island. Stay in line, don't push or shove, never raise your voice or argue—just get through processing as quickly as possible.

Once inside the front door, Marcello stopped and gaped at the enormous room. At the top of the grand stairway before him, three doctors in white coats peered down at the arriving immigrants, observed them as they climbed the stairs, then wrote notes on clipboards. His stomach clenched. Marcello nudged Dominic with his satchel. "Look up there. Those are the doctors."

"What are they doing?" Dominic asked.

"I'm not sure."

Gripping their bags, they climbed the steep stairs side by side. Marcello felt eyes boring through him and glanced up once. He was certain the doctors were studying each passenger and making some determination about their health. When they reached the top, he and Dominic were herded in a group between waist-high railings to the first doctor's examination.

The line was at a standstill. Marcello craned his neck but couldn't see why they weren't moving. "What's taking so long?" he muttered to Dominic. They inched forward a few steps, then stopped. Their slow progress only increased his anxiety. Were the exams more thorough than those his brothers had experienced? Would he and Dominic be examined for something he didn't know about, something worse than the eye disease? The line crept forward until it was Marcello's turn.

The doctor beckoned him forward and started the exam by checking Marcello's posture, having him turn slowly in a circle. The doctor examined Marcello's face, looked down his throat, and into his ears. He pressed his fingers on the sides of Marcello's neck, sliding them along the jawline.

"Lift your pant leg," the doctor said and showed Marcello what to do.

Bewildered, Marcello did as he was instructed, and the doctor examined his lower leg. After writing something on his clipboard, he pointed Marcello to the next exam station.

"They look at our legs? What for?" Dominic gave Marcello a quizzical look. Marcello shrugged his shoulders.

The next station had a line longer than the first and moved as slowly. The air was heavy with the sweaty smell of the unwashed, anxious immigrants. When Marcello reached the front of the line, the doctor spoke to him. "I'm going to examine your head. Lean forward."

Marcello shook his head to show he didn't understand. The doctor took Marcello's head between his hands and inspected Marcello's scalp. Marcello felt him spread the hair apart on his head and lean close before moving to another place on his head, then another. He took both Marcello's hands in his and inspected his fingernails and the front and back of his hands. The doctor wrote on his clipboard and nodded to Marcello to follow the flow of immigrants for the final exam: the dreaded eye exam.

Marcello had heard the doctor would check his eyes with a strange instrument. They were looking for trachoma, found only by examining the underside of the eyelid. Would it hurt? How long would it take? Marcello's heart pounded wildly by the time he faced the eye doctor. He wiped his clammy hands on his trousers and tried to slow his racing heart with a deep breath. The doctor held an instrument that looked like one of Luisa's crochet needles with a round hook on the end. As he brought it to Marcello's eye and touched his eyelashes, Marcello instinctively jerked back.

"Hold still."

Marcello guessed what the doctor had said.

The doctor brought the instrument toward his eye again while he held the back of Marcello's head and pulled back the eyelid. Marcello clenched his teeth while the doctor looked at the underside. He released the eyelid and repeated the procedure on the other eye, then he removed the instrument. Through watering eyes, Marcello saw the doctor write something on his clipboard. With a wave of his arm, the doctor pointed Marcello toward the main room down the hall. The exam was over.

Marcello released the breath he'd been holding and felt the weight on his shoulders lift. He'd passed! Giddy with relief, he turned and grinned broadly at Dominic, who was waiting behind him.

"Your turn. You'll pass, I know it."

Beyond Dominic in the next line, Marcello spotted the old woman who had stood beside him on deck early that morning. The doctor examining her put a streak of white chalk on her coat and motioned for an attendant to come over and pull her from the line. The woman cried out and struggled to wrench her arms free, but her efforts failed. Her companion, a young woman, put an arm around her and coaxed the elderly woman to come with the attendant. Both women wept as they were led away. Marcello stared in disbelief.

He was still staring after the women when Dominic joined him. "What's wrong?"

"That old woman . . ."

"Who?"

"The one I saw on deck, the one who was bent over. She got pulled from the line. I don't think she passed the doctor's exam."

"That's terrible." Dominic turned around, trying to locate the woman.

"I was feeling so relieved to pass the eye test, and then all of a sudden I saw her pulled out of line. They marked her coat." Marcello kept his gaze where the woman had disappeared in the crowd. "She was so happy this morning. She cried at the sight of America, you know?"

"Maybe she won't be forced to go back—maybe she's sick and has to stay in the hospital until she's better." When Marcello didn't respond Dominic said, "There's nothing we can do for her. Come on, we need to finish getting our papers processed."

Marcello didn't move.

"You coming?" Dominic asked.

Marcello wasn't listening. He began walking toward where he had last seen the old woman.

"Marcello, where are you going? What are you—" Dominic ran after him.

"I just want to see where they're taking her," Marcello called over his shoulder and quickened his pace as he wove around the lines of immigrants.

"Marcello, stop." Dominic caught up and stepped in front of him, blocking his path. "What good will it do to find out where they're taking her?"

"She's old, Dominic. She's won't have another chance at America. You didn't see her face. She was terrified."

"I'm sorry this happened to her, but you can't change what's happened, Marcello. Look at us. We barely understand what's happening ourselves."

Dominic was right. What help could he possibly offer the woman? "It's not right." Marcello's voice trembled. He turned and walked back to the doctor who had marked the woman's coat and leaned into him. *"Non e giusto, non e giusto!"*

An official in a black uniform was making his way toward the commotion Marcello was creating. Dominic grabbed Marcello's arm and yanked him away. "Stop it. The police are coming!" He pulled Marcello into the crowd away from the doctor and waited until the uniformed official passed by. "That was too close." Dominic's eyes were huge as he implored Marcello. "What did they tell us on board ship about not causing any trouble?"

"I know." Marcello looked away.

"Do you want trouble? Because we came that close." He held up his index finger on top of his thumb in front of Marcello's nose.

"No." Trouble was the last thing Marcello wanted, but it didn't change what had just happened. Today was a day of joy for him, a day of despair for the old woman.

"We've got to go to that big room at the end of the hall and finish our processing."

Marcello followed Dominic to a cavernous room where they were bombarded by voices echoing wildly off the walls in a jumble of languages. Winding their way through a maze of roped walkways, they reached the benches in the middle of the room, dropped their bags, and sat.

Dominic eyed Marcello. "You calmed down?"

"I'm fine." Marcello leaned against the back of the tall bench and stretched out his legs. He sighed. "Feels good to sit. Seems like we've been standing all day. Hey, Dominic, what are you doing?"

Dominic had kicked off one of his shoes and was rubbing his foot. "A blister. Damn sock has a hole in it."

"I don't care. Put your shoe on. The stink is . . ." He pinched his nose for effect.

Dominic sighed dramatically, put his shoe on, and tied it. "I don't think my feet smell any worse than anything we smelled on the ship."

Marcello's stomach suddenly growled, shifting his focus from Dominic's feet to his own empty stomach. He opened his satchel and dug through wrinkled clothes that smelled of garlic until he found the last of the salami wrapped in brown paper. "You got anything left to eat?"

"Crackers, such as they are." Dominic opened a small box, sifted through the crumbs, and handed Marcello three crackers.

Marcello finished the salami and was about to eat the last cracker when he noticed a little boy in patched trousers sitting on the opposite bench, watching him eat. Marcello thought he was about two years old, the age Tony would be in a couple of years. He leaned over and held out the cracker.

"You want it? Here." The boy stared back with a longing expression, then looked up at the dark-haired woman beside him. A thin shawl draped her narrow shoulders. She nodded, and the child grabbed the cracker and gobbled it up. The woman said something to Marcello. He didn't understand what she said but nodded to her and smiled at the boy.

"Do we know what these are for?" Dominic fingered the tag pinned to his coat.

"It has something to do with when we go back there." Marcello gestured toward officials behind a row of tall desks at the far end of the hall. "That's where they ask us questions."

"Are they going to ask us to read? Do you think it'll be something hard? I'm not very good."

"My brothers got through all this." Marcello's arm swept the room. "And we will, too."

An hour dragged by. An official wearing a starched collar and serge jacket called Marcello's name, motioned him to his desk, and examined the tag. He smelled heavily of musky cologne. Marcello watched the man page through a ledger until his finger stopped on Marcello's name. To Marcello's relief a translator put the gibberish of English into Italian. A series of questions were fired at him:

"What's your name?"

"How old are you?"

"Married or single?"

"What is your calling or occupation?"

"Are you able to read or write?"

"How much money do you have?"

"What is your final destination in the United States?"

"Who is your sponsor? Name? Address?"

"Have you ever been in prison? The poorhouse?"

The questions were easy to answer. It was the intimidating manner of the official that made Marcello uneasy. Was the man pushing him so he'd make a mistake in his answers? Was there going to be a trick question? The official studied Marcello and peppered him with more questions, twenty-nine in all, verifying what was already in the ship manifest. He handed Marcello a card and told him to read it. *Is this the trick?* Marcello wondered. He looked at the card in his shaking hand. The passage was in Italian, and he read it easily.

With their papers approved and stamped, Marcello and Dominic fled the great hall—fearful an official could jerk them back into another line—and hurried down a stairway to the main level to exchange their money and buy train tickets to Chicago. Marcello slipped the ticket into his shirt pocket. His fingers brushed over the coin his father had given him and he smiled. Papa and Mama wouldn't believe everything that had happened to him today. He'd write a letter to the family after they caught the train to Chicago.

They picked up their bags and exited through the double doors. The day that began early on the deck of *La Provence* had faded into evening. They looked at each other as joyful smiles spread across their faces. Marcello breathed the fresh evening air, his first breath as an American, and his spirits soared. The barriers of class and background fell away; the promise of America was his for the taking. He tipped his head back and shouted, "*Siamonell' America, Dominic.* A-mer-i-ca!"

The door was open.

CHAPTER 6

Marcello wanted to tell his family everything—how majestic the Statue of Liberty was, how vibrant New York City was, how triumphant he felt after processing through Ellis Island—but the words were beyond the capacity of his fourth-grade education. As they rode the train from New York to Chicago, he wrote his first letter home. He sharpened a pencil with his pocketknife and used the top of his suitcase as a writing surface. The train swayed gently, and he concentrated on each letter to form it perfectly.

Dearest Papa, Mama and Luisa,

Dominic and I are here safe. I am so happy to be in America my new country. I miss you all. I will write again from Kansas. Don't worry about anything. I love you so much.

Your loving son and husband
Marcello

He kissed the paper, folded it, and slipped it into an envelope. "Where can I buy a stamp?" he asked Dominic.

"Probably at the train station. When we get to Chicago, we'll look for a place to buy one."

"If we can make ourselves understood," Marcello said.

"Just hold up your envelope and point to the empty corner." Dominic smiled, pleased with his solution.

"Not bad," Marcello said, nodding, "for an immigrant." He nudged Dominic in the ribs.

They stood beside track seven in the busy Chicago train station. The Kansas City Zephyr hissed and spewed white smoke across the waiting crowd as the brakes screeched and the hulking engine ground to a halt.

"It's about time—almost two hours late." Marcello pointed at the massive clock hanging at the end of the platform above the depot entrance. He shifted uneasily and looked at Dominic. "Dominic—"

"Marcello—" Dominic spoke at the same instant. The lifelong friends smiled sadly at each other. The time had come to go their separate ways. Dominic's uncle lived in Cumberland, Wyoming, one of three mining towns clustered in the southwest corner of the state. Although four of Marcello's brothers lived in the same town, Marcello had decided to take the mining job his older brother Giovanni had written about near Pittsburg, Kansas.

Dominic looked Marcello in the eye and began again. "You're sure this is what you want? You can change your mind."

"My best chance for a job right now is in Kansas. I wish you'd change *your* mind and come with me."

"If the mines aren't hiring in Cumberland, I'll find work on a farm. I can live with my uncle."

"We'll both do all right." Marcello stared at the planks in the platform, searching for words. He looked up. "I'm glad we came together."

"I *did* keep you from punching that doctor in the nose at Ellis Island. Who knows what would've happened otherwise. You do remember that policeman, don't you?"

"Yeah, well, you'd still be wandering around in the fog at Le Havre looking for the shipyard if it weren't for me. You have no sense of direction."

"That's not true and you know it—"

A lone conductor walked the length of the platform and hollered, "Boooard!"

They stopped kidding and grew silent. "I'll miss you, Dominic."

They grabbed each other in a hug as passengers pushed past them to board the train. Marcello struggled to control his emotions. They'd relied on each other to go this far, but from here on out, he was traveling through the unknown alone. He'd miss his friend. Marcello stepped back and gathered his bags. "I'll write after I get to Kansas. Thank you, my friend. God be with you." He got in line to board the train.

"God be with you, Marcello," called Dominic. "Good luck to us both."

Marcello leaned toward the window as the train chugged south through eastern Kansas. The autumn sun gleamed on the yellow ocean of wheat nodding in fields beside the tracks. Leaves fluttered on stands of trees scattered on the rolling hills. He was eager for the reunion with Giovanni and wondered if his brother had changed much in the two years since he left home.

The conductor's voice startled Marcello from his thoughts. What had he just said? Ticket? Marcello understood a few words—good day, money, food, toilet, goodbye—from listening to the onslaught of English in the conversations around him and observing the Americans. The conductor punched Marcello's ticket and returned it to him. Ticket, ticket. Marcello added it to his mental list of mastered words as he slipped the ticket into the safety of his shirt pocket. He would make Giovanni teach him English.

He smiled. He'd be there in two hours.

★ ★ ★ ★ ★

"Giovanni, sono qui!" Marcello grabbed Giovanni and kissed him on both cheeks.

"*Benventi in America, fratello!* It's so good to see you." Giovanni grinned, and the brothers clapped each other on the back. For the first time since he left Monastero, Marcello breathed easy. The anxiety of the crossing, processing at Ellis Island, struggling to understand English, and board the right trains fell away. His journey was over.

Giovanni wore denim overalls and a plaid wool jacket. He and Marcello shared the same brown eyes and dark hair, but Giovanni stood two inches taller and was several pounds heavier. "I know exactly how you feel. How are you? Tell me about your trip."

"That was the longest twelve days of my life. The food was terrible, the water tasted like rust, but the smell—"

"I remember the smell." Giovanni nodded. "It was indescribable. How about Ellis Island? Any problems?"

"Just like you had written, not bad except for that horrible eye exam. I thought that doctor was going to take my eyeballs right out of my head. 'Hold still, Mr. Immigrant. This won't hurt a bit. Let me gouge your eye out with this sharp hook. You won't feel a thing.' " Marcello concluded with an exaggerated shudder, which sent the brothers into a fit of laughter.

Giovanni picked up Marcello's bags and carried them to a wagon in front of the train station. "You look good, Marcello. You've grown up in two years." He slapped Marcello on the back. "I bet you're hungry. Let's get something to eat." They walked to a small café beside the station.

The brothers sat at a quiet table in the corner as other passengers filled the cafe. "How are Mama and Papa?" Giovanni pulled off his jacket.

"They're all right. Papa still tends the cows and Mama keeps house, but they've slowed down. They wanted me to stay home and take care of them. The day I left was the worst day of my life. Mama cried so, I felt like I was punishing them." Marcello lowered his eyes.

"Don't feel bad, Marcello. They hurt when we leave, but they understand why we go. I felt their sadness more than my own when I left, but it helps to know they are happy for our success here."

"Leaving Luisa and Tony . . ." Marcello's voice trailed off. "I can still see Luisa waving goodbye to me. I didn't know it would be this hard."

"You're homesick. Your family is on the other side of the ocean."

"I try not to worry about Luisa and Tony, but I think about them and Mama and Papa all the time." Marcello cleared his throat. "I'm glad they're all together. They can take care of each other and keep each other company."

A young woman in a white apron over her dark woolen dress came to their table. Giovanni spoke in English to order sandwiches and coffee. "Your English is good," said Marcello. "You'll help me learn?"

"My English is all right. I get by. I can't read it worth a damn, though. Don't know if I ever will. But I can help you learn how to speak a little, sure." Giovanni reached across the table and playfully punched Marcello's upper arm. "It's great you're here. I miss the family."

"Mama worries you won't find a wife and have a family," Marcello said.

"Well, now that you brought it up . . ." Giovanni paused.

"Yes?" Marcello raised his eyebrows and smiled. "Tell me."

"I have my eye on someone. Her name's Agostina."

"Agostina? She's Italian?"

"What else? She's the daughter of one of the miners. Only seventeen."

"Seventeen? And you're twenty-five. She's just a *bambina.*"

The waitress brought a tray with their food and two steaming mugs of coffee. Marcello hadn't eaten since breakfast. He grabbed the sandwich and bit into the thick slices of ham and cheese wedged between slices of fresh-baked bread. He closed his eyes as he relished the best food he'd eaten since he left home.

"What about you? Ready to start work?" Giovanni stirred cream into his coffee.

Marcello spoke with his mouth full. "Ready." He swallowed and wiped his mouth. "How soon can I start? Who will teach me what to do? I never asked you about tools or—"

"Whoa, Marcello, slow down. One thing at a time. You'll bunk with me at my boardinghouse. Tomorrow we'll see the mine supervisor. He'll probably pair you with me to start out." Giovanni's face grew serious. "It's important who you work with. Your partner means everything—your coal output, your safety, but most important, your survival. It's a dangerous business."

"I know it's dangerous. You can teach me everything about mining, I'm ready to start." Marcello leaned across the table. "I'm anxious to earn money to bring Luisa and Tony here as soon as possible."

Giovanni put his sandwich down and looked evenly at Marcello. "It'll take a couple of years to save money for their passage. You know that, don't you?"

"Are you sure?" Marcello chewed another mouthful and washed it down with coffee while he contemplated Giovanni's words. "I can save faster than that, maybe in a year and a half. I'll work extra to earn more money." He brushed crumbs from his mouth and drank the last of his coffee.

"I'll give you the three-minute tour of town before we go to the boardinghouse." Giovanni stood and smiled. "Come on, brother—I mean partner."

Situated on the rolling prairie with scant trees in the southeast corner of Kansas, the town looked lonesome to Marcello. No mountains embraced it. The main street ran from the train depot toward ramshackle clapboard houses where the miners lived. The general store stood out as the largest building, square and plain, with two boardinghouses on each side. A half mile beyond was the mine.

On his first day of work, Marcello stood at the mine entrance, a large hillside opening propped up by thick timbers. A pair of rails on the ground sloped downward into the maw of the dark tunnel. He adjusted the carbide lamp attached to his cap while he waited with Giovanni and a dozen miners for the ride into the mine. The extra weight from the lamp felt odd, and he readjusted the cap after tipping his head side to side, up and down. The miners climbed into a wagon pulled by a pair of mules, set their tools and lunch pails on the floor, and sat.

"Hadn't counted on spending money *before* I started work," Marcello said. He'd paid a dollar and eighty cents for his overalls at the general store and leased his tools from the mining company for three dollars a month. Every penny of his one dollar, fifty cents daily wages was crucial.

"Don't worry, Marcello," Giovanni assured him. "Everybody starts out this way. You'll earn it back soon enough."

The mules strained forward, and the wagon bumped over the rutted path into the dark tunnel, bringing a rush of cool air over the miners. Marcello slowly turned his head and watched the light from his lamp bounce off the jagged walls. They passed under wooden beams supported on each side by thick timbers as the sound of clopping hooves echoed off the tunnel walls.

He stared over his shoulder at the shrinking circle of light that was the mine entrance. He had an absurd impulse to grab the disappearing daylight and drag it with him into the tunnel in order to stay connected with the outside world. Each clop of the mules' hooves carried them deeper into the tunnel, until the shafts of light disappeared and darkness filled the void. A shiver went down Marcello's spine.

He leaned toward Giovanni and whispered, "Thank God for these lamps."

"You don't want anything to happen to your lamp," Giovanni answered. "Besides your partner, it's your best friend. That metal flask they gave you?"

"The one I put in my overalls?" Marcello fingered the bulge in his side pocket.

"Don't ever come down here without it. That's your extra carbide. You don't ever want to run out."

The wagon stopped in a large open space. Tunnels branched off with empty coal cars beside each entrance. The miners grabbed their tools and fanned out to the tunnels, their lights dancing off the ebony walls like fireflies that disappeared into the night.

"Follow me," Giovanni said and pointed to one of the tunnels. Instead, Marcello watched the handlers turn the mules around to lead them back up the slope, to fresh air and daylight. A feeling of panic rose inside him. He had a desperate thought to walk all the way back to the surface, out the mine entrance and never look back. How bad would that be? He hadn't really started to work yet. Would it be so terrible to change his mind? Since he had entered the mine, he couldn't shake the feeling that something was very wrong.

Marcello turned in time to see Giovanni stoop and disappear into the tunnel he had pointed out. No, he couldn't justify walking away. Not after pinning everything—his future, his family's future—on becoming a miner. He'd have to face his fear and lick it.

"Hey, wait for me." Marcello hurried to the entrance and inched his way into the tunnel. At five feet, nine inches, Marcello was too tall to stand upright inside the tunnel and was forced to tip his head down. Suddenly his light dimmed, and the space around him darkened. His heart thudded with a burst of adrenaline. "What's wrong with my lamp?" Marcello fought to keep his voice steady.

Giovanni turned, his light blinding Marcello for a moment. "Keep your head up. Lamp doesn't work if you lean over. You all right?"

"Yeah . . . sure." Marcello swallowed hard. "How am I supposed to stand up in here?" He lifted his head and the lamp brightened.

"Get down on your knees. If we knock down this ceiling, it'll be easier. Then we can load the cars."

"How much do they hold?"

"Four tons. We each have a car. Think you can fill one on your first day?"

Marcello heard the challenge in Giovanni's voice. "Let's get started and find out."

Giovanni went to his knees and made short swings with his pick, skillfully chipping away at the ceiling. Marcello imitated his brother, but as he struck the ceiling, sharp chips and shards fell on his face, chest, and thighs. He kept at it, in spite of the coal dust that irritated his eyes and nose. A deep breath brought on a spasm of coughing.

"See all this dust we're stirring up?" Giovanni continued to swing his pick.

"You mean that stuff I just sucked into my lungs?"

"It's real flammable. Can start a fire in no time."

"Trying to scare me, brother? First it's about my lamp going out, now it's about starting a fire."

"Just want to make sure you know what's what." Giovanni halted his work and turned toward Marcello. "Never be careless down here. That's how accidents happen."

"I'm convinced." Marcello chipped away at the black rock overhead and wiped debris from his eyes and mouth with his bandana. He spat on the floor, wiped his face again, and continued to swing his pick, not at all confident his new occupation was the right one for him.

Marcello collapsed onto his bed. He had just finished his first week at the mine—six days of work, ten hours each day. Tomorrow was Sunday, and he planned to sleep the entire day. Their room had two beds with plenty of blankets, a chest of drawers, and two wooden chairs. His brother sat in the one beside the window that faced the western sky where the last streaks of daylight faded into dusk.

Giovanni struck a match and lit a cigarette. "Tired?" Smoke circled his head.

"You could say that." Marcello struggled to keep his eyes open.

It had been a week unlike anything he'd experienced. After the first day, he and Giovanni opened a new tunnel with a ceiling so low, they worked lying on their sides, soaked in mine water that pooled on the floor. Each evening Marcello peeled his wet overalls from his aching body and draped them over a chair to dry overnight. The next morning, he pulled on the overalls, still damp and filthy, headed to the mine and crawled into the wet tunnel again.

Marcello looked at his hands. The creases between his thumbs and index fingers were raw and oozing. "Big mistake not buying gloves." He rolled on his side and faced Giovanni. "Are we about done in that tunnel?"

"Think so. How's your head?"

"It's gonna be a goose egg." Marcello rubbed the knot on his forehead, the result of falling rock, when he caught Giovanni in a half smile. "What's so funny?" He rolled onto his back and tried to find a comfortable position for his aching body.

"Nothing's funny, Marcello. You're being initiated."

"Initiated?"

"What it's like to be a miner. You did a good job this week, working in a tunnel like that." Giovanni stood and stretched.

"You going out?"

"To Agostina's."

The rest of Giovanni's words floated away as Marcello closed his eyes and felt his muscles relax. He drifted to sleep, but instead of restful darkness, he found himself in the mine surrounded by jagged tunnel walls. His arms struggled to lift his pick overhead and swing at the walls of an endless tunnel. The pick grew too heavy to lift. Chunks of coal fell from overhead until everything collapsed on him in a thundering crash.

He threw his arms up with a jerk and his eyes shot open. Marcello didn't move. He stared at the ceiling and waited for his heart to stop racing.

Chapter 7

December

Heavy, wet snowflakes fell from the gray clouds that draped the Italian hilltops. Luisa shivered. Her errand to the village to sell eggs rewarded her with more than she could have hoped for. She clutched the letter in her coat pocket and quickened her steps up the path to the house. Bursting through the front door, she pulled the letter from her pocket and waved it in the air.

"A letter from Marcello!"

"Good, good." Marcello's mother smiled broadly and set her mending aside. "It's been too long."

"Nearly three weeks. I've marked the days on the calendar." Luisa took off her coat and shook the snowflakes from her headscarf that left wet drops on the dirt floor.

"Come sit, Luisa. Read it to me."

Christmas was three days away. Luisa and her mother-in-law were up early to bake panettone, their traditional holiday bread studded with nuts and dried fruit. Three golden loaves cooled on the kitchen table. Tony slept near the fireplace in a makeshift cradle, a rectangular wooden box cushioned with layers of quilt scraps. Luisa moved a chair beside the fire and tore open the envelope.

2 December, 1915

My dear Luisa and Tony,

I'm sorry I haven't written more often. By the end of

the day I'm tired and fall into bed after supper. The first weeks were hard but Giovanni helps me learn about mining. He also teaches me English. I can say things like what time is it and how much does it cost. There's three other Italians in our boardinghouse, two from northern Italy one from the south. Giovanni has a special girl and visits her every Sunday.

I wish I had money to send for Christmas. I've gotten two paychecks and paid my bill at the general store. Next month I'll start to save money and send some to you.

I miss the family so much. It helps to keep busy so I don't have time to be homesick. I think of you my beautiful Luisa every night before I go to sleep. Give Tony kisses from me and my love to Papa and Mama, Alfonso and Batista. Happy Christmas.

Your adoring husband,
Marcello Corsi

Luisa pressed the letter to her chest. "A letter from Marcello." She leaned over Tony and whispered, "A letter from your papa. He sends you his love." Luisa brushed her lips across Tony's forehead, then carefully refolded the letter and pocketed it in her skirt.

"We must celebrate." Luisa jumped up and went to the cupboard for a bottle of wine. "He sounds good, don't you think?"

"Yes. It's good Giovanni helps Marcello in the mine."

"They work so hard . . ." Luisa found two glasses, then suddenly whirled around. "I just realized something."

"What's that?"

"Marcello sent us the perfect Christmas gift. His letter. Tomorrow I'll visit Mama and read it to her. She'll want to know his news."

Luisa brought a glass to her mother-in-law. "To Mar—" His

name caught in her throat and tears flooded her eyes.

"I know, my dear. Christmas without Marcello."

Luisa brushed away the tears and began again. "To Marcello." They clinked their glasses and sipped the wine.

Marcello's mother pulled a hanky from the sleeve of her dress and wiped her own eyes. "Read it again, Luisa."

That evening Luisa read Marcello's letter to the family as they sat around the dying embers of the fire. It was late. She kissed Mama and Papa and wearily climbed the stairs carrying Tony, drowsy and heavy in her arms. She gently laid him in his crib at the foot of the bed and tucked his cotton blanket around him. His eyelids closed, and Luisa stroked his downy hair, singing softly until he fell asleep. In the quiet, she read Marcello's letter one last time. *He misses me, he misses us,* she thought. *He's safe and well.* She smiled sadly and traced his words with her finger. Tears threatened.

She caught sight of her reflection in the cloudy mirror above the dresser and saw no signs of the change taking place inside her. She turned her profile to the glass and smoothed her dress over her middle, relieved she wasn't showing yet. She cast a worried glance at Tony and wondered if nursing him would take away from this baby. If only God had waited to bless them with another baby until she was reunited with Marcello. And when would that be? How awful to be pregnant during a crossing—or worse, to give birth at sea.

The secret was hers to carry alone as long as she could. She wouldn't tell Marcello; not yet.

Marcello hadn't told Luisa the whole story in his Christmas letter.

The miners were paid by the weight of their carload of coal at the end of each day. Four miners claimed management had cheated them and quit their jobs the first of December. They said the owners had rigged the scales to weigh less than the actual weight and, as a result, paid the miners less than they earned. Even though Marcello couldn't understand what the miners said at work, he felt the tension, saw the sideways glances, heard the whispers behind backs. When he overheard conversations, he watched the men. Their faces were hard with anger.

"They changed the scales? This is terrible. Can they get away with it?" Marcello's voice rose as he talked with Giovanni in their room before supper. He paced in the narrow space between their beds.

"You haven't heard the latest news," Giovanni said.

Marcello paused and waited for Giovanni to continue.

"This afternoon the owners spread the word they had been falsely accused and hadn't rigged the scales."

Marcello wrinkled his brow. "Who's telling the truth?"

"That's the problem. I believe the miners, but we have no proof. I also heard that more men will quit. But that's not the worst of it."

Marcello sat down at the foot of his bed and eyed Giovanni. "Worse? What can be worse?"

"Most of the men I've talked to have decided to go on strike. They want to close down the mine."

"What? No! When?"

"First day of January."

"But that means . . . no more paychecks." Marcello felt as though someone had kicked him in the stomach.

"That's right."

"The owners should pay us what we earn, but to strike? Is that the only way to settle this? Do *I* have to strike?"

"The miners stick together. The strike is more successful if we do."

"But I need the money."

A voice floated up the stairs from the dining room. "Supper's ready."

"Let's eat. I'll tell you the rest at supper."

The enticing aroma of fried potatoes and seasoned corned beef greeted the miners as they filed into the dining room lit by kerosene lamps. Marcello and Giovanni sat at the trestle table set with crockery plates and cups for the eight miners who roomed at the boardinghouse. Mrs. Humphrey, their plump landlady known for her high-quality cooking, brought bowls of corned beef hash, carrots, and turnips from the kitchen and placed them beside baskets of corn bread and biscuits on the table. Their hands and faces freshly washed, but coal grit still under their fingernails, the men dished up portions for their plates and passed the heaping bowls around the table.

Marcello leaned toward Giovanni. "Finish what you were telling me."

"We went on strike a year ago. There were boys, not even twelve years old, who worked in the mine, and we were all against it. We closed down the mine. It lasted 'bout ten days before the owners gave up, let the boys go, and hired men in their places." Giovanni took a helping of hash and handed it to Marcello.

"I have to think about Luisa and Tony. I can't quit." Marcello shoveled hash on his plate and passed the dish.

"I don't think you understand, Marcello. I've been through a strike before—"

"I don't think *you* understand, Giovanni." Marcello felt the color rise in his face, and his voice rumbled. "Don't tell me what to do. I have a family that depends on me and you don't." The room became silent, and Marcello felt all eyes on him. He avoided the stares, passed the carrots, and slathered his biscuit with butter. Marcello dug into his food but found the delicious meal tasteless as he struggled over the thought of a strike. He ignored Giovanni the rest of the meal.

When the men finished supper, Mrs. Humphrey and her daughter cleared the dishes. Chair legs scraped across the rough plank floor as the men pushed away from the table to stretch out their legs. Marcello engaged the talkative miner next to him, a young Italian with rippling muscles who had worked at the mine for a year after emigrating from a village near Napoli. The English speakers—three from England and one from Wales—sat at the other end of the table, their fair heads bent together as they talked, their faces telegraphing concern over labor issues. Suddenly a fist slammed against the table followed by a stream of English that Marcello didn't understand, except for one word—*hell.*

He nudged Giovanni. "What did he say about hell?"

"He said, 'I'll go back to work here when hell freezes over.' "

Marcello frowned. "What does that mean?"

"That means," Giovanni said, "he'll never work in this mine again."

The rumors festered among the miners like an infected boil. Anger grew until the miners unanimously agreed on a course of action—to strike on the first day of January. When Marcello saw their solidarity and determination, he abandoned his plan to cross the picket line and reluctantly joined the cause. He hoped Giovanni was right, that the strike would only last a week; two at the most.

In the freezing dawn on January 1, 1916, the miners gathered in the street in front of the general store and marched to the mine. They pulled up short when they rounded the corner to the entrance. Before them stood two dozen men armed with bats and truncheons.

Marcello was bewildered. He nudged Giovanni. "What's this?"

"Strikebreakers," Giovanni muttered angrily.

"Where'd they come from?"

"The mine owners hired them. They mean to stop us."

The surprised miners hesitated for only a moment. The leaders of the march charged the strikebreakers, who raised their weapons and clubbed the miners to the ground. Chaos erupted. More miners charged but were beaten back, their fists no match for the clubs. The strikebreakers moved into the crowd, beating the miners at will. Marcello and Giovanni ducked and covered their heads, falling over the men behind them. The miners fell back. Some scattered, others helped the injured to their feet and led them back to town. Marcello and Giovanni lifted a half-conscious miner to his feet and supported him back to their boardinghouse. It was the engaging young miner from Napoli, his head split open from a truncheon's blow.

Women tended to the injured, applying salve to wounds and tearing their aprons into bandage strips. The miners, furious after the attack, spread the word from the boardinghouses to the shanties along Main Street for the miners to arm themselves. They would march tomorrow, and they would be prepared.

In the early light next morning, the miners armed themselves with shovels, picks, and bats and marched to the mine. Wives, mothers, and sisters followed at a distance, their coat pockets bulging with rocks. One carried an American flag; others banged on pots in support of the striking miners.

Trembling with cold and fear, Marcello gripped his shovel as they approached the strikebreakers lined up at the mine entrance. He'd never backed down from a fight, but those had been between schoolboys, nothing this formidable or violent. Angry shouts rang out, and the two sides collided in battle. A strikebreaker ran toward Marcello, his bat raised. Marcello ducked and swung his shovel into the man's chest. Stunned, the strikebreaker fell back; a second blow from Marcello sent the man to his knees.

Rocks hurtled through the air and rained down on the strikebreakers. The miners held their ground and pushed back until the fight turned in their favor. They encircled the strikebreakers so they couldn't escape and chased them to the train depot, barricading them inside. With a raucous "Hurrah!" the miners raised picks and shovels in the air and marched back to the mine in triumph.

Emboldened by their success, the miners picketed in large numbers every day, while remaining vigilant to the possible return of the strikebreakers. When the threat of violence passed, Marcello had another worry—how to live without a paycheck. He made inquiries in town for odd jobs at the blacksmith's barn and the general store but found nothing. He cleared his debt at the general store, but continued to pay four dollars for room and board every other week. He watched his savings dwindle and quietly panicked. The strike showed no signs of ending, and by the end of the month, it was clear what he had to do. He wrote a letter to his brothers in Wyoming and broke the news to Giovanni.

"I can't wait any longer. My savings are almost gone, and I can't find any work in town. I've decided to leave."

"Where will you go?" Giovanni's face registered concern.

"Cumberland."

Giovanni nodded. "To the brothers."

"I can stay with family while I look for work. If I can't get hired at the mine, maybe I can work on a farm like Dominic. What about you, Giovanni? Is it safe to stay here?"

"After the first attack, we put some men out to snoop around. They have ways of getting information. We won't be surprised again."

"What about the strike? Ever think of leaving?"

Giovanni hesitated. "I can't go with you."

"Why not?"

He looked at Marcello and a smile slowly spread across his face. "Agostina. I've asked her to marry me. We'll settle here near her family."

Marcello's eyebrows shot up. "Get married? Giovanni, that's wonderful." He pumped his brother's hand before they broke into laughter and hugged. "It's time you settled down before you're an old man. You and Agostina will be happy."

"Thanks, Marcello. We might have to live with her folks if this strike continues much longer."

"You've always made things work out. I know you will this time, too."

"You have enough money to get to Wyoming?"

"Yes, if I don't wait around here any longer."

"Let me know what it costs. I'll help you out."

"You've already helped me, Giovanni. You taught me how to be a miner. I couldn't have asked for a better partner, even if you are my brother."

Giovanni jabbed Marcello in the arm.

The night before Marcello left town, Agostina's family crowded together in their tiny miner's quarters and after a dinner of roasted polenta, raised their glasses to wish him well on his journey to Wyoming.

"God be with you, Marcello." Agostina kissed him on both cheeks. "We'll miss you."

Marcello swelled with gratitude for their kindness. "Thank you for this wonderful send-off." He gazed at Agostina's parents and younger siblings gathered around. "My brother's a fortunate man to join this family."

Giovanni drew Agostina to his side and smiled at her with

pride. "I'm the happiest man in the world." Her dark eyes glowed and she leaned into him, a delicate figure beside his broad chest.

Marcello eyed them with envy. "Mama and Papa would give you their blessing."

Marcello gave Giovanni and Agostina privacy to say good night on the porch and walked back to the boardinghouse alone, his heart aching. A tumbleweed gusted down the street and grabbed at his pant leg. The fullness of Giovanni's life with Agostina and her family amplified the emptiness in his own. The gulf between himself and his family gaped, a chasm that overwhelmed him. As he passed the clapboard saloon, bright lights and raucous voices spilled out the doorway into the street. He had never felt more alone.

The next morning Marcello boarded the train to Kansas City, set his cardboard suitcase on the overhead rack, and sank into a seat beside the window. As the train pulled out, Marcello watched the little mining town of Pittsburg disappear into the prairie, just as his first chance for success had disappeared. He slumped in his seat.

His plan was a failure. The timing of the strike couldn't have been worse. He understood success in America meant hard work, but he'd never dreamed that work would be taken from him. He fingered the two dollars in his pocket, all that was left of his earnings. Five precious months wasted. All his hopes now resided in Cumberland, the place that offered him a second chance. He prayed this was the right decision. He couldn't afford any more mistakes.

He pulled his cap down over his eyes and hid in despair.

CHAPTER 8

March

The conductor steadied himself as the train rocked from side to side. "Next stop, Kemmerer, Wyoming," he repeated, walking down the aisle.

Marcello leaned against his seat as he looked at the steel-gray sky with weary eyes. He had never seen such barren landscape—no trees, no grass, no water. He drew a deep breath and prayed there were rich veins of coal under the endless hills of sand and a trustworthy company in charge of extracting it.

The train ground to a halt at the station. Marcello grabbed his bags and made his way down the aisle to the door. His pulse quickened when he stepped onto the platform, scanning the crowd for one of his brothers. Michele, Angelo, Giacomo, and Luciano mined coal in Cumberland five miles away, and one of them would meet him at the station. Marcello turned up his jacket collar against the sharp wind.

"Marcello! Over here!" He turned and saw Luciano striding toward him, waving his arms, a big smile on his face.

"Luciano!" Marcello shouted. The brothers grabbed each other and kissed on both cheeks. "It's so good to see you."

"It's good to see you, too, little brother." Luciano stepped back and looked at Marcello from head to toe. "Eight years is a long time. You hadn't started shaving when I left. Look at you now, all grown up."

Nearly thirty, Luciano was smartly dressed, a dark wool coat over his shirt and trousers. His copper-brown hair and hazel eyes set him apart from his dark-haired siblings. Marcello had always looked up to him, the ambitious, confident brother, the one who left home first for America. He gazed with admiration. Luciano could do no wrong.

Luciano led Marcello to his buckboard. "How are Mama and Papa?" They stowed the bags and climbed aboard while Marcello fed him news of the family.

"Sorry things didn't work out in Kansas," Luciano said, "but you should have come here in the first place, like the rest of us."

"I thought working with Giovanni in Kansas—"

"Little brother, I've been here eight years. I know how things work and how to get things done. Take advantage of it. Listen to me like you did Papa."

Marcello stared straight ahead.

Luciano cast a quick glance at Marcello and softened his tone. "I wasn't going to preach to you on your first day here. I'm just offering advice. And help."

A gust of wind swirled dust into their faces. Marcello wiped his eyes and pulled his cap down before shoving his hands into his pockets. "Does the wind always blow like this?"

"You'll get used to it. There's a blanket under the seat." Luciano guided the horse down Main Street past the First National Bank, the Kemmerer Hotel, and the Golden Rule Store.

"Kemmerer's a lot bigger than Pittsburg," said Marcello and draped the blanket over his legs.

At the end of Main Street, Luciano flicked the reins as they passed the livery stable and took the road out of town. "Julia thought you'd be hungry. There's a basket behind you. Eat something."

"I'm starving." Marcello rummaged through the basket and pulled out squares of corn bread. "How's the family?"

"The boys are growing fast. Always into mischief." He winked and smiled with pride.

Marcello wiped crumbs from his mouth and glanced at Luciano's clothes again. "You're all dressed up. Doesn't look like you just came from the mine."

"I don't work there anymore."

Marcello's eyebrows shot up. "I didn't know you quit."

"I'm not sorry to leave the mine. Been working at a saloon in Silverton since fall.

"Where's Silverton?"

"Three miles the other side of Cumberland. Next month, I take over as the manager of the saloon." Marcello watched his brother's chest swell with pride. "You'll have to come see it, it's really something. Two pool tables, a long bar with big mirrors on the wall behind it, gaming tables. My plan is to buy it eventually and hang a big sign out front that says"—he paused for effect—"Silverton Saloon, Lucas Corsi, Owner."

"*Lucas* Corsi?"

"It's American. We've decided to use Americanized names. I like Lucas for my business. Michele goes by Mick and Giacomo is Jim."

"And Angelo?"

"He's still Angelo, can't talk him out of the old ways."

Marcello stared at his brother. "Lucas . . . Lucas." He tried to make the new name fit but failed. "I can't call you Lucas. It's not you. It sounds—"

"American," Lucas interrupted. "That's where we live, and that's what we are. Being American is very good, Marcello. You'll see."

"I'm not changing *my* name," said Marcello.

"You might think diffcrently when you get tired of Americans mispronouncing your name. How does a name like . . . Mark sound?"

"Like it belongs to somebody else."

Lucas tossed back his head with a laugh.

The horse clopped down the road between rocky hills and ravines dotted with sagebrush. Stubborn patches of snow clung to the sandy hills. White clouds scudded across the sky, and Marcello shivered in the sharp March wind. He'd need warmer clothes.

An hour later, Lucas halted the buckboard on a rise in the road to give Marcello a sweeping view of the prairie and a sloping valley below. "There's Cumberland."

A high rocky ridge rose on the east. On the west side, six tall smokestacks shot high into the sky above a cluster of wooden buildings beside a railroad track. In between was a treeless town of identical clapboard houses standing in rows like a child's blocks in a giant sandbox. The rooflines angled in relief to the gently sloping hills. The single dirt road leading into town branched off into dusty streets. Beyond the town, rocky crevices and scraggly brush scattered into the dun-colored distance.

Lucas turned onto a rutted path leading to a weathered frame house, a barn, and two small outbuildings. A rusty windmill in the front yard squeaked as it spun in the relentless wind.

"This is Mick's place. You can stay here as long as you want. He should be home from the mine by now." They hopped off the buckboard and walked to the front porch.

Marcello grabbed Lucas's arm and stopped. "You should know," he said, looking Lucas in the eye, "things were bad for me in Kansas. I'm broke. I need to start work as soon as possible."

"We suspected as much from your letter. It'll be all right, Marcello. Family will help. But I've got to tell you," he said as his face grew somber, "work hard, or you'll be on your own. We don't put up with lazy, no-good little brothers." He flashed his trademark smile and draped an arm over Marcello's shoulders.

As they mounted the porch steps, the front door opened and Mick stepped out, his arms spread wide, a broad grin on his face. "*Benvenuti,* Marcello. Come in." Mick steered Marcello into the living room overflowing with family. "Marcello is here!" His brothers with their wives and children descended on him in a welcoming throng.

"It's about time you came. We knew you'd end up here," they chorused with hugs and back slaps as they huddled around Marcello.

Marcello could only smile, dazed by the outpouring of love. "What a welcome. It's so good to see . . ." He inhaled suddenly and blinked away the tears welling in his eyes. "To walk through the door and see all of you, it's like coming home."

"You must be chilled to the bone," said Mick's wife, Theresa, with a look of concern. "Come warm up." Tall and slender with thick brunette hair pinned back in a bun, she guided him to the potbelly stove in the center of the room where a grinning Dominic waited to welcome him.

They shared a big bear hug and pounded each other on the back. "I thought you were working on a ranch," said Marcello. "When did you start at the mine?"

"About a month ago. I wasn't sure I'd like to work underground, you know? But it's been a good move. It pays better, too." He paused, and his face grew serious. "Things didn't sound good in your last letter. I'm glad you came to Wyoming."

Marcello held out his numb hands to the welcoming warmth of the stove. "Turned out to be a bad decision. Thought I'd be ahead by working in Pittsburg."

Angelo eased through the crowded room and stood beside Marcello. His brothers had changed little in the years since they emigrated. Angelo was broad-shouldered, as strong as he was reliable. His handlebar mustache was the same charcoal black as his thick, wavy hair. "It's tough to run into a strike so soon after you emigrated." He stroked the end of his mustache, his expressive face full of concern. "You'll settle in fine."

"Luciano lectured me about going to Kansas instead of coming here."

Angelo gave him a small grin. "Did he try to talk you into changing your name?"

"How did you know?"

"He's completely devoted to America, which is fine. Now me—I'm good with Angelo." He slapped Marcello on the back.

A plank table was laid for supper with tin plates, cups, and baskets of bread. He sniffed the aroma of simmering tomatoes, onions, and garlic from the kitchen: the mouthwatering smells of home. Mick disappeared and returned with bottles of wine and glasses.

"Are they hiring at the mine?" Marcello asked, taking a glass from Mick.

"They expanded operations last month," Mick said. "They need more diggers." Mick was the tallest, towering over his brothers at six feet with a lanky build. A shock of dark hair fell over his forehead. He still possessed his easy smile in spite of balancing the hard work at the mine with operating a farm. He was identical to Marcello in the penetrating warmth of his brown eyes.

"What about wages?" Marcello asked.

"The union was organized about a year ago. Our contract is eight hours a day, three dollars a day."

Marcello's eyes widened. "What? I don't believe it! I was making half that in Kansas."

"Welcome to Union Pacific Coal," said Jim and clinked his glass to Marcello's. "Last strike was six years ago."

Teased as a youngster for being the only redhead in the family, Jim was two years older than Marcello and never missed an opportunity to remind him of it. He was slim and muscular, and his lively blue eyes reflected his mischievous personality. The brothers were all married now, except for Jim, who was still too carefree to settle down, but not opposed to looking.

Marcello leaned into Jim and noticed a bruise through his red stubble. "What happened to your chin?"

Jim grinned. "Some rowdies at the bar. Had to settle a dispute."

Marcello laughed. "Still the same old Jim."

Chatter from the kitchen ceased as the wives carried platters of sausage and polenta covered in marinara to the table. Theresa smoothed her calico apron and waved the family toward the table. "Come eat." She smiled. The children filled their plates and sat on the floor near the stove while the adults pulled out chairs at the table.

"Before we eat . . ." Lucas raised his glass. "To new beginnings." He nodded to Marcello.

Reeling in the joyous reunion with his family and from the good news that he would earn the astonishing salary of three dollars a day, Marcello dared to hope his fortune was changing. He raised his glass with the others.

"Where do I buy a warm coat?"

When Luisa's skirts could no longer hide her pregnancy, she'd had no choice but to confide in Marcello's parents. They were overjoyed. They urged her to write Marcello immediately, but she resisted. She wanted to wait until he was settled before sharing the news. Although he never complained in his letters, she knew from what he didn't say that those first months were difficult. Her intuition was confirmed when Marcello wrote about the strike in Pittsburg and his abrupt move to Cumberland. The last thing she wanted to do was add to his worries.

"Luisa, you must tell Marcello. He should know about the baby." Marcello's mother was resolute.

"I will, Mama." Luisa reached for her mother-in-law's hand, callused from a lifetime of hard work, and covered it with her own. They had finished churning butter in the cool early morning and sat on a bench by the front door. Tony crawled in the grass under the pear tree bursting with the first blossoms of spring, a white dome against the blue sky.

"Feeling all right?" Mama gave Luisa a concerned look.

"A little tired, but I'm fine." Luisa saw Tony grab a fistful of grass and poke it in his mouth. "No, no, Tony." She jumped up and grabbed it before he swallowed. "He puts everything in his mouth and then crawls away from me as fast as he can. Such a busy boy."

"Before long you'll be busier than you can imagine. Tony will be walking, and you'll have another little one to care for." Mama's eyes twinkled, and she lifted Tony onto her lap. "What do you want, Tony, a little brother or sister?"

Tony looked at his *nonna* with a drooling grin that exposed bits of grass. With a laugh, she wiped his mouth and hugged him.

Luisa rested her hand on her growing belly. "I think this is a little girl. Doesn't kick as much as Tony."

"You're far enough along, I should be able to tell if it's a boy or a girl," said Mama. "Look at me." Everyone on the mountain knew Mama Corsi predicted the sex of babies with amazing accuracy. Young mothers anxious to know if their firstborn would be a boy or a girl made it a point to visit Mama during the last months of pregnancy.

After studying Luisa's face for a considerable while, she spoke. "It's a girl."

"I'd love a little girl. So would Marcello." Luisa spoke wistfully and allowed herself to dream. She would buy pink yarn at Donato's and knit her a special blanket. Luisa would braid her hair in the morning and share little secrets before bedtime. She would teach her to bake bread, knit warm slippers, and grow butternut squash. Their little girl would be a playmate for Tony and a darling for Marcello to spoil.

"You're right. It's time to tell Marcello. I'll write a letter tonight."

A stabbing pain in her belly jolted Luisa from sleep. When her head cleared, she was seized with panic. It was too soon. The baby wasn't due for two months! She pulled herself up when another pain descended, sharper than the first.

"Mama, help! Something's wrong." Tony stirred in his crib.

Events hurtled out of control. The pain gripped with ferocious teeth, and Luisa doubled over. The bed was wet.

"Mama, help!"

Mama appeared. "Dear God!" She covered her mouth at the sight of the bloodstained sheets. "I'm here, child."

"It's too soon, it's too soon," Luisa cried through clenched teeth and bore down no matter how hard she tried not to.

Two pushes. When the pains stopped, Luisa took a deep breath. Mama shouted, "Papa, hot water!" She wiped damp strands of hair from Luisa's face.

Wave after wave, the contractions descended. They came closer together, in greater intensity until the pain was unbearable, unending.

"It's time to push, Luisa."

Luisa felt herself fading away, unable to resist the dark shadows closing in on her. Her eyes grew dim. She couldn't see Mama.

"Baby's close, Luisa. Push."

"I can't . . . I can't . . ."

Mama's voice cut through the darkness. "Yes, you can. Push hard. Now!"

Luisa cried out and bore down in one endless contraction,

and the baby was born into Mama's arms, a perfect little girl with thick dark hair. Instead of rosy pink, she was ash gray. Immediately Mama laid her on the bed and grabbed a towel from the commode. She wiped mucus from the baby's nose and mouth and rubbed the tiny body with gentle urgency, but the baby made no sound.

Luisa pulled herself up to see the baby and gasped. "She's not crying. She should be crying!"

"She's not breathing," Mama said.

Luisa's heart hammered; tears flooded her eyes. This couldn't be happening. "Help her, Mama, please—" She choked with fear.

Mama didn't seem to hear, so intent was she on massaging the tiny chest and uttering prayers for the baby to breathe.

A cry escaped from the crib. Was that the baby? Luisa realized it was Tony and, in the chaos, prayed her newborn would cry like her big brother. Please, God, make her cry. From somewhere far away she heard Papa's voice.

Mama looked into the baby's mouth and nose again. She rubbed her back and chest, desperate for sound to escape the tiny mouth, but there was none.

How much time had passed? It seemed like forever. It seemed like no time at all. Suddenly Mama stopped her futile effort.

"Don't stop!" Luisa cried angrily. She forced her attention away from the baby to Mama, refusing to accept what she dreaded most.

Mama seemed to move in slow motion. With great tenderness, she swaddled the baby and held her close. Looking into the tiny face, she touched her cheek and kissed her forehead. Tears coursed down Mama's cheeks as she gently placed the baby in Luisa's arms.

An icy cold washed over Luisa, and she shook uncontrollably. Mama brought a shawl from the wardrobe and wrapped it around Luisa's shoulders. Luisa shook so hard, Mama reached for the baby, but Luisa clutched her too tightly. All Mama could do was put her arms around Luisa and hold them both until the shuddering ceased.

Luisa sat motionless. Mama spoke urgently about the afterbirth, but her words were far away, and Luisa took no notice. She looked into her baby's perfect face. "No . . . no . . . no." She pulled the lifeless bundle to her breast and rocked back and forth. "Holy Mother!" She bent her head over her stillborn daughter and sobbed.

Chapter 9

Marcello and Jim climbed out of the wagon in front of the mine office with the other men and slapped coal dust off their jackets and overalls. Eager to collect his wages, Marcello quickly wiped grit from his face and hands with his bandana.

Inside the crowded office a thin man with an air of importance stood behind the desk.

"Name?" the paymaster asked, peering over his wire-rimmed glasses at Marcello.

"Marcello Corsi."

The man ran his finger down the list in his ledger. "Fifteen dollars." He reached in the metal cash box when Marcello stopped him.

"Could you bank twelve dollars of that?" Marcello asked.

"Certainly. First National Bank of Kemmerer?"

Marcello nodded. The paymaster made a notation and wrote a receipt he handed to Marcello along with three silver dollars, the balance of his weekly earnings.

"Thanks." Marcello slipped the coins into his shirt pocket while Jim was paid.

"Say, Marcello." Isaac Johnson, their blond crew chief, joined them from across the office. "Just wanted to say you're doing a good job. Your output's gone up steadily since you got here."

"Thanks, boss," Marcello said.

"That's because he's working with the best," Jim deadpanned. "I taught him everything he knows."

"Is that so?" Isaac's chuckle lit up his bright blue eyes. "Whatever the reason, keep it up. See you fellas Monday."

Marcello and Jim headed to the Cumberland Saloon for a beer with Angelo and Mick. Since Union Pacific prohibited the sale of liquor in town, the saloon stood just outside of town, a simple wood frame building identical to the miners' houses. The large room was finished with rough plank floors and walls. A bar ran along one side of the room; the shelves behind it were cluttered with bottles of spirits. Mismatched tables and chairs covered with a thin layer of coal dust crowded the middle of the room, dimly lit by kerosene lamps.

Mixed among the miners were cowboys, sheepherders, and drifters who passed through southern Wyoming, some of them employed by ranchers, some looking for work, and some content to drift. All of them were fond of the drink and the prostitutes who lived in the small house next to the saloon. When they weren't serving drinks, the scarlet ladies were in and out of the saloon after dark with conspicuous regularity.

Gritty, tired, and thirsty, Marcello and his brothers sat at one of the tables and downed their first gulps of beer in silence.

"Ahh," Jim sighed after a long swallow.

"I agree," Marcello said and wiped his mouth on his shirt-sleeve.

Jim leaned back in his chair and stretched his arms overhead. "Finally, Friday. No work tomorrow."

"Some of us don't get Saturday off," said Mick. "If you're looking for something to do, I could find work for you on the farm."

"No, no. Not me." Jim protested, holding up both hands. "What about you, Marcello? Any plans?"

"Working on the farm with Mick." Marcello paused. "But I do have something to announce."

"Oh?" said Angelo.

"Today, for the first time, I banked some of my wages. Twelve dollars in all."

"Hey, brother, good for you." Mick reached across the table and jabbed Marcello's arm.

"From here on out, I should be able to set aside money for Luisa and Tony." Marcello raised his glass in a toast and took another swallow of beer. He tipped his chair back on two legs and looked around the saloon at the miners, dirty-faced, hunched over their drinks. It was then he noticed four strangers at the bar. "Hey, who are they?" He jerked his head in their direction.

"Never seen them before," said Angelo. "I'd guess they work for a rancher around here. Or just passing through."

Felt hats partly obscured their weathered faces. Marcello eyed their dusty chaps and pointed boots, gear he'd seen before on local cowboys. They tossed down their drinks and rapped their glasses on the bar for refills. While they waited for the next round, the men leaned against the bar and surveyed the room. One of the men locked eyes with Marcello. He said something to his friends and nodded at the Corsis' table. After the cowboys downed their refills, they crossed the saloon and circled the table where Marcello and his brothers sat.

"Well, what we got here?" One of the men bent over the table, reeking of whiskey and horse sweat. His nose angled to one side of his pockmarked face, and his lip curled back in a sneer. "I believe we got us a bunch of wops here, that's what I think."

"I think you're right," one of his friends said. "Or maybe they're dagos." The men burst into laughter. One of them leaned into Jim's face. "Tell us what you are, wops or dagos," he hissed.

Jim came out of his chair, but Angelo grabbed him by the arm. "Sit down, Jim. These boys are going back to the bar to drink, aren't you?" He gave each man a stony stare.

"Oh, this one knows how to talk American," said the one with the crooked nose and turned his attention to Angelo. "You a smart dago or a stupid wop?"

Mick stood up, towering over the man and leaned into his face. "Question is, do you *understand* American? Because we just said you were going back to the bar." Talking in the saloon ceased. Marcello could feel the stares of everyone in the room on them. It was dead quiet.

The bartender grabbed an ax handle from under the bar and slammed it against the wood. "You fellas hold it right there."

The cowboys ignored the warning and exchanged a knowing look. They hovered beside the table a moment, then leaned in and spat into the glasses of beer. The table erupted. The brothers swung their fists, delivering sharp jabs and punches. The cowboys pounded back. The table overturned; glasses shattered on the floor and splattered beer. Marcello threw his fist into a cowboy's nose and heard it crack. A sharp blow to his own jaw dazed Marcello, and he fell backward over a chair, then leapt up, raging, lunging with an uppercut to the cowboy's jaw. Vaguely aware of more bodies joining the brawl, Marcello pummeled the cowboy's gut with his fists.

"Stop! Stop it, all of you!" The bartender and a brute of a man who helped keep order in the saloon rushed into the fight, stepped between flying fists, and pulled the men off each other. "Get out of here now! Go! And you," he said, pointing his ax handle at the cowboys, "don't come back. Hit the trail."

The cowboys snatched their hats from the floor. They cast hateful glares at the Corsis and cursed loudly on their way out. "Dirty eye-talian bastards! Don't think we're done." Crooked Nose spat in their direction before he disappeared out the door.

Marcello and his brothers picked up broken glass and straightened overturned furniture while the room watched in silence. The Corsis nodded appreciation to the few who had joined them in the fight. Gradually the murmur of conversation and the sound of clinking glasses resumed.

Mick brought pieces of the busted chair to the bartender. "Sorry about this. We'll pay for it."

"Damn right you will," said the red-faced bartender. His bald head was beaded with sweat. "And don't come back here until you have the three dollars to replace it."

"That's a day's wages," Mick protested.

"Maybe next time you won't be so quick to throw punches." The bartender turned his back and grabbed a broom.

His heart still pounding from the fight, Marcello approached the bar and threw down two silver dollars. "This should pay for it." He glared at the bartender.

"I said 'three dollars.' " The bartender returned Marcello's glare.

"My brother owns a saloon. He says chairs don't cost more than a dollar-fifty."

"Oh, really?" The bartender puffed himself up. "And who is your brother?"

"Lucas Corsi, Silverton Saloon."

The man's face slackened. He gave Marcello a hard stare, took the coins, and walked away.

The brothers left the saloon and assessed their damage: Jim's bloody nose, Mick's split lip, and Angelo's swollen eye. Marcello put his hand to his jaw and slid it side to side, then opened and closed his mouth a few times. His jaw was sore, but he still had all his teeth.

"Mio Dio!" Marcello exhaled. "Those men are crazy. Will they be back?"

"We'll never see them again, but we'll see others like them," said Angelo. "They're no-good drunks. They've already moved on to find another fight in another saloon."

Jim said, "There's nothing we can do about it—"

Mick finished the sentence. "Except be ready the next time it happens."

"You just said they wouldn't be back," Marcello protested.

"There are more crazy drifters out here than just those four," Mick said.

Angelo and Jim said good night and walked down the dark street toward the miners' neighborhood. Before they disappeared, Jim called over his shoulder. "Hey, Marcello, you throw a damn good punch." He waved and kept walking.

Marcello couldn't help admiring Jim's dismissive attitude. "That's Jim. Sees the fight as just another Friday-night brawl."

"They're a nasty lot, those cowboys," said Mick. "But like Angelo said, nothing'll come of it. They're gone."

When they arrived at the farm, Marcello helped Mick bed the horse down. As they walked back to the house, Marcello stopped. "Think I'll stay outside for a while. Not ready to sleep yet."

Mick looked critically at Marcello. "How bad does your jaw hurt? Want some laudanum?"

Marcello touched the swelling. "It'll be all right."

"The lantern's here on the porch if you need it. Try to get some rest." Mick gently squeezed Marcello's shoulder before he mounted the steps and went inside.

The moon lit Marcello's way to the barn; the earth burst with the dampness of early spring. He found a mound of clean straw in one corner and stretched out on his back, fingers laced behind his head. As much as he wanted to forget everything that had happened in the saloon, he couldn't. Images of the fight played over and over in his head, the faces of the cowboys and Crooked Nose looming in grotesque detail. *Parassiti! Un porco!* The more he relived the brawl, the angrier he got. He hoped his brothers were wrong about the cowboys never coming back to town. He wanted those men to return to Cumberland, so he could finish the fight. He balled his hand into a fist and slammed it into the straw.

His thoughts suddenly turned to his family. Would Luisa and Tony be safe here? The cowboys had just exposed an ugly side of Cumberland, one he'd never seen before. Was moving here another bad decision?

Slivers of pale moonlight streaked through the gaps in the plank siding and laced across the barn floor. Marcello closed his eyes, and his breathing slowed. The smell of hay, the odor of the barn, the lowing of the cows took him back to Monastero with such clarity, he felt if he reached out, Luisa would be there beside him, and all of this would be just a bad dream.

Chapter 10

"I'm glad you came with me," Luisa said to her sister, Angelica, as they placed wild asters from the meadow on the baby's grave.

"You're alone too much—you need company." Angelica and their brother Roberto lived at home and cared for their widowed mother. Although never married, Angelica had a lifetime of experience helping raise the children in the family. Luisa was the youngest of seven, and Angelica, the oldest daughter, had never hesitated to offer motherly advice.

They sat in the grass beside the grave and looked across the valley at the changing shades of green on the tree-covered hills. The brilliant June sun lit up Angelica's auburn hair and accentuated the sprinkling of freckles on her cheeks. The sisters differed in coloring but shared the same round face and wide-set eyes.

A wrought-iron fence enclosed the tiny hillside cemetery, cared for by the families on the mountain. On her first visit after the burial, the barren mound of dirt over the grave tore at Luisa's heart. She fled the cemetery, unable to bear the sight. Angelica had planted grass that now softened the grave with new growth. Papa fashioned a cross from scraps of wood, and Batista carved the inscription: Sophia Corsi, 10 April 1916.

"I don't mind coming here by myself. And I'm not alone. Marcello's parents—"

"You know what I mean. You haven't visited us for weeks. Mama misses you. We all do."

Luisa looked into her lap, fidgeting with her fingers. "Tell Mama I'm sorry. I don't mean to stay away. It's just . . . coming here every day keeps my baby's memory alive. I have to do this."

"Mama and I worry about you. It's been two months since . . ." Angelica's words trailed off.

Luisa looked up, her brow furrowed. "Two months, and I still don't have an answer. Why did this happen? I had no trouble carrying Tony. Why with this baby?" She drew a breath. Her expression turned sorrowful. "What if I never have another baby?"

Angelica wrapped her arms around Luisa. "You'll have more babies."

"You don't know that." Tears welled in Luisa's eyes.

"I *do* know it," insisted Angelica. "Our mama lost two babies. Look at how many more she had. Same with Mama Corsi—she lost one and had six strapping boys after that."

"What if I'm not strong enough for the trip to America? The crossing is difficult, and it's a long way to Wyoming."

"You have your strength back—you're healthy enough."

"But if something happens to me on the way, who would take care of Tony?"

"I know losing the baby broke your heart. Mama says the sadness, at least some of it, stays with you forever. But it lessens over time." Angelica grasped both of Luisa's hands. "You're letting it take over your life. Some days I hardly recognize you."

Luisa wiped her cheeks with the back of her hand. "Maybe I should leave Tony with Marcello's parents and send for him later."

"Don't be silly, Luisa. You could never leave Tony behind." A soft breeze sent wispy clouds across the sky and rustled through the trees. "Have you told Marcello?"

"I tried to. I tore up the letter I wrote the night before the baby was born. I waited a few weeks and tried again. It was hopeless. I cried so much, I couldn't finish." Luisa's voice was a whisper. "Little Sophia."

Angelica spoke softly. "She's in God's heaven. Try to find peace in that." When Luisa didn't answer, Angelica asked, "Are you ready to go home?"

Luisa stared off into the distance. She twirled a loose strand of hair, a habit the sisters shared when lost in thought. She turned to Angelica, a pleading sadness in her eyes. "Is God punishing me?"

Luisa brought small bouquets to the baby's grave every day through the summer and into the golden autumn until the winter rains came. Gray clouds shrouded the hillsides, and the village huddled under drenching rain that changed to wet snow. The days stretched endlessly, each one more dismal than the day before. An unshakable heaviness settled over Luisa. She woke up tired, her limbs burdened by invisible weight. The feeling spread deep inside and wrapped itself around her heart.

Luisa stumbled on the path, lost her balance, and rolled to the bottom of the hill. She found herself in a ravine of brambles that tore her legs and ripped her skirt as she yanked it from the thorns. Willing her legs forward, she climbed the hill, frantically searching for the path. Maybe at the top, she could see where he was. Shadows closed in around her and the path disappeared. It was late, and she should turn back, but not before she found him. Huge boulders appeared. She climbed over them, clutching at the smooth surfaces, and slid backward. She stood and ran up the hill again until she gasped for air and staggered to her knees. *Where are you, Marcello?* She screamed his name, but nothing came out of her mouth.

Luisa sat up in bed, her heart pounding, her gown drenched with sweat. The candle stood cold in its holder on the nightstand. Through the window the sky was black and showed no signs of a winter dawn. She wiped sweat from her forehead with the sleeve of her nightgown. She knew the dream too well.

Luisa pulled her knees to her chest and dropped her head as tears spilled down her cheeks. No matter how hard she tried, she couldn't find Marcello. It was a terrifying dream, but worse to wake to the painful reality of his absence.

Luisa remembered the Montrose family that lived farther up the mountain. After their third baby was born, the mother took to bed and didn't rise to care for any of the children, not even the newborn. Frantic with worry, the father asked for help from the women in the village. Luisa knew she had to pull herself out of the mire before she became that mother.

She made herself walk to the village and buy skeins of yarn at Donato's store. On cold, sunless days, she knitted scarves for the family and sweaters for Tony as he outgrew his baby clothes. She offered to take the cows to pasture after milking in the morning. When butter needed churning, Mama was grateful for her help. Luisa took on the bigger share of the housework, whether it was making soap, boiling laundry, or baking bread.

Still, at the end of the day or on Sunday afternoons when chores were done and life stood still, she couldn't escape the heartbreaking reality of living each day without Marcello. She tried not to think about the months and years stretching endlessly before her, but she did. Not knowing when they'd be together again was almost unbearable.

Luisa opened her eyes to streaks of daylight slanting through the window. She hoped it signaled a day of sunshine and an end to the cold rain that had soaked the village all winter. Lacking the will to get up, she rolled onto her back and stared at the weathered beams supporting the sagging roof. On the wall beside her bed hung a calendar of the Madonna and Child from San Nicolao Church in the village. Her eyes rested on April fifteenth. Marcello had been gone exactly a year and a half. It seemed like a lifetime.

Tony slept peacefully in his crib at the foot of her bed. She sat up and watched his chest rise and fall, listening to his tiny puffs of breath, and whispered a prayer of thanks for a healthy child.

Leaning against the headboard, she pulled the quilt up under her chin against the chill in the loft. Next month would bring another milestone: Marcello's twenty-first birthday. She wanted to send him something special. New trousers? Not practical. Work clothes? Practical, but not for his birthday. She closed her eyes. A new sweater? Not with warm weather coming. Tony stirred. His quiet jabbering brought a smile to her lips. Just before drifting off, she sat upright, her eyes wide. What a wonderful idea!

With a glimmer of purpose in the day ahead, Luisa swung her legs out of bed and pulled on a wool dress. She lifted Tony from the crib and hugged him. "Let's get you dressed and see if Nonno and Nonna are up."

Marcello's father brought an armload of wood into the house as Luisa came downstairs carrying Tony on her hip. He set the wood on the hearth and added a log to the crackling fire. "Just saw a pair of finches," he said, brushing his hands on his pants. "The first sign of spring."

"Glad to see you're up early," Mama said. "Feeling better?"

"I *am* feeling better," said Luisa. "What can I do?"

"Slice the bread. I'll make coffee."

Luisa went to the cupboard for her apron and set a loaf on the cutting board. Before she could cut the first slice, she spun around, bursting to share her idea. "I've thought of a surprise for Marcello's birthday."

"Oh?" said Mama.

"A photograph of Tony. It's been a year and a half since Marcello's seen him, and I know he'd love to see how much Tony has grown. Then I thought, why not have a photograph of the whole family—both of you, me, Alfonso, and Batista with Tony? What do you think?" Luisa paused and eyed Marcello's parents, trying to gauge their reaction. "I know it will be an expense, but I'll make extra trips to the village to sell eggs and chestnuts, maybe churn butter to sell.

Marcello's father turned to Tony, who teetered beside him on wobbly legs. A gentle smile creased his weathered face and he nodded. "Marcello would like to see his son. What do you think, Mama?"

"It's a good idea." Mrs. Corsi's eyes shone as she spoke to Luisa. "We'll find a way to pay for it. The photographer in Lanzo, the one who took Marcello's photograph before he left—we can use him. He's fair with his price. Maybe he'll trade for produce."

Luisa smiled with genuine joy for the first time in months.

Luisa looked through the wardrobe, but already knew there was only one dress to wear for this picture—her dark blue Sunday dress with leg-o'-mutton sleeves. It was her only piece of clothing from a store, and she treated it with such care, it looked as new as the day she bought it.

She dressed Tony in a white smock. He wiggled from side to side on the bed as she poked his arms through the sleeves. "Young man, you are too wiggly." She buttoned the smock and scooped him up into her lap.

"Hold still." Tony waved his arms above his head, trying to grab the brush from his mama. When she finished, Luisa frowned at the wispy ends of hair that refused to lie flat. She licked her fingers and pressed the strands in place. "All done." She planted a big kiss on his cheek and carried him downstairs.

The family climbed into the horse-drawn cart and bumped down the winding road into Lanzo, to the photographer's studio, on a narrow, cobbled street. A bell on the door jangled as they stepped inside, and the photographer led them to a large room at the back of his studio. Marcello's father and brothers adjusted their collars and tugged at their coat sleeves; Marcello's mother smoothed the wrinkles from her skirt. Papa and Mama sat in chairs in front of a pastoral scene hanging from the ceiling. Alfonso and Batista stood behind them. Luisa bounced Tony in her arms and hummed quietly until the photographer motioned for her to stand next to the brothers.

"Now, everyone, look this way." The photographer ducked his head under the black cloth behind the camera, then reappeared. "Ready? Hold still . . ."

Luisa held her breath. *Happy birthday, my darling.*

CHAPTER 11

The wrapping paper fell away, and Marcello found himself staring at his family. His loved ones, half a world away, came to life in Mick's Wyoming farmhouse. He marveled at their images and ran his fingers over their faces. To his great relief, Mama and Papa hadn't aged since he'd last seen them. His brothers' faces reflected strength and vitality. He could rely on Alfonso and Batista to care for Mama and Papa.

The sight of Luisa cut through him with a stab of longing. She looked beautiful, her hair swept back from her face, her eyes wide and expressive, her lips turned up ever so slightly. He ached for her. Tony's chubby cheeks and curly dark hair brought a smile to his lips. The infant he had kissed goodbye was now a thriving, healthy child. Comfort washed over him.

He set the photograph on the small table beside his bed. Whenever he was discouraged with the slow progress of saving money, whenever his aching body begged for rest, looking into the faces he loved made him work harder to bring his beloved Luisa to his arms.

A sharp wind whipped the dark clouds building in the western sky and kicked up the snow on the low hills around Mick's farmhouse.

"More snow tonight," Mick said as he and Marcello mounted the steps on the back porch. They stomped snow off their work boots and unbuttoned their coats. The door flew open.

"Uncle Marcello, there's a package for you!" Anna was breathless.

"Come see." Ida grabbed Marcello's hand, and together his nieces led him into the front room brightly lit by kerosene lamps. A cardboard box bound with string sat on the plank table.

The room smelled of fresh pine. Yesterday Mick and Marcello had chopped down an evergreen from a clump of scrub pines and brought it inside to stand in front of the window. The girls had ripped pages from the old Montgomery Ward's catalog destined for the outhouse and cut strips of paper they glued into chains. The tree dripped with them.

"Mama said it's from Aunt Luisa." Anna's voice rose dramatically. "From Italy!"

"It's your Christmas present." Ida's eyes sparkled with excitement. "I can't wait for tomorrow."

"Neither can I," said Anna.

"Ah, but you *do* have to wait." Marcello's smile grew wider as he picked up the box and gently shook it.

Theresa came from the kitchen, wiping her hands on her apron. "They've been watching for you ever since the post came." She turned to the girls. "I told you not to bother your uncle when he came home. Come help set the table for supper. *Fretta.*"

Marcello retreated to his small bedroom off the kitchen, grateful for a moment alone. He sat on the bed and hugged the box to his chest. He'd open it tomorrow, but he wanted to cherish the package from Luisa in private. He looked at the postage stamps and wondered how she'd paid for sending the package. She must have saved an extra lira here and there from produce she sold in the village. It would have taken her weeks to save enough money.

It occurred to him she might have tucked a letter inside,

which meant news from home. His eagerness to hear from Luisa overcame his resolve to wait until Christmas, and he opened the package. A letter was on top.

30 November 1917

Dearest Marcello,

Merry Christmas my dear husband. We are all well. I pray this is our last Christmas apart. I miss you so but wait patiently for the day you send for us. I know you work hard every day to earn money for our passage.

I asked Sister Margarita to help me write a letter. I stayed after Mass last Sunday. She's a good teacher and helped me with spelling. I asked her to help me learn English, and she said yes.

I have exciting news. Roberto has decided to accompany me to America! You know how I have worried about finding a male traveling companion. His friend Carlo Finni will travel with us, too. Mama will be very sad to see us leave, but Angelica will be here to care for her.

Tony is healthy and grows bigger every day. All his first teeth are in. When he smiles his dimples look like yours. We say prayers for you at bedtime, and I tell him Papa waits for us in America.

Take care of yourself Marcello. I hope my sweater keeps you warm this winter. I miss you with all my heart. Nothing will make me happier than the day we are together again.

Your loving wife,
Luisa Corsi

Marcello lifted a green wool sweater from the box. He pulled it over his head and ran his hand over the soft, even stitches. He pictured Luisa beside the fire after a long day, knitting a gift for him, love in every stitch. That was so like her—never too tired to think of others. Wrapped in her splendid sweater, Marcello's heart nearly burst. It was an embrace from across the ocean.

He turned his gaze to the family portrait on the bedside table and smiled. "It's perfect, my dear Luisa." He ran his hands over the sweater once more before he pulled it over his head and carefully returned it to the box. He would share his gift from Luisa with Mick's family on Christmas morning. It deserved to be opened a second time.

By the end of winter, Marcello wrote Luisa he had saved the seventy-five dollars needed to pay for ocean passage, and almost half of the fifty dollars for train tickets from New York to Kemmerer. Luisa was overjoyed and danced around the cottage, the letter clasped to her heart. The good news came as the daffodils pushed through the earth, and white blossoms burst from the pear tree. The spring air was sweet with promise.

On an unusually warm May afternoon, Luisa trudged up the path to her mother's whitewashed cottage and called out, "Roberto, Angelica." The path from Monastero to Coassolo where her family lived wove around thickets of dense shrubs and through groves of wild chestnut trees. She wiped away trickles of sweat from her forehead with the back of her hand and brushed bits of weed off her skirt. The door swung open.

"There you are!" Angelica smiled, her arms open for a hug. "Mama will be happy to see you. She talks about your Sunday visit all week."

Luisa stepped inside. "Where's Roberto?"

"Right behind you," a deep voice rumbled.

Luisa turned to see her brother duck his tall frame through the doorway. He set a basket of eggs by the door. Roberto had dark eyes just like Luisa, but in his, there was a permanent glint of mischief. He sported a carefully trimmed mustache that made him look older than his twenty-two years. "The girls in the village find me irresistible with my new mustache," he had told his sisters with an air of importance.

Luisa hugged Roberto. "How's Mama?"

"She doesn't have much energy today."

"Come." Angelica motioned for Luisa to follow her to the room at the back of the house. Their mother was asleep on a narrow bed with a cotton blanket draped over her tiny frame. A breeze through an open window cooled the room.

Luisa leaned over the bed. "Mama."

Her mother stirred and opened her eyes. "Luisa." She sat up, pulled Luisa close and kissed both her cheeks. "Where's Tony?"

Luisa sat on the edge of the bed. "His little legs can't walk this far. I'll bring him next week when we ride in the cart." Luisa eyed her mother critically. "How are you?"

"Some days good, some days . . ." She waved her hand dismissively. "Tell me your news. Have you heard from Marcello?"

Luisa grinned and pulled a letter from her pocket. "A letter came yesterday."

"Good news, I hope," said Roberto. He sat on the floor at the foot of the bed and stretched out his long legs.

"Read it to us," said Angelica and pulled up a chair.

Luisa unfolded the letter. "His health is good, and he's busy at the mine. But here's the exciting news." She cleared her throat to emphasize the next words. " 'There are houses in town that belong to the coal company for miners and their families. One of them will be available soon, and I'll move in.' " Luisa felt herself flush with happiness. "A *house,* just for us." She beamed at her family before continuing. "He says it will cost eleven American dollars a month."

"How much is that in lira?" Angelica asked.

"I don't know, but the house has two bedrooms and a big kitchen."

Luisa's mother nodded. "Sounds nice, dear."

Luisa continued. "Let's see . . . the town has added another pool hall . . ." She stopped reading and looked up, puzzled. "Roberto, what's a pool hall?"

He shrugged. "Not sure."

"Wonder why they need two of them?" She turned the letter over. "The company plans to build a doctor's office."

"A doctor's office in town." Angelica was impressed. "You are fortunate."

"Does he say when he'll send for you?" Roberto asked.

"That's the best part—in about three months." Luisa's excitement bubbled over. "Three months, Mama!"

Her mother tipped her head to one side and studied Luisa. "You look happy, my dear. That does me good." She patted Luisa's hand. "You should be with Marcello." She tried to smile, but Luisa saw sadness in her eyes. "Soon we'll have to say goodbye."

A soft breeze stirred the gauzy curtains at the window. Luisa wrapped her arms around her mother. "Yes, Mama," she whispered. They sat silently for a long while, the warbling of a finch in a tree outside the window the only sound.

The pots of flowers outside Donato's store withered in the August heat. Luisa pushed open the shop door, a basket of zucchini on each arm.

"Hello, Mrs. Donato," said Luisa, setting the baskets on the counter. She wiped her damp brow with a swipe of her forearm. "Such a hot day."

"You brought zucchini," Mrs. Donato said, her short plump figure covered in a work apron. "That's good. We're almost out." She disappeared beneath the counter and reappeared with the scales.

"I wondered . . ." Luisa paused and raised her eyebrows.

"If the mail's come?" Mrs. Donato winked at Luisa as she placed squash in the scale's metal bowl.

"Yes." Luisa broke into a smile.

"As a matter of fact, my mister is in the back right now sorting it. He should be done soon."

"Is someone asking about the mail?" a voice boomed from the back room. Mr. Donato appeared, as tall and thin as his wife was short and round, and walked to the counter, a letter in his hand. "I believe there's something here for you today, my dear."

"Oh, thank you, thank you!" Luisa snatched the letter from his hand and immediately felt herself redden with embarrassment.

"I know you're anxious for news from America," he said. "Go read it, find out he's all right."

"Don't leave without your money." Mrs. Donato dropped four coins into Luisa's hand.

Luisa's feet barely touched the floor on her way out the door. The afternoon sun slanted across the piazza as she quickened her steps past the villagers. She perched on the wide stone steps of the church and tore open the envelope. A banknote fell into her lap. She stared at it. With trembling hands, she held Marcello's letter as her eyes raced over his words.

". . . money for you and Tony for reservations on the train from Lanzo . . . passage from Le Havre to New York . . . train to Kemmerer, Wyoming."

The words swam before her eyes.

". . . we'll be together soon . . . we can start again, dear Luisa."

A sob escaped her mouth. "It's here. It's finally here." She jumped up and wiped the tears from her cheeks. She ran across the piazza, her hair tumbling loose from its pins, past the villagers' curious stares, past Donato's store to the path home, clutching the banknote of one hundred twenty-five dollars.

CHAPTER 12

An old beat-up chair and a small side table from the previous tenants stood in the empty miner's quarters when Marcello took possession. He walked through the three rooms, mentally taking notes, and decided to cobble together enough furnishings so Luisa wouldn't arrive to an empty house. But he needed to do more. He wanted to welcome her to their new home with just one piece of furniture that wasn't a cast-off. Something special to mark the beginning of life in their new country. He would buy the best wood his budget could afford and build a dining table.

Two weeks after he mailed Luisa the banknote, Marcello drove Mick's wagon to the lumberyard in Kemmerer and selected quarter-sawn oak for the table and a thick piece of maple for a cutting board. On the weekends he cut, sanded, and fashioned an oblong dining table big enough to seat his brothers and their wives for Sunday dinner. He pictured Luisa using the cutting board to dice vegetables, the table to roll out dough and stuff chickens. He'd whittle toys for Tony here and play cards with his brothers on Saturday nights. He wasn't building just a piece of furniture; he was crafting the place that would become the heart of their home.

The late afternoon sun dipped behind the hills at the farm while Mick milked the cows. Contented lowing repeated through the barn. Marcello swatted away flies as he stared at the tabletop lying upside down on a tarpaulin on the barn floor.

He had attached three legs and raised his hammer to nail the last one in place. His hand slipped, and the hammer slammed onto his thumb, splintering the wood at the nail hole. *"Dannazione!"* He shook his hand in the air to throw off the pain.

Mick appeared at his side, a bucket of fresh milk in each hand. "Need help?"

"The leg is giving me fits. Keeps splitting."

"Let me hold it." Mick lowered the buckets to the floor. "Give it a quarter turn and try again."

Marcello raised his hammer, and on the second swing, the top of the leg split as the nail went through. *"Stupido,"* he muttered. He yanked the nail out with the claw and repositioned the leg. One, two, three swings, and splinters of wood popped off the top of the leg as the nail pushed through. Marcello threw his hammer to the floor and glared at the table, hands on his hips.

Mick picked up the splintered leg. "You've been at this since morning. Time to call it quits."

"There's so much left to do," Marcello argued. "I have only three weekends to get the house ready before Luisa comes. I still have to sand and varnish the table and—"

"Papa, Uncle Marcello, supper's ready," Ida sang from the back porch.

"Let's eat, Marcello. There's always tomorrow." They leaned the table against the wall, the offending leg beside it, and headed to the house for supper.

Refreshed after a good night's sleep, Marcello returned to the barn the next morning after Mass. He repaired the leg, turned the worst side inward, and hammered it in place on the first try. With Mick's help, they righted the table and stood back to examine it.

"If you don't look too close, it looks fine," Marcello said, viewing the table from every angle. *"È finito,"* he proclaimed, and waved his hammer in triumph. He turned to Mick. "What's that American saying about the tunnel and the light?"

" 'I see the light at the end of the tunnel.' "

"Yes, yes, that's it. I've sent Luisa money for her passage and now"—he swept his arm to the table with a flourish—"I've finished the first piece of furniture for our home. I see the light in the tunnel."

"The light *at the end* of the tunnel," Mick corrected.

"That's what I said." Marcello grinned ear to ear. The arrival of his family was at hand. He could taste it.

Luisa stood in front of the clothes piled on her bed, both hands on her hips, and declared, "We have work to finish." She and Angelica had started sorting and mending at sunup the day before and were nearly finished with their task. When they weren't chattering or laughing, Luisa hummed happily.

Tomorrow she would leave for America.

Besides clothes for herself and Tony, Luisa packed her most treasured possessions in Mama's humpback trunk built by her father: her wedding quilt, a portrait of Marcello's parents, her first communion cross, and her sewing basket with knitting needles.

Angelica folded Luisa's nightgown. "Marcello will be happy to see this again." Her dimples appeared in an impish grin.

"Angelica!" Luisa pretended to be offended, but their grins turned to laughter. "Marcello won't be the only one happy. Sharing his bed is long overdue."

With the trunk packed, Luisa stuffed skeins of yarn wherever she found empty spaces in the corners, then stood back to take stock. "Let's hope it closes." She pulled up the massive lid and let it fall, banging the metal latches as it slammed shut. "We did it!" Luisa shouted, buoyant with success. "We make a good team."

Angelica clapped her hands. "Well done."

Luisa stared at the trunk, solidly latched, and suddenly felt something in her own life latch permanently. She turned to Angelica, and they both recognized the enormity of the moment. "I wish I could take *you* with me, just like everything else I need. You would be such a comfort." Luisa sank to the bed and gazed at the loft that had been her bedroom for the last three years. "Don't tell Mama," she said.

"Don't tell her what?" Angelica sat next to Luisa.

"That I'm scared. Scared of crossing the ocean, of what the ship will be like, of finding my way to Wyoming. I don't know enough English."

"Roberto and Carlo will take care of you. You'll be safe."

Luisa continued. "I have prayed for this day for three years. I'm so happy, but—" She stopped. "I dread tomorrow. How do I say goodbye to you and Mama? How?" She put her hand to her lips and swallowed the emotion rising in her throat.

Angelica blinked away tears. "I don't know, Luisa. We'll just do it. Mama and I pray you have a safe journey. Like Marcello's mother, we hope we will see you again someday, God willing."

They embraced. Luisa held on to her sister, knowing that after tomorrow, she would never see her again.

Angelica's navy suit was her pride and joy, years old but good as new. She insisted Luisa wear it to America. "It's very warm and fits you. You need it more than I do."

Tony's sweater and knickers made him look every bit a three-year-old. Even though it was a mild September day, they planned for the cold voyage ahead and wore their only coats over their traveling clothes.

Luisa steeled herself for the farewells on the day of departure, but soon realized there was no way to prepare for the heartache when she and Marcello's parents said goodbye.

"You've loved me like your own daughter. I'll remember that forever." Luisa's voice broke and tears filled her eyes.

Marcello's parents embraced her and Tony, not wanting to let go. "We are your family," said Papa. "Go to Marcello, take care of each other."

Luisa wept with Mama, remembering how Mama had begged Marcello not to leave three years before, but he'd left anyway. Now children were leaving again. Marcello's mother had delivered Tony and their stillborn daughter. She had comforted Luisa for three long years. She had given unconditional love. There were no words for the bond they shared, nor words for Luisa's depth of love and gratitude.

Roberto hefted Luisa's trunk into the back of the cart, and they bumped along the rutted road from Monastero to their mother's home. Mama was sitting up in bed, a shawl around her tiny shoulders, when Luisa, Tony, Roberto, and Angelica gathered in her bedroom.

Luisa sat on the bed and pulled Tony alongside her.

"Everything's ready then?" Mama asked.

"It's all in the cart—the trunk, our bags, everything," said Roberto.

Mama gazed from Roberto to Luisa. "I want you both to promise me something."

"Anything, Mama," said Roberto.

"Promise you'll look after each other."

"Of course we will," said Luisa.

"Roberto, take care of your sister. Traveling alone with a child on such a long trip, she needs you. There are men who might take advantage."

Roberto nodded solemnly "Don't worry, Mama. I'll protect her."

Mama turned to Luisa. "Your brother has the heart of a youth. He likes the girls, but he's looking for a wife—"

"Mama," Roberto protested.

She held up her hand to silence him. "Choose your wife wisely, Roberto. You are a good son, and I want you to have a good life in America. Come here." She opened her arms, and Roberto leaned in and hugged her. She kissed him on both cheeks. "Godspeed, my dear son."

"I love you, Mama." Roberto stood and wiped his eyes. He turned to Angelica and gave her a long hug.

"Tony, it's time to say goodbye to Nonna," said Luisa. "Come give her a big hug and a kiss." Tony hugged his grandmother as she held him close and covered his head with kisses.

Roberto held out his hand to Tony. "Come outside with me while Mama says goodbye to Nonna." They left the room, hand in hand.

Luisa silently thanked Roberto for his thoughtfulness. He understood exactly what she needed at this moment—time alone with Mama. Luisa swallowed before speaking, hoping to steady her voice. "Thank you for your trunk, Mama. I know it will bring me good luck in America. You should see how well we packed. You'd be proud."

"I'm proud of you for many reasons, Luisa. You're brave to travel across the ocean, facing so many unknown things."

"I won't be alone."

"Roberto and Carlo will look after you, but it's not the same as making the journey with your husband. You have a lot of courage, my dear, no matter what you say."

Luisa could hold her emotions in no longer. She bent her head and tears fell. "I'm not brave, Mama. I'm scared."

Mama pulled her youngest daughter into her arms and stroked Luisa's hair.

Luisa let her tears flow as she felt her mother's gentle touch. All her life, everything was made right in her mother's arms. Here she was safe; here she found comfort.

"I used to do this when you were a little girl, remember?" Mama whispered.

Unable to speak, Luisa could only nod, cherishing Mama's gentle caress for what she knew would be the last time. At length, Luisa wiped her cheeks and straightened. Through her tears, she studied her mother's face and memorized her soft brown eyes, wrinkled cheeks, and snow-white hair. When Luisa was a child, there hadn't been money for a family photograph. Her mother's declining health during the past two years had kept them from making a trip to the photographer in Lanzo. Now it was too late. Luisa had no picture of Mama to take with her, no locket with her image. Nothing. Luisa held her mother's hand. "I carry you in my heart, Mama. You are always with me. I love you."

"And you are in my heart, Luisa. I love you." Her cheeks were wet with tears.

Luisa stood and embraced Angelica before whispering goodbye. With Roberto at her side, Luisa left the tiny cottage, holding Tony's hand, and followed the path down the hill, leaving the family she loved and the only life she'd ever known, just as Marcello had done three years before.

Chapter 13

September

The sight of their ship waiting at the dock took Luisa's breath away. The morning sun illuminated the name, *La Savoie,* emblazoned on the side and the two large smokestacks that reached into a sparkling blue September sky. Tony clutched her hand and stared wide-eyed at the shouting dockworkers, the stevedores hauling cargo onto the ship, and the crush of immigrants waiting to board with them. Luisa inhaled the salty air with deep breaths and a smile spread across her face.

She bent close to Tony and whispered, her voice filled with emotion, "That's the ship that will take us to America."

The metal gate clanked open. Trailing behind Roberto and Carlo, Luisa and Tony inched up the gangway in the press of steerage passengers. Tony was suddenly sandwiched between two men. Luisa yanked him back to her side before he was swallowed by the crowd and lifted him into her arms. She carried him on board, both arms tightly around him, and crossed the deck. Even in the open air, the odor of unwashed bodies nearly overwhelmed her. When they reached a darkened stairwell, she set Tony down, and they clattered down the metal steps to the lowest deck. A uniformed attendant directed Roberto and Carlo to a passageway on the right, Luisa and Tony to the opposite direction on the left.

"What's this?" Luisa frowned.

"They separate the families and the single men. Marcello

wrote about this. You and Tony are with the families down that way." Roberto pointed to the passageway on the left and handed Luisa her satchel. She'd heard about this, but didn't want to face it. They'd eat and sleep in different dormitories, and now it was time to go their separate ways.

The thought of traveling without Roberto at her side terrified her. "I can't do this. I don't know anyone else." She squeezed Tony's hand until he winced.

"You'll be with other families," Carlo offered.

Her frown deepened. "But they don't speak Italian," Luisa protested.

"Some do. I heard them," said Roberto. Irritated passengers behind them pressed against their backs. "We'd better move along." Roberto and Carlo turned toward the men's dormitory.

Luisa didn't budge. "Can we meet on deck after we're settled?"

"Yes," Roberto called as he moved farther away. "Tony, be a good boy for your mama."

The wave of passengers pushed Luisa and Tony down the passageway like leaves swept downstream and deposited them in a cavernous room dimly lit by gas lamps. Slatted vents allowed slivers of light into the gloomy space. Trestle tables and rough wooden benches ringed the walls, and rows of iron beds stacked two deep filled the remaining space in the center of the room.

Luisa was shocked by the number of people already crammed into the space. They swarmed past her and crowded between the berths to claim beds. Confused and anxious, they juggled bundles of clothing and satchels, hollering at one another in languages she'd never heard before. She had to act quickly. She wove her way through the horde to a bed on the outer edge of the sleeping area with a hammock suspended from a beam beside it.

"Tony, sit on this bed." She set her satchel into the hammock and claimed their space.

No sooner had Luisa secured their beds than a burly man threw a suitcase on the bunk above her head and waved to a woman with three children. Luisa froze. This stranger—a man, no less—would be sleeping in the bunk directly above her, barely an arm's length away. If that wasn't frightening enough, he was overweight. Would his bed come crashing down on her as she slept, crushing her between bunks?

She sneaked a glance at the family. The man had dark hair and a thick mustache, his shirt and trousers threadbare but clean. The mother looked haggard. Strands of dark hair straggled from under her kerchief. She chose a bed across from Luisa and pointed at three open bunks for the children. Their clothes were tattered and patched. Luisa suddenly felt conspicuous in Angelica's navy suit and lowered her eyes.

After the woman secured her bunk, she turned around. Luisa raised her eyes, and the woman spoke. *"Buongiorno?"*

Luisa jumped up with a smile of relief and pumped the woman's hand. *"Si, buongiorno, buongiorno!"*

Before going up on deck, Luisa stowed her satchel on top of her bunk, hoping to keep her food away from rats, and immediately started to worry about the safety of her belongings. Any one of the hundreds of passengers could ransack her things while she was gone. *At least my money is safe,* she thought, touching the small cloth pouch with her lira pinned to the inside of her suit jacket. Realizing there was no way to secure her bag, Luisa decided to trust the other passengers and pray they were honest.

"Let's find Uncle Roberto and Carlo."

They stepped out of the stairwell into the fresh morning air. The deck was packed. Some passengers leaned against the railings to wave farewell or milled about the promenade, while others enjoyed strolling the deck. Luisa scanned the crowd. Roberto was a head taller than most men; she thought it would be easy to find him. "I don't see him, Tony. Come with me."

Luisa clasped Tony's hand, and they walked the deck until they came to a metal barricade. "I guess this is as far as we go." She looked beyond the barricade to a spacious deck where passengers sat on lounge chairs. The women wore coats with fur collars and matching hats trimmed with satin. The men sported topcoats over vested suits. Even at a distance, Luisa could tell the clothes were expensive and the shoes made of fine leather. Moments ago, she'd felt overdressed in front of the family from Palermo. Now, wearing her sister's nicest suit, she looked across the barricade and felt every bit the peasant from Italy.

She squared her shoulders and lifted her chin. "Let's turn around." They hadn't gone far when Luisa spotted Roberto and Carlo talking with what looked like a family—a father, mother, and two daughters.

Roberto waved. "Luisa, come here." He turned to the father and mother and introduced them to Luisa. "This is Mr. and Mrs. Barra."

Luisa nodded and shook hands. "Nice to meet you."

"They're from Napoli," said Carlo. "These are their daughters, Elana and Tina." Luisa guessed Tina was about her age and Elana a few years younger. Both pretty girls. She noticed Roberto flashing his most attractive smile and speculated the girls were the reason he and Carlo had struck up a conversation with the family.

Luisa turned to Roberto. "You were right. I've already met an Italian family, and they have bunks next to ours."

"See, what did I tell you?"

"They're from Palermo. Their dialect is different, but we understand each other."

Three low-pitched blasts from the ship's bridge stopped their conversation. Luisa started. "Are we leaving?" A quiet rumble resonated from deep within the ship.

"Let's stand at the railing," Carlo said.

"We don't have anyone to wave to," said Tina.

"Doesn't matter," Roberto replied. "It's exciting. Come on."

They wedged in at the railing, Luisa and her family, the Barras, and hundreds of others from steerage to watch the ship ease away from the dock. Luisa's heart pounded as a farewell cheer rose from the crowd on shore. Her wait was over. In spite of the thrill in that moment, a strange sadness tugged at her heart. This was goodbye to Italy. Like Marcello, she would always love Italy, for it marked the place of her beginning. America would mark a second beginning for her, and she couldn't reach Marcello soon enough to embrace it. Luisa felt the ship's gentle movement beneath her feet. She looped her arm through Roberto's and tipped her head to the sky.

"We're on our way!"

Luisa lined up early for supper. After the chaotic noon meal, she was determined to hold her place in line. If that meant planting her feet and using her elbows, so be it. A ship steward and men in their dormitory helped keep order by yanking back those who broke the line.

Ship attendants dished out boiled fish and potatoes into their dinner pails as Luisa and Tony passed through the food line. They hurried to find seats at one of the tables quickly filling with passengers. A dark-skinned man with long hair, wearing a soiled tunic, spoke to Luisa as he squeezed in beside her. She didn't understand him and shrugged with a faint smile. His unwashed body smelled and forced Luisa to turn her attention to Tony.

"Eat your supper," Luisa urged.

Tony picked at his food. "It doesn't taste good." He frowned.

"Eat, or you'll be hungry. And drink your milk." Luisa brought a bite of fish to her mouth, and her stomach recoiled at the strong odor. No wonder Tony didn't want to eat it. She forced herself to swallow the fish and found the potatoes tasteless and mushy. Tony drank his milk but refused to eat. Fortunately for both of them, Luisa had packed food for their journey. She pulled a hunk of bread stashed in her skirt pocket, ripped it in two, and shared it with Tony.

Tony fell asleep in his hammock as soon as he closed his eyes. Luisa went to the lavatory, changed into a wool skirt and cotton blouse, and carefully folded away her suit for their arrival in America. She pinned the cloth pouch with her lira to the inside of her skirt and returned to the darkened dormitory. Stowing her satchel at the foot of her bed, she fell onto the bunk, exhausted.

She closed her eyes and listened to the hum of conversations that floated through the dormitory. A baby cried, and a mother sang a simple tune with strange-sounding words. Luisa pictured the mother rocking her baby as she repeated the lullaby, but the crying persisted. She rose onto her elbow and looked at Tony asleep in the hammock, his arm wrapped around his rag dog. With a sigh of envy, she lay back down on the rustling straw mattress and pulled the gray wool blanket over her head to muffle the squalling. The ship rocked gently, and she fell in and out of sleep all night.

When Luisa woke, her stomach rumbled with hunger, and she looked forward to breakfast until she saw the porridge. She shuddered at the runny offering in her bowl and wondered if it was last night's potatoes disguised as breakfast. Her appetite vanished, and she ate a chunk of bread while Tony found the porridge agreeable. He cleaned his bowl and his mama's, too.

When they rose from the table, the ship heaved sharply, and passengers collided with one another. Luisa looked through the slats of a vent and saw waves swell against a black sky. Thunderclaps exploded. By the time they rinsed their dishes in the lavatory and returned to their bunks, the ship pitched and rolled violently. The wooden beams in the dormitory gave a threatening creak, and bags slid out from under bunks across the floor. Passengers cried out in alarm and grabbed on to bunk rails to steady themselves. Luisa heard someone retching.

"Mama!" Tony's face telegraphed his fear. Luisa put her arm around him and grabbed hold of her bunk. She searched the huge room for something to fasten her gaze on, but everything in the dormitory was moving. The room tilted and blurred until Luisa could no longer sit upright. She fell over on her bunk and closed her eyes. The pitching intensified as the ship began another upward climb, followed by a crashing descent.

"Mama, are you sick?" Luisa felt Tony's breath on her cheek as he whispered into her ear.

"I'll be all right in a minute." She felt Tony slide to the foot of her bunk. The ship tipped upward again, and she held her breath, gripping the edges of her bunk before the ship—and her stomach—plunged down.

Luisa kept her eyes shut and breathed through her mouth to avoid the smell of vomit that fouled the air. The coolness of a wet cloth on her forehead forced her eyes open. It was Matilda, her new friend from Palermo. She bent over Luisa and adjusted the cloth.

"Has the food made you sick?"

"I don't know what's wrong with me. When the ship started to rock, I began to feel terrible."

"Lie still. I think you're seasick."

Luisa looked at Tony sitting at the foot of the bunk and saw his lips quiver. "I'll be all right, dear. Come here." She opened her arms, and he crawled into them. "Don't you worry." She stroked his hair as he nestled beside her.

"Tony, would you like to play with my children for a while? They're over there." Matilda nodded toward one of the tables at the far end of the dormitory. The children sat with a man playing a concertina.

Tony stood and sniffed back his tears. "Can I, Mama?"

"Of course you can."

"Can I take my dog?"

"Yes. Be a good boy." As they started to leave, Luisa grabbed Matilda's hand. "Thank you so much." She fought back tears. Her voice wavered.

Matilda patted her hand. "You rest."

The ship rolled and pitched through the rough seas for the remainder of the day. What began as an occasional moan among other passengers became cries of misery as seasickness spread throughout the dormitory. Lying on her straw mattress, plagued by the pain between her eyes and waves of nausea, Luisa's thoughts turned dark. She thought it might be preferable to die, not forever, but just a few moments to stop the nausea and the searing pain in her head. If she had known beforehand it would be this horrible, would she have made the crossing? Even in her misery she knew it was an absurd question. She would do anything to be with Marcello again.

She pulled the cloth from her eyes and leaned on her elbows to look for Tony.

Matilda sat across from her on the opposite bunk. "How are you?"

"Horrible." Luisa scanned the dormitory. "Where's Tony?"

"Playing with my children. He ate supper with us, doesn't seem to be seasick at all."

"Supper? It's that late?" Luisa lay back and closed her eyes again. "Thank you for taking care of him. I don't know what I'd do . . ."

Luisa drew a line through October first on the pocket calendar from her satchel. She kept a record of the days since they had boarded the ship—a line through each day at sea, a circle around the days she was seasick. There were eight lines and eight circles on her calendar.

Overnight the heavy seas gave way to favorable winds and a clear sky. Through an open vent in the dormitory, Luisa saw sunshine. "Let's go up for air after lunch, Tony. It looks like a beautiful day." It was the first time since they had departed over a week ago that Luisa felt well enough to go up top.

Tony hurried up the stairs ahead of her and ran onto the deck.

"Slow down, young man, or you'll run into someone."

Tony disappeared from view, and Luisa quickened her steps to catch up. She rounded a corner and smacked into Carlo.

"Oh, Luisa, I'm sorry. I didn't see you." Carlo reached for her arm to steady her. "Are you all right?" The wind had blown his dark hair over his forehead, and his expressive gray eyes registered concern.

"I'm fine. I should be the one to apologize. I think *I* ran into you." She looked over Carlo's shoulder and called out when she spied Tony. "Come back here right now." Luisa turned her attention back to Carlo and realized he still held her arm.

He quickly removed his hand from her arm. Luisa thought he was blushing ever so slightly. "I—we've been worried about you. Are you much better?"

"I am, thank you. Matilda and her family have been a godsend. They looked after Tony when I couldn't get out of my bunk, which has turned out to be every day since we left. But today," she said, spreading her arms wide, "today is calm and beautiful, and I feel like a new person."

Tony ran up to them. "Mama, I found Uncle Roberto. Come on." He tugged at her skirt.

Luisa looked past Carlo and saw Roberto and Tina a short distance away against the inside wall of the deck, talking with their heads bent together. They held hands.

Luisa was incredulous. "What is Roberto thinking? He's known that girl for seven days and will probably never see her again." She looked at Carlo. "Here we are on our way to America, and he's taken up with a girl he hardly knows on her way to—where are they going?"

"They have relatives in New York City." Carlo smiled. "I wouldn't say he's taken up with Tina. He's just flirting."

"That's how my lovestruck brother gets into trouble—by flirting. I told Mama I'd keep an eye on him. I didn't think he'd need rescuing so early in our trip. I need to speak to him."

Tony pulled Luisa by the hand along the deck with Carlo following behind until they reached Roberto and Tina. "Roberto, we've been looking for you." Luisa forced a smile and turned to Tina. "Nice to see you again, Tina."

"Luisa!" Roberto immediately dropped Tina's hand, and his face reddened like a schoolboy caught snitching sweets. "You're better, I hope?"

"Much better. Matilda told me you and Carlo brought Tony on deck for air while I was sick. Thank you."

"It was the least we could do." Roberto tousled Tony's hair.

"I'm sorry you've been sick." Tina looked genuinely concerned. "My mother and sister haven't been well, either."

"I don't ever want to feel that horrible again," Luisa said.

"If you can stand four more days," said Carlo, "we'll be in New York."

Out of the clear blue sky, a cinder landed on Luisa's coat sleeve. She jumped back and brushed it away just as another cinder landed on Tony's jacket and another on Roberto's shoulder. "What's this?" Luisa looked up at the smokestacks high above their deck spewing cinders from deep inside the ship's furnace and shook her finger at them. "Don't spoil my chance for fresh air. I've waited eight days for this."

"We'd better go below," Roberto said, and they hurried to the stairs, ducking the shower of cinders.

Luisa stepped into the dark stairwell. "I can last a few more days." The ship plunged forward suddenly, and she reached for the railing.

Carlo caught her. "Watch your step."

"I'm fine, Carlo."

It was the second time that afternoon he had prevented her from a fall. Luisa thought it odd he was suddenly so attentive. On both occasions he steadied her longer than necessary before releasing his hand from her arm. *Did* he do that, or had she imagined it? He and Roberto were very concerned about her health, and rightly so. She had been extremely ill. She gripped the railing at the top of the stairs and began the descent. The smell of stinking air rising through the stairwell dismissed any thought of Carlo.

"Only four more days."

Chapter 14

Luisa hugged Matilda and whispered, "I don't know what I would have done without you."

"You would have done the same for me if I had been sick," Matilda said. They stepped apart and picked up their bags.

The two families had processed through Ellis Island and lingered together, hesitant to part. They hugged one last time and promised to write before Matilda and her family left to meet relatives in Manhattan. Luisa watched them depart with an unexpected sadness after knowing them only twelve days. The endless hours cramped together in steerage had forged a special kinship Luisa would never forget.

Roberto remained stoic when he and Tina said goodbye, despite the tears she shed. Her family planned to live with relatives on Mulberry Street in the Little Italy section of New York City. Roberto said he might come back to visit someday, but Luisa thought Tina and Roberto both knew better.

It was impossible to sleep on the overnight train ride from New York to Chicago. When they arrived at the Chicago station to change trains, they found seating on one of the carved oak benches in the waiting room and slumped together in bleary-eyed silence.

Luisa rolled her head from side to side and rubbed the back of her neck. She gazed at the magnificent waiting room, and a sense of awe replaced her weariness. Polished marble floors glistened as the parade of passengers in morning coats and brocade dresses hurried by with tapping heels and rustling skirts. At the edge of the sitting area, massive marble columns with leaves chiseled into the bases climbed to the lofty ceiling. Stained-glass windows high above scattered blue, green, and gold beams across the floor like precious gems. A marble fireplace at the far end of the room was flanked by two curved stairways that led to balconies overlooking the waiting area.

Roberto broke the silence. "Have you ever seen such a beautiful place?"

"I was thinking the same thing," Luisa answered.

"It's like night and day, this place and our quarters in steerage," said Carlo.

Luisa smiled at the irony. "That dark, stinky hold. I get sick just thinking about it. But this building . . ." She looked around in wonder and was at a loss for words.

"We've always heard everything's bigger and better in America," Carlo said.

"This proves it," Roberto nodded. "Look at the statues and marble floors. It's like a palace."

"The hardest part of the trip is behind us, don't you think?" Luisa hoped they concurred. "We survived the crossing, thank heaven, and all that business at Ellis Island. Once we catch this train, I will finally relax."

Tony tugged on her coat sleeve. "Mama, I have to go."

Luisa didn't want to move her aching body. "All right." She sighed. "We should use the lavatory before we board the train anyway. How much time before our train leaves?"

Roberto looked at the huge clock suspended from the ceiling. "Thirty minutes. We'll find our gate when you come back."

"You know how to find the lavatories? There're just down this hall." Carlo pointed the way.

"We'll find them." She and Tony wove through the maze of benches in the waiting room to a hallway. She watched women going through a door labeled Ladies Room and followed them inside. A row of porcelain sinks with shiny fixtures lined one wall and wrapped around a second one. Two rows of oak-paneled doors closed off each toilet stall. She stared in disbelief.

Luisa ran her hand across the sink fixtures. "Who would imagine a lavatory like this?" She pictured the wet floor and filthy wipe rags of the latrines on their ship. The memory of the stench threatened to return.

After using the toilets, they washed up. Luisa leaned over the sink and caught the stream of water with both hands. She gently splashed her face, relishing the access to fresh water, which the ship didn't have. She splashed her face again, delighting in the luxury. The water trickled into the corners of her mouth, and she smiled. It wasn't salty.

Tony splashed at the sink and clapped his hands under the streaming water. "What's that funny noise?" he asked, looking up at the high ceiling.

"An echo."

With a glint in his eye, he unleashed a string of high-pitched noises that bounced off the lavatory walls.

"Tony, stop! Too noisy," Luisa scolded. Women in the lavatory turned and stared at them with disapproving frowns. Luisa felt her cheeks burn and lowered her eyes while she and Tony finished washing. She snatched up her satchel, quickly ushered Tony through the door into the hallway, and hurried back to the waiting room.

As they drew near the bench where they had been sitting, Luisa stopped. Roberto and Carlo were gone. So were their bags. "Where did they go?" She turned in a circle and scanned the crowded waiting room. "They should be right here."

"Where's Uncle Roberto?"

"I'm looking for them." Luisa eyed a woman sitting at the end of the bench and approached her. *"Scuzi, cerco due uomini."*

She pointed to the empty seats.

The woman held up her hand to stop Luisa. "I don't understand. Sorry." She looked away.

"Where are they?" Luisa whispered under her breath. "They wouldn't leave without us." She took Tony's hand and walked to the edge of the waiting room, searching the face of every man she passed. Her chest tightened. She had to find them. She couldn't locate the train without them.

Luisa shuddered. The train!

How much time before their train left? She looked at the clock and realized she hadn't noticed the time when she left for the lavatory. Her mind raced. She thought of the tickets. That would tell her what time the train left. She dropped her satchel to the floor and pulled the tickets from the inside pouch.

"Mama, where's—"

"I told you, I don't know. Hush!" She studied the tickets and looked up at the clock. The train left in fifteen minutes. She had to find the train by herself.

Fear crept up from deep inside. Who could she ask for help? No one understood her.

She took Tony's hand and walked quickly from the waiting room to the hallway. "Maybe they went to the lavatory." She tried to convince herself they were just around the corner and quickened her steps. Tony trotted beside her to keep up.

She spotted a man dressed in a dark uniform with brass buttons and rushed to him. *"Scusi, mi sonoperso."* The man shook his head and pointed down the hall to a counter with workers stationed at windows where long lines of passengers waited.

Luisa's heart sank at the sight. She didn't have time to wait. She ran to the nearest line with Tony in tow. The time on the clock above the counter showed ten minutes before their train left. Her pulse surged. She stared at a large board above the counter filled with words and times and numbers that made no sense. Blinking back tears, she looked up and down the lines of people, seeking a friendly face that might help her. What would she do if they missed their train? How would they get to Wyoming?

"Miss, may I help you?" The people in front of her had moved on, and a woman behind the window was speaking to her. Luisa stepped forward and tried to control her quivering voice. *"Si, mi sonoperso."*

"Pardon?"

With shaking hands Luisa pushed her tickets toward the woman and pointed to the time printed on them. The woman looked at the tickets and turned to the clock. "Your train leaves in five minutes. You'll miss it if you don't hurry. Track nine."

Luisa shook her head and choked back a sob. *"Non capisco."*

"Track nine." The woman pointed back down the hallway and to the right. "Go that way. Track nine." She held up nine fingers and pointed a second time down the hall and to the right.

Luisa nodded. *"Si. Grazie."* She grabbed Tony's hand, and they flew down the hallway, turned right and kept running. Her satchel grew heavy and banged against her leg. She felt Tony slowing, and tugged on his arm. A waiting room loomed ahead at the end of the hall. They ran to the entrance, and Luisa saw an open iron gate at the opposite end of the room that led outside to a covered platform. "This way, Tony." She pulled him through the waiting area to the gate and out to the platform. Large overhead signs numbered each track. She saw the sign for track nine in the distance.

"Come on, we're almost there."

Tony was out of breath. "I can't run any more, Mama."

"Yes, you can."

Tony didn't move. "I'm too tired."

Luisa leaned down, her face inches from his and pointed to

their track. "We're going to race to that train over there, and I'm going to beat you if you don't run as fast as you can." Tony's eyes grew big with the challenge, and he shot toward their train like a rabbit.

When they reached the track, Luisa spotted Roberto and Carlo pacing the length of the train. "There they are!" shouted Carlo. He ran to Luisa and grabbed her satchel while Roberto scooped up Tony, and the four of them chased down the empty platform to the porter who was closing the door to the last car. *"Attendere, attendere!"* they hollered. The porter opened the door and helped them aboard, picked up the step stool from the platform, and closed the door.

They stood together, shaken and out of breath. Roberto turned to Luisa, his face grave with worry. "What happened? We waited, but you never came back."

"What happened to *you*?" Luisa struggled to speak between gulps of air. "When we came back from the lavatory, you were gone."

They found four seats facing each other and fell into them as the train jerked away from the station. Luisa took a jagged breath and brushed away loose strands of hair. Her fingers trembled. "I was so frightened, Roberto. I—"

Roberto reached over and gave her arm a gentle squeeze. "You made it. You found the train."

Luisa shook her head at the thought of her near catastrophe. "I tried to find help, but no one understood me."

"We waited as long as we could," said Carlo. "We couldn't find anyone to help us, either."

"Once I understood where to go, I dragged this poor child through the station as fast as I could." Luisa leaned over and kissed Tony on the top of his head. She suddenly jerked upright, her eyes wide. "Oh, no! My trunk!"

"We have it, we have it." Carlo leaned forward to reassure her. "We loaded it on the train with our belongings before you found us." He eyed Luisa with sympathy.

Roberto spoke. "I think I know how you got lost. The lavatories are in the center of the station, right? And there's more than one way in and out of both lavatories. I think you came out a different door than you went in and ended up in the other waiting room."

"Other waiting room? You mean there are *two*?" Luisa fell back against her seat, exhausted.

She scolded herself for not learning more English before she left for America. Sister Margarita had helped her, but Luisa's limited vocabulary had not been enough to prevent the fright she had just experienced. The importance of understanding English smacked her full in the face. She was not prepared to take care of herself in her new country, nor could she rely on others to help her.

She wouldn't make that mistake again.

The train gathered speed over the barren plateau, clicking off the miles in southern Wyoming. The cars rocked from side to side; black smoke poured past the windows. Luisa put the bread and cheese left from their lunch into her satchel and leaned back against her seat. Roberto dozed, and Tony kept watch out the window. In a few hours they would be in Kemmerer.

"You must be excited," Carlo said. He was sitting opposite her.

"Excited?"

"We're almost there."

Luisa didn't answer at first. She couldn't begin to describe all the emotions she felt—excited, nervous, relieved, apprehensive. "All I've cared about for the past three years is the day Marcello and I would be together again. That day is here. I've never been happier."

Carlo smiled, but Luisa saw sadness in his face. She frowned. It wasn't the first time she'd noticed this expression. "Is everything all right?"

"Yes. Why?"

Luisa hesitated. "We're close to the end of our journey, and yet you seem . . . sad. Are you worried about something?"

There was a long silence.

"No, not worried, just preoccupied."

Luisa raised her eyebrows. "About what?"

"About what happens next. My uncle works in the Spring Hill mine. I'll move in with him and look for work. With any luck, I'll find something soon." Carlo gazed out the window but continued to speak. "During the crossing . . . Roberto and I were worried about you. You were so sick, and there was nothing we could do for you. We both felt helpless."

"You spent time with Tony," Luisa said. "That was help enough."

He turned from the window and faced her. "Roberto's been a lifelong friend. I think of you and Roberto as family. How is it I never got to know you until we made this trip together?"

Luisa was taken aback at his candor. She chose her words carefully. "This journey is unlike anything that's ever happened to us. It's changed our lives forever. After living through something like this, you see your friends in a new light."

Carlo cleared his throat. "I hope you won't think me impolite if I say you faced the difficulties of this trip with courage. Your husband is a fortunate man."

Their eyes locked. Luisa felt her face flush.

"Mama, look." Tony jumped up from his seat and pointed out the window. "What's that?"

Luisa turned away from Carlo, relieved for the interruption, and leaned toward the window. "They look like deer." They watched the graceful brown animals run on slender legs over a hill and disappear. "I wonder if it looks like this at our new home. What do you think, Tony?"

"I don't see trees."

Neither do I, Luisa thought. They hadn't seen a tree since they left Nebraska.

She stared out the window past the arid landscape and her thoughts returned, as always, to Marcello. How much had he changed in three years? Mining was hard work. Had it made him stronger, more muscular? Had he lost weight? In his letters he'd written that men who work the mine for years ended up pale and stooped. She prayed Marcello would always be strong and healthy.

Her gaze rested on Tony. She ran her fingers through his dark, curly hair. She could hardly wait for Marcello to see him. He would be thrilled to see his baby had grown into a fine boy. Impulsively, she wrapped her arms around Tony and hugged him.

"Mama, stop." Tony tried to pull away from her hug. As he squirmed, Luisa tickled him in the ribs, and he doubled over in laughter. When she stopped, Tony grinned at her and said, "Do it again." She found his ticklish spot and laughed at his uncontrollable giggling until her sides hurt.

"Enough tickling," she gasped, holding her stomach. They flopped back against the seats. Luisa couldn't remember the last time she had laughed like this.

After the overnight train ride, Luisa had taken extra care fixing her hair this morning, combing it softly away from her face into a loose coil at the base of her neck. Her pierced earrings dangled from her ears in delicate loops. She ran her hands over the skirt of Angelica's suit, smoothed out the wrinkles, and adjusted the jacket. Lifting her feet slightly, she gave a critical look at her black buttoned shoes, scuffed but presentable.

And what would Marcello think of *her.*

For three unbearable years, she'd ached to be with him. In a few hours she would look into his warm brown eyes that always made her feel she was where she belonged, where nothing in the world mattered except the two of them. How she needed that assurance. Would he look at her the way he used to, his eyes reflecting his love for her? Or would she and Marcello be strangers, changed over time and awkward with each other?

It wouldn't be much longer. Her stomach was in knots.

The train screeched to a stop and hissed, announcing its arrival in Kemmerer.

"Do we have everything?" Carlo asked as they picked up their bags from the overhead rack.

Roberto double-checked the rack and under their seats. "We have it all." He looked at his sister. "Are you ready?"

Luisa quickly pinched her cheeks to give them color and inhaled nervously. "Ready."

Roberto gave her a reassuring smile and led them down the aisle to the end of their car and through the door to the exit compartment. The porter opened the door and pulled down the steps to the platform.

"Do you have your dog, Tony?" Luisa asked.

He held up his raggedy companion.

"Good. Now, be careful going down the steps."

"Now we can see Papa?"

"Now we can see Papa."

They climbed down the steps to the platform. Luisa's heart hammered in her chest. She stood on her toes, searching for Marcello in the small crowd gathered next to the train. People around her shouted greetings as they shook hands and hugged one another.

"Do you see him?" Roberto asked, peering at the crowd.

"Is Papa here?" Tony looked up at his mother.

"I'm looking." For a moment, Luisa feared she might not recognize Marcello.

Luisa turned the other direction and caught her breath. There he was, walking to them with long strides, smiling his beautiful smile. He looked exactly as he should, his dark hair tousled by the wind, his arms open wide. Marcello engulfed her and Tony in a single embrace and held them tightly. Luisa fell into his embrace and buried her head in his shoulder with a sob, still clutching Tony's hand.

"Finally, you're here," Marcello whispered and bowed his head against hers. "The wait is over." Luisa cried softly, feeling Marcello's strong arms wrapped around her, his face against hers. She tipped her head back, and he kissed her. He smiled into her eyes and bent down to his son. "Good day to you, Antonio. I'm your Papa."

Luisa laughed through her tears at the puzzled expression on Tony's face. She leaned against Marcello's chest, and he pulled both of them back into his arms, where they stood motionless. The days, months, and years slowly fell away in the silence as they held on to each other.

★ ★ ★ ★ ★

Part Two: 1918-1921

★ ★ ★ ★ ★

There is no substitute for hard work.

—Thomas Edison

Chapter 15

Marcello wanted to hold on to them forever.

When he finally released Luisa and Tony, he stood back and absorbed their every detail, like a starving man nourished by their presence. "What a sight to see—my wife and son standing before me." Marcello felt a hand on his shoulder and turned. It was Roberto. "Welcome to America." He hugged his brother-in-law. *"Come stai?"*

"Molto bene," said Roberto with a smile, clapping him on the back. "It's so good to see you, Marcello." He turned to Carlo. "This is my friend, Carlo Finni, from Coassolo."

"How do you do," said Carlo, extending his hand.

"Nice to meet you," Marcello replied, warmly grasping his hand. "I can't thank you and Roberto enough for taking care of Luisa and Tony. They couldn't have made the journey by themselves."

"I'm glad I could help," said Carlo. He stole a glance at Luisa. "You have a wonderful family, Marcello."

Marcello, not hearing, stared at Luisa, overwhelmed by the sight of her, unable to look at anything else, unable to move. "You look beautiful," he whispered, lost in the joy of her presence. She smiled, her eyes misty with tears.

Roberto cleared his throat.

Marcello apologized with an embarrassed grin and brought himself back to the task at hand. "Let's collect the bags. The wagon's behind the station."

Tony peeked from behind Luisa's skirt and watched the men stow baggage in the back of the wagon. Roberto and Carlo hopped on and sat among the bags. Marcello walked over to Tony and crouched next to him. "How old are you?"

Tony held up three fingers.

"Would you like help into the wagon?"

Tony eyed his father with a skeptical expression and nodded.

Marcello lifted Tony into his arms. "You are so big, I can hardly pick you up. You must have strong muscles." Tony gave a shy grin, and Marcello gently squeezed his son's upper arm. "You *do* have big muscles."

They climbed aboard and sat on the front seat, Tony between Marcello and Luisa. With a snap of the reins, Marcello guided the horse down the street toward the road to Cumberland. The sun sparkled between the clouds floating across the October sky. A light wind swirled the dirt in little eddies along the barren ground. Luisa turned up her coat collar and put her arm around Tony as the wagon jolted over the rutted road.

"How far is it to Cumberland?" Roberto asked.

"About an hour," said Marcello. "I'll take you to my brother Angelo's house. We'll eat supper there with the family. We invited your uncle, Carlo." Marcello paused and turned to Luisa. "Tell me about the trip."

"There's so much to tell," she answered. She spoke over her shoulder to Roberto and Carlo. "Where should we start?"

The three of them took turns recounting the grim conditions in steerage, Luisa's seasickness, the processing at Ellis Island, and their nearly disastrous separation at the Chicago train station. As their story unfolded, Marcello's heart sank when he heard Luisa had been seriously ill nearly every day of the crossing. Were it not for the kindness of strangers like Matilda from Palermo, who knew how she would have managed. He freed one hand from the reins to grasp Luisa's hand.

"You had a difficult crossing. I'm sorry."

"We're together now." Luisa covered his hand with hers. "That's all that matters."

His heart nearly burst.

At a rise in the road, Marcello pulled the wagon to a stop. It was the same place Lucas had stopped three years previously for Marcello's first view of Cumberland. "There it is," he said with a wide sweep of his arm. He pointed to the east side of town. "Those are the miners' houses I told you about, and if you look to the west, the entrance to the mine is just past the smokestacks." He glanced at Luisa but couldn't gauge her reaction to Cumberland, so unlike the village she had left in Italy. It must seem so foreign to her, he thought, just as it did to him when he first arrived. He renewed his hope she would like their house.

"Cumberland's bigger than I expected. How many people did you say?" Luisa asked.

"About three hundred."

Roberto gave a low whistle. "Much bigger than Monastero."

"The land is so flat," Carlo said.

"It's called prairie."

"Back home you can see across the valley from one hill to the next," said Roberto. "This is so different."

"There's no grass or trees," said Luisa, eyeing the sandy soil. "Can you grow anything here?"

"I haven't tried," said Marcello. "But Mick keeps a few cows, and they do all right with just the scrub grass."

Marcello flicked the reins, and the horse pulled forward. "This is the only road into town. A train comes every morning from Kemmerer with empty coal cars and leaves every night with full ones. We sell it all to the railroad. America needs coal, and Cumberland supplies it."

As they approached town, they passed a square clapboard building with a narrow porch across the front, a door in the center, and windows on each side.

"That's the Catholic church," said Marcello.

"That's the church?" Luisa's voice rose. Marcello's mind flashed to the golden stucco church that had been the heart of Monastero for hundreds of years. The tower bell chimed every half hour, a comforting reminder for the villagers of their shared heritage. He could tell this primitive building didn't look like a place of worship to Luisa.

They passed a second building beside the church, identical to it. Marcello spoke over his shoulder to Roberto and Carlo. "And that's the saloon."

"Is the church next to the saloon for a reason?" Roberto chuckled.

"There's always a few who stir up trouble, church or no church," replied Marcello.

The horse ambled down Main Street, a rutted dirt road, while Marcello gave a commentary on life in the coal-mining town. Two large buildings faced each other on opposite sides of the street. Marcello nodded to the one with a flag pole in front. "That's the town hall, for meetings and dances." The one across the street was twice the size of the miners' houses, with rough lap siding and a large sign above the double front doors. "That's the company store. You can buy just about anything you need there—food, clothes, tools, gunpowder. The boardinghouse is around the corner, Roberto. My brother Jim lives there. We'll get you set up with a room."

Tony tapped Marcello's arm. "Where's our house?"

"We're almost there, Tony. You and Mama can see it soon."

After leaving Roberto and Carlo at his brother's house, Marcello drove the wagon one block over and pulled up in front of their own house. Anxious to see inside, Luisa and Tony hopped down and hurried to the front door with Marcello close behind.

Luisa stepped into a sizeable room with pleasant light from two windows, one beside the front door and one on the opposite wall that looked toward the open prairie. The only furniture stood in the center of the room—a large dining table with six chairs. The oak wood was rubbed to a golden sheen. "Oh, Marcello." She moved beside the table and ran her hand over the polished surface. "It's the most beautiful table I've ever seen."

Marcello stepped beside her and slipped his arm around her waist.

"When did you find time to build it?"

"On my day off."

"You work so hard in the mine, and then you build something like this." Luisa's face glowed.

"Don't look too close at the legs," Marcello advised with a grin.

She tipped her head sideways. "I don't see anything wrong with the legs. Besides—" Luisa looked beyond the table and gasped. "A stove." Against the far wall stood a cast iron stove with buckets of kindling and coal on the floor beside it. Luisa clasped her hands to her chest. "You didn't say anything about a stove."

Marcello smiled as Luisa approached the stove and opened the door to the firebox. "Wood goes in here?"

Marcello nodded. "Once the fire is lit, we use coal for fuel."

She opened door to the oven. "For baking?" She closed the oven door, then opened it again for a closer look. A shelf across the upright back of the stove held a saltbox and pepper grinder. She whirled around. "I've never seen one before. You've cooked on it? Does it warm the house?" She turned back to the stove and ran her hand along a compartment on the side. "What's this?"

"The water reservoir. When the firebox is lit, water heats up. Think of that, Luisa—hot water for washing."

"Mama." Tony stood in the doorway of the next room and motioned to his mama. "My bed?"

"That's your room," said Marcello. "Do you like it?" He and Luisa followed Tony into his room and watched him climb onto the bed, his rag dog in tow. A nightstand with a kerosene lamp stood beside the bed, a small window above it.

"I like it," said Tony and lay down, wiggling under the cotton covers, trying out his new bed.

"And there's one more room to see," said Marcello. He took Luisa's hand and led her through the doorway into the last room, their bedroom.

A patchwork quilt covered their bed. Luisa slid her hand over the iron headboard. "This is more than I expected, Marcello." The only other furniture was a simple chest of drawers; on top sat the family photograph Luisa had sent Marcello, beside a kerosene lamp. She went to Marcello and pulled his arms around her waist. "You've made a fine home for us."

Marcello gently pulled back and searched her face. "Will it be all right? We don't have much, but I can build a cupboard for the kitchen. I bought the beds at the company store, and the chairs I found here and there. Rosa and Theresa helped with the bedding—"

Luisa put her finger to Marcello's lips to silence him. She smiled, tears brimming in her eyes. "It's perfect. Thank you, husband."

Marcello pulled her tight against his chest. He buried his face in her hair, loosening her hair pins. "Dear, Luisa. Can you possibly know how much I've missed you? How long this time has been without you?" He nuzzled her ear and felt the intake of her breath. He kissed her hair, her neck, the tears on her cheek.

"Waiting for you has been the hardest thing I've ever done," Luisa whispered. She held his face in her hands and covered him with kisses.

Marcello's hands moved down her back. "The ache for you—it was more than I could bear."

"I know . . . I know," she murmured.

Marcello leaned back and looked through the doorway into Tony's room. "Our son is sound asleep right where we left him." He turned back to Luisa. "That means, my dearest wife . . ." He scooped her off her feet, carried her to their bed, and laid her on the quilt.

". . . that you're going to make love to me . . ." Luisa pulled him down to her.

". . . over and over again," he whispered. "We'll be very late for supper."

CHAPTER 16

Marcello woke before daylight. He felt Luisa next to him and gently slid his body closer, laid his arm around her waist and matched her breathing, breath for breath. It wasn't a dream. He was touching her, holding her, everything he had longed for during those endless three years. What he wouldn't give to stay right here and never leave. Just the two of them like this. Forever.

With eyes closed and head nestled beside Luisa's, a smile spread across his face as his thoughts returned to yesterday. Yes, they had been very late for supper, and everyone at Angelo's knew why. When he arrived with Luisa and Tony, he raised knowing smiles and winks from his brothers, which he did his best to ignore. His family welcomed Luisa and Tony with a feast of roast chicken and wine, while the children played late into the evening.

Marcello didn't know how long he lay in bed, but the next time he opened his eyes, he saw traces of daylight through the window. Forcing himself from the bed, he pulled back the warm covers and put his feet on the cold floor. He dressed and went to the kitchen to rekindle the fire, leaving the bedroom doors open to allow heat to spread throughout the house. The coffeepot was bubbling when he noticed Luisa at the bedroom doorway.

"I tried not to wake you. Go back to bed. It's still early."

Luisa's unbraided hair spilled over the cotton shawl wrapped around her shoulders. Her nightgown brushed the floor as she walked sleepily to Marcello and wrapped her arms around his waist. "Can't let you go off to work without a proper goodbye." She kissed his cheek and hugged him tightly. "I hate to see you go."

"I'd love to stay here with you, believe me." Marcello raised her chin and kissed her lips. He took her in his arms and marveled at how perfectly their bodies fit together. He nuzzled her hair. "My boss won't allow me to miss work two days in a row," he whispered.

"I know, but I wish otherwise." Reluctantly, she released Marcello and gravitated to the warm stove. "Nice fire. Let's see if I can cook on this fancy stove," she said, and reached for the iron skillet.

When Marcello finished his breakfast of biscuits, bacon, and coffee, he pulled on his coat, put on his miner's cap, and picked up his lunch pail.

"What's that?" Luisa stared at the small lamp attached to the front of Marcello's cap.

"My lamp. Stays lit the eight hours I'm in the mine."

Luisa shook her head, amazed. "I have some catching up to do. First a cook stove with an oven, now a lamp on my husband's head."

"You and Tony have a good day settling in." Marcello kissed her cheek. A grin spread across his face. "I'll see you tonight, *cara.*" His eyes full of mischief, he patted Luisa's bottom and kissed her again before walking out the door.

He hadn't changed one bit. Luisa was struck by her enormous relief at this realization, the same feeling she'd had yesterday at the station. Her shoulders relaxed as she gazed out the door. The early-morning sun peeked over the rocky ridge and lit the tops of the smokestacks in the distance like candles. She watched her husband stride down the street with a lamp on his head, swinging his lunch pail and whistling.

After breakfast, Luisa unpacked her trunk. Humming happily, she moved clothing into the dresser, assigning the bottom drawer for Tony's clothes and the other four drawers for Marcello and herself. Their coats would hang on the hooks by the front door, her apron on a peg beside the stove. She decided to store her quilt, knitting basket, and yarn in the trunk, which she pushed to the foot of their bed. Mama's trunk looked right at home there.

"Tony, let's go outside. I want to look in the root cellar."

The cellar was a dugout under one side of the house that Marcello had reinforced with timbers. He'd built a small door. Luisa brushed aside the cobwebs, ducked her head, and stepped inside the cave-like space to take inventory: potatoes, onions, and a large bunch of turnips. Cured meat hung from an overhead beam. What had Marcello called these birds? Then she remembered. Sage hens. He said they were everywhere in Wyoming. Bottles of homemade wine covered in a layer of dust sat on a crude wooden shelf, just like the wine cellar back home. The thought of home brought her comfort with a touch of sadness, and she made a mental note to write Mama and Angelica now that they had arrived.

When she stepped out of the root cellar, she spied Tony filling his coat pocket with rocks.

"Look, Mama." Tony held up a flat stone with sharp edges that came to a point at one end.

Luisa bent over for a closer look. "It looks like someone carved it."

"Good morning."

Luisa looked up and saw Rosa, Angelo's wife, walking through the backyard with her children, Stefano and Ginny. Outgoing, with an easy smile, Rosa had welcomed Luisa as one of the family at supper last night. Luisa liked her immediately.

Now, as the morning sun caught glints of gold in Rosa's auburn hair, she realized Rosa reminded her of her own sister, Angelica. "Good morning. Look, Tony, we have company."

Rosa nodded at the basket on her arm. "Leftover food from last night. I thought you'd be busy unpacking. Now you don't have to worry about supper."

"How kind. Come inside. Coffee's still warm." Luisa turned to Tony. "Why don't you play outside with your cousins?"

"Good idea," said Rosa and followed Luisa into the house. "Soon enough the snow will pile up, and we'll be stuck inside with cabin fever."

"Cabin fever?" Luisa's eyes widened. "What's that?"

"It's not a real fever," Rosa assured her. "It's just an expression. Means being forced to stay in the house when the weather's bad."

Luisa poured coffee into two cups and brought them to the table with spoons and a bowl of sugar. "Does that happen often?"

"Seems like we have at least two or three big snowstorms every winter. Snow is so deep, you can't leave the house for days. The rest of the year isn't so bad. Summer breezes keep the heat down." She stirred sugar into her coffee. "So, are you settled?"

"The clothes are put away, and I checked the root cellar. We have flour, sugar, and lard but I can't find any cornmeal."

"You know about the company store, yes? You can buy it there. I'll take you tomorrow and show you how to use American money."

"Would you? That would be wonderful." Luisa told Rosa about her panic when she was lost in the Chicago train station. "I know a little English, but not enough."

"Marcello will help you. We all will." Rosa chatted about Cumberland and explained which rancher sold the freshest eggs and milk, what time Mass was on Sunday, and how fortunate they were to have a doctor in town two days a week.

"Marcello wrote about the doctor. We *are* lucky." Luisa sipped her coffee. She set her cup down and looked at Rosa. "Can I ask you something?"

"Of course."

Luisa paused before continuing. "Wyoming is so different from what I expected. When I looked out the window this morning, I wondered if I could grow flowers. Or have a vegetable garden. And there are no trees, no shade. It's so bare—nothing like the mountains back home." She leaned toward Rosa. "Do you get used to it?"

Rosa smiled, a wistful look on her face. "Angelo and I have been here four years. It was very hard for me at first. We were so excited to be in America, but I was homesick that first year. I missed my parents, I missed our village, I missed Italy."

"You did?"

"Oh, yes." Rosa nodded seriously. "A lot of wives get homesick, but we don't write home about it. But you know something?" Her eyes lit up. "It got easier with time. We've made good friends with other immigrant families. They become like a new, bigger family." Rosa paused. "Marcello will make a good living here with Union Pacific."

Although she had known Rosa less than a day, Luisa sensed this was someone she could confide in. "Thank you for telling me this. Ever since I got here I've had mixed feelings—overjoyed to be with Marcello, but disappointed with the countryside."

"You're not alone. Many of us felt like that when we first got here." Rosa reached over and patted Luisa's hand. "Give it time. I think Cumberland will grow on you."

The children tromped inside, interrupting their mothers to show them their wide-ranging collection of rocks. Stefano told them Tony's pointed rock was an Indian arrowhead, hunted and prized by the neighborhood boys. They sat at the table and munched on slices of bread from Rosa's basket until it was time to leave.

Luisa and Tony stood at the kitchen window and watched Rosa, Ginny, and Stefano walk to their house on the next street. Luisa suddenly brightened. She couldn't do anything about the drab landscape, but she could do something about their colorless kitchen. "I'll make curtains! That's what I'll do." She smiled and stepped back, hands on her hips, and pictured the window flanked with color. If Marcello agreed they could afford it, she'd buy material when she and Rosa went shopping tomorrow. Luisa's gaze moved to the bare floor, and she tapped her foot on the tight, even planking. How nice to be through with dirt floors. After she made the curtains, she'd save scraps to make a rag rug.

"Tony, it's time to meet Papa." Luisa put on her coat and gloves.

"Where?"

"We'll walk down the street to the mine where those big smokestacks are. He doesn't know we're coming. We'll surprise him."

"A surprise?" Tony quickly put on his coat and cap. They stepped outside and headed down the street toward the towering smokestacks.

Luisa had heard about the mines in northern Italy but had never seen one. She and Tony stared at the mine entrance and the pair of rails on the ground that sloped downward into the dark tunnel.

"Is Papa in there?" Tony pointed toward the mouth of the mine.

"Yes. He's digging coal with the other miners." They leaned toward the black hole, eager for something to happen. A horn mounted on a tall pole beside the mine blasted three times.

They jumped at the same instant, then burst into laughter at their surprise.

Presently Tony jerked on Luisa's skirt and pointed to the mine entrance. "Look, Mama, I see stars."

Out of the darkness came the flickering lights from the miners' caps as they rolled to the surface in the transport car, the mantrip, as Marcello had called it in his letters. It came to a halt at the entrance, and eight men covered in coal dust climbed out with their tools. They wiped their faces with bandanas, coughed and spat on the ground to clear their lungs. Luisa stared at the men, but coal dust masked their features, and she couldn't distinguish Marcello from the others. Another carload of miners arrived shortly after the first, and more men climbed out.

"Where's Papa?"

"I don't know. I can't tell . . ." A third load of miners arrived and dispersed. Luisa searched for Marcello in the sea of blackened faces. From the last car, a familiar figure walked toward them.

"Well, look who's here. I didn't expect to see you."

"Oh, *there* you are," Luisa said, relieved and just a little embarrassed she'd had difficulty recognizing her own husband.

Tony jumped up and down and shouted, "Surprise! We surprised you!"

"You sure did." Marcello rumpled Tony's hair.

Tony studied his father's face with knitted brows. "Papa?"

"What?"

"You're dirty."

"I know." Marcello smiled, his teeth bright against his blackened face. "Should I wash up when we get home?"

Tony nodded vigorously.

"All right then. Let's go."

The wind began gusting in the twilight as they held hands

and walked through the miners' neighborhood to their clapboard house for supper.

30 November 1918

Dear Mama and Angelica,

We are in good health and hope you are too. Sorry I haven't written in so long. We are busy. Marcello plans to build a big kitchen cupboard with shelves for dishes and cupboards for storage. I'm making rag rugs for the kitchen and bedrooms.

Tony is well. He was very shy around Marcello at first. Now he wants to do whatever his papa is doing. Marcello made him a horse out of an old beer keg. He loves to play on it.

The weather has turned very cold. Every morning Marcello builds a fire in our stove to warm the house. He tells me the miners keep a jug of whiskey under their beds for a quick nip in the morning. It helps them warm up before they go to the mine. We don't have a jug under our bed yet.

Roberto is fine. He comes to our house for dinner on Sunday. He is good friends with Dominic and Marcello's brother Jim. They live in the boardinghouse. They are all bachelors looking for wives but don't worry. I keep my eye on Roberto.

Luisa put her pen down and rubbed her hands together. She went to the stove and stirred the embers in the firebox before adding more coal, then wiped her smudged fingers on her apron. Glancing out the front window, she saw Tony playing tag with the neighbor boys. They didn't seem to mind the cold temperature and brisk wind as they chased about, escaping the reaches of the playmate who was "it." She adjusted the green and white gingham curtains at the window. The bold colors brought cheerfulness to the room, exactly what she'd intended. She nodded with satisfaction and sat at the table to finish her letter.

There are many Italians in Cumberland. There are also Poles, Finns, Greeks, Russians, English, Welsh and Irish. All the children seem to mix easily, and Tony has playmates. The family next door is Russian. Elsa is a good friend and speaks in English to me. If I don't understand, she shows me what she's talking about. Sometimes we forget, and she speaks Russian and I answer in Italian. Then we laugh.

There is a grocery in Silverton that sells salami, sausage and all kinds of cheese. They deliver to Cumberland. The Italians give them a lot of business.

I pray for your good health. I think of you every day and miss you. Please write when you can.

Your loving daughter and sister,
Luisa

Chapter 17

Frozen snow blanketed the ground. The temperature hovered near zero as Marcello dressed and ate breakfast. He poured a second cup of coffee and swallowed the hot liquid, its pleasing warmth spreading inside.

"Sure you don't need an extra shirt?" Luisa asked.

"My long johns are enough. Temperature in the mine isn't too cold."

Marcello shrugged into his heavy coat, pulled on his cap, and carried the empty water bucket out the door. His boots crunched on the snow that had buried the plank walkways in front of the houses weeks ago. He reached the well at the end of the street and struggled with the frozen rope before lowering the bucket. Rumors circulated that the company planned to use a nearby reservoir to provide water hydrants for each street in town.

"Water from a spigot. I'll believe it when I see it," Marcello muttered, his breath hanging like a cloud in the frigid air. He turned up his collar and walked back to the house with a full bucket.

He prided himself in overcoming the obstacles life threw at him. Hadn't he learned enough English to make his way in America? Hadn't he saved enough money to bring his family here? Hadn't he found a steady job despite layoffs and strikes? After all he'd accomplished, there was one challenge that brought him to his knees: Wyoming winters. Just when he thought he had life under control, winter arrived and forced him into submission with bone-chilling cold and piercing winds that went straight to his soul.

Marcello set the water bucket beside the stove. "One less chore for you today."

"And a mighty cold chore. Thank you." Luisa slipped her apron over her head and tied the strings behind her waist. "Baking bread today. It'll be ready by suppertime."

"Sounds good." He kissed her cheek and left, hurrying to shut the door behind him.

Luisa set two pans of dough on the top of the stove and covered them with dishtowels. By early afternoon the sweet aroma of yeast filled the kitchen as the dough crowned high in the pans. She set them in the oven and added chunks of coal to the firebox.

Tony wiped a spot of moisture from the front window and peered out. "Can I go outside?"

Luisa came to the window and saw Uri and Anton from next door running around with their mouths open, catching snowflakes on their tongues.

"You want to eat snow, too?"

"Please, Mama?"

"Bring me your coat and mittens."

She helped Tony with the buttons on his coat, pulled his cap over his ears, and sent him out to play, noting the fat snowflakes before closing the door.

She busied herself tearing scraps of material into strips for a rag rug. Glancing out the window, she watched the three bundled figures blaze trails that crisscrossed the yard through the snow. The flurries thickened into a steady snowfall.

An hour later, Luisa poked her head out the doorway. "Time to come in," she called, but her words were sucked away by the wind. "Tony! Inside!" she shouted. Uri and Anton waved goodbye, and Luisa ushered Tony inside, forcing the door shut against the wind.

"Goodness, your clothes are soaked." She helped him put on dry overalls and draped his snow-caked coat and pants across a chair beside the stove. The sky grew darker, and Luisa decided to refill the coal bucket before Marcello came home from work.

She put on her coat and gloves, pulled her woolen hat down over her ears, and picked up the bucket. "I'll be back in a minute, Tony," she called over her shoulder and stepped outside. She sucked in her breath against the fierce wind and stood dazed, enveloped in white. Her head bent, she hugged the front of the house with short steps and turned the corner. A furious blast of wind smothered her into another standstill. She inched her way to the back of the house until her foot slid across an exposed icy patch, and she grabbed the siding to keep from falling.

Through the spinning snow, she could make out the shape of the outhouse and the large compartment attached to it that stored coal. How many times had she crossed the yard, never giving it a second thought? Now it looked so far away. Too far away.

As she moved away from the house, the storm's fury jerked the bucket from her hand and knocked her to her knees. She felt for the bucket and curled her fingers around the handle. The wind roared in her ears, daring her to get up. Luisa stood and regained her balance. Head down, eyes tearing, she leaned into the wind with one arm outstretched, searching for the outhouse. Icy needles stung her face. Her breath came in freezing gulps, burning her lungs.

Where was the outhouse?

She stopped and raised her head. A dark shape loomed. She trudged forward, buffeted by the wind, until her hand collided against the side of the outhouse. Exhausted, she dropped her bucket and fumbled for the handle on top of the coal bin. Grabbing with both hands she hoisted the lid up. She forced her fingers to wrap around chunks of coal and dropped them in the bucket until it was full.

Her legs wobbled. Lugging the bucket, she felt her way around the corner of the outhouse to the door and pushed herself inside. With a great heave, she forced the door shut and sagged against it. Shaking with exertion, she waited for her pounding heart to slow while the storm battered the tiny shelter.

"I made it. I made it." Regaining her breath, Luisa stomped her feet, rubbed her arms, and beat her hands together, trying to bring life to her frozen limbs. "I made it out here. I can make it back." She waited several minutes before she gathered her courage and stepped out into the whiteness.

The outline of the house guided Luisa through the blinding snow as she fought across the backyard. The bucket, heavy and unwieldy, banged against her leg. It started to slip from her hand, and she stopped to grip the handle to keep the coal from spilling into the white nothingness around her. She plunged forward in clumsy steps, the snow up past her knees. Around the corner of the house, to the front porch, through the front door, she stumbled into the house and forced the door shut. With a relief she had never known, she leaned against the door and closed her eyes.

Thank God.

Luisa set the coal bucket down with a thud and unclenched her frozen fingers, rubbing feeling back into them. She pulled off her hat and coat, shook off the snow, and hung them by the door. What had Rosa said to her after she first arrived? Cumberland would grow on her if she just gave it time? If these first three months were any indication, not only was Cumberland *not* growing on her, but she was taking a strong dislike to the place.

Huddling beside the stove, her shawl pulled tight, Luisa drank steaming tea and trembled with cold and fear. Her chore could have been deadly. What if she had lost her way? What if she had fallen and not had the strength to get up? The cold might have forced her to give up and close her eyes and . . . Luisa shuddered. What was this place Marcello had brought her to?

Loud pounding on the door interrupted Luisa's worries. She unlatched the door and recognized the Silverton grocer covered in snow. The delivery bobsled and team of horses stood in front of their house with a driver wrapped in blankets. "*Santo cielo,* come in, come in."

"Just finishing our deliveries, Mrs. Corsi," he said and stepped inside. "You're our last one. Weather wasn't near this bad when we started out this morning." He handed her four packages. "Two cheddar, one salami, one sausage."

"It was much trouble for you. Thank you." She went to the cupboard and reached for the tin canister on the top shelf. "Can you warm up? Your friend, too?"

"No thanks. We're anxious to get back to Silverton."

Luisa counted the money into the deliveryman's hand, proud of paying the correct amount when he nodded his head.

"Thank you, ma'am."

"Be careful." Luisa glanced out the window at the storm.

"Yes, ma'am. Lived around here a long time, so we know what to expect. You have a good evening." He left, and Luisa latched the door behind him.

She went to the bedroom and checked the pocket watch Marcello kept on the dresser: five o'clock, time for the miners to get off work. They should have let the men leave work early.

Be safe, Marcello. Please be safe.

Luisa forced her worry aside and busied herself peeling vegetables. The onion sputtered in bacon fat and released a comforting aroma. She added it to the large pot of chicken stock simmering with potatoes, carrots, and beans. After slicing the salami and cheese onto a platter, Luisa brought the kerosene lamps to the kitchen table.

"When will Papa come home?" Tony dumped his wooden soldiers on the table and watched her light the lamps.

She gave Tony a reassuring smile. "He'll be here soon." She turned the bread out onto the cutting board and sliced it.

Tony ran to the front window and pressed his nose against the pane. "Look, Mama, it's snowing a lot." Luisa went to the window and caught her breath. Snow was piled up to the windowsills. She saw nothing beyond but a curtain of white surrounding the house. A growing dread gripped her. How would Marcello find his way through the storm? She peered over Tony's shoulder and searched in vain through the swirling white for the men returning from work.

Be safe, Marcello. Please be safe!

Luisa heard footfalls on the porch. The door burst open, and Marcello stumbled into the house in a gust of snow with the two deliverymen. Breathless and red-faced, they stomped their boots and beat snow off their coats as Marcello pushed the door shut and latched it.

Luisa nearly collapsed with relief. "Marcello!" She threw her arms around his neck, ignoring his snow-caked clothes. Frost covered his brows and lashes; his cheeks were blotched red.

Marcello pulled off his frozen gloves and wiped his face. "That's *some* storm."

"You must warm up," Luisa urged Marcello and the deliverymen. The men peeled off their coats and moved to the warmth of the kitchen range. They stood a long while, facing front, then back, then front again toward the radiating heat and rubbed their hands together. Luisa brought them towels to dry their faces.

"How did you ever find your way home?"

"We almost didn't," said Marcello. "I was leaving the mine when I met up with the delivery sled. They were heading out of town."

"We decided it was too risky to go back to Silverton," one of the men said. "Your husband said we could stay the night. My name's Nash, ma'am." A stout man, he extended his hand to Luisa, whose small hand disappeared in his beefy grasp.

"And I'm Lewis," said the other man of slight build, his face covered in blond whiskers. "We're mighty grateful."

Marcello rubbed his neck with the towel. "I climbed onto the sled, and they turned the horses around to come back here. Couldn't see your hand in front of your face, so we took turns walking beside the horses, guiding them the best we could. Every so often I'd feel for the walkway with my foot to make sure we were still in the street."

"We made it to the company barn and bedded the horses for the night," said Nash.

"We waited a spell and hoped the storm would let up," said Lewis, his hands extended toward the stove. "Your husband was sure he could find your house, even in the blizzard."

Luisa shared a worried look with Marcello. *"Tramontana."*

"Si," Marcello nodded. He saw Nash and Lewis's bewildered expressions and translated. "It means 'cold wind from the north.' "

"You're right about that," said Nash. "Could say it was freezing wind from the north."

"You're safe. That's all that matters," said Luisa. She moved beside the stove and lifted the lid from the simmering pot. "Soup's ready. You must be hungry."

They settled sat around the table and silently devoured the sandwiches and steaming soup. Luisa was heartened to watch Marcello eat with such relish.

"Soup's real good, ma'am," said Nash.

"Warms a body from the inside out," Lewis added as he sopped the last of his soup with a hunk of bread.

"There's plenty." Luisa stood. *"Mangia."*

Marcello grabbed her hand before she went to the stove. "Thank you." His face was strained with emotion, a mixture of worry and exhaustion. And regret? Luisa couldn't tell.

After supper they moved their chairs around the stove. Marcello noticed a ridge of snow under the front door and stuffed the gap with rags. When he returned to his chair, he lit his pipe and billows of fragrant smoke floated to the ceiling. Tony brought his blocks from the bedroom and built a tower for his wooden soldiers beside his mother's chair. Grateful to replace the stress of the storm with their usual evening rituals, Luisa picked up the scarf she was knitting and set to work.

"You know," Nash began, "this reminds me of a storm five years ago."

"Winter of 'fourteen?" asked Lewis.

"That's the one. It come up so fast, ranchers lost cattle. But the worst thing was losing my neighbor, old Bill Farnsworth."

Luisa's eyebrows rose. She still had difficulty understanding English when it was spoken too fast. "What?"

"My neighbor. He lived alone. Went out to get coal before the storm got bad. Least that's what we think happened. He never made it back to his house."

"Never made it back?" Luisa's knitting dropped into her lap. She looked at Marcello for an explanation and turned back to Nash. "You mean . . ."

"Yes, ma'am. We went to check on him the day after the storm, found him lying in the snow not ten feet from his front door, frozen, his bucket beside him. Must have gotten lost in the blizzard trying to get back to his house."

Marcello gave Luisa a look of concern. "But that doesn't happen often, does it?"

"No," said Lewis, "but something like that makes you respect Mother Nature. She's in charge when the blizzards come." He turned his head to the side and pointed to his ear. The portion that curved across the top was missing. "Lost this to frostbite when I was just a kid. Lucky that's all I lost."

The wind rose to a crescendo and beat against the house. The men stopped talking, and Luisa held her breath as the house shuddered. Marcello gave her a reassuring look. The wind subsided as quickly as it had blown up, the men returned to their conversation, and Luisa's knitting needles clicked again. They stayed up late into the night, the warmth of the kitchen wrapping them in a blanket of security against the storm raging outside.

Supplied with quilts, Nash and Lewis expressed their gratitude again before retiring to sleep in Tony's room. Marcello picked up Tony, who had fallen asleep in Luisa's lap, and carried him to their bedroom. The three of them huddled together under the blankets, warming the cold bed.

"Do you think the storm will be over by morning?" Luisa whispered.

Marcello reached across Tony and searched for her hand. "Can't know for sure, but the wind seems to be dying down."

"Marcello, I was frantic."

"I know. I'm sorry." He squeezed her hand. "But here I am, and everything's all right. And tomorrow, when the storm has passed, there are three strong men here ready to dig out."

"I don't know what I'd do . . . if something happened to you."

"Nothing's going to happen to me, I promise. It's a big storm, but we're all safe."

"What about that man who died, frozen to death at his front door?"

"That was years ago in a storm worse than this one."

"Worse than *this*?"

"Yes. Now, no more worrying. Try to sleep"

"I love you."

"I love you, too. Always."

Luisa burrowed deeper under the covers and closed her eyes. Would tomorrow be her first day of the cabin fever?

Tony stood on his toes and rubbed frost from the window. "It's not snowing. Can I go outside, Mama?"

Luisa squinted at the dazzling brightness of the morning sky. The landscape sparkled in every direction. "We'll go out after Papa and our friends clear a path. Come and eat breakfast."

After bacon and eggs, the men put on coats, gloves, and caps and shoveled paths from the front door to the street and the outhouse. When Tony saw the neighbor boys playing in the snowdrifts, he ran for his coat.

Luisa stood on the front porch wrapped in her heavy coat and wool hat. The fierce wind had blown itself out, leaving a cloudless dome of cerulean blue overhead as pure and fresh as the icy cold air. Snow draped the houses in drifts like a tapestry spun with gold that glittered and swirled from rooftops, across windows and doors, around the houses to the prairie beyond. There was a hush over everything, as though nature itself was in awe of the beauty. She shaded her eyes against the sunshine while she watched Tony plod through the snowdrifts until he was stuck up to his waist and shrieked for the fun of it. Yesterday's fears were gone, replaced with delight in the brilliance of the wintry creation.

When the company store reopened the next day, Marcello came home with a hank of rope.

"What's that for?" Luisa asked.

"You'll see. Come out back in about ten minutes."

Bundled up against the cold, Luisa trudged through the shoveled path around the house to the backyard, where she found Marcello with a big grin on his face. He had hammered a nail to the house and another nail to the outhouse, bent them into hooks, and strung the rope between.

"Now we have a lifeline."

Chapter 18

April arrived, and pleasant breezes from the south released Cumberland from the icy grip of winter. As the snow retreated, the Corsis and their neighbors emerged from their homes, optimistic with the arrival of spring. By the end of the month, the creek that ran through town filled with runoff. Mud oozed in the streets, beside the walkways, and around the houses. When tufts of green sprouted in the brown prairie, and the meadowlark sang its morning song, Marcello took down the rope in their backyard.

Buoyed by the change in weather, Marcello and Luisa resumed Cumberland's favorite pastime—socializing with neighbors.

"Any visitors tonight?" Luisa asked. She took off her apron and hung it on the wall peg.

"Jim, Roberto, and Dominic," said Marcello.

"Good," Luisa nodded. "Better the bachelors play cards here than find trouble at the saloon."

Marcello stole a glance as she settled in the rocker. She seemed happy, or at least contented, which was a great relief. Winter had been difficult for her. She hadn't been herself, and he assumed it was the brutal weather but wondered if it went deeper than that. All he knew for sure was that as the weather improved, Luisa seemed happier.

"Anybody home?" Roberto called. He pushed open the door and walked in with Jim and Dominic.

"If you're ready for some serious poker, you found the right place," Marcello answered. "I feel lucky tonight." He rubbed his hands together in anticipation.

"Nice to see you, gentlemen." Luisa smiled at Jim and Dominic. "You too, Roberto," she teased and turned up her cheek so her brother could kiss her.

"My favorite little sister," said Roberto and pecked her cheek before joining the others at the table.

"Glad you're feeling lucky," said Jim. "We don't want a repeat of last week."

"Forget last week." Marcello shuffled the cards.

"Over, but not forgotten." Dominic gave Jim a sly grin.

"What happened last week?" asked Roberto.

"We'd been playing poker for hours," Dominic began.

"Dominic . . ." Marcello stopped dealing cards and stared daggers at his friend.

Jim took up the story. "Marcello hadn't won a single hand. When he looked at the cards he'd just been dealt . . ." Jim convulsed with laughter.

"He turned red as a boil," said Dominic. "He scooped up all the cards and threw 'em in the stove."

"You did?" Roberto turned to Marcello.

"You'd have done the same thing. Miserable night of cards," Marcello muttered. "Lucky for you guys I have more than one deck. Now, can we play?" He finished dealing, picked up his cards, and suppressed a smile as he stared at a very promising hand.

As play began, the room grew silent except for the slap of cards hitting the table, the grumble of disappointment or the shout of triumph at the end of each hand.

Marcello brought out a bottle of wine. "Ready for some dago red?" he asked and filled glasses without waiting for an answer. Calling the Italians' homemade wine "dago red" began as an insult from some of the old-timers, but Marcello shrugged off the affront and turned the moniker into one of pride. He made excellent wine. No one in Cumberland ever turned down a glass of it, no matter what it was called.

The hour grew late, and Luisa set aside her mending with a yawn. "I'm going to bed." She kissed Marcello's cheek and said good night to the others before retiring.

Jim pulled four cigars from his shirt pocket and passed them around the table. After the men lit up, smoke rose above their heads in a thick veil. Marcello turned up the kerosene lamp and opened another bottle of wine. He was on a winning streak and generously refilled the empty glasses. Roberto was on his fourth glass of wine when he asked no one in particular, "What do you think about me getting married?"

Play stopped. Jaws dropped. Marcello found his voice first. "How much wine have you had?"

"I thought you knew how this worked," said Jim. "You see"—he leaned close to Roberto and spoke with exaggerated simplicity—"you need a *woman* to get married."

"Very funny. I know I need a woman, and I've come up with a plan." He paused. The others waited. "I'm twenty-two. I can't wait for a wife forever. What I'd like is one of those, what you call, mail-order brides. Joey Mecina just married one. She came out to Cumberland from back East somewhere, pretty as can be, and now he's a married man."

"I don't think that's a good idea," said Dominic. "What if you order one and don't like her when she shows up? What then?"

"What other choice do I have? Every woman in Cumberland is either married or still in pigtails."

"Roberto, you've been here only four months," said Marcello. "A mail-order bride is worse than an arranged marriage like we had back home. You don't want to do this."

"But it *could* work," Roberto insisted.

"Even if she turned out to be a nag?" asked Jim.

"Or ugly?" Dominic added.

"Maybe I could find out what she looked like before she got here. Is that possible?"

"Hmm. This gives me an idea," said Jim. He studied Roberto. "You sure you want to get married, or as they say here, 'tie the knot'?"

Roberto's eyebrows shot up. "They tie you in a knot?"

"No, no, no. That's just an expression. It means to get married," said Dominic.

"I'm ready for marriage. Remember that Italian saying, 'How poor is a home without a woman.' Well, my home needs a woman, and I'm not a bad catch, if I do say so." He struck a dignified pose and ran a finger over his trimmed mustache.

"I think there's a way we can find a wife for you," said Jim, a gleam in his blue eyes. "Marcello, didn't you have one of those mail-order bride books around here?"

"What?" Marcello frowned.

Jim went to the cupboard and found what he was looking for on the top shelf. "Here it is." He picked up the Montgomery Ward catalog and brought it to the table. "This is what you want."

Marcello was speechless. He looked at his older brother and began, "Jim, that's—"

"—just what he's looking for," interrupted Dominic, picking up where Jim left off.

"Now wait a minute," Marcello began.

Roberto was already flipping through the pages of the catalog. "I can't believe this," he exclaimed. "Look at all these women. There must be dozens of them—all beautiful." He looked at Jim and Dominic. "All these women are brides?"

"Well, let's have a look," said Jim and pushed the playing

cards aside. They bent their heads over the catalog as Roberto pored over each page. "What about this one?" Jim pointed to one of the models.

"Hmm . . . no, I like dark hair." He continued to turn pages, studying every woman. On page nineteen, he stopped and stared at a pretty brunette with dark curls that framed her perfect oval face and a heart-shaped mouth. "Oh, now this one"—he tapped the page—"she's beautiful. What does it say about her?"

Dominic leaned over Roberto's shoulder. "Says she's twenty years old . . ."

"Perfect," Roberto said with enthusiasm.

". . . and she lives in Chicago. That's where you have to send the order."

"How much does this cost?" Roberto looked ready to burst with excitement.

"Three dollars and eighty-five cents," said Jim. "That's a good deal. You can't do better than that."

"*I* might want to marry her myself," said Dominic.

"I saw her first," said Roberto, pulling the catalog out of Dominic's reach.

Marcello watched the ruse unfold in disbelief. Jim and Dominic were very convincing, and Roberto—always after a woman—was a willing participant. But he was Luisa's brother, and Marcello didn't want this crazy scheme to find its way back to his doorstep and upset Luisa. "All right, boys, you've had fun with Rober—"

"Marcello, are you going to deny Roberto a wife?" Jim was indignant. "All he has to do now is fill out the order form."

"I'll help him buy the money order at the post office on Monday," said Dominic. He clapped Roberto on the back.

"Roberto," Marcello began, "I hate to tell you but that's not a mail—"

"I didn't know it would be so easy," said Roberto, ignoring Marcello.

Jim grabbed the wine bottle and topped off the glasses. "This calls for a toast," and raised his glass. "To Roberto and his new bride."

Marcello sat at the kitchen table polishing his boots. Tomorrow was Sunday. After frequently missing Mass during the bitterly cold winter, they could once again enjoy the walk to church. He rubbed a rag with soot from inside the stove into the scuffed leather, spitting when needed to even out the polish.

Luisa came inside after watering the seedlings beside the porch. "Roberto's headed this way." She took off her coat and hung it by the door. "He usually doesn't come this early. Dinner won't be for another hour."

"Maybe he's bored. Dominic and Jim are probably sleeping late." Marcello went to work on his other boot when the door burst open.

Luisa whirled around. "Roberto—" Without a word he tossed a small package onto the table. "What's that?" she asked.

Hands on his hips, jaw clenched, Roberto scowled at the package. After a moment, he reopened the package and dumped a navy-blue dress with white polka-dots onto the table.

"What in the world?" Luisa looked at Roberto.

"Oh, no." Marcello fell back in his chair.

Roberto fixed his fiery gaze on Marcello. "Did you know this would happen?"

"What's going on?" Luisa looked from Roberto to Marcello.

"Roberto, listen . . ." said Marcello.

"Oh, I'm ready to listen, all right." Roberto folded his arms across his chest and waited, stone-faced.

"Sit down." Marcello pulled out a chair at the table. Roberto didn't move. "Please, sit." Marcello watched Roberto sit stiffly on the edge of the chair. "Yes, I knew what Dominic and Jim were doing. But if you remember, I tried to make you listen to me. You were so determined to buy a wife, you refused to hear me."

"Buy a wife?" Luisa turned to Roberto. "What's he talking about? What have you done?"

"A mail-order bride. I thought I was choosing a bride from that book of yours. Least that's what Jim and Dominic told me." Roberto spat out the words. "Turns out I was ordering a *dress.*"

"Now hold on." Marcello held up his hands in protest. "It was one in the morning in the middle of a poker game when you brought up the subject of marriage. Hardly the time for a serious discussion."

"That doesn't make it right. You played me." Roberto was defiant.

Luisa pulled up a chair beside him. "Are you so desperate to find a wife that you'd do that?" Roberto was silent. "What did we promise Mama before we left home?"

"To look out for each other. I've done that for you."

"Yes, you have. And I feel this is my responsibility to you. Finding a wife is not like choosing which trousers to buy."

"That's not fair," Roberto shot back.

"Don't be foolish." Luisa's voice rose. "You'll regret it if you choose the wrong woman to marry, and so will I."

Luisa turned to Marcello. "And you. To not put a stop to such nonsense—I'm angry with the both of you."

"It was just a joke, Luisa. There's no harm done." Marcello reached across the table for her hand, which she quickly withdrew to her lap.

Marcello turned to Roberto. "So you didn't know what a catalog was. So, what? Think of it as a harmless introduction to life in Cumberland. Believe me, I've heard about initiations that weren't funny at all. I can tell you a story about a miner back in Kansas that will make what happened to you seem silly."

Roberto glared at Marcello, silent.

"A new miner came soon after I arrived. On his first day of work the two men training him thought it would be fun to take him into the mine and leave him there to fend for himself. He'd never been in a mine before. He didn't know the layout of the tunnels, how to work his lamp properly—nothing."

Roberto looked up at Marcello, interested, but still silent.

"Fortunately, he didn't panic. He found his way back through the tunnels to the main haulage way. Some other miners found him and brought him out."

"You never said anything about this before," said Luisa. "That's horrible."

"It could have been deadly. After turning corners once or twice in those narrow tunnels, most new miners are lost." Marcello held up the dress. "This was just a joke about a mail-order bride." He paused. "No bad feelings?"

Roberto said, "I was serious about finding a wife. Jim and Dominic knew that."

Luisa laid her hand on his arm. "You're serious about finding a wife, yet look how you went about it. During a game of poker. And you took the word of Jim and Dominic."

"Yes, but—"

"It takes time to find the right girl. Don't give up. You'll find someone."

"I just want a wife and a family. I don't think that's too much to ask."

"Family is what everyone wants," Luisa said. She studied her brother's defiant expression. The cuckoo clock interrupted their discussion and she stood, smoothing her apron. "It's time to start dinner. We're having your favorite, Roberto—roast chicken."

Roberto picked up the dress, stuffed it into the package and headed to the door.

"Where are you going?" asked Marcello.

"Some unfinished business. Need to talk to Jim and Dominic about this."

"I'm making dumplings to go with the chicken," Luisa called after him.

The door banged on his way out.

Chapter 19

A thunderous crash rocked the tunnel. Marcello dropped his shovel and covered his head before he was plunged into darkness.

Silence.

Pain seared his left shoulder. His chest pressed against the wall, Marcello waited until the sound of rock hitting the floor stopped before he dared move.

"Jim? Jim?"

Silence.

Marcello's pulse raced. The silence was terrifying. "Jim! Sully!" As he lifted his head, his lamp flickered and illuminated a thick blanket of explosive coal dust boiling up in the tunnel. The warning Giovanni gave him his first day in the mine screamed in his head. "Be careful around coal dust. The slightest spark sets it off." He ignored the warning for a few more precious minutes of lamp light.

"My arm!" hollered Sully. "It's caught."

Marcello heard Jim cough. "I'm all right," Jim sputtered. "You okay, Marcello?"

"I think so." Marcello turned his lamp toward the sound of Sully's voice. "Can't see you, Sully," he shouted, and immediately coughed on the dust he'd sucked into his lungs. He covered his mouth and nose with his gloved hand.

"Marcello." It was Jim. "Douse your light. We can't take a chance with the dust."

"How will we see?"

"We'll feel our way."

"That's impossible—"

"Turn it off—now!"

Marcello fought the urge to ignore Jim and find his way through the tunnel to Sully. Instead, he extinguished his lamp.

Total darkness.

Jim coughed to clear his lungs. "I'll make my way over to you."

Marcello coughed. "No, get out of here while you can. I'll help Sully."

"Don't be crazy. I'm not leaving . . . keep talking."

Marcello heard the stumble of Jim's footsteps. "Be careful, Jim . . . take it easy . . . take it easy." He continued to talk and extended his arms toward the footsteps, hoping to make himself easier to find.

"I think my arm's broken." Sully's voice resonated with pain.

"We're coming, Sully," Marcello said. The inhale of dust sent him into a spasm of coughing.

"Ahh!" It was Jim.

"What happened?"

"Twisted my ankle. Rocks are everywhere."

Jim's footsteps came nearer. "You're close," said Marcello. "You're—" Jim collided into him, smacking him in the face. They grabbed onto each other until both were steady.

"Sure you're all right?" Marcello asked.

"I'm okay," Jim said. He inhaled and coughed. "Now to find Sully."

"Over here." Sully's voice was faint.

Marcello and Jim turned toward the sound of Sully's voice. They felt along the jagged tunnel wall, Marcello in front and Jim behind with his hand on Marcello's shoulder. Marcello prayed the ceiling would hold. He put out a hand to feel his way forward as they stepped through the debris. His eyes burned, and his throat was parched from breathing dust.

"My arm . . ."

"We're coming, Sully," Jim said.

Marcello counted steps as they moved forward for a sense of their location in the tunnel. On the tenth step his foot landed on Sully's boot, and he caught himself before toppling over. He and Jim knelt beside their friend and ran their hands over his body. His clothing was dry, which meant he wasn't bleeding, but his arm was buried up to the shoulder.

Marcello and Jim removed the rocks one at a time and set them aside, mindful that a rock fall could set the tunnel ablaze. No friction, no sparks. No sparks, no fire.

"Sullivan! Marcello! Jim!" The sound of voices penetrated the dust and debris from the far end of the tunnel.

Marcello turned toward the voices and called out, "Sully's hurt."

"We're coming."

"Think you can walk out of here once your arm's free?" Jim asked Sully.

"I know I can. Nothing wrong with my legs."

It was nerve-racking to take it slow. Marcello repeated the warning in his head to stay focused—no friction, no sparks, no fire. "Can you move your arm yet?" he asked Sully.

"I'll try."

Marcello heard the scraping of rocks and a cry of pain.

"No."

"I can tell why," Jim said. "Marcello, feel right below his elbow."

Marcello ran his hands over a huge rock pressing on the lower half of Sully's arm. His heart sank. "I feel it."

"Put your hands under it. We'll lift it together and set it beside me. Ready?"

"Ready." They lifted the rock, but as they moved it away, it slipped from Marcello's grip and fell against the tunnel floor.

Caro Dio. Marcello's heart hammered loud enough to echo through the tunnel.

"My arm's free," said Sullivan. He leaned forward. Marcello and Jim wrapped their arms around him and helped him to his feet. "Let's get out of here before this place explodes."

With Marcello in front, they felt along the tunnel wall and stumbled through the black void toward the sound of voices and the open end of the tunnel.

Marcello dreaded telling Luisa about the ceiling collapse. It didn't disrupt work in nearby tunnels, and the next shift was already reinforcing timbers across the ceiling. Tomorrow would be like any other day in the mine, but that didn't make facing Luisa any easier. He rested his hand on the front door latch, thinking of ways to downplay the incident.

Luisa sat at the table mending a pair of overalls. She looked up, surprised. "Is it five o'clock already? I didn't hear the whistle."

"No, I'm home a little early."

She eyed him critically. "Marcello, you're filthy, head to foot."

"We had some trouble at work."

Luisa's brow furrowed as she stood. "What trouble?"

He hung up his jacket on the hook by the door, his back to her.

"And what happened to your shirt?" She crossed the room and felt the tear that ran across his shoulders.

He turned to face her. "Banged up a little. Part of the ceiling where Jim and I were working came down."

"Oh, no!" Alarm flashed in her eyes.

"Don't worry. Most of the fall landed behind us, but we both got hit across the shoulders pretty good."

"Take your shirt off—let me have a look."

"I'm fine. Really. Another fella in our tunnel injured his arm, but Jim and I are fine."

"Take your shirt off." Luisa's mouth set in a determined line.

Marcello didn't argue. He pulled off his shirt and sat at the table. He heard Luisa's initial intake of breath. When she didn't say anything, he wondered how bad it looked. After a moment, she spoke. "You have a very big bruise, most of it on your left shoulder," she said. "The skin's broken. It needs to be cleaned."

She brought a bar of soap, washcloth, and basin with warm water from the range to the table.

"Dannazione di tuttiall'inerno." Marcello's frustration boiled over.

"Language, Marcello."

"Until today I've never gotten more than scraped knuckles and a sore back at the mine."

"And I'm thankful every day it's never been worse than that," Luisa said. She dipped the washcloth in the basin and rubbed soap onto it. Marcello winced as she touched his shoulder. "Sorry, dear." She gently dabbed the abrasions.

Marcello sat quietly while she washed his shoulder. "I don't understand how this happened."

"It was just an accident, wasn't it?"

"Yes."

"Marcello . . ." Luisa paused.

He turned around to look at her.

"Were you careless today?"

"No. Never. I do everything possible to prevent accidents. I check my lamp before work, I carry extra carbide, I follow work orders. Jim and I always pay attention to the tunnel we're working."

"Then you mustn't blame yourself."

"But I keep wondering if I missed something. Was a crossbeam ready to give way, and we didn't notice it? If there was some way to prevent what happened . . ." He tipped his head back and closed his eyes. He heard the crash, saw the darkness, felt the panic.

Luisa brought a towel to the table and blotted his shoulder. "Was the tunnel unsafe?"

Marcello opened his eyes and pushed the memory away. "The company keeps careful watch on crossbeam supports."

"You're making too much of this. You're a good worker." She leaned over and kissed his cheek. "One accident won't change that."

Marcello hoped she was right.

Marcello sat in the rocker and listened from the kitchen to the bedtime story Luisa told Tony before she tucked him in. He tamped tobacco into his pipe, struck a match, and puffed until the tobacco glowed. His evening ritual gave him little pleasure. Smoke drifted out the open window into the April night. Had his promising future disappeared today like the wisps trailing out the window?

His grand plan to move up to management and gain higher status now seemed naïve. The ceiling collapse forced him to acknowledge a new obstacle in his path: an incident report. His crew boss said it was routine protocol and told Marcello he had nothing to worry about. But Marcello couldn't ignore that the possibility of a promotion was diminished by what had happened. Would he now be viewed as one of those immigrants with limited potential beyond swinging a pick and filling up a coal car?

After worrying all week, Marcello was anxious to get away for a day. Saturday dawned bright and breezy. He borrowed a wagon from his neighbor, Oleg, and drove Luisa and Tony to visit Lucas, Julia, and their two young sons in Silverton.

"Can't wait to show you some changes I've made," said Lucas, leading both families from his house down Main Street to the whitewashed clapboard saloon.

Julia, petite and energetic, leaned close to Luisa. Her coal-dark eyes sparkled as she whispered, "Lucas is so proud of his business."

Lucas unlocked the front door and welcomed the families inside, bowing at the waist with a wide sweep of his arm. They stepped into a large room with windows across the front facing the street. Two pool tables occupied the center of the room, with a scattering of tables and chairs around the perimeter. Three massive mirrors and shelves lined with bottles of spirits covered the wall behind the bar of dark wood. A brass footrail ran the length of the bar, with spittoons on the floor at each end. Lucas walked to the bar and nodded at the cash register.

"È bello," said Luisa.

Tony's eyes widened as he stared at the shiny register.

"Is that silver?" asked Marcello.

"No, it just looks like it." Lucas smiled, his chin raised proudly.

"Well, that's a mighty fine cash register," said Marcello. He ran his hand over the surface of the raised metal design. Centered on top of the register in black letters surrounded by silver scrollwork was a name plate: Lucas Corsi.

"I know how it works!" bragged six-year-old Frank, Lucas's oldest son.

"So do I," said younger brother Peter, and they ran behind the bar and reached for the keys.

"Hold it," said Lucas. "What did I say?"

"Don't touch the new register," Frank said. He and Peter withdrew their hands and looked hopefully at their father.

Lucas walked behind the register. "You can each have a turn—but just this once." When it was Tony's turn, Lucas lifted him and helped press down on one of the keys. Tony stared with fascination when a number popped up in the glass window at the top of the register. When Lucas pulled a lever and the cash drawer flew open with a loud chime, Tony giggled with delight.

While Lucas showed Marcello and Luisa the newly installed gaslights, the boys discovered the pool cues and pulled them from the rack. With shrieks of laughter, they chased each other around the pool tables, jabbing the make-believe swords in the air.

"Boys!" Julia hurried over to Frank, Peter, and Tony and retrieved the pool cues. "Those aren't toys. They belong to the pool hall and cost a lot of money."

"Let's go home, boys, said Luisa. "You can play outside until dinner." She and Julia grabbed their sons' hands and herded them out the door.

"There's something else I want to show Marcello before we leave," Lucas called after them. He walked to the back room and returned with two amber-colored bottles. "Have a seat," he said, gesturing to one of the tables. They opened the bottles, clinked them together, and drank.

Marcello wiped his mouth with the back of his hand. "Is this a new brand of beer?"

"I've started to brew my own," Lucas answered. "What do you think?"

"You brewed this? It's good." Marcello downed another swallow. "How do you make it?"

"I boil the mash in the kitchen. Julia can't stand the smell and opens every window in the house. It ferments in the basement, then I bottle it." Lucas studied the bottle and smiled with satisfaction. "This is my best brew."

Marcello gazed around the pool hall. "I envy you, Lucas. You're realizing your dream in a big way. Me, I don't know if

I'm going forward or backward."

"The ceiling collapse? From the gossip I've heard, you have nothing to worry about."

"What gossip?"

"From some of the regulars who play pool."

"Did they say anything about *me*?"

"No—just that the collapse wasn't very serious, and the tunnel was repaired."

Marcello took a long drink, leaned forward, and spoke in a low voice. "Right after the ceiling fell, I couldn't find Jim. All I could think of was getting the hell out of there. I didn't know how we'd do it in total darkness." He fell back in his chair as though a great weight had been lifted, like a man who had just confessed his sins to a priest. "I was terrified. I haven't said that out loud to anyone, not Jim, and especially not to Luisa."

Lucas looked Marcello in the eye. "Are you still afraid?"

"I'd be lying if I said no. I worry at night about going to work the next day. When I ride the mantrip into the mine I look at every cross beam like it's ready to give way. My heart pounds, my hands shake—I'm glad it's dark so no one sees."

Lucas sat up in his chair, his eyes bright. "Come work for me. My business is growing. I still make most of my wine, and now that I'm brewing beer, I've hired a neighbor. There's more than enough work."

"Thanks, but I—"

"I can't pay as much as the mine right away, but you could work for me and learn the business. When I open my next saloon, you could manage it and earn even more money."

Work for Lucas? The thought had never crossed Marcello's mind. He had chosen to be a miner and was good at it. The pay was better than anything else he could earn as an immigrant. Marcello eyed his oldest brother's earnest expression. "I'm not ready to give up on mining. I have a plan."

"What kind of plan?"

"To work for a promotion to crew chief and then management."

Lucas took another swallow of beer. "Be realistic, Marcello. Even if you get a promotion, you'll never get rich working at the mine. The people who make money are the ones *selling* things to the miners—like the company store and the saloons."

"Like you." Marcello's voice was thoughtful.

"Like me."

Marcello fingered the neck of his bottle in silence.

"Don't answer right now. Keep your options open, that's all I ask."

They drained the last of their beer and thumped the empty bottles on the table. Marcello wiped his mouth. "Damn good beer, brother. Get ready for lots of business. The locals will knock down your door."

When they stood to leave, Lucas put a hand on Marcello's shoulder. "I'm serious about you working for me. You could make a decent living, and it won't threaten your life every day." He paused. "I don't want anyone in our family to pay the ultimate price for being a miner."

The gravity in Lucas's voice sent a shiver down Marcello's spine. His brother's warning followed him out the door as they walked back to the house, the soft summer morning suddenly chilly.

CHAPTER 20

Sunlight streaked over Oyster Ridge, the rocky hills on the east side of town, and lit the rooftops of Cumberland. Angelo and Marcello strode down the street to the mine, their work boots thumping on the plank walkway. They heard stirrings of the summer morning behind the closed doors of the miners' homes—the clatter of kettles, the muffled voices. Two boys filled water buckets at one of the neighborhood hydrants, recently installed by the company. Except for a handful of miners, the streets were empty.

"You're serious about trapping coyotes?" Marcello asked Angelo.

"I don't have any traps yet, but I can buy them at the company store. My neighbor has trapped the past two years. Said he'd show me how it's done. Between coyotes and badgers, there's money to be made."

They turned the corner onto the main street when Marcello abruptly stopped. "What was that?"

"What?" Angelo frowned.

Marcello held up his hand to quiet him. "Did you hear something?"

Angelo listened a moment. "No."

Marcello paused again for a moment, then shrugged. "Guess it was nothing."

They continued down the street. "What do you use for bait?" Marcello asked.

"Well, the best thing—" Angelo stopped suddenly. "Wait. I *do* hear something. Sounds like—"

"A child?" asked Marcello. They followed the sound that grew louder as they neared one of the miner's houses. They approached the front porch and stopped dead in their tracks.

"What's this?" Angelo was incredulous.

Curled up behind sagebrush in front of the house was a little girl with blond curls, no bigger than a toddler. She was whimpering. She raised her head when she saw them and looked up with sorrowful eyes. She wore overalls with a thin blanket around her shoulders, held in place by a safety pin. A crust of bread was clutched in her tiny first. Then Marcello's jaw dropped.

A rope around the child's waist was tied to the porch railing.

"*Caro Dio,* who would tie up a child?" Angelo untied the rope, and Marcello picked up the little girl. "It's all right," he said gently, but the child burst into tears. Marcello bounced her in his arms. It was then he noticed the note. "Angelo, look."

Angelo unpinned the scrap of paper and squinted at it. "It's hard to make out, but I think it says, 'Please take care of her because I can't.' " Angelo gave Marcello a look of amazement and strode to the front door. It was unlocked, and he pushed it open. "Hello, hello," he called. "Anyone here?" There was no answer.

"Try next door," Marcello said.

Angelo banged on the door of the next house. Presently, a fair-haired man with stooped shoulders leaned out.

"Do you know who this is?" Angelo pointed to the next yard where Marcello stood with the child in his arms. "We just found her. She was tied to the porch."

"Oh, my God," said the neighbor. "That's the Ketolas' child." They hurried across the yard to Marcello.

"Do you know where the parents are?" Marcello tried to

soothe the child. "Shh, shh. We'll find your mama and papa."

"A strange pair," he said. "She's nice enough but has been real sick. Terrible cough. I told him to take her to the doc, but he had strange notions. Didn't believe in doctors. Now that I think about it, I haven't seen her for quite a spell." He mounted the porch steps and peered in the front window. "Looks like they just up and left."

"The note sounds like they're not coming back," Angelo said. The child's crying had quieted, but she coughed and sniffed. Angelo took out his handkerchief and wiped her runny nose.

"What should we do with her?" Marcello looked at the neighbor. "Your wife, could she look after her?"

"My wife took sick. Went back to Nebraska to stay with her sister till she's better."

"What about Luisa?" Angelo looked at Marcello. "Rosa can help, too, until we know what's happened."

"Someone has to take care of her, poor child." Marcello eyed the child's dirty, tear-stained face, unable to fathom abandoning a child, and shook his head. "We have to report this."

Luisa was washing breakfast dishes when she heard the front door open.

"Marcello? Why are you—" Her curiosity heightened when she saw him holding a little girl. "Who's this?" She wiped her hands on her apron.

"Angelo and I found her on our way to work."

"Found her? She's lost?"

"She belongs to a family on the next street, but there's no sign of them."

Luisa's frown deepened. "What do you mean? Someone must know where they are." She took the child from Marcello and smiled at her. "Why don't we wipe those tears." She set her on the table next to the basin.

"She was tied to the porch."

Luisa spun around, stunned. "What?"

"There was a note that said 'look after her because I can't.' "

Luisa struggled to understand. She turned back to the child, a lump rising in her throat and whispered, "They *left* you? How could they?" After wringing out a cloth, she gently cupped the child's chin and wiped away the dirt and tears. Showing no emotion, the little girl stared at her with the bluest eyes Luisa had ever seen. "You must be hungry. Would you like milk?"

The child sniffed and blinked her eyes, her long lashes dripping with tears.

Marcello and Angelo reported the discovery of the child to Mr. Hopkins, the mine supervisor. Officially, there was no indication Henri Ketola had left Cumberland or Union Pacific Coal, but pieces of information surfaced by midday. He'd emigrated from Finland and worked for Union Pacific less than a year. Other Finnish miners said his English was poor, and he kept to himself. No one knew the extent of his wife's illness or the name of his child. Before the end of the day, a handwritten flyer was posted in the mine office urgently seeking information on the whereabouts of the Ketola family.

Arriving home that evening, Marcello brushed coal dust off his clothes on the porch. He smelled stew and biscuits before he opened the front door.

"Papa." Tony ran to him and hugged his legs. Marcello swung Tony up into his arms.

"Such a nice welcome. How's my boy?"

"There's a girl here," said Tony with a frown, pointing to the child. She wore a clean shirt and a pair of overalls Tony had outgrown. Luisa set the table and held the little girl on her hip.

"How is she?" Marcello asked Luisa.

"She's been clinging to me all day." Luisa shifted the fussy child to her other hip.

"I'm sorry this was forced on you, Luisa. We had to find someone to carc for her right away."

"It's all right, I don't mind. She had a good nap after I fed her and gave her a bath." Luisa smoothed the little girl's blond curls. "Poor thing. What can she be thinking?"

After Marcello washed up, they sat at the table, Luisa holding the wiggly girl in her lap. "I'm anxious to know what you found out." She blew on a spoonful of stew and slipped it into the open mouth of the little girl.

Marcello recounted what he'd learned about the Ketolas and the efforts by the company to locate the parents.

"They're Finnish?"

"Seems so." Marcello looked at the child, who had nestled against Luisa's chest. "She likes you. She feels safe with you. Has she said anything?"

"She makes sounds, but I can't tell if she's babbling or speaking in a language I don't understand."

"How old do you think she is?" Marcello asked.

Luisa brought another spoonful of stew to the child's mouth. "Not yet two years, I'd guess."

"When's she going home?" Tony looked from his papa to his mama.

"We don't know," answered Luisa. "Her mama and papa aren't home. There's no one to take care of her."

"Did you play with her?" asked Marcello.

"She didn't want to." Tony scowled at his supper. Marcello pushed away from the table and patted his lap. Tony slid from his place and climbed up, smiling as though his proper place in the family had been restored.

"You could help us take care of her." Luisa raised her eyebrows with the invitation. "That would be a nice thing to do."

Tony didn't answer, but eyed the little girl with a mixture of skepticism and resentment.

"Mr. Hopkins asked if she could stay with us for a few days until they know more. If he can't locate the parents or relatives, he'll find an orphanage. Angelo told me Rosa could help look after her. Is that all right?"

"I'll walk to Rosa's after supper, and we'll talk," said Luisa. Marcello saw the concern on her face. "What could have happened to the parents, Marcello? Look at her. How could they leave her?"

"Their neighbor said the mother was sick. Maybe she's near death, and it's only him to care for both of them. The note did say '*I* can't look after her.' "

"But to leave your own flesh and blood? How could they?"

"Truth is, we don't know how desperate the parents were. Maybe they thought she had a better chance to survive with someone else, even strangers. All we know for certain is they're gone."

Luisa stared into the blue eyes of the child and her heart ached. "We don't even know your name. What should we call you? Piccolo? Cara? Luisa brought a spoonful of potato to the child's mouth. "*Mangia,* Cara."

"English . . . Italian . . ." Marcello wondered, "Do we know anyone who speaks Finnish?"

The little girl slept on a pallet beside Luisa and Marcello's bed. The first night she cried out in her sleep so often, Luisa slid out of bed and lay down beside her on the floor, holding her the rest of the night. Tony hid all his soldiers and blocks under his bed, refusing to share with her. Only after Luisa sternly explained the little girl had no toys, no parents, and no house to live in, did Tony grudgingly give up one of his soldiers and four blocks.

Marcello invited a Finnish miner and his wife to their home to talk with Cara. She sat on Luisa's lap and stared at the strangers. The couple spoke in a kindly manner with words Marcello and Luisa didn't understand. Cara showed an interest, and there was a flicker of recognition in her eyes. When the miner's wife said *"aiti,"* the child sat up straight in Luisa's lap. She looked between the man and his wife and repeated the word. *"Aiti, aiti, aiti."* She became agitated. *"Aiti,"* and suddenly burst into tears.

Alarmed, Luisa cradled Cara and rocked her, trying to stop her sobbing. Near tears herself, Luisa asked, "What is she saying?"

The wife shook her head sadly. *"Aiti,"* she replied, "means mother."

Two weeks went by. Mr. Hopkins called Marcello into his office and explained they had found no leads on the Ketolas. He wasn't hopeful they would find the missing parents, but would wait until the end of the third week, when he'd contact authorities at an orphanage in Rock Springs.

Marcello was worried. Although he was proud of Luisa's willingness to step in and care for Cara, the little girl's attachment to Luisa was now proving problematic. So long as the child was near Luisa or could hear her voice, she was content. Any separation brought on inconsolable anxiety. Cara had chosen Luisa, and Marcello hadn't planned on that.

"Mr. Hopkins is contacting the orphanage next week." Marcello said the words matter-of-factly, sitting across the table from Luisa in the late evening before they turned down the lamps and retired.

Luisa was suddenly anxious. "Already? I thought he was still trying to find the parents."

"He's put in a lot of time looking for them—more than I

thought he would. It's time for her to find a permanent place." Marcello looked Luisa in the eye to gauge her reaction.

Luisa looked away and said nothing. Finally, she spoke. "I have something to tell you." She stared nervously at her clasped hands. "I should have told you long before now."

Marcello frowned. "Told me what?"

Her words came slowly at first, but once she started, every detail, every suppressed memory poured out in a torrent. She told him everything about the first year after he left Italy—the surprise at her pregnancy, her decision not to tell him, the birth and death of their daughter, the deep melancholy she experienced afterward.

"She was born early. So tiny and beautiful, a perfect little face and delicate fingers." Luisa's eyes brimmed with tears. "She never took a breath."

Marcello leaned over, his head in his hands. He said nothing.

"I'm sorry I didn't tell you, Marcello. I could not put pen to paper without weeping. I was heartsick." She wiped her eyes. "When I was finally myself again, I stopped trying to send you word and put it out of my mind. Or tried to."

Marcello walked to the window, where he stared into the night. After a heavy silence he said, "You should have told me."

"Perhaps." Luisa's voice was barely audible. "I named her Sophia."

"Sophia?" Marcello's voice was distant. "A baby I never knew about. Where is she buried?"

"The family cemetery. I visited her grave every day."

Marcello shoved his hands into his pockets and turned. "Is that why you want this new little girl, to replace the one you lost?"

"Don't you see?" Luisa rose from the table and went to him. "Finding this child was no accident—it was meant to be. I know this as surely as I'm standing before you. We lost our baby girl, but this little girl is here now. She needs us. I can't let her go—I won't let her go."

Marcello thought of his escape from the accident at the mine only two months ago. "What if something happens to me, Luisa? The next time there's an accident, I might not be so lucky. You'd be left with *two* mouths to feed."

"Marcello, imagine what it's like to walk away from your child—forever. If her mother is alive, she's praying desperately her daughter will be saved and cared for. If we do this, I believe the mother will know it. Somehow, she will have a sense of it. We must do this for her, for the child and . . ."

He finished her thought. "And for you?"

The look on Luisa's face and the tone of her voice told Marcello she had already made her decision. He moved away from her and sank into a chair. He struggled for words. "We had a baby." He stood and paced in slow steps beside the table, sorting through the deluge of information. "You want to keep the child and raise her as our own?"

"I already feel she is ours."

Marcello stopped and faced her. "We'll have more children, Luisa, many more. You know that, don't you?"

"I know only this for certain—we're not promised anything in this life."

"But to take in someone else's child . . ." His forehead creased. "I . . . there's so much to consider. What about her parents? What if we grow to love her and her parents return? I need to think about this." He gestured absently in the air as though the pieces of Luisa's revelations were scattered about the room, upsetting the balance of their universe, and he was burdened with restoring order.

Louisa stood and wrapped her arms around him. She leaned her head against his chest. "I love you, Marcello Corsi. You are a good man with a good heart."

Marcello remained rigid, his arms at his sides. "I have to think."

Later that night after Luisa was in bed, Marcello stepped out on the porch for air. He stared into the night sky studded with stars and thought about the baby Luisa had named Sophia. When he was little, his mother told him a story that each star in the sky was an angel. He had forgotten the story until tonight, but now he searched the heavens for baby Sophia's star. His thoughts turned to the little girl asleep in their house. Surely her mother worried about her—who had found her, was she all right, who cared for her? Or did the mother give in to her greatest fear that her child was gone and belonged to the scatter of stars in heaven. Perhaps the mother herself was now a star.

Marcello closed his eyes against the weight of the night and went inside.

Chapter 21

Cara had been with them three weeks. Separation from Luisa no longer frightened her, and she slept soundly through the night. She was curious about Tony and followed him around the house, often mimicking him. When Tony discovered she found him entertaining, he became more tolerant. It pleased him to make her smile. Given the stressful days after they found her, Marcello was surprised at how well she had adapted.

Soon her stay with them would end. Day after tomorrow Mr. Hopkins planned to contact the orphanage. Marcello found sleep difficult. The Corsis faced a life-changing decision they didn't agree on: Luisa wanted to adopt the child and he didn't.

He'd formed a strong bond with Tony. It hadn't been easy to be the father of a three-year-old who didn't know him. Tony overcame his shyness and warmed to his father as time passed. Now he followed Marcello like a little shadow, often getting underfoot, which Marcello didn't mind one bit. Their family had settled in nicely, only to be upended at the prospect of adopting the child of strangers.

"Wouldn't it be better if a Finnish family adopted her?" he asked Luisa one evening.

"No one in town has come forward," she said. "Most of the Finns are bachelors, and the rest of the families already have more than enough children."

"But maybe an orphanage could find a Finnish family for her."

Luisa bristled. "She has a family now—you, me, and Tony."

"Luisa—"

"It doesn't matter to her whether we're Finnish or Greek, so long as we love her. Besides, isn't this country supposed to be—what do they call it—the melting pot where all these ethnic groups come together and live side by side? That's what Cumberland is." She paused a moment and her eyes glimmered as an idea struck her. "We could be a melting pot *in* a melting pot."

Marcello and Luisa knew about orphaned children. Back home in their village, injury or illness claimed mothers and fathers, sometimes in their prime. Relatives or neighbors in the close-knit communities took in these children and raised them as their own. Why would it be any different here?

Tony came from the bedroom into the kitchen wearing his pajamas. "Can you tell me a story, Papa?" He climbed into Marcello's lap, jiggling the rocker as he settled himself.

"Don't you look cozy," Luisa said as she joined them, carrying Cara dressed in her nightgown. Cara left Luisa's arms, toddled to the rocker, and did something she'd never done before. She climbed onto Marcello's lap next to Tony.

Marcello's eyes widened.

"What do you think of that?" Luisa met Marcello's gaze with one, equally surprised, of her own.

Marcello shifted in his rocker, arranging the children comfortably in his lap. "A story? All right, just a short one." Tony nodded, and the little girl took her cue and nodded with him. "Once there was a very big tortoise . . ." Tony nestled against Marcello's chest and Cara did the same. He embellished the fable of the tortoise and the hare into the adventures of an odd assortment of animals. The tortoise's best friend, a woodchuck, worked with him in a Wyoming coal mine with a rabbit, a duck, a pig, and a cow, all of whom came from faraway countries.

At the story's end, Tony slid off Marcello's lap with a yawn and padded after Luisa to his bed. Marcello looked down at the girl, her head against his chest, her eyes closed. He carried her, heavy with sleep, to her pallet and tucked the blanket under her chin. Instead of leaving, he sat on the floor beside her. Usually sore or exhausted after a day at the mine, Marcello rarely put the children to bed. Tonight was different.

A roll of thunder rumbled in the distance. He watched Cara's chest rise and fall. She stirred, and blond curls fell across her cheek. Staring at her sleeping face, a thought came to him: nothing about the child made her undeserving of a family to love her. Not one thing. She had come to Marcello and Luisa in a way they could never have imagined. Whatever dark forces had wreaked havoc in her life, she needed a family. She deserved a family.

Marcello thought back to the night Luisa had told him about their stillborn daughter. In the same moment, she told Marcello she wanted to adopt the little girl. In his mind, the two events became one. He associated the shock and sadness of their baby's death with adopting this child. Losing their baby held its own grief that had to heal in its own time. Adopting this little girl was its own act of love.

He kissed Cara on her cheek and stood.

The smell of rain floated through the open front door. Marcello found Luisa on the front step and sat beside her. The pink and purple cosmos she had coaxed from seeds swayed on feathery stalks in the rising breeze. They sat in silence, captivated with the billowing clouds, building one on top of another, illuminated from within by flashes of lightening.

Marcello didn't know how to start, his thoughts so jumbled. "I'm sorry if I seemed distant these past weeks. When you told me about losing our baby, I was shocked." Marcello shook his head. "I was angry, I was sad." He reached for Luisa's hand. "You lost the baby without me beside you, without me even knowing about it."

He heard Luisa take a breath and felt her hand cover his.

Marcello turned to her. "When you said you wanted to adopt Cara right after telling me about the baby, I was overwhelmed. I couldn't see things clearly."

Luisa squeezed his hand. "Now that you know about the baby, we can remember her together. That's the way it should be."

"But that doesn't answer the question about Cara."

"No."

"When I said we'd have more children—"

"I remember."

"You were right. We don't know what the future holds. But one thing I do know. I intend to provide for all our children, whether we have a houseful or just two."

Luisa let his words sink in. "Just two? What are you saying, Marcello?"

He spoke softly. "You are right. We should call her Sophia."

He pulled Luisa close and felt the tears that spilled down her cheeks.

At ten o'clock, Marcello poked the embers in the stove, and Luisa had carried the lamp to their bedroom, when heavy pounding on their door broke the silence.

"Marcello, open up! It's Angelo." The pounding grew louder.

Marcello opened the door and Angelo rushed in, breathless and rain soaked, carrying a lantern. "There's trouble."

"What's wrong?" Marcello asked.

"Jim and Dominic and Roberto—"

"Roberto?" Luisa quickly crossed the room.

"They're in jail."

"What?" Luisa cried.

Marcello grabbed his jacket off the hook. "What happened?"

"That's all I know—heard it from my neighbor." Angelo raked his fingers through his wet hair.

"Let's go," said Marcello.

Luisa grasped his arm, a pleading expression on her face. "Please be careful."

"I will." He mustered a reassuring smile before heading out the door.

Angelo's lantern threw dim light on the dark, muddy street as they raced to the jail at the edge of town. "There was a huge fight at the saloon." Angelo's voice was tight. "Didn't want to say so in front of Luisa."

"Dear God," Marcello muttered.

Their boots sloshed and thumped on the rain-slicked walkway. Through the drizzle, they saw a mob of men in front of the jail and quickened their steps. They elbowed their way to the front of the crowd and stopped.

The front door of the jail was smashed and tossed aside on the floor. Marcello and Angelo stepped inside the shambles, broken glass crunching under their boots. The desk was overturned, chairs were broken and tossed, windows were shattered, papers strewn about. The jail cell that cordoned off a corner of the room stood intact, but the door hung open, the cell empty.

Marcello turned to the men who had followed them inside. "Anybody know what happened?"

One of the men Marcello recognized from work spoke up. "Somebody told me a bunch of Italian cowboys broke in here and let them out. Word spread real quick after the fight that something like this would happen. They sure tore up the place."

Marcello's mind raced. "Where's the sheriff?"

The men looked at each other and shrugged in silence.

Marcello's gut churned. An empty jail and no sheriff—what had happened? Fearing the worst, he spoke under his breath to Angelo. "This is bad. Where do you think our boys are?"

"Don't know. Back at the boardinghouse?"

"If something happened to that sheriff . . ." Marcello didn't want to finish the thought.

Kerosene lamps lit up the boardinghouse when Marcello and Angelo raced into the front room. The boarders crowded around the couch where Jim, Dominic, and Roberto sat.

"You all right?" Angelo leaned close and eyed each of them.

Marcello didn't wait for answers. "What happened?"

"Questo e terribile!" Dried blood covered the bridge of Jim's nose. "We were at the saloon minding our own business. A bunch of no-good drifters started it. Called us dagos. They wanted a fight."

Dominic held a bandana to a cut above his right eye. "They started it, Marcello. You know how it works—they start it and we get blamed."

"That figures," muttered Marcello and set his jaw. "What happened after the fight?"

"Somebody went for the sheriff. He and a couple of men took us to jail."

"But none of the troublemakers," Jim continued, "just the *eye-talians.*" Bitterness dripped from his sarcastic pronunciation.

"We just came from the jail," Angelo said. "It's destroyed."

Jim, Dominic, and Roberto exchanged looks.

"I wouldn't believe it if I hadn't seen it with my own eyes," Jim said. "Some Italians work on the ranches north of town. A couple of them were in jail with us. Their friends rode into town, broke them out and us with them."

"What about the sheriff?" Marcello's temples throbbed as he

listened to the account.

"Those guys had guns." Dominic removed the bandana from his forehead, the gash on it no longer bleeding. "The sheriff tried to stop them, but they knocked him around pretty good. That's when he ran for it. Didn't even take the keys. They were still in the desk."

"So the Italians unlocked the cell and let us out, and then they wrecked the place," said Roberto "They were crazy mad."

"Was that the last time you saw the sheriff?" Marcello asked.

Roberto nodded and rubbed his swollen knuckles. "This whole thing is *stupido.* It was just a bar fight. That sheriff was trying to be a big man, but he's just a coward."

"He might be a coward, but he's still the law in Cumberland." Marcello gave each of them a piercing stare. "You're in big trouble." The room was silent.

"So what do we do now?" Dominic sounded contrite.

"I think, if the sheriff comes back, you should go back to jail," said Angelo.

"What?"

"Never!"

"No!" The three men hollered over each other.

"Stop!" Marcello shouted, holding up both hands. Jim, Dominic, and Roberto grew silent again. "We don't know what the law will do about this. They might be here first thing tomorrow to arrest you. If they don't come, the three of you should talk to your boss. Tell him your side of the story—how the fight started, the arrest, the breakout, everything.

Roberto edged forward, anxious. "That will make things worse for us."

"Maybe, maybe not. One thing is in your favor. The sheriff ran off. He might be in more trouble than you."

After Marcello went home and told Luisa what had happened, she fretted into the early hours of the morning about

Roberto's impending arrest. The authorities never came, so Jim, Dominic, and Roberto went to their boss's house to explain what had happened.

"I swear they started it," Jim said while Dominic and Roberto looked on. Isaac listened patiently while Jim continued. "It was a bunch of drifters, they were drunk. They called us all kinds of names. They pushed us into a fight."

After Jim explained the arrest and jailbreak, Isaac spoke. "This is serious business." He gave them an intense look, his blue eyes sharp. "First thing Monday, go to the office and tell Mr. Hopkins what happened. Take someone who saw the fight to vouch for you."

On Monday morning, Marcello went to the mine as usual and worked alone while he waited nervously for Jim to join him. Marcello worried about the outcome of the meeting. Jim had a temper and, if angered, Marcello knew he could make a bad situation worse. He wasn't as worried about Dominic or Roberto—they were angry but would cooperate.

He'd been at work about an hour when Jim entered the tunnel. Marcello immediately stopped loading his coal car. "What happened?"

"It was good we took someone to stand up for us. The bosses listened, and I think they believe us—not like that stupid sheriff."

"I hope you didn't call the sheriff stupid in front of your boss."

"Give me some credit, Marcello. I know better."

"Did they say what you should do now?"

"They think the sheriff in Kemmerer will be in charge. Dominic asked if we'd have to go back to jail, but they didn't know. Said we might have to pay for damages. Those damned drifters started the whole thing, and they're long gone. Nothing will happen to them. Makes my blood boil!"

"Me, too, Jim . . . me, too." The memory came flooding

back—the saloon fight he and his brothers had been in years earlier with cowboys who were just looking to stir up trouble. The image of Crooked Nose came into focus with stark clarity. All these years later, Marcello's fists clenched at the memory of the insults. "So there's nothing you should do?"

"Not right now. We wait and see."

"Maybe it'll be settled fairly." Given the past, Marcello knew the chances of that were slim.

"Before we left, our boss gave us some advice."

"What's that?"

"He told us to stay out of the saloons."

Chapter 22

With the addition of Sophia to their family, Luisa's spirits soared. She sang to the prairie as she hung out the laundry, while Tony and Sophia chased each other around the freshly washed sheets whipping in the wind. On baking day, she sold loaves of bread to bachelors at the boardinghouse with Sophia toddling along beside her. Not even Roberto's run-in with the law diminished her happiness. The sheriff ordered Jim, Dominic, Roberto, and the Italians working at the Prescott Ranch to pay for damages to the jail. He added a stern warning: any future brawls meant jail time. Luisa turned the page on the troubling event along with her initial dislike for Cumberland. Perhaps she had been hasty in the assessment of their new home. She would give Cumberland another chance.

Elsa poked her head through the doorway. "Luisa, you ready?"

Tall and strong, with bright green eyes, their Russian neighbor was as hard-working as she was friendly. Her hands bore calluses from the trips when she'd driven their wagon to Kemmerer for supplies while her husband lay ill with pneumonia. She patiently conversed in English while Luisa learned the language, yet couldn't resist teaching Luisa a smattering of Russian. Elsa was the first friend Luisa made outside Marcello's family.

"Almost ready," answered Luisa. She slipped two bills and five coins from the tin canister in the cupboard into a leather coin purse and stepped outside with Sophia in tow. Tony charged down the street with Elsa's boys, Uri and Anton, toward the shouts of children playing tag.

Sophia's golden curls bounced as she step-hopped between Luisa and Elsa, supported by the clasp of their hands. They walked at their leisure down the wide dirt street through the miners' neighborhood. The women of Cumberland personalized the identical houses with pots of flowers on the front steps and bright curtains at the windows. One husband had built a three-tiered birdhouse that stood near the walkway. A handmade wooden bench sat beside an open front door.

"Now *this* is the weather I like," said Luisa and took a deep breath of fresh air scented with sage. She tipped her head and welcomed every delicious ray of sun on her face as it teased with the promise of more warm days to come.

"Have I told you about Mr. John?" asked Elsa.

Luisa shook her head.

"He has a general store in Kemmerer and brings merchandise here once a month to sell. You can bargain with him."

"What is bargain?" asked Luisa.

"You offer to pay less than his price. Sometimes he says yes, sometimes no."

Luisa nodded. "I know this. We call it c*ontrattare sulprezzo.*"

Elsa leaned close to Luisa and whispered, "We call him Cheap John—but not to his face."

A gathering of women stood at the end of the street, their skirts rippling in the morning breeze, their brightly colored bonnets bobbing like wildflowers in the sunshine. Mothers carried infants in their arms or in slings fashioned from shawls. In the distance a large covered wagon laboring under a heavy load rumbled down the dusty road toward them.

Luisa, Sophia, and Elsa reached the shoppers as the wagon pulled to a stop. Two men hopped down, walked to the rear of the wagon, and unloaded large cases they set on the ground in rows. As soon as the men opened the display cases, the women swarmed around them to look at the merchandise.

Elsa nudged Luisa, amused. "Like chickens at the feeder, don't you think?"

A pudgy man with wiry red hair bristling on top of his head and under his chin barked orders at the crowd. "Step back. Give me some room. Move back," he commanded, strutting back and forth, the rooster in charge of the feeder.

"Is that Cheap John?" Luisa whispered to Elsa. Holding up his baggy brown pants were the brightest red suspenders Luisa had ever seen. "He wears them to match his hair, yes?" she giggled.

While scolding the shoppers for interfering with his job, John worked quickly, and when the last case was opened he announced, "Now, I'm ready."

Luisa scooped Sophia into her arms as the women rushed forward in a wave. They tried on bonnets and gloves and scrutinized the shirts and trousers for size and quality, chattering in a myriad of languages. They admired dress shoes and examined the quality of work boots. Household utensils—spoons, ladles, spatulas, sifters, skillets—clattered as the women pawed through the cases. They jostled for position, holding bolts of gingham and cards of yarn to be measured and cut.

"*Nadal stoja,* Thaddeus," a mother implored her squirming son as she held trousers up to his waist.

Two women beside Luisa conferred over a pair of work boots. *"Ce parereaveti?"* One of the women turned to John. "How much?" she asked.

"Two dollars and fifty cents."

"Pay you two dollars."

"Two dollars and twenty-five cents. No less," John replied.

The woman shrugged and paid John, took her purchase, and moved on with her friend.

Luisa and Elsa inched their way to a case piled with neatly folded shirts. An elderly woman beside them inspected several shirts, then chose one and held it up.

"Kóotoc? Kóotoc?" she asked.

"Eighty cents. That's a fair price."

She shook her head, put the shirt down, and left.

Luisa lowered Sophia to the ground and quickly picked up the shirt the woman had just rejected. "This is Marcello's size." She ran her hand over the white cotton, admiring the fabric. All Marcello's shirts were flannel, fit for work. He could wear this one to church or for Sunday dinner when the family came. An extravagance, yes, but she rationalized he could wear it for years.

"If you see something you want, buy it before someone else does," said Elsa.

With women pressing against her to look at the merchandise, Luisa decided not to bargain, paid for the shirt, and moved to the next case. "Oh, look at these," she exclaimed. A pair of brown and amber combs displayed in a case with hairpins and ribbons caught her attention. "What do you think, Sophia? Pretty?"

Sophia nodded. "Pretty."

"How much are they?" Elsa asked.

Luisa held up the combs and raised her voice over the clamor. "Cost, *per favore*?"

"Forty cents," John hollered.

"Thirty cents," Luisa countered.

"Forty cents, no less," John responded. "Those are special combs."

Luisa shook her head. "Too much," and returned them to the case. "I'll wait till next month." She turned to leave and bumped into a woman behind her. *"Scuzie,"* Luisa said and stepped back.

The woman stiffened, her posture rigid, and gave her a hard

look. Her shirtwaist and bonnet looked new. She had alabaster skin and piercing blue eyes that scrutinized Luisa with disapproval. Her gaze traveled to Sophia. Luisa instinctively grasped Sophia's hand under the withering stare of the women.

"So *you're* the family," the woman sniffed, returning her gaze to Luisa. "It isn't right, the child not with her own kind."

"Excuse me?" Luisa frowned.

They eyed each other until the woman sniffed again and muttered under her breath, *"Ulkomaalaisia."* She glared at Elsa before turning away and disappeared into the crowd.

Luisa stared after her. "Who is she?"

"Never seen her before," said Elsa. "Might be Finnish."

Luisa's eyes narrowed. "Did she say I'm not kind?"

Elsa didn't respond at first. "She must be new to Cumberland. Don't give her another thought."

"She has bad manners," Luisa said.

Elsa lowered her voice. "I've heard the Finns plan to build their own town hall on the other side of town." Wanting to change the subject, Elsa stood on her tiptoes and looked over the crowd. "Luisa . . . where are the boys?"

At that moment, Luisa heard Tony's excited voice above the crowd. "Mama, come look." They found the boys huddled around a case of pocketknives and watches. The knives gleamed against the black cloth in the display, their blades spread open like fans.

"Tony, you're too young to have a knife."

His face fell. "Please, Mama."

Luisa took his hand and led him and Sophia to a case of toys: penny dolls, wooden clowns, paper snakes and stick candy. The scowl on Tony's face disappeared when he spied a bright blue whistle. "Can I have that?" Luisa nodded and gave him two pennies from her coin purse.

She turned to Sophia. "And what would you like, little one?"

Sophia leaned over the case and pointed to a tiny wooden doll.

With new toys in their hands, Tony and Sophia followed Luisa until they found Elsa and her sons. Elsa was haggling with John's assistant over the price of boys' shoes, when an angry outburst exploded over the crowd. Luisa and Elsa leaned through the shoppers for a closer look.

"I said that was my final price. Take it or leave it!" With hands on his hips, Cheap John faced a tiny, dark-haired woman holding a pair of trousers. A hush fell over the crowd.

"No, too much," she retorted, wagging her finger in front of his nose.

John leaned in and pushed her finger away. "You understand English? I said that was my final price."

"Not good," she said, standing her ground. "Too much money."

The crimson color in John's neck spread to his face. "I'm done!" he thundered. He grabbed the pants from her hands and tossed them into the case. He walked past each case and slammed the lids with a bang. "No more sales," he shouted and waved his arms for emphasis. He hollered to his assistant, and they loaded everything back into the wagon.

The tiny woman trailed behind John, shaking her finger and scolding him in her native tongue. Unhappy with the abrupt end of shopping, a handful of women joined her and clustered around John's wagon, squawking disapproval.

"This has happened before," Elsa whispered to Luisa and gave her a knowing wink. "Cheap John will drive his wagon across town and start selling there like nothing has happened. He'll be back here, same day, next month."

Cheap John rumbled off in his wagon in a cloud of dust. The crowd dispersed, except for the disgruntled shoppers who began a brisk walk across town to his next stop. Elsa and Luisa made their way back to their houses, pleased with their purchases,

Anton and Uri racing alongside, Tony tooting his whistle, and Sophia clutching her doll. A lone cloud floated overhead, momentarily covering the sun. A shiver ran down Luisa's spine.

"Thank you for helping me shop, Elsa. I—"

A blaring horn split the morning quiet.

Elsa froze in her steps.

Luisa took a step, then stopped when she realized Elsa hadn't moved. "What is it?"

The color drained from Elsa's face. "Oh, no."

"What's wrong? Luisa's eyes darted toward the mine, the source of the noise, then back to Elsa. "I don't understand." She had never seen such a look on her friend's face. "What does this mean? *Per favore!*"

"An accident at the mine."

Chapter 23

The horn wailed, bringing life in Cumberland to a halt. Luisa pushed against the panic rising inside her. Tony stopped blowing his whistle and covered his ears. "Mama, what's that noise?" Sophia ran to Luisa and clutched her skirt.

"What should we do?" Luisa searched Elsa's face for an answer. "Should we go to the mine? Should—"

"No, we wait here." Elsa grabbed Luisa's hand. "The men will be sent home, except for the ones who need to help."

"Mama . . ." Sophia tugged on Luisa's skirt.

"Un momento." Luisa placed her arm around Sophia's shoulder and turned back to Elsa. "How do we find out what happened?"

"We'll wait until Marcello and Oleg come home."

"Wait?" Luisa's voice rose. "I can't wait!" It was unthinkable to stand there and do nothing. But when she looked at Tony's troubled face and Sophia clutching her skirt, she knew Elsa was right.

The horn quit blaring as suddenly as it had started, leaving a pall of desperate silence in the void. Luisa sat beside Elsa on her porch step and stared down the street. Women who moments ago had chatted and bartered in good-natured combat with Cheap John stood mute in doorways or sat silent on front steps, every head turned toward the mine in a sisterhood of dread.

"You're sure it's an accident?" Luisa asked.

"It's the only time the horn sounds."

"Do you think it's bad?" Luisa feared the answer but wanted to know the truth.

"It's impossible to know until we talk to someone from the mine." She squeezed Luisa's hand.

Luisa sat in silence, her mind racing with unspeakable scenarios. She grasped Elsa's hand tighter, grateful for the comfort of her friend. She closed her eyes and begged the Holy Mother to protect Marcello and Roberto. She prayed for Angelo, Jim, Mick, Oleg—for every miner she knew and every miner she couldn't name.

It began as a trickle, the men in their blackened pit clothes leaving the mine in groups of two and three, then growing in number and fanning out into the streets of town. Luisa and Elsa stood and took a few uncertain steps toward the street, searching for Marcello and Oleg.

Elsa saw them first. "There they are!" she cried. She and Luisa flew down the street to their husbands. Marcello dropped his lunch pail and caught Luisa as she flung herself into his arms, spilling tears on his shoulder.

"I'm all right," he murmured in her ear. She held him tight to reassure herself he wasn't injured.

When she released him, Luisa took his face in her hands. "Thank God you're safe!" She held him close, not wanting to let go, and thanked the Holy Mother with her whole heart.

"What happened?" asked Elsa. She and Oleg stood nearby, their arms entwined.

Oleg shook his head. "The ceiling in the south tunnel collapsed. Some men are trapped."

"Trapped? Do they know who?" Luisa looked at Marcello.

"They don't know for sure. The rescue has just started but . . ." Marcello looked at the ground.

His hesitation alarmed Luisa. "But what, Marcello?"

He raised his gaze. "It's the tunnel where Roberto works."

Luisa clenched her fists and pressed them to her mouth to keep from crying out. Marcello pulled her into his arms until her trembling ceased.

"Roberto has to be all right. He *has* to be." She pulled away suddenly and looked at Marcello. "What happens now? How do they get the men out?"

"I'll go back. Maybe I can help."

"I'm coming with you," Luisa said.

"No, Luisa."

"I must come."

"But the children . . ."

"Don't worry about Tony and Sophia," Elsa said. "We'll take care of them."

When Marcello and Luisa reached the mine, families of the trapped miners huddled together, faces taut, gazes locked on the entrance to the mine. A few stood apart, refusing to believe their loved ones were caught in the cave-in. The sooty smell of coal belched from the tunnel and hung in the air, the dust settling on the ground.

"Wait over there," said Marcello.

"Marcello! Luisa!" Marcello's brother Angelo and wife, Rosa, rushed toward them through the crowd.

Rosa put her arms around Luisa. "I'm so sorry."

Angelo's face was etched with worry. "What can we do?" he asked Marcello.

"Stay with Luisa while I find Isaac." Marcello's crew chief was part of the first aid crew. If anyone could give him reliable information, it would be Isaac. Marcello spotted him in a makeshift emergency area under an open tent and hurried over.

"Isaac, what's happening? Any word on the men?"

"The diggers sent out two loads of rock already. It'll take time to open the tunnel." He wound a cloth around the hand of an injured miner and reassured him, "That will hold you until the doctor comes." He turned back to Marcello. "Your brother's down there?"

"It's Roberto, my brother-in-law." The words stuck in his throat. "He was in the tunnel that caved. My wife's desperate for news."

Isaac shook his head. "It's a bad business. They brought out a few injured—the ones near the tunnel entrance—but it's slow."

"What can I do?"

"Stay with your wife. If the tunnel keeps crumbling, we'll need another shift of rescuers—but don't say anything about that to your wife."

Marcello nodded and walked back to the anxious families. Luisa grabbed his arm the minute he reached her. "What news?"

"They brought out a few men, but their biggest job is to remove rock." He put his arm around her.

"They know what they're doing," Angelo said to Luisa with confidence.

"We've been through this before," added Rosa. "A cave-in four years ago, before Marcello got here."

Marcello eyed the supervisors at the mine entrance and read their somber faces, strained to the breaking point. He knew Roberto was in total darkness, the blackest black imaginable. It was terrifying to be alone in such darkness, and Marcello prayed someone was with him. Was he buried in rock? Could he move his head? His arms, his legs? If he got out alive, would he lose a limb? He wouldn't be the first miner to suffer an amputation that ended his means to earn a living. The thought of Roberto buried under rock gripped Marcello's gut.

"What's that for?" Luisa's voice brought Marcello back to the moment. They watched coal cars loaded with timber rumble back into the mine.

"The crew reinforces the tunnel with new cross beams as

they clear it. Prevents more cave-ins." He turned to Luisa and tightened his arm around her. "The rescue team is good at their job."

Marcello knew Roberto ached for water, his throat parched from coal dust. But Marcello worried about something deadlier than Roberto's thirst—blackdamp. The odorless gasses could kill in seconds. How long before the oxygen in Roberto's tunnel was gone? How many breaths did he have left? Instinctively Marcello inhaled and felt a stab of guilt breathing the limitless supply of fresh air surrounding him.

Shouts erupted from the entrance. The mantrip emerged, and a supervisor yelled for help. In the first car, two injured men supported a third slumped between them. Gashes on their heads bled heavily onto pit clothes, bright red on black. Behind them, two men lay motionless on the seats of the car.

"Get stretchers!" Isaac yelled.

Marcello ran to the car, praying Roberto would be in it. The crew lifted the unconscious men onto stretchers and rushed past Marcello. He glimpsed a mangled arm hanging grotesquely off the side of a stretcher. The other injured men climbed out and leaned heavily on first aid workers as they made their way to the tent.

With a sinking heart, Marcello walked back to Luisa and shook his head. Minutes later a second mantrip clattered from the mine with a team of diggers who reported to the supervisors. Family members desperate for information shouted questions in a frantic torrent.

"Where's my husband?"

"Did you find my boy?"

"How long before you get them out?"

A supervisor approached the relatives. He pulled down the blackened bandana that covered his nose and spoke, his voice strained. "We're reinforcing the tunnel as we go so it will be safe when we bring the men out. It will take the rest of the afternoon, maybe into the night." He wiped black streaks of sweat from his forehead. His tone softened. "We're doing everything we can. That's all I can tell you."

Luisa inhaled sharply, and Marcello wrapped his hand over hers. Family members around them exchanged hushed words and embraces. Some decided to leave their vigil at the mine and return later in the day. A young woman beside Luisa began to weep and walked away, leaning on an elderly man.

"Go home, Luisa," Marcello said. "The children need you."

Luisa stared at the mouth of the mine and said nothing.

"I'll come for you the minute I know anything."

Luisa spoke, her eyes fixed on the mine. "I'll go . . . for a while."

Marcello hugged her. "Try to eat something. There's no telling when they'll reach Roberto. If he's badly injured, we'll bring him to our house so you can take care of him." Marcello knew that, with each passing minute, the odds of rescuing Roberto alive dropped. But in his heart, he wanted to believe a lifesaving rescue was possible for Luisa's sake. He glanced at the sun and gauged two hours had passed since the cave-in. His pulse surged. They had to find Roberto soon.

"If you hear news about Roberto . . ." Luisa choked on his name.

"I promise."

Marcello turned to Angelo and Rosa. "Take her home. Stay with her."

Angelo nodded. Rosa linked her arm through Luisa's and the three walked away.

Marcello kept watch at the mine. Coal cars loaded with rock rumbled to the earth's surface fifteen times before he quit counting. Dirty, exhausted workers climbed out of the mantrip and walked on unsteady legs to the first aid tent for food and drink. A fresh rescue team immediately rode back into the mine, followed by cars hastily filled with timber to reinforce the collapsed tunnel. Marcello helped injured miners at the first aid tent, always on the lookout for Roberto. A steady stream of families brought sandwiches and coffee for the rescue workers and blankets for the injured.

"Marcello! Thank God you're all right." Lucas jumped off his buckboard and ran toward him. "Just got word. Our brothers?"

"They weren't in the mine, but—"

"Who?"

"Roberto."

"*Caro Dio.* How long's he been down there?"

"Happened a little after eleven."

Lucas's eyes widened. "After the first hour, they'll run out of air."

"I know." Marcello clenched his fists. "But Luisa doesn't."

The rescue dragged on, like drips of water from a leaky bucket. A load of rock, a word from the supervisors. Over and over, the same events dripped out of the bucket. A load of rock, no news, more rock. Drip, drip, drip. Marcello wanted to scream. He wanted the mine to gush forth with lifesaving water, all the men washed out in a mighty river of salvation. Then he could run back to Luisa and tell her, "They found Roberto. He's alive! All the men are saved!"

He rolled his head side to side to relieve the tension in his neck and gazed at the sky. The sun that gleamed so brightly at dawn now struggled to hang in the western sky, as though the heavens themselves were weary. Shadowed by guilt, Marcello returned home, exhausted and frustrated. He had walked out of the mine unharmed while Roberto remained imprisoned underground.

Angelo and Rosa insisted Marcello's family eat supper with

them that evening. Meals with Angelo's family were usually full of chatter and laughter, but not this night. Even the children sensed their parents' anxiety and ate silently, their faces serious.

"They brought an extra team of diggers from Spring Hill. Doc Chapman is there with the first aid crew," said Marcello. "They've made progress, but I don't think we'll hear anything more until early tomorrow."

"Tomorrow? The longer they take . . ." Luisa caught her breath and covered her mouth with her hand.

"Maybe it will be sooner," Angelo said. "Sometimes they get an unexpected breakthrough. Maybe the cave-in only separated Roberto's crew from the mouth of the tunnel."

Luisa wanted desperately to believe him, but Angelo's eyes shifted away after he spoke.

Rosa reached for a platter of butter biscuits and passed it across the table to Luisa. "Eat, Luisa. I made these just for you."

Luisa took a biscuit and brought it to her mouth, but the thought of eating threatened to choke her. "I can't. I'm not hungry." She set the bread on her plate.

Marcello remained positive. "They'll send someone the minute they have any news, no matter what time."

Luisa turned to him. "How long's it been?"

Marcello checked his pocket watch. "Almost eight hours." A frightful reality settled over the table and no one spoke.

"It's the waiting." Luisa's voice trembled. "The waiting . . ." She buried her face in her hands.

Marcello reached out and put his arm around her shoulders. "I'll go back after supper."

Luisa looked up and quickly wiped away the tears. "I want to come with you. It's better than sitting here." Luisa turned to Rosa. "Could Tony and Sophia stay here until we come back?"

"Leave them here tonight—they'll be fine. Go to the mine."

Tony brightened. "Can we stay, Mama? Please?" He looked hopefully at cousins Stefano and Ginny and then at his mother.

With a sense of relief, Luisa silently mouthed "Thank you" to Rosa and turned to Tony. "You and Sophia can stay. Be good for Aunt Rosa."

Luisa and Marcello kept vigil with the other families gathered at the mine. More loads of rock came to the surface, but no more men were found. The sky darkened, and Luisa reluctantly agreed to go home. Too exhausted to undress, Luisa fell into bed. She reached over and laid her hand on the cot where Roberto would recover from his injuries. She'd put her treasured wedding quilt on it, a gift from Mama. Marcello changed out of his pit clothes and collapsed beside her. They stared at the ceiling in the heavy silence of the night.

Marcello fell into a tortured sleep of dark tunnels and falling rock. He took gasping breaths in a choking cloud of coal dust when banging on the front door yanked him from the nightmare. Even in the fog of waking, he remembered something was wrong.

Roberto.

In one motion, he swung his feet to the floor, rushed to the kitchen, and unlatched the door. It was Isaac.

"What's happened?" Luisa rushed to the door and stood beside Marcello.

"They found Roberto." Isaac's voice was heavy. He looked at Luisa. "I'm so sorry."

Luisa sagged against Marcello. "No! No!" she screamed, sending her anguish into the dark night.

The Union Pacific Coal Company sent a train to Cumberland to take the bodies of the seventeen dead miners and their families to the cemetery in Kemmerer. Work at the mine halted for a day of mourning. Over one hundred miners, along with Marcello's family, rode the train with Luisa, Marcello, and the other bereaved families.

Luisa gazed absently out the window at the passing countryside. Forty-eight loads of rock before they found him. Forty-eight . . . forty-eight . . . forty-eight. The train clicked over the tracks in rhythm to the number that pounded in her head. The cave-in had happened so fast, Roberto had no chance to save himself. Just like his new life in America, it was over before it started.

After the train pulled into the Kemmerer station, Luisa stepped onto the platform, a black shawl draped around her shoulders. The air was heavy with the scent of rain. She stared at a row of horse-drawn wagons waiting beside the tracks and watched the seventeen caskets lifted onto the wagons. One by one the horses pulled away from the station.

The local band led the procession of mourners from the station, playing a somber tune that washed over the town. Luisa clasped hands with Marcello and followed the wagons that creaked over the uneven path from the edge of town up a steep hill to the cemetery. The procession came to a halt among the scrub pine trees scattered at the top, the horses and wagons silhouetted against the bright sky as they waited to relinquish the brave souls to the earth.

The wind blew off the prairie and whipped Luisa's skirts as she stood dry-eyed at the graveside, her last drop of emotion wrung out. She placed her hand on the rough pine box.

It was all wrong. Roberto was young and strong, his whole life ahead of him. He should find a wife and live out his days with a family at his side. She'd promised Mama to look after him, to keep him safe, but she was helpless to protect him from something as fearsome as the mine.

Luisa raised her head. The scene horrified her. So many sobbing women, so many caskets. How could her brother be in one? She heard a child wail, "Daddy!" How many daddies were dead? How many husbands and brothers? How long before Union Pacific forced that crying child and his family to leave their rented home and face life with no means of support?

The weight of grief robbed her breath. Luisa leaned over Roberto's coffin and sobbed, "*Mi perdoni, mi perdoni.* I'm so sorry, dear brother." The box was lowered into the ground. She tossed in a handful of dirt and bent her head as fresh tears spilled on the rough planks of the coffin.

Chapter 24

Black ribbons hung on the front doors of the deceased. A stream of neighbors brought baskets of food to Luisa's family and offered their condolences in the days after the tragedy.

Ethnic differences eased with heartfelt sympathy and offers of assistance. Touched by the kindness of close friends and people she barely knew, Luisa accepted their condolences, concealing her grief until she was alone to weep in private. She moved through the days' chores in a fog, and drifted off to bed early in the evenings, long before Marcello joined her. Her emotions swung between sorrow and anger. Roberto had been killed before realizing any of his dreams—a wife, a family, a life in America.

She blamed God. Hadn't she prayed for Marcello and Roberto's safety every morning when they left for the mine? Wasn't she faithful enough for God to hear her prayers? She found no answers, not in the candles she lit for Roberto, nor in her pleadings with God. For reasons she couldn't fathom, God had turned away from her, and that made her heart ache even more.

Luisa shuddered with a new fear: she couldn't shake the plain fact that Marcello risked the same fate as Roberto. She was as powerless to protect her husband as she'd been to protect Roberto. She could not bear the thought of facing life without Marcello.

The summer days melted into autumn. Luisa forced herself to

put all her energy into the family. As Tony's English grew while he played with the neighborhood children, Luisa picked up his new words and made them her own. Sophia was a busy toddler, curious about everything, quick to mimic those around her. When Sophia joined the family, she came with just the clothes on her back. Rosa had generously given her Ginny's outgrown clothes, but by midsummer the dresses were too short, the shirts too tight. Luisa knew it was time to add to Sophia's wardrobe.

"Marcello, I'm going to the store. Need anything?"

Tony magically appeared at Luisa's side. "Mama, can I have a candy?" he asked.

"Candy?" Sophia chimed in.

"I wasn't asking *you two.*" Luisa leaned over the children, both hands on her hips. "Have you been good enough for a special treat?"

Tony nodded so earnestly, Luisa burst into laughter.

Marcello kissed Luisa's forehead. "It's good to hear you laugh."

Luisa tied a white kerchief around her hair, patted the coin purse in her skirt pocket, and stepped outside. The flowers by the porch withered under the early morning sun, and she made a mental note to water them when she came home. Shading her eyes, she glanced heavenward. The sun was always there, firing up the morning sky at first light, beaming brilliant and golden as it paraded across the heavens, sliding reluctantly into sunset each evening, shimmering red-orange. She still wasn't accustomed to its enormous presence with no trees or towering mountains to tame it. A layer of dust on the walkway muted her footsteps. She cooled herself by pushing up the sleeves of her blouse.

She turned the corner to Main Street and saw brisk activity at the company store, typical for a Saturday. Luisa passed a man hefting a sack of lime into his wagon parked out front before she pushed open the double doors. A host of languages spun together in a hum that reverberated through the store. She stepped around a barrel of brooms and shovels and angled down the aisle between shoppers to the dry goods on the back wall. She ran her hand over the bolts of cotton, picturing a smock for Sophia, and reached for a blue fabric with tiny yellow flowers, the same color as Sophia's curls.

"*Buongiorno,* Luisa."

She whirled around. "Carlo."

"What a coincidence. I was going to call on you and Marcello today after I finished buying supplies. How are you?"

Luisa hesitated momentarily. With the death of Roberto still stinging, she couldn't utter the expected "I'm fine" without effort. She summoned a smile and said, "I'm doing well. How are you?"

His expression became serious. "Please accept my condolences for Roberto. I'm so sorry. You and Roberto were very close. This must be hard for you."

Luisa saw such sadness in Carlo's eyes that her own eyes misted with tears. "Thank you, Carlo. You're very kind."

"I thought the funeral was a wonderful tribute. There were so many people there, I barely got a chance to speak to you."

"It seemed everyone in Cumberland came. I was glad for that."

"Since the funeral, I've thought back to our years growing up." The corners of his mouth turned up in a wistful smile. "We were always in trouble when we were boys. Remember when we hid the neighbor's goat in your shed?"

Luisa smiled at the memory. "Mama was furious with you two. She always said, 'When those two are together, there's trouble.' "

"We had such big dreams when we came here." He shook his head, unable to continue.

Luisa couldn't speak for the lump in her throat; she simply nodded as she blinked back tears.

"I'm sorry. I didn't mean to upset you." Carlo touched her arm for a moment before withdrawing his hand.

Luisa took a deep breath and cleared her throat. "You must come for dinner sometime, Carlo. You and your uncle."

"I'd like that, but my uncle's in poor health. Consumption. That's why I haven't called on you sooner."

"I'm sorry to hear that. I hope he recovers."

"But I do have some good news." He brightened. "I'm engaged to a fine woman from Kemmerer. She works at the J. C. Penney Store."

"That's wonderful. You deserve to be happy." Luisa swallowed the emotion welling up inside her. "Be happy. That's something you could do to honor Roberto. Enjoy every moment of your life. Take nothing for granted."

"I will." He moved back a step. "I should be going. Give my best to Marcello." He held her gaze for a moment. "It was good to see you again, Luisa." He nodded his head awkwardly, turned, and walked away.

Luisa stared after Carlo. She saw an image of Roberto walking beside him as the inseparable youngsters they had been back home on the mountain. The happy image blurred with her tears. Even though she was on the mend, Luisa longed for the day when the ache in her heart would be healed.

Early one Sunday morning after Mass when the autumn sky was buttery yellow, Angelo and Lucas brought their wives and children to Marcello's for a family outing. They hiked a short distance past the edge of town, to a sandy ridge where an underground spring fed a tiny creek that sparkled along a grassy bank. Luisa, Rosa, and Julia spread blankets under a lone willow tree beside the creek and unpacked picnic baskets. Marcello and his brothers set off with their shotguns to hunt sage hens, and the children scattered in search of treasures to unearth.

"Don't go any farther than the ridge of the hill," Luisa called after the children. She and Sophia sat on the blanket with Julia, baby Marco, and Rosa. Puffs of cottony clouds floated overhead, creating shadows on the sandy landscape as they scooted across the sky. A pair of red-tailed hawks circled and swooped high overhead.

"I'm glad we have the day together," said Julia, cradling Marco in her lap. "It gives us a chance to talk. How are you . . . since the accident?"

Luisa looked away for a moment. "I keep busy with the children and the chores, but it's so hard . . ."

"We feel bad for you, Luisa," Julia said. "Everyone in town feels the loss."

"One minute I'm fine, then suddenly I'm terribly sad or angry." Luisa frowned in puzzlement. "I know it was an accident, but it would help if I could make some sense out of it."

"Sometimes," Rosa said, "we can't find reasons for the awful things that happen because there aren't any—they just happen. Our babies get sick, sometimes they die. Our husbands and brothers are killed in the mine. Don't trouble yourself trying to find meaning in the accident."

"And don't think for a minute God punishes us with these terrible things." Julia's dark eyes flashed. "God weeps with us in our sorrow." She leaned over and gently squeezed Luisa's hand.

Luisa pulled Sophia into her lap and stroked her curls. "You'll think I'm crazy," she said hesitantly, "but I've thought about asking Marcello if we could go back home. To Italy." She lifted her gaze to the lonesome willow overhead, doing its best to provide shade, and thought of the pear and plum trees back home. Had they blossomed already? When she was a child, she thought heaven couldn't be any prettier than their hillside when the trees were full of blossoms.

Rosa and Julia sat in stunned silence. Far away a thrush trilled. Finally, Rosa spoke. "You're not crazy," she said quietly. "I remember dreaming about going back to Italy when I was so homesick my first year here. And you're grieving for your brother—"

"It's not just that," Luisa interrupted. "I'm convinced the same thing will happen to Marcello, and the only way to avoid that is to go back home." The wind rustled the leaves on the lone tree. Luisa tucked a loose strand of hair behind her ear.

"In time you'll feel better, Luisa," said Julia. "Then you'll be able to make a good decision about the future. Give yourself more time."

The shouts of the children drew their attention to their husbands, who crested the brow of the hill. "Look what Papa's got!" cried Tony, running toward Marcello, who held up a string of hens. The children followed their fathers to a bare spot on the bank near the blanket.

Marcello laid the hens on the ground.

"Time to build a fire," said Lucas. "Each of you bring an armful of brush," he directed the children. The fathers piled branches and brush inside a circle of rocks, lit the fire, and placed a wire grate on top.

"Are you going to help Mama pluck the hens?" Marcello teased Tony.

"Ick." Tony turned up his nose. "I want to go hunting."

"You can hunt when you're bigger, maybe next year." He tousled Tony's hair.

The men readied themselves for another round of hunting. "Be back in an hour or so," said Angelo. They headed to the rocky ridge and disappeared. The children scattered in the opposite direction, this time in search of coyotes and prairie dogs.

The women rolled up their sleeves and set a kettle with spring water over the grate. When the water boiled, they scalded the hens and plucked the feathers. A second pot of water was set to boiling while the hens were washed in the spring, then placed in the pot with a generous portion of wine, salt, and pepper and covered.

The enticing aroma of sage and wine drifted from the kettle as the hens simmered. By the time Marcello and his brothers returned with another string of hens, the meal was ready to eat. The children filled cups with cold water from the spring. The family loaded their plates with fresh bread, cheese, and tender meat swimming in broth. Except for the smacking of lips and an occasional *delizioso,* they ate in contented silence.

After the meal, the parents reclined on the blankets and watched their children dig for arrowheads and skip rocks in the creek. A pale crescent moon appeared high in the afternoon sky, opaque against blue. Luisa and Marcello leaned against the tree.

"A nice day," said Marcello.

"Very nice." Luisa nodded. "I needed a day like this." She reached for Marcello's hand and, in the soft breeze of the afternoon, felt more peace than at any other time since Roberto's death a month ago.

The hours slipped away, and the moon brightened. The distant howl of a lone coyote floated across the prairie on the night air. The families gathered up their trophies—two strings of sage hens, stashes of rocks, three arrowheads, and a bouquet of wilted wildflowers—and followed the brilliant light of the moon home.

Chapter 25

December

Marcello stood at the head of the dining table in the kitchen, his immaculate white shirt starched and pressed, his curly hair combed in place. The room was ablaze with lamps and candles that cast bright light on the faces of the people gathered for Christmas dinner. Steaming platters of roast beef and gravy, potatoes, carrots, and fresh-baked bread with apple butter sat on the table. Mince pie, molasses baked apples, and roasted chestnuts warmed on the shelf over the stove. The overflow of children sat cross-legged on the scrubbed plank floor.

"This is the way *Natale* should be celebrated, with *famiglia.*" He gazed around the table at his brothers and their wives and stopped when he came to Luisa. "It's been a year of happiness and sadness for us." They exchanged a knowing look, and Luisa nodded. "We were blessed when we found Sophia. Now we have two wonderful children, and Tony has a little sister." He smiled at the children before continuing. "Our sadness came with the loss of Roberto. We miss him every day. Luisa and I depended on you when we came to Cumberland and again when Roberto died. We'll never forget that. Thank you." He raised his glass. "To good health and good fortune in the coming year."

Lucas cleared his throat. "Our families have earned a good living this year. That's not true for everyone. Let's be thankful for our work and our success."

"May Cumberland never run out of coal," said Angelo, a broad smile beneath his thick mustache.

"And our cows never run out of milk," Mick added with a grin.

Marcello spoke. "To Mama and Papa." His voice wavered as he spoke their names. "We love you and miss you, especially today. *Buon Natale.*" The Corsi family raised their glasses to salute the holy day. They passed platters of food around the table and filled their plates. The room echoed with conversation and laughter while the family savored the meal and the time of leisure together.

It was late afternoon when Luisa circled the table offering second helpings of mince pie. Mick held up his hands in protest. "I can't eat another bite. Besides, we should leave while it's daylight."

Theresa nodded. "The cows need milking, even on Christmas." She helped Julia and Rosa clear the last of the dishes.

"We should be going, too," said Lucas, "before the wind kicks up." He extended his hand to Marcello. "It's been a wonderful day. Thank you."

Three loud raps sounded on the door, and Jim burst into the room with Dominic and their friend Sal. "*Buon Natale,* or should I say Merry Christmas?"

"Look who's finally here," said Marcello, ushering the trio in from the cold. "We ate hours ago."

"Lost track of time. Been celebrating with the Magnettis. Then we went to Fiori's house." Jim handed Marcello a jug. "Merry Christmas, brother."

"Homemade?" asked Marcello.

"What other kind is there?" Jim clapped him on the back and grinned.

"You boys hungry?" asked Luisa. "There's plenty of food."

The company departed while it was still daylight, but the

bachelors celebrated late into the evening. They opened more wine and took turns offering toasts; the later the hour, the more bizarre the tributes.

"To Luisa's mince pie." Sal belched as he raised his glass and slopped wine onto the table.

Dominic's eyes were glazed with drunkenness. "To good cards at the poker table." He clinked glasses with Sal.

"Know what's wrong with Cumberland?" Jim asked with a serious expression. "Too many bachelors and not enough women."

"We need more women," Sal said.

"To more women," Jim shouted and raised his glass with Sal.

Marcello struggled to keep his eyes open. He pulled his watch from his shirt pocket. "It's time you boys went home."

Dominic, who appeared to be dozing, struggled to lift his head off his chest. His eyes wandered and failed to focus on Marcello. "What?"

"It's almost midnight." Marcello hoped his sharp tone would cut through the wine-induced fog.

"But we jus' got here," Sal slurred.

"Tomorrow's a work day," Marcello continued.

Jim sat upright in his chair. "Work! Oh, God. I forgot."

Marcello eyed Jim critically. "Can you make it to the boardinghouse?"

"I'm fine, but those two—" Jim nodded toward Dominic and Sal. "I don't think so."

Sal attempted to stand up, weaved back and forth, and collapsed back into his chair.

Marcello sighed. "I'll help you." He and Jim put on their coats, helped Dominic and Sal with theirs and pulled the two friends to their feet. Marcello supported Dominic out the front door, followed by Jim with Sal leaning heavily against him.

The foursome shambled down the cold, dark street to the

boardinghouse two blocks away. Dominic stumbled and leaned into Marcello just inches from his face and whispered, "You're the bes' friend I've ever had, Marcello. You really, really are."

Marcello's eyes watered at the stench of wine on Dominic's breath. "Keep moving your feet, Dominic. We have another block to go." Marcello turned to Jim, who was laboring with Sal's slumping body. "How you doing?"

"Terrible. He keeps falling asleep." Jim hollered in Sal's ear, "Hey, wake up, *uomo*!"

The boardinghouse was in sight. Marcello trudged Dominic to the door, pushed it open with his foot and shoved Dominic inside. Jim guided Sal, who stumbled through the doorway and immediately fell on top of Dominic who was sprawled on the floor in front of him.

Jim looked sheepishly at Marcello. "*Mi dispiace*. I'm sorry . . ."

Marcello held up his hand. "It's all right, it's *Natale*. You better get some sleep. Morning will be here before you know it."

Sunshine pierced Marcello's eyelids. He rolled out of bed and fumbled for his pocket watch on the dresser. He'd overslept. He dressed quickly in the cold bedroom and hurried to the kitchen, wiping the sleep from his eyes. There wasn't time for breakfast, so he put cheese and bread in his lunch pail and shrugged on his coat.

He stepped outside and squinted against the brilliant sun, his head pounding. The street was empty. A wave of panic sent him toward the mine in quick strides. Where was everyone? Was he the last one to work? He gulped the bracing air and lengthened his stride. When he reached the mine, he stopped short. The site was deserted except for a few crew bosses loitering at the mine entrance. He spotted his crew chief.

"Hey, Isaac. Where is everyone?"

"Don't know. They sure aren't *here*." Isaac leaned against an empty coal car. "You're only the second digger to show up."

"What?"

"Might not have enough workers to operate the mine today."

Marcello blinked against the sunshine and tried to make sense of what Isaac said. Last year on the day after Christmas, a dozen diggers didn't come to work, barely noticeable compared to the huge absence today. It appeared the whole town had a hangover this year.

A half hour later the bosses decided it was pointless to operate the mine. Marcello picked up his lunch pail and walked home through the sleepy streets of Cumberland. He didn't know if it was his imagination, but his head didn't throb, and the sun didn't glare in his eyes. He began to whistle.

Marcello's good mood disappeared later that afternoon when Angelo stopped by the house. "When I got to work, Isaac was locking up the office. Said the mine was closed, so we went home."

"Anyone with you?" asked Marcello.

"Sven and Kubicek. After we got home, we started to hear rumors."

"Like what?" Marcello frowned.

"That something big would happen because of the poor showing at the mine this morning."

"Who said that?"

"Neighbors. Some of them claim they heard it from our union reps."

"Let's hope they're wrong."

"We've lost a day of wages," Angelo said.

"Not good." Marcello's frown deepened.

When Marcello arrived at the mine the next morning, rumors whipped through the rank and file like a blast of winter wind. The most persistent rumor was that the diggers who had failed to show up for work would be laid off. "You watch," they said. "Management's going to teach us a lesson."

Marcello and Jim stood a few feet apart in a new tunnel, using augers to drill holes in the wall for shot-firers. At the end of the day, the shot-firers would fill the holes with black powder and set off a fuse. Tomorrow, he and Jim would clear the tunnel and dig into the newly exposed coal.

"Do you think they'll lay off the diggers?" Marcello asked.

"There are too many of us," Jim answered. A heavy spray of dust fell from the ceiling and forced the two men to cover their eyes.

Marcello wiped his face with his bandana. He turned to Jim, the beam from his lamp illuminating his brother's face. "I overheard a couple of old-timers at lunch. They said the union bosses would call for a strike if *anyone* was laid off. If they lay off fifty or sixty diggers, the mine will come to a standstill."

"Unless they bring in diggers from Spring Hill or some other mine around here. Angelo told me there's a union meeting tomorrow night at the hall."

"All this talk of layoffs and strike is no good." Marcello leaned into his auger as it met resistance in the wall.

"You and Angelo are caught in the middle of this, aren't you?" said Jim.

Marcello stopped working. "What do you mean?"

"Both of you came to work yesterday. Anyone who showed up won't get laid off. Be ready for the diggers to give you a hard time if you don't support them in a strike—if it comes to that."

The diggers in Cumberland would demand solidarity, just as the strikers had back in Kansas. Marcello's gut churned, remembering the strikebreakers wielding bats against the miners. He pulled his drill from the wall and moved farther into the tunnel. "The last thing any of us can afford is a strike."

"I'm with you. All I want is a steady job." Jim turned toward

Marcello. "It was stupid of me to miss work because I was hungover. That's going to end."

"Really?"

"Really. I can't risk losing my job."

Marcello smiled to himself and wondered how long Jim's new attitude would last. His smile quickly faded at the thought of the growing dispute between management and union. He prayed this wouldn't be a repeat of the strike in Kansas. He leaned into the auger, his mouth set in a grim line.

Chapter 26

Marcello couldn't sleep. He stared at the ceiling and replayed the conversations from work until his pulse raced. He punched his pillow and rolled onto his side but couldn't stop worrying.

What if there was a layoff? The miners would strike in retaliation. Then what? Would Union Pacific negotiate, or would they fire all the strikers? Marcello suddenly had a chilling thought: Union Pacific owned the houses, the general store, the school—everything in Cumberland. If he lost his job, he and his family would be out in the cold. Literally. Everything he had gained was threatened. Everything he had promised Luisa hung in the balance, and once again the wolf would lurk at their door.

First thing the next morning, Marcello found Isaac at the mine office and pulled him aside. "What have you heard about a layoff?"

"Nothing official. Our men meet with management this afternoon. The union meeting for tonight is postponed—for now," Isaac said.

"That's a good thing, isn't it? That they're talking?" asked Marcello.

"Better than not talking."

"What do you think will happen?"

"It's anybody's guess. These rumors are a problem." Isaac looked Marcello in the eye. "One rumor leads to another, people get riled up, and that's when bad things happen."

Marcello ran his fingers through his hair. "I'm really worried.

I have a family to support and I can't . . ." He glanced around and noticed two miners standing nearby who quickly looked away when Marcello made eye contact.

"Maybe we'll know something by the end of the day," Isaac said.

Marcello checked with Isaac before he left work, but the representatives were still meeting with mine officials. That night he vented his frustration to Luisa as they prepared for bed. "I don't know any more today than I did yesterday." Marcello placed the lamp on the bedroom dresser.

Luisa sat on the bed and unbraided her hair. "You'll hear something tomorrow. Be patient."

"This waiting is making me crazy. I want to know where we stand." Marcello put his grimy overalls into the wicker basket beside the door.

Luisa pulled on her nightgown and tied the ribbon at the neck. "I know this is hard for you, but try not to worry, dear."

Marcello extinguished the lamp, and they climbed into bed. "I have good reason to worry. Remember that strike I told you about in Colorado? The company forced the miners and their families out of their houses." Marcello remembered every grim detail of the Ludlow massacre. A tent city crowded with striking miners' families living with meager rations in unbelievable filth had sprung up around the mine. The culmination was a deadly fire at the hands of the Colorado National Guard that burned the tent city to the ground. Twenty-six men, women, and children perished. Marcello shuddered. "God forbid that would happen here."

"That was over five years ago and has nothing to do with Union Pacific or Cumberland. How many times have you said Union Pacific is a good company, and they do right by their workers?"

"I know, but—"

"And," Luisa interrupted, "don't most of the men feel the way you do?"

"Yes, but there's a few troublemakers. I worry they'll bully others into a strike." Marcello paused. "Instead of striking, they should be glad this is a decent place to work. Nothing like that mine in Kansas."

Luisa held his hand and gently rubbed his callused palm. "The only thing you can control is what *you* do. Work hard the way you always do, and hope there's no layoff or strike."

Marcello rolled onto his side and faced her in the darkness. "I shouldn't worry you with troubles at the mine." He brought her hand to his lips and kissed it.

"I pray this will turn out all right."

"I wish I was as certain as you are."

"Get some sleep, *caro. Buono note.*"

Marcello rose early the next morning. It was dark outside the frosty kitchen window when he reached for his coat.

"Work doesn't start for another hour. Sure you've had enough to eat?" Luisa wrapped a bacon sandwich and placed it in his lunch pail.

"I want to talk with Isaac and not have people eavesdrop on our conversation." As he pulled on his coat, he caught sight of a piece of paper stuck under the front door. He picked it up and read a scrawled message.

All the miners stick together—or else.

"What the . . . ?" Marcello frowned.

"Something wrong?" Luisa set out bowls for the children's breakfast.

He quickly stuffed the note in his pocket. "Just found a note I had forgotten about." He pulled on his cap and gloves and picked up his lunch pail. "See you tonight."

"Maybe you'll have good news today." She crossed the room

and kissed his cheek.

"Hope so." He knew otherwise but forced a smile for Luisa and left.

Word circulated through the mine, and the union called a meeting at the end of the shift at the Catholic church. Dirty and disheveled, the miners filed in, filled the chairs and lined the walls. Jack Phillips, the union representative, stood in front of the group, sleeves rolled up, hands on his hips.

"There've been lots of rumors the past couple of days," Phillips began, "and I want to set the record straight. Negotiations didn't start well. They were ready to lay off every digger who failed to come to work, said they'd bring in replacements to keep the mine open. We said if they did that, we'd call for a general strike."

Phillips coughed to clear his throat. "We know they can't find replacements if they fire all of us. We made a proposal of our own: deduct a day's wages and no layoffs. Management countered with an offer to deduct three days' wages for no layoffs. We countered with two days, but they refused. Said being irresponsible has to stop. That's their final offer."

The miners muttered and shifted in their chairs. Phillips held up his hands to quiet them. "Do you want to accept their offer?"

A lanky young miner with dirty blond hair that hung to his shoulders jumped to his feet. "I think we should refuse their offer and go on strike, show management we mean business. They're pushing us around." He looked around the hall and acknowledged the men who nodded in agreement.

"Your name is?" asked Phillips.

"Logan, Greg Logan." He nodded to Phillips and sat.

Ian McGregor, who lived down the street from Marcello, rose and folded his thick arms across his muscular chest. "Let's don't be too quick to strike. Christmas celebrating is out of control. We didn't come to work, because we were hungover. That's irresponsible. The boss man's offer is fair. Better to give up three days' pay than lose my job."

"That's the coward's way out," a voice shouted from the crowd. "We have to stand up for ourselves."

Ian's face turned red. " 'Tis a fool who doesn't think this is a good offer, not a coward," he fired back.

Marcello listened to the miners argue. He shoved his hands into his pockets and his fingers curled around the note left under his front door. He held it, his anger slowly boiling until he couldn't contain it.

He shot up from his chair. "Mr. Phillips, I want to say something." Heads turned in his direction, and the room quieted again. Marcello felt his color rising. "I have a family to support. I can't let them down. I need my job. I'm also part of *this* family"—he looked around the room at the weary faces blackened with coal—"and I don't want to let you down, either. I've always supported the union, but I want to make this clear—when it comes to voting for a strike, *I'll* decide how to vote. I'll be damned if anyone threatens me."

He pulled the note from his pocket and held it in the air. "This was left under my door last night. It says, 'All miners stick together—or else.' " He paused and let the words sink in. "Whoever wrote this, say it to my face like a man. Don't go sneaking around like a coward."

Marcello scanned the faces in the room and saw solidarity until his eyes rested on a man beside Greg Logan. The man's dark hair was shot with gray, and his expression was a penetrating sneer. Marcello had never spoken to the man but had seen that look directed to certain miners before, himself included.

Marcello balled up the note and threw it on the floor. "That's what I think of your threat."

The hall was silent.

Angelo jumped up. "I got one of those, too. Who else got one?"

Hands rose in the air, several miners stood up. A commotion broke out at the back of the hall between two men who argued until one threw a punch.

"Break it up!" Phillips shouted. "Anyone who fights, I'll have you thrown out." Two crew bosses pushed through the crowd to the disturbance, grabbed a man, and hustled him outside.

The hall quieted, and further discussion continued without incident. The members voted by a wide margin to accept three days' dock in pay in exchange for no layoffs. When they filed out of the meeting, Marcello could tell from the hard stares he received that the matter was far from settled.

Marcello nodded toward Greg Logan. "You know him?" he whispered to Angelo.

"No, but he looks like trouble."

"How about the guy with him?"

"Name's Barrett Jones. Been here since the early days."

"Looks like he's trouble, too," Marcello said.

Angelo nodded. "Acts like he's the boss."

The brothers turned up their coat collars and walked home through the dark streets. When they reached the end of the block, they stopped before parting ways to their houses. "At least the vote turned out right," Angelo said. "Things should calm down now."

"Most of the men agree with us," Marcello said. "Numbers are on our side."

"That's good."

"Good enough to keep the peace?" Marcello asked.

CHAPTER 27

July

An early morning cannon blast from the hillside overlooking Cumberland announced the arrival of Independence Day. Luisa came into the kitchen with Sophia on her hip. Dressed for the heat, Luisa wore a floral print summer dress and wide-brimmed straw hat, Sophia a yellow pinafore and calico print bonnet.

"Well, don't my boys look nice," she said, noting Tony's best shirt tucked into his pants and Marcello's Sunday shoes, cleaned and polished. "Tony, come here." She licked her fingers and pressed his curly cowlick until it lay flat. "That's better. Now we're ready."

"The Gilbert's ram was loose again," said Marcello. "I'll look outside."

Luisa sighed in exasperation. "Why can't they keep him in his pen? He roams the streets, the boys tease him, and now he's meaner than ever." Luisa clucked her tongue at the cause of the trouble: an ornery old ram whose huge horns had earned him the name Il Diavolo. "Last week he butted Mr. Pappas in the rear."

"Butted?" Tony snickered before he burst into laughter.

Marcello leaned outside and scanned the street. "Don't see him."

They joined the stream of neighbors in their Sunday best walking to the town hall. The flag in front of the company store snapped in the summer breeze under a cloudless blue sky.

Tony skipped beside Luisa. "Papa said today's America's birthday."

"And because it's a holiday, Papa doesn't have to work," Luisa said.

"Is there a holiday tomorrow?" Tony asked.

Marcello chuckled. "Only today."

When they reached the hall, Marcello led his family through the packed room to empty seats near the front. Patriotic bunting draped the wall behind a raised platform with American flags at each side.

Mr. Hopkins, the mine foreman, strode to the podium. "Welcome to the Union Pacific Independence Day celebration. The day's activities include footraces and games with prizes for the winners, a baseball game with Spring Hill miners, and will conclude with a dance tonight at the hall, followed by fireworks." Murmurs of excitement rippled through the crowd. "Also, the Catholic church is sponsoring an ice cream social and cake-baking contest from noon till five."

Tony tugged on Marcello's sleeve. "Can we go?"

Marcello put his finger to his lips and nodded to the podium.

Mr. Hopkins cleared his throat. "I'd like to make a special announcement. Cumberland has hired a music director to organize our very first band. Please welcome our new director, Mr. Ernesto Lavero."

The crowd clapped enthusiastically as a portly man in a three-piece suit stepped to the podium. "Thank you, ladies, and gentlemen." He smiled and held up both hands to quiet the audience. "I'm excited to start the Cumberland Concert Band and look forward to making music with you. I'd like to honor Independence Day with a patriotic song. Please stand and join me in singing 'America.' Union Pacific has generously donated flags for our celebration today. If the boys in the back would pass them out now . . ."

Chair legs scraped the floor as the crowd stood and passed flags down the rows.

Tony's eyes widened when he took his flag from Marcello. "I can keep it?"

"It's yours."

Tony ran his fingers over the tiny cloth flag attached to a wooden dowel and beamed at his papa.

In a booming baritone, Mr. Lavero began to sing. *"My country 'tis of thee . . ."*

Everyone joined in, blending in various dialects and off-key melodies. Tony and Sophia raised their flags and waved them in sweeping circles.

"Sweet land of liberty, of thee I sing . . ."

The room fluttered with flags. Tony climbed onto his chair and lifted his flag toward the ceiling. Marcello scooped Sophia into his arms so she could do the same.

"From every mountainside, let freedom ring." Mr. Lavero held the last note in a crescendo, his face red and arms wide in an embrace of the hall. The audience burst into applause and ear-piercing whistles.

The program concluded after remarks from Mr. Lavero, and the crowd worked its way toward the exit. Holding Tony's hand, Marcello stepped into the packed aisle and jostled the man beside him. He turned, ready to apologize, and froze.

It was Barrett Jones, the miner Marcello suspected of writing the threatening note months ago. A head taller than Marcello, Jones had steel gray eyes that glinted hard as rocks. They eyed each other in silence. The hair on the back of Marcello's neck bristled.

Marcello planted his feet. "Do you have something to say to me?"

Jones narrowed his eyes but said nothing.

Marcello waited. After months of threatening looks from

Jones, Marcello's patience had ended. "I'm tired of your sneers. I'm tired of the rumors. Say it to my face."

Jones pulled himself to full height. "You don't know how it works around here. Me and my boys decide how things are done, not you or some other greenhorns."

"The union decides how things are done—after we vote."

"Ha!" The laugh was caustic. "Shows how little you know."

Marcello stepped closer. "Stop making trouble."

Jones eyed Marcello, then glanced at Luisa and the children. "This your family?"

Marcello tensed. "Why?"

"Nice looking wife, children." A smirk crossed his lips.

"Leave my family out of this."

"Or what?" He leaned forward.

Marcello didn't flinch. "You don't want to find out. I have a *very* big family."

Jones balled his fists. Marcello readied himself to dodge a punch. When Jones didn't move, Marcello tightened his grasp on Tony's hand and led Luisa and Sophia out the door.

Once outside, Luisa grabbed Marcello, a look of alarm on her face. "Who was that?"

"One of the troublemakers I told you about." Marcello glanced over his shoulder, but the man had disappeared. Marcello ran his fingers through his hair and manufactured a smile for Luisa. "He's harmless, just talks big." In truth, Marcello knew nothing of the kind. He thought the man capable of anything, but would never admit that to Luisa. Wanting to put the incident out of mind, he crouched beside Tony and Sophia and changed the subject. "Do you like your new flags?"

"I love mine," Tony said and waved his flag wildly as proof.

"Take good care of it. Remember, it's not a toy, it's our flag."

Luisa watched miners' families drift toward the tent beside

the Catholic church at the end of the block. "Anyone hungry?" she asked.

"Me," shouted Tony and Sophia in unison.

Marcello hoisted Tony onto his shoulders. "Let's go." Luisa picked up Sophia, and they hiked up the street.

Inside the church tent, Marcello's family sat at a long table crowded with parents and children and ate bowls of freshly churned ice cream. Marcello saw Barrett Jones enter the tent, then turn around and leave. Marcello fought the urge to follow him, but decided it was wiser to stay close to his family. Later, the Corsis joined a backyard celebration, and Marcello was so distracted watching for Jones, he jumped at the mere tap on his shoulder from his neighbor Oleg. When Marcello walked his family to the baseball game, he sensed someone following, only to whirl around and see no one.

At twilight, the families of Cumberland piled out of their houses onto porches and blankets, every face turned toward Oyster Ridge. While Marcello's family waited to watch the fireworks from their front porch, he searched the faces in the fading light. He didn't see Jones, but that didn't mean he wasn't there. Which shadow could Jones be hiding in, watching them?

Marcello looked protectively at his children. Tony's rumpled shirttails hung out; his dirty hands still clutched his flag. Sophia's curls were a windblown frizz, her chin sticky with ice cream. Their happy faces brought a smile to Marcello's lips and worry to his heart. How easy it would be to hurt defenseless children. He resolved no harm would come to his children, not while there was breath in his body.

From the first explosion, Tony and Sophia sat motionless, their eyes wide as the fireworks burst to life, adorning the black sky with dazzling jewels. Blasts thumped in a fiery trail from the ground to the sky and exploded in fountains of red, blue, green, and gold.

When the fireworks ended, a hush fell over the town, and the Corsis sat speechless. Luisa slipped her arms around the children. "Wasn't that beautiful?"

"Can they do it again?" Tony asked.

"Again," Sophia demanded.

"You'll see them next year," Marcello promised.

"We had quite a day, didn't we?" Luisa pulled the children close and gently rocked them while she hummed their favorite song about a cuckoo bird. Tony sang the words with Luisa, and Sophia clapped in time to the music. After four verses, Luisa told the children it was long past their bedtime, and they followed her inside, too tired to protest. Marcello waited behind and stood at the door for one last look at the emptying street. Inside, he studied the latch on their door. He would replace it tomorrow with a stronger one.

Two weeks later as the sun crested over Oyster Ridge, Luisa ran to the outhouse just before she threw up her breakfast. She leaned over the hole and retched a second time. Hopeful her stomach was empty, she waited, her throat burning with bile. A centipede scuttled over her shoe and disappeared through a crack in the floor. She wiped her mouth with a rag and brushed a strand of hair from her damp forehead. Luisa left the stench of the outhouse and stepped outside into the fresh air.

This was the fourth morning she'd thrown up. There was no ignoring the nausea any longer. She was pregnant. In spite of her roiling stomach, her heart soared. With each step back to the house, she took deep breaths. Tony barreled around the corner and flew past her. "Tony, what—"

"Gotta go." He dashed to the outhouse and slammed the door.

Amused, Luisa shook her head. Tony had a habit of waiting until the last minute before he went to the outhouse. It happened so often, Marcello nicknamed him "the streak."

Once inside, Luisa dressed Sophia and cleaned house. She and the women of Cumberland constantly battled coal dust and insisted husbands remove their pit clothes after work before they came inside. Marcello promised to build a small room off the back of the house where he could change clothes and wash up. In the meantime, Luisa swept the floor and wiped down the furniture every day to keep the level of griminess bearable.

As she emptied the dust pan into a bin, she paused. She strained and thought she heard someone calling. Luisa went to the window that faced the backyard and caught her breath. Pacing in front of the outhouse was Il Diavolo, and Tony was nowhere in sight. Her thoughts raced. Suddenly the outhouse door opened, and Tony poked his head out. "Mama! Help!"

Luisa put her hand to her chest. "That dreadful beast!" She grabbed the first thing she saw—her rolling pin—and stormed outside. The outhouse stood at the far corner of the yard. If she distracted the ram, Tony could run for the house. She looked around for something else to throw and spied a chunk of wood beside the root cellar. With her eyes on the ram, she moved cautiously, picked up the wood, and stuffed it in her apron pocket along with some rocks.

Armed with her missiles, Luisa prayed her aim was good enough to hit Il Diavolo. Out of the corner of her eye, she saw movement beside the house next door. "Is someone there? I need help." She took her eyes off the ram for a quick glance at the back of the house and was disappointed no one was there. She gathered her courage and called to Tony. "Get ready to run."

Tony's head popped out again. "Okay."

Luisa mustered a mighty yell and waved her arms. "Hey, hey, heeeey!"

The ram turned and stared at her. He took a single step

forward. Luisa held her breath and clutched a rock.

"Hey, hey, hey!" She waved her arms again.

The ram took another step, lowered its head, and charged. Luisa let loose with the rock that glanced off his side like a pebble skipping water. Tony saw his chance and streaked to the house. Luisa stepped backward, took aim, and heaved the wood, which hit the ram squarely on the nose. It halted. Luisa threw the rolling pin at him for good measure, grabbed her skirt, and ran for the house.

Once inside, she gathered Tony in a hug. "You all right?"

Tony nodded and looked up at her, his eyes filled with admiration. "You got him, Mama."

"I was lucky. I usually have terrible aim."

Sophia came over to them and hugged Luisa's legs. "Mama."

"Know what, children? It's time to lock up Il Diavolo permanently, or I'm cooking us mutton stew!"

Tony giggled.

Luisa looked up and froze. She stared into a face at the back window. She blinked, and the face was gone. It happened so fast, she wasn't sure if it was real or her imagination. Her heart skipped, then pounded wildly. "Who in the world?" She threw open the front door and ran to the back of the house. No one was there. She walked back to the front porch and eyed the empty street, strangely quiet but for the moaning wind. Luisa tried to remember the face—man or woman, young or old—but the image was a blur. A shiver ran down her spine. She hadn't imagined seeing the face.

That evening while dressing the children for bed, Luisa couldn't decide what to do. Should she tell Marcello about the face at the window? Mama said dwelling on dark thoughts made them come true. Luisa wanted no shadows hovering over this pregnancy. Nothing should spoil the joy of telling Marcello she was expecting another child. But when Luisa relived the sudden terror of seeing that face and the threat she felt to herself and the children, she knew she had to tell Marcello.

Bedtime was delayed when Tony couldn't stop talking about Il Diavolo. He told his papa how the bad old ram scared him into hiding in the outhouse, how Mama saved him by throwing the rolling pin, how he ran to the house, and how Mama would fix mutton stew if Il Diavolo ever came back. When Tony finally exhausted the story—and himself—Luisa turned down the bedside lamp, kissed the children good night, and returned to the kitchen.

The summer breeze floated through the window and nudged the curtains as Marcello sat in the rocker, puffing his pipe. Luisa was ready to burst with her news.

"I can't wait any longer. Marcello, I have something to tell you."

Her husband pulled his pipe from his mouth. "I'm not surprised—your smile gives you away."

Luisa went to him, sat on his lap, and draped her arm around his shoulders.

"This *is* good news, and you haven't said a word." He gave her a mischievous grin.

Her smile widened. "I'm pregnant."

For a brief second, he said nothing, then his eyes misted over. "That's wonderful," he whispered. He pulled her close and kissed her. "How long have you known?"

"A week or two—morning sickness."

"When will the baby come?"

"Next spring—sometime in April."

Marcello cupped her chin and looked into her eyes with a serious expression. "I want you to take care of yourself."

"I will."

"No more run-ins with the ram." He kissed the tip of her nose. "I'm so happy."

"So am I." Luisa ran her hand over her stomach. "I think I'm already gaining weight. I'll be huge if this keeps up."

"All that matters is that you and the baby are healthy."

Luisa laid her head on Marcello's shoulder. "Just think, Marcello." She felt her face flush with happiness. "Our first child born in America." A moment later she lifted her head. "I have something else to tell you. It's probably nothing . . ."

"Oh?"

"This morning after I chased off the ram and we were back in the house, I could have sworn someone was watching us through the back window."

"What?" Marcello's voice rose.

"I only caught a glimpse, and then it was gone. I went outside and looked, but no one was there."

Marcello frowned. "If you think you saw someone, you probably did. I'll talk to the neighbors. Maybe Oleg and Elsa saw someone hanging around the neighborhood." Worry clouded his face, and Luisa knew they were both thinking the same thing.

Barrett Jones.

Marcello pulled Luisa close.

CHAPTER 28

December

Luisa turned the jug upside down and waited for the thick, syrupy liquid to ooze out. None came. "We're out of molasses."

"Baking gingerbread again?" Marcello already knew the answer. In her fifth month of pregnancy, Luisa's biggest craving was for gingerbread, warm from the oven with cream dribbled over the top.

Luisa managed to button her wool coat over her expanding stomach and pulled on her knitted hat. "I'll be back soon."

"Don't take too long. Sky looks full of snow."

Luisa picked up the empty jug, kissed Marcello on the cheek, and left.

Inside the company store, she caught the familiar aroma of coffee beans and fresh cheese mingled with the smell of leather boots and tobacco. A potbelly stove warmed the store. For a Saturday morning, the store was nearly empty, and she easily navigated the piled sacks of flour and cornmeal to the counter in front of shelves lined with tins of fruit, spices, and cookies. Luisa set her jug on the counter.

"More molasses?" Everyone in town knew Mrs. Henderson, a pleasant woman whose family ran the store. Today she wore a plaid hunting jacket over her dress for extra warmth.

"Seems all I want to eat is gingerbread." Luisa gave an embarrassed smile.

Mrs. Henderson filled Luisa's jug under the tap of the molasses barrel behind the counter.

"Good morning, Luisa." Mrs. Broski, Luisa's petite neighbor, bundled in a heavy coat, sidled up to the counter, her round face animated.

Luisa turned. "Good morning. How are—"

"I'm fine, thank you, but my Janna has been very ill. Worst case I've ever seen."

"What did she—"

"The croup. She was so sick. I was up with her day and night for a week."

"Is she—"

"Better? A little. The worst is over, but I'll tell you, the only thing worse would have been if our youngest child, Thaddaeus, caught it . . ."

Luisa nodded.

". . . and if you or your children catch the croup . . ."

Like Donato's store back home, the company store was the heart of the town's news and gossip. Luisa knew Mrs. Broski loved dispensing both.

". . . and Doc wasn't in town, so I . . ."

Luisa caught sight of the dark sky outside and slowly backed away. "I really should be going—"

"—I have the best remedy." When Mrs. Broski paused for a breath, Luisa saw her chance. She picked up her jug, smiled, and hurried to the cash register.

When she stepped outside, Luisa was surprised at the sudden drop in temperature. The leaden sky threatened snow. She shivered and pulled her hat down over her ears. Hugging the jug to her body, she walked down Main Street past the boardinghouse and rounded the corner. She leaned into the biting December wind blowing down the deserted street.

The man came out of nowhere and blocked her way. Luisa stared up into the face of Barrett Jones and gasped. Her heart pounded with a painful explosion of adrenalin. He loomed so close, a threatening sneer on his face, it made her skin crawl. Her mind raced, and she looked for a way to escape but stood frozen with fear. She forced herself to speak, her voice loud. "Excuse me," she said, and stepped around him.

He laughed and stepped in front of her again. "Excuse me, is it? My, my, aren't you the fancy one."

She looked around frantically for an escape. "You're in my way." Her heart pounded.

"Don't be in such a hurry. It's about time I got to know you." He glanced up and down the street, then grabbed her arm.

"Let go!" Luisa pulled against him. His grip tightened. She flung the jug at him, but he ducked, and it thudded to the ground.

He yanked her from the walkway to the rear of the boarding-house and breathed in her face, his breath stinking of alcohol. "You're a pretty little thing, even if you are eye-talian."

Luisa's heart pounded in her ears. "Help! *Help!*" She screamed as loud as she could, but the wind sucked her cries away.

He clamped his hand over her mouth and pinned her against the house, banging her head on the siding. "Shut up!" His hand groped under Luisa's coat across her stomach. Revulsion surged through her, and he gave her a sickening smile. "That's the way I like my woman—with big bellies." He moved his hand to his trouser button.

Luisa couldn't breathe, couldn't scream. Tears coursed down her face. She forced her jaw open and bit down with all her strength on the filthy hand over her mouth.

He howled and pulled his hand away long enough for Luisa to wrench an arm free and claw at his face. She screamed until he slapped her across the face and grabbed both her wrists.

Stunned, Luisa's field of vision narrowed to a dark tunnel with Jones's contorted face at the center. She fought to free her wrists but was no match for his strength.

Suddenly, powerful arms pulled Jones off her and threw him to the ground. Ian McGregor stood over Jones and landed a punch full in his face. "You scum!" McGregor roared and punched Jones again. "Leave her alone!"

Jones stared up from his sprawl on the ground, his nose bleeding. "I didn't do nothing," he growled. He got to his feet, stood, and glared at Ian before he turned and walked away.

Luisa shook uncontrollably. She felt Ian's arm support her while she gasped for air. Ian waited, his arm firmly holding hers. When air returned to her lungs, Luisa looked at Ian through her tears. In a million lifetimes, she'd never find words to thank him.

Ian seemed to read her thoughts and nodded with a whisper, "Let's get you home, Mrs. Corsi."

As they neared the house, Ian hollered for Marcello and pushed open the front door. The minute Marcello saw Luisa leaning on Ian, he was on his feet. "My God. What happened?"

Luisa fell into a chair and Marcello knelt beside her. Tears spilled down her cheeks. Tony and Sophia rushed from their bedroom and stopped short when they saw their mama crying. Sophia burst into tears and ran to her, burying her face in Luisa's lap. Tony hung back, blinking tears, then ran to his mama.

"It was Jones got her." Ian spoke as though apologizing for uttering something so hideous.

"No! Luisa, did he—" His face turned crimson.

"He didn't hurt me," Luisa's voice caught, "or the baby." She shuddered and sobbed into Marcello's arms.

"I heard her scream, thank the Lord. Was putting my boots on the back porch," said Ian. "Gave that miserable wretch a face pounding—begging your pardon, ma'am." He nodded at Luisa.

Marcello held her tight until her sobbing eased. He brushed strands of hair from her face, then turned to the children. He pulled a handkerchief from his trousers and wiped their noses. "Go to your room while I talk to Mama." When the door to their bedroom closed, Marcello gently took Luisa by the shoulders. "Look at me," he said tilting her head until she looked into his eyes. "Are you sure you're all right? Do you want me to get Doc?"

Luisa shook her head and choked back a sob.

Marcello's mouth set in a grim line. He went to their bedroom and returned with his revolver. He stuck it in his waistband, his expression unlike anything Luisa had seen.

"I'm taking you and the children next door to stay with Elsa and Oleg until I come back."

Luisa clutched his arm. "Where are you going?"

"To find Jones."

Fear rippled through Luisa. "Don't leave me! Please don't leave me."

Marcello's eyes blazed. "This has to end."

"He's evil, Marcello. Stay away from him."

"Do you want to look over your shoulder for Jones every time you leave the house? When you go for water? When you walk to Rosa's? Wondering if he's watching, waiting for another chance to—" Marcello's anger left him speechless. "This is up to me, Luisa. I'm going after him."

Marcello stormed down the street with Ian at his side. He took no notice of the deepening snow. Coal smoke spewed from the stovepipes on the miners' houses, into the swirling wind. "Jones lives in the boardinghouse on Main Street, right?"

"So far as I know." Ian tried to match Marcello's stride. "What are you going to do?"

"End this—now." Marcello picked up his pace.

They ran up the front steps of the boardinghouse and pushed open the door. Two miners sat beside a potbelly stove in the front room reading the weekly newspaper. They looked up with mouths open, startled by the angry intruders. Drab upholstery covered the easy chairs and the sofa along the opposite wall. A long plank table surrounded by mismatched chairs took up the adjoining dining room. Pots and pans clattered behind the closed kitchen door. The aroma of flapjacks lingered.

They climbed the stairs, two at a time, to the rented rooms. Marcello flung open the nearest door and hollered, "Barrett Jones!" The room was sparsely furnished with a bed and chest of drawers. It was empty. He worked his way down the hall, banging doors open, hollering for Jones, finding only miners irate at being rudely awakened.

"Where is he?" Marcello yelled in frustration.

"The kitchen? The back porch?"

They pounded down the stairs, boots clattering, in time to see Jones flee the house. Marcello leaped down the last three stairs and ran out the door with Ian on his heels. They stopped at the bottom of the porch steps and peered into the swirling snow. Jones was nowhere in sight.

Marcello shouted above the whining wind. "Go around to the back. I'll go this way," he pointed in the opposite direction. They separated, and Marcello edged around the side of the house. When he turned the corner, Jones tackled him and slugged him in the face. Marcello struggled for footing on the frozen ground and swung his fists, missing his target.

Jones landed a blow to Marcello's jaw that snapped his head back. Contempt spread across Jones's face. Marcello ran at him, throwing frantic jabs. Jones threw his elbow into Marcello's stomach. Gasping a breath, Marcello butted Jones's head and backed him up against the house, punching until Jones lost his balance and fell to his knees.

Marcello kicked Jones in the ribs. When Jones fell forward, Marcello grabbed his hair, yanked his head back, and punched his face. Blood spurted from Jones's nose, and he fell backward.

Marcello landed on Jones and straddled his body. He pummeled him, yelling with each blow, "My wife, my wife, my wife!" He couldn't stop. He felt unhinged. Again and again he rammed his fist into Jones's bloody face, screaming wildly until his voice broke. Tears of rage stung his eyes.

"Stop, Marcello. Enough!" Marcello felt Ian pulling him off Jones. Marcello swung at Ian with full force. Ian clamped down on Marcello's arms until they went limp. Blood streamed from his nose and oozed from his knuckles. One of his eyes was swelling shut.

Still heaving from rage, Marcello leaned over Jones and glared into his dazed eyes. "Come near my family again, and I'll kill you."

Ian pulled Marcello away from Jones and led him to the street. They stumbled over chunks of broken glass poking through a mound of snow. The molasses jug.

Marcello clenched his fists.

"Leave him," Ian warned. "He got the message."

Marcello stood immobile, staring at the jug. He looked up at Ian. "I didn't thank you."

"No thanks needed. You'd have done the same for my misses."

"You saved Luisa." Marcello's throat tightened.

"Come on home now," said Ian. "You've had a day."

Marcello nodded. He took a few steps and stopped. "I have to stop by the store first, bring home a jug of molasses."

CHAPTER 29

February

Marcello and his brothers settled into easy chairs in Lucas's living room after a Sunday dinner of fried chicken and biscuits. The chatter of their wives and the clatter of dishes floated from the kitchen.

Lucas unbuttoned his vest. "That was nice. Julia wanted a family get-together while the roads are still passable. Surprising how little snow we've had for February."

"Glad we could make it," Marcello said. "Luisa won't be traveling by wagon after today—too bumpy for her condition."

Lucas nodded. "Between that and the weather, it's hard to get out in the winter."

"I bet snow flies any day," Angelo said.

"Followed by cabin fever." Marcello chuckled. "The first time Luisa heard that expression, she thought it was a real sickness."

"Theresa will tell you it *is* a real sickness," Mick said, crossing his long legs. "It's no fun being snowed in at the farm."

Marcello sighed happily, his stomach full, surrounded by his family in the comfort of Lucas's home. He slid his hand over the chair's deep green upholstery and stretched out his legs on a patterned area rug in shades of brown and blue. Lucas's well-appointed home seemed a million miles from the backbreaking labor and grit of the mine.

Moments like this held new meaning for Marcello after

Jones's attack on Luisa. Since that day, Jones had kept his distance at the mine, his mocking demeanor no longer directed at Marcello. But Marcello knew one fight wouldn't change a man like Jones, who'd revealed the depth of his depravity. Marcello kept his eyes and ears open and held true to his threat—he *would* kill Jones if he came near his family.

No one at the mine spoke of the attack, but in the close-knit community, everyone knew their neighbors' business. Marcello noticed subtle indications from fellow workers—a nod of acknowledgment, a glance that revealed understanding, even sympathy. The unspoken support heartened him. He believed any one of these men could have been Ian McGregor on that horrible day.

"How's business?" Jim's question brought Marcello back to the moment.

The brothers waited for Lucas to answer. He watched the eight young Corsi cousins outside playing tag around the bare trees.

"Prohibition has changed everything." He spoke in a matter-of-fact tone and leaned back in his chair. "Without spirits for sale, there's no reason to come to the saloon. I have to find another way to make money. Adapt."

Marcello had seen this before. Lucas had the ability to appear composed even while grappling with a serious problem. "How?" Marcello asked.

All eyes were on Lucas. "I've given this a lot of thought. You probably won't like my plan, but I've decided to make my own liquor."

"What?" Marcello sat up in disbelief.

"Stop right there." Angelo held up both hands in protest. "You're not going to do something that's—"

"Illegal," Jim blurted out.

"You'd be taking a huge chance, dodging the law." Mick

stood, hands on his hips.

"Like I said, I've given this a lot of thought. My plan is reasonable."

Mick lowered himself into his chair, and the room became quiet. The brothers exchanged worried looks.

Marcello broke the silence. "Do you even know how to make whiskey?"

"I'm building a still in my basement," said Lucas.

"Since when?" Jim was incredulous.

Lucas went to the kitchen doorway and glanced at their wives washing dishes before returning to his brothers. "Follow me." He opened a hallway door and led them downstairs to the basement. He had a collection of barrels, a kerosene stove, a copper boiler, and a heap of what appeared to be unusable pieces of copper. Sacks of sugar were piled against the wall.

"You're serious about this," Angelo said.

"Absolutely." Lucas appeared the proud owner of a new invention.

Jim's face registered interest. "Maybe you're on to something, Lucas. This could be the start of a booming business."

"Hold on, Jim," said Mick. "There's lots to learn about this business before it turns a profit." He bent his lanky frame over the stove and boiler, then straightened. "Suppose you make something good enough to drink. How will you sell it?"

"You mean distribute it," Lucas said, "without being caught?"

"Something like that," Mick answered.

"I'll start small, with a few friends. When output increases, I'll work out a bigger distribution network."

Marcello looked around the sizeable basement and imagined his enterprising brother expanding his venture. He poked through the pile of copper tubing and coils. "How do you turn this into a still?"

Lucas pointed to the copper in Marcello's hand. "That piece

is soldered on top of the boiler. The goose neck attaches to the tubing that coils into the barrel."

"What about a recipe?" asked Angelo. "I've heard some moonshine isn't worth spit."

"Yeah, you don't want anyone to go blind from it," Mick said.

"Bad for business." Jim tried to look serious, but his eyes twinkled.

"True enough," Lucas said. "I have a recipe that's floated around town for a while. I'll start with that. Next time you're here, I'll let you be the first to sample my moonshine."

Marcello asked the only real question he had. "How dangerous is bootlegging?"

"I'll find out." Lucas smiled at Marcello's skepticism. "Seriously, more folks around here break Prohibition than obey it. There's probably a dozen bootleggers around Silverton, and they're not criminals, they're friends. No one's been in trouble."

"Not yet, anyway," interjected Angelo. He stroked his mustache, an absent-minded habit when deep in thought.

"Always the cautious one." Lucas acknowledged Angelo.

"And you're the risk-taker?" Marcello asked.

"When it comes to my business, I don't make foolish decisions." Lucas paused. "I don't have to tell you to keep this quiet—even from your wives."

"You can't make a still and just leave it in the middle of your basement." Angelo frowned.

"I'm working on that. First, I have to build the still. I'll worry about hiding it later."

Lucas chose a bottle from a shelf, heavy with bottles of homemade wine, that ran along one wall. The brothers returned upstairs, and Lucas brought glasses from the oak breakfront in the dining room. "At least we can still make our own wine." He filled the glasses. "Even though we have to buy a permit now."

"Count yourselves lucky," said Jim. "Being a bachelor, I'm not allowed to make as much as you."

"You know what that means?" Marcello teased. "Find yourself a wife."

"I'll make that a solemn duty," Jim said with a straight face. The brothers laughed.

Lucas raised his glass. "To new ventures."

Marcello watched the April rain beat against the windows. A lightning bolt split the night sky and the house shuddered with thunder. When he wasn't poking the coals in the firebox or refilling the kettle on the stove, he sat in the rocker, shifting for a comfortable position, but found none. Doc said it wouldn't be much longer. Rosa and Elsa had come earlier in the day when the contractions began, and by supper, Marcello fetched the doctor. Doc divided his time between Cumberland and Spring Hill and, to Marcello's great relief, this was his day in town.

Luisa cried out from behind the bedroom door. Marcello flinched, relieved that Tony and Sophia were next door. He added chunks of coal to the firebox and glanced at the cuckoo clock ticking away the minutes with unhurried indifference. Despite the risks of childbirth, Marcello found himself grateful for this moment. Luisa had carried the baby the full nine months, and that meant everything.

A tiny wail pierced the silence. His head snapped toward the bedroom. He heard raised voices and hurried footsteps on the other side of the door. He expected Rosa or Elsa to come from the bedroom, but the door remained closed. Minutes ticked away until he could stand it no longer. He went to the door and pressed his ear against it.

More voices, more footsteps.

He shoved his hands in his pockets and paced the room, stopping to glance out the window into the rain-soaked night.

He moved to the bedroom and waited, his eyes riveted on the door. Suddenly Rosa opened it, relief on her face. "She's fine."

Marcello released the air from his lungs. "Thank God. And the baby?"

"You're in for a surprise," said Rosa.

Elsa came from the bedside. "I'll bring the children to see the babies, if that's all right."

"Babies?" Marcello's gaze turned immediately to the bed. Luisa's eyes were closed and beside her, wrapped in flannel, lay two babies. "Twins?" Marcello's jaw fell.

Doc dried his hands at the commode. "Congratulations. You have two healthy sons. The second one gave us a scare, but he's breathing fine now."

Marcello stood still, dumbfounded.

Doc rolled his sleeves down and buttoned the cuffs. "Two for one." He smiled kindly at Marcello and patted him on the shoulder.

Luisa opened her eyes. "Two boys. Can you believe it?"

Marcello was at her side. "No, I can't." He took her hand and leaned close to the sleeping babies, amazed. "Two miracles; two fine boys." He kissed her forehead. "Are you all right?"

Luisa managed a smile. "I'm tired."

"You're a strong woman," Doc reassured her. Rosa tucked a wool blanket around Luisa.

"Look who's here!" Elsa stood at the door with Tony and Sophia, damp from dashing through the rain, their faces eager with anticipation.

"Come see the babies." Luisa motioned them to the bed.

Sophia moved close to her mother and eyed the two bundles. "Two babies?" She peered at one of the babies and furrowed her brow. "This one doesn't have hair."

"It will grow." Luisa patted Sophia's hand.

Tony looked from one baby to the other. "They look alike,

Mama . . . what are their names?"

"I'd like to name one of them Roberto." Luisa lifted her gaze to Marcello. "What do you think?"

"Roberto would be happy for his nephew to carry his name."

Sophia darted from the room and returned with two little animals Marcello had carved for her and Tony. She placed one on top of each swaddled baby and looked up at her father.

"*Bene,* Sophia." She clapped her hands at his approval.

Marcello scooped her up into his arms. "Three boys and a girl. How about that?"

★ ★ ★ ★ ★

PART THREE: 1925–1926

★ ★ ★ ★ ★

Truth is your truest friend, no matter
what the circumstances are.

—Abraham Lincoln

Chapter 30

October

The day the twins turned four was the day Luisa discovered her first gray hair. Marcello teased her about it, which didn't help. He remembered her dismay at the discovery until she recalled her mama's hair had been streaked with gray as far back as she could remember. They sat beside each other on the porch and watched a game of "Pum Pum, Pull Away" while Luisa snapped the last harvest of beans. Two teams of neighborhood children faced each other in the wide, dusty street. When one team chanted "Pum, pum, pull away," the other team tried to run through their opponents to the opposite end of the street without being tagged.

"The twins are growing fast." Marcello smiled. Four-year-old Roberto and Tomas insisted they were old enough to chase up and down the street with the big kids. They were fiercely protective of each other, but complete opposites when it came to rules: Roberto followed them. Tomas ignored them.

Tony, the tallest and swiftest of his sixth-grade friends, dodged his opponents and dashed untouched down the street. Marcello admired his competitive nature, just as Luisa was touched by his affection for every stray animal that sought safety under their porch. With his slim build and mop of dark hair, he looked more like Marcello every day.

Sophia held her own while others gave chase, her blond curls flying behind her. She loved the large bows Mama pinned in her hair every morning, which were bedraggled by day's end after playing with her brothers. Like them, she ran barefoot in the warm evening, glad to be rid of the outgrown shoes that pinched her feet.

Marcello pulled his pipe from his overalls and examined the bowl. "Empty." He stood with effort and stretched his back. It had been a brutal day at the mine. When he came home, he stripped his pit clothes in the shed he'd built off the back of the house and scrubbed his grimy face and neck with lye soap. Pain had shot down his back when he leaned over the basin to rinse his face.

Luisa looked up as she snapped the last of the beans. "Sore?"

"It's nothing." He twisted side to side in another stretch and moved to the door.

Luisa followed him into the kitchen. She set the basin on the counter and pulled up a chair at the table. Chores were finished, and there was nothing to delay their discussion, which had begun the evening before. Marcello lit his pipe and sent a cloud of smoke to the ceiling. He sat beside Luisa and noticed she was fidgeting with her fingers.

She took a deep breath to summon courage and looked him in the eye. "The bootleg is a bad idea."

Marcello couldn't believe his ears. In Italian families, it was unheard of for a wife to contradict her husband. If Luisa's mama had been there, he knew she'd scold Luisa for such shameful outspokenness. An angry furrow creased his brow. "I explained that last night."

"It's trouble."

"Like I said, there won't be any trouble."

"It's against the law." Luisa showed her husband a defiant face.

Marcello drew a tired breath. The last thing he wanted was an argument with Luisa. "Folks in Cumberland and Silverton still make their own wine, like they have for years because the sheriffs issue permits for it. They also know the locals make whiskey and don't stop it. In fact, some of them *buy* it, even though it's illegal." He frowned, the frustration in his voice growing. "I don't know what you're worried about."

"The revenuers raided Flatbush last week and busted the stills—that's what I'm worried about." Luisa's eyes flashed.

"Revenuers never come around here. Besides, the Silverton sheriff has known Lucas for years, counts on him to help out the miners when times are hard. Lucas might as well be the mayor. All he wants is a place to store his whiskey until he sells it. The sheriff doesn't care. Why should we?"

"We don't have anywhere to put it," Luisa challenged.

"I'd make a place for it, a new dugout."

"Marcello!" Luisa gasped. "What if Lucas is caught by somebody besides the sheriff?"

"He won't be."

"You don't know that." She sat tall in her chair and crossed her arms.

Marcello leaned forward, trying to keep his voice low so prying neighbors couldn't hear him. "Mick has been storing whiskey in his barn for over a year. Jim helps Lucas move his whiskey. There hasn't been any trouble, *capire*?" He leaned back, a satisfied look on his face.

Luisa paused and tucked a loose strand of hair behind her ear. "Why didn't you tell me?"

Marcello ignored the question. "Did you forget we'll make money storing it? Lucas will pay five dollars each month. That buys new shoes for Roberto and Tomas." He grabbed one of the twin's shoes from under the table and shook it in the air. "No more holes, no more hand-me-downs. How can you say no?"

"This is about more than new shoes. It's about being a father.

"What do you mean?" Marcello was incredulous. "*I'm* their

father! I provide for them!"

"How can you provide for them if you're in jail? What would we do? Tell Lucas no."

Marcello's face flushed hot. "I won't."

"Marcello—" Angry tears glistened in Luisa's eyes.

"He's my brother!"

"And I'm your wife!" Luisa jumped to her feet. "The one you swore to love and honor, the mother of your children."

Her words stung. *"Basta!"* Marcello stood and slammed his fist on the table. "That's the end of it!"

Luisa turned on her heel, her face set like stone, and went to the bedroom. The lock clicked behind her. Marcello stormed out the front door, slamming it with a force that loosened the hinges. He sank to the front step and winced as he leaned his aching back against the railing.

How dare she question him! How could Luisa think he would ever do anything to put her or the children in danger? What did she take him for? His jaw clenched. He labored every day to the point of exhaustion, knowing the mine could break his bones and savage his lungs, and for what?

His family.

How could she not see everything he did was for the family? Why was she acting this way? Marcello chewed on the stem of his pipe. Three years ago, he had opened a savings account at the bank, one of the proudest days in his life. They lived frugally, so he could set aside five dollars each month for savings. He kept the passbook in the top drawer of the dresser and double-checked the bank's figures after each deposit, which now showed two hundred and five dollars. Storing moonshine would mean five dollars more each month without backbreaking work at the mine. It would buy shoes for the children and help Lucas at the same time.

He stared into the October sun until it sank below the

horizon. Winter lay in wait beyond the waning days of autumn, and that meant new coats, new boots. The decision was made for him: he would store moonshine for Lucas—with or without Luisa's approval.

The next morning anger from their argument lingered in the air like a storm brewing on the horizon. Marcello shot a glance at Luisa and swallowed his coffee. "The train bringing grapes from California comes today. Who wants to go with me?"

"I do! I do!" Tony and Sophia chimed together.

"Can we go now?" Tomas jumped up from the table, and his spoon clattered to the floor.

"Finish breakfast, then we go," said Marcello. He buttered a biscuit and looked across the table at Luisa. Neither of them spoke of yesterday's argument. "Want to come with us?"

"I have work to do." Luisa looked away.

As soon as they finished breakfast, the children ran outside and climbed into neighbor Oleg's wagon. Tony and Sophia sat in the back beside empty wooden crates. Tomas and Roberto crawled inside two of the crates and giggled at each other as Marcello slapped the reins, and the wagon rumbled down the street.

"There it is!" Sophia squealed. A lone boxcar sat on a siding of track beside the mine office. Marcello pulled up beside neighbors unloading their children and empty crates from their wagons.

Tony leaped to the ground. "I'll get our grapes," he called over his shoulder and dashed off to the crowd of children beside the boxcar. Two burly workmen shoved open a large sliding door, reached into crates of fresh grapes, and passed them into outstretched hands. Tony reached on his tiptoes and came away with two bunches. "Over here!" He waved to Sophia and the twins. They plopped down on a patch of grass away from the boxcar to eat.

Tony dropped three grapes in his mouth. "Just like I remembered." He savored the tangy sweetness.

"Yummy." Sophia closed her eyes, an expression of joy on her face.

Roberto swallowed a mouthful. "The grape train should come every day."

"Umm-hmm." Tomas swiped away juice dribbling down his chin.

Marcello paid for his grapes, and the children helped load the crates into the wagon. When they returned home, Marcello had the children help fill a tub with water and lugged the wine press from the root cellar with Tony's help.

Marcello wiped dirt and cobwebs from the press. "Tony, you turn the handle." He turned to Sophia and the twins. "Your job is to wash the grapes and put them in the press." The twins each grabbed a bunch of grapes and dunked them vigorously into the tub. Water flew everywhere.

"Stop it," Sophia scolded and backed away.

"No playing," Marcello spoke sternly. Tomas gave Roberto a daring look and, when Marcello turned away, splashed again. "Tomas, I heard that!" Marcello turned around with a withering stare that caused Tomas's head to droop.

They worked through the morning and transformed the grapes, popping and squirting in the press, into thick juice laced with skins that would turn the juice red. When the bucket at the bottom of the press was full, Marcello emptied it into a barrel in the root cellar to ferment.

By midday, Roberto and Tomas looked hopefully at their papa for signs it was time to stop. Roberto dropped a handful of grapes into the press and wiped his hands on his pants. "Papa, how much longer?"

Marcello glanced at the sun. "It's almost time to eat."

"I'm tired. Can I stop now?" Roberto offered a forlorn face.

"Me, too," Tomas said, letting his head droop dramatically.

Marcello looked at the stack of crates. "I suppose—" The twins didn't wait for him to finish and took off in a burst of newfound energy.

"Papa?" Tony raised his eyebrows.

"We'll finish up this afternoon."

Marcello herded the children back to the grape press after dinner. Luisa was glad they were busy because she had something important to do. She lifted her skirts to avoid snagging them on sagebrush as she picked her way through their yard to Angelo and Rosa's house.

"Rosa?" Luisa leaned through the open doorway to the sweet aroma of warm chokecherry jelly.

"You came at a good time. Just finished." Steam rose from the boiling pot where Rosa clamped her tongs around the last jar and set it on the counter beside Mason jars dripping from the water bath, sparkling ruby red with jelly. "I'm ready to sit." She wiped a trickle of sweat from her brow with her apron and led the way to the back porch.

They settled into rockers and looked across the gentle hills awash in shades of brown dotted with yellow goldenrod and white saltbush. The sky was a cloudless blue. Rosa pushed up her sleeves and fanned herself with a Munson Funeral Home cardboard fan, stirring her auburn locks. "Canning is hot work. Would you like—" She stopped and looked at Luisa with a frown. "You all right?"

"No." Luisa bit her lip.

"What's wrong?"

"Marcello."

Rosa sat up. "He's not sick?"

"No, nothing like that." Luisa didn't know if Rosa knew about Lucas's bootleg operation. She hesitated. "It's Lucas. Do you know about—"

"His bootlegging?" Rosa avoided Luisa's gaze. "Yes."

"He wants to store it at our house."

Rosa gasped. "You, too?"

Luisa grabbed Rosa's hand. "He asked Angelo?" They stared at each other in shared amazement.

"A few days ago. I'm sick with worry." Rosa fell back in her rocker.

"Mick and Jim are already involved. Marcello says he's going to do it, even though I don't want him to." Luisa's voice quivered, and she pulled a handkerchief from her skirt pocket. "I'm furious, but I don't know how to stop it."

"Angelo hasn't given Lucas an answer yet, but I'm afraid he'll say yes. I want nothing to do with bootlegging." Rosa swept away the horrible notion with a wave of her arm.

"Marcello says the sheriff won't make trouble. How does he know that?" Luisa threw her hands in the air. "There might be a lot of trouble. What if the sheriff is like the police back home in Lanzo?" A shudder ran down her back.

"Nobody's as bad as the *poliziacorrotta.*" Rosa thought for a moment. "I think the sheriff's a decent type. He treated Jim and Roberto fair."

"That doesn't make Marcello right about this, choosing his brother over the children and me like we don't matter."

"You know that's not true."

"Then why doesn't he listen to me?" Luisa stood and paced the porch.

"The Corsi men are the head of their families. That's the only way they know how to act." Rosa's tone was one of resigned acceptance.

Luisa stopped pacing. "Marcello trusts Lucas completely, as if he's right about everything."

"What do you think?" Rosa waited.

"No one's right all the time, not even Lucas."

"He's the oldest, and all the brothers look up to him. He's a smooth one, I'll give you that. Sometimes I think he could charm the horns off the devil."

"Lucas said he'll pay us. I'd rather do without the extra money than put the children in danger." Rosa nodded, her eyes brimming with understanding. Luisa sank into the rocker and spoke in a whisper. "If Marcello went to jail, how would we survive? We'd lose the house. I'd have to find somewhere else to live, take in boarders, do laundry, mend clothes."

"Luisa, stop. Don't think like that."

"But we can't know the future." She glanced down at her handkerchief, which was twisted into a ball, then returned her gaze to Rosa. "What are you going to do?"

Rosa sat tall. "The only thing I *can* do is tell Angelo I don't want any bootleg liquor in our house." She slapped the arm of her rocker. "We'll stand together on that, you and me."

"I promise you," Luisa said, seething, "if I think the children are in danger, I'm taking them somewhere safe."

Two weeks later while Sophia played in the backyard, she noticed the cows. Marcello had bought three milking cows from Mick last spring, which they kept in the company barn near their house. "What's wrong with them?" she asked her brothers. Instead of grazing in the fields, the cows wandered through the neighboring yard to the street behind their house.

Roberto and Tomas shot marbles in a dirt patch beside the house. Roberto looked up and followed her gaze. "Don't know. Never seen *that* before."

"Why are they walking funny?" Sophia cocked her head to one side and studied the cows with her brothers.

The first cow lumbered forward on unsteady legs, then stopped and swayed. It leaned heavily to one side but remained upright. The cow behind it veered from side to side and bumped into the first cow that had stopped in its path. The last cow lurched and fell on its hindquarters when its back legs buckled. The first cow resumed walking and plowed into the neighbor's outhouse. It bellowed but didn't move, its massive body leaning precariously against the outhouse for support. The second cow staggered to a ditch that ran between the yards and stopped to eat something.

"Roberto, get Papa!" Sophia yelled. She ran to the cow and saw its large, rough tongue lick a gooey purple mass covered with mud. "Ick! What's that?"

Moments later Marcello was beside the cow with a rope he looped around its neck. "Come on, Bossy, come on," he urged the cow and gently pulled on the rope to guide it away from the ditch. Marcello led the lumbering cow to a stall in the barn, where it collapsed on the hay and closed its eyes. He scratched the cow's ears. "You're all right now," he said, and left it to sleep. He grabbed a shovel and headed back to the ditch.

"Papa, what's that?" Tomas pointed with a disgusted look as Marcello buried the slimy glob.

"Grape pulp." He threw on the last shovel of dirt and packed it down. "That should take care of it, so long as they can't smell it."

"Is that what made them walk funny?" asked Roberto.

Marcello nodded. "They love it, but it can make them sick, even drunk."

"Where'd it come from?" Sophia stared at the freshly covered hole.

"The bottom of a wine barrel. Somebody threw it out in the ditch."

Sophia looked up when she saw her mother come from the house. "Mama, come quick. The cows are drunk! Papa said so."

"Someone threw pulp in the ditch," Marcello called as Luisa

crossed the yard.

"Oh, no! How bad are they?" She eyed the two incapacitated cows with a worried frown.

"They'll be okay. One's in the barn. I can get that one next." He nodded toward the cow leaning against the outhouse. It made a feeble attempt to bellow and blinked sleepily. "The other one might be a problem if it keels over completely."

"No milk for supper tonight," said Luisa.

Marcello winked. "Not unless you like wine in it."

Chapter 31

"My deal."

Jim shuffled the worn cards and dealt hands to Angelo, Vito, and himself. Jim and Vito played poker every Saturday night at Vito's, a bachelor house on Main Street next to the boarding-house. They sat in mismatched chairs around an old second-hand table, scratched and dented from years of use, their light a single bulb hanging overhead. A rough-hewed sideboard held a dimly lit kerosene lamp that spilled light on bottles of spirits and glassware.

Angelo stood and stretched. "Be back in a minute." He shrugged on his coat and left for the outhouse in the backyard.

Jim finished the deal and pulled a pouch of tobacco and cigarette paper from his pocket.

"What happened to your hand?" Vito asked.

"Got caught between coal bins yesterday." Jim ran his hand over his raw knuckles. He tapped tobacco onto the paper, rolled it, and struck a match. Smoke drifted toward a window etched with frost, while outside a November snow fell from the dark sky.

"More?" Vito refilled his glass with wine and held the bottle, waiting for Jim's reply.

"Sure."

Vito emptied the bottle into Jim's glass. "Anything new in the search for a missus?" he asked, arching his dark bushy eyebrows, a teasing smile on his face.

"I'm not searching," Jim said, "and even if I were—which I'm not—I get enough ribbing from my brothers."

"I know. That's why I asked." Vito chuckled.

"You, of all people—you've been a bachelor forever."

"I've been a bachelor so long, no one bothers me about it anymore."

"Lucky you. I'll trade my brothers for some peace and quiet on the subject." Jim took a swallow of wine.

What Jim hadn't told anyone was he'd found a girl, maybe *the* girl, without even searching for her. He'd bumped into her, literally, at the company store and sent her armful of canned goods rolling across the floor. As he helped retrieve her items, she thanked him with the most beautiful smile he'd ever seen, a smile that made her green eyes sparkle. He made a point of returning to the store at the same time a week later. She was there shopping, clearly pleased to see him again. He wanted to think she had been waiting for him.

Jim was enamored. It was impossible to keep a person's private life from gossip in Cumberland, but he and the girl managed to find time together over the next weeks without drawing attention to themselves. Yesterday everything changed. Ailene invited him to Sunday dinner with her family. Jim was surprised he didn't feel pressured by the invitation; he welcomed it. Tomorrow the Italian bachelor would call on the daughter of an Irish family. That would give Cumberland something to talk about. He smiled.

Angelo returned to the table and rubbed his hands together. "Cold out there." He glanced at Jim. "What are you grinning about?"

"Probably has another winning hand," Vito grumbled, looking at his hard-earned money piled in front of Jim.

The smile still on his face, Jim focused on his cards. "It's a game of skill, gentlemen." He fingered his winnings to emphasize his point.

"Think you're smart," Angelo said. "Play."

Heavy pounding on the front door interrupted the game. Frank and Sal, friends of Jim's from the boardinghouse, burst into the room in a blast of cold air, their coats covered with snow. Everyone in town knew about the hatred between Frank and Vito. Some said they feuded over who controlled the local moonshine market. Others said their hatred went back to the early days of the mine, when both men had fought over the affections of the same woman, who spurned them both.

Frank swayed where he stood, holding a bottle of moonshine, his bloodshot eyes focusing on Jim. "Knew you'd be here."

"Oh, God, not *you.*" Vito muttered under his breath. He confronted Frank. "You can't bust in here. Get out!"

"Aw, come on, Vito." Sal's face was flushed, and his eyelids drooped. "We jus' wanna have a drink with Jim and you. No harm in that." Sal fell into an empty chair and leaned toward Jim. "How 'bout it, Jimmy? Have a drink with us."

Frank raised his bottle. "It's g-o-o-d stuff."

"Thanks, but I'll stick with wine," Jim said, eyeing Frank and the moonshine.

"You sayin' my shine's no good?" Frank lurched to the table.

"No, Frank." Jim held up his hands in protest. "I'm sure it's good."

Vito stepped in front of Frank. "You heard him. He doesn't want a drink, and I don't want you in my house."

Frank's eyes narrowed. He leaned into Vito and growled, "Who the hell you think you are, givin' me orders?"

Vito's face was inches from Frank's. "This is my house. Who the hell do you think *you* are?" He jabbed his finger in Frank's chest.

"I sure ain't no Sicilian scum like you!" Frank spat on the

floor at Vito's feet. "Always think you're better 'n everybody else. Only thing you're good for is the Black Hand."

Vito, enraged at the Mafia reference, lunged at Frank, his fists balled. Jim and Angelo grabbed his arms before he landed a punch. A glass fell from the table and shattered on the floor.

"You don't wanna fight me," Frank snarled. "I'll beat you good."

Vito struggled against Jim and Angelo. "I'll give you a fight!" Vito yelled at Frank.

"Hey, hey!" Jim held Vito until he stopped resisting. "Calm down."

Vito shrugged him off and left the room.

Tension hung in the air as Jim and Angelo locked eyes, their faces anxious. Jim took a deep breath and turned to Frank. "Will you leave if I have a drink with you?"

Frank lowered himself into a chair, and Jim brought glasses to the table. With an unsteady hand, Frank splashed moonshine into the glasses, gave a silent toast, and tossed down his drink. "Told you it was good." He wiped his mouth on his sleeve.

Suddenly Vito appeared from the bedroom, waving a revolver. He pointed it at Frank and Sal. "I told you to leave. I'm not telling you again—get outta here!"

Sal jumped out of his chair, alarm on his face. "Vito, put it down! We're leavin'."

"Hell we are," shouted Frank, knocking over his chair.

Jim jumped in front of Frank. "Put the gun down, Vito."

Vito's eyes blazed. "As soon as he leaves."

Frank reached around Jim for the gun at the same moment Jim tried to push the gun away.

The gun went off in one loud explosion.

The blast sent Jim backward. Angelo caught him before he fell to the floor.

Vito stood dumbfounded, the gun smoking in his hand, staring at Jim

"Bastardo!" Frank yelled. He lurched forward and wrapped his beefy hands around Vito's neck, shoving him to the floor, knocking the table over.

Angelo held Jim, unable to believe his eyes. Smoke curled from the singed hole in Jim's shirt, blood bubbling out with his every breath. "My God, you shot him!" Gripped with fear, Angelo bent close to his brother. "I'm going for help, Jim."

He ran into the dark street, through deepening snow, straight to Marcello's house on the next block. Angelo bounded up the front step and shoved open the door. Marcello sat by the stove smoking his pipe, Luisa beside him sewing.

"Jim's been shot!" Angelo gasped.

"What?" Marcello leapt to his feet.

Luisa's mending basket fell from her lap to the floor.

"At Vito's. He's hurt bad."

Luisa turned to Marcello, her face flooded with fear.

Marcello grabbed his coat. "We'll bring him here. The children—"

"I'll take them to Rosa's," said Luisa.

Marcello and Angelo bolted into the night. The miners' houses along the street gave faint light in the swirling snow. Wind sucked ribbons of smoke from the chimneys. They ran to Vito's, frigid air burning their lungs with each breath. Marcello leaped the steps to the open front door and stopped in the doorway. The sight paralyzed him. On the floor, littered with broken glass and overturned furniture, lay two men. Frank and Sal hunched over one of the men. The sight hit Marcello like a physical blow.

The man was Jim.

Marcello dropped to his knees beside his brother. A crimson stain pooled in the center of his shirt. *"Oh, mio Dio!"*

Jim's eyes were open. "Marcello . . ." His voice was a whisper. "Stupid fight . . ."

Marcello gripped his hand. "Don't talk. We'll get Doc."

"Hurry." Jim gave a feeble smile.

Marcello turned to Angelo. "Get Doc."

Angelo disappeared out the door.

Sal knelt beside Jim and rocked back and forth. "Oh, God, oh, God."

Frank swayed as he gained his feet. "Vito's fault. Shot him point blank." He stumbled to where Vito lay, his battered head bleeding onto the floor. *"Idiota!"* he yelled and kicked Vito in the ribs.

Vito screamed and rolled onto his side, clutching his ribs.

"Stop!" yelled Marcello. He ran to the bedroom and yanked blankets off the bed. He shouted at Frank and Sal, "Help me, *rapidamente!*" They placed Jim on the blankets, lifted him from the floor and edged out the door. Jim moaned with every jostle of the blanket.

Snow was past their boot tops, every step an effort. They stumbled with the dead weight of Jim's body. Jim swayed in the blanket, loosening their grip on the corners. Sal faltered, and Jim cried out in pain. Marcello yelled at Sal, "I swear, there'll be hell to pay if you drop him!"

As they neared the house, Luisa threw open the door, and the men brought Jim to the kitchen table, trailing snow from their coats and boots. The bulb hanging over the table cast dim light on Jim; the blankets and his shirt were soaked with blood. Luisa clamped her hand over her mouth to stifle a sob. Sal and Frank recoiled from the sight.

Marcello ripped open Jim's shirt. Blood spurted from a gaping hole in the center of his chest. Luisa reached in the cupboard for cloths that Marcello pressed over the wound. They were soaked instantly. She ran from the room and returned with all their linens. They tumbled from her shaking hands onto the table. She gripped a chair to steady herself.

Marcello threw the bloody cloths aside, the coppery smell of blood overwhelming the kitchen, and pressed a fresh folded towel over the wound. "Hang on. Doc's coming!" Jim's color was fading. Never taking his eyes off Jim, Marcello exploded in anger, "What in God's name happened?"

"It was an accident." Sal choked back a sob and cowered near the door.

"Damn Vito told us to get out." Frank's voice pulsed with drunken anger. "Wasn't our fault."

Marcello turned away from his brother and stared fiercely at the pair. "It *was* your fault. You're so drunk—"

"You weren't there," Frank persisted.

"Enough!" Marcello roared. "Get out of my house."

Sal pleaded. "Marcello—"

"Scappate via!"

Sal grabbed Frank's arm and pulled him out the door into the night.

Luisa stood beside Marcello and reached for the towel. "Let me do that."

Marcello backed away and drew a shaky breath. His hands were covered with blood, and he wiped them on his pants.

Jim fought for breath and whispered, "You were right." His hand moved, and Marcello grabbed it.

"About what?" Marcello leaned close.

". . . should have settled down." Jim coughed, and bubbles tinged with blood trickled from the corner of his mouth.

"You'll have time for that—you'll find a girl and get married." Marcello's face belied his words.

Jim whispered, "Ailene . . . her name's Ailene."

Marcello frowned. "Ailene?" He turned to Luisa, bewildered.

Luisa shook her head. "I don't know . . ."

Marcello put his lips near Jim's ear. "You're going to make it. Doc's coming."

Jim eyes fluttered. ". . . I can't."

"Yes, you can. Hang on, Jim!" Marcello's voice caught in his throat.

Jim closed his eyes. Marcello bent over him, watching for the rise and fall of his chest. He placed his fingers on Jim's pulse. "It's barely there."

"What else can we do?" Luisa pleaded.

"All I know to do is slow the bleeding and keep him warm."

"Hold the towel." Luisa disappeared and quickly returned with a blanket she tucked over Jim. She placed a clean towel over the wound. "The blood's slowed." She turned to Marcello with a desperate look. "That means . . ."

Marcello clutched Jim's hand and looked at the clock. "Where's Angelo?" He rushed to the door, threw it open, and stepped into the frigid air. He stared down the deserted street, shaking in the cold. "Angelo! Doc!" His voice disappeared into the wind and snow.

"Marcello," Luisa called, "come inside."

Marcello latched the door and pushed away a shiver. "I let in too much cold." He scooped coal into the stove until the kitchen was warm again. He frowned at the single light bulb dangling over the table. "Doc will need more light." He lit the kerosene lamp from their bedroom and placed it next to Jim. In the flickering light, Marcello shuddered. Jim's face was too pale. Time was running out. He clenched his fists. "Why aren't they here yet?"

Chapter 32

Marcello paced beside Jim as each precious minute vanished. His breathing became ragged and came in small gasps.

Luisa reached for Jim's wrist, and panic spread across her face as she searched for his pulse. "I can't find it." She looked helplessly at Marcello, her eyes filling with tears.

Marcello placed his fingers on Jim's neck and willed his brother's heart to beat. He felt a push on his fingertips. "There it is."

They heard voices and footfalls on the porch. Luisa ran to the door and threw it open. "Hurry, Doc!"

Doc Chapman was beside Jim in an instant. Angelo followed and leaned over Doc's shoulder as he pulled away the bloody towel.

Angelo choked. "Do something, Doc. Please."

Doc placed his stethoscope on Jim's chest. After a moment, he moved it to the left and bent his head, listening. He moved the stethoscope back to the first position and reached for Jim's wrist. Thirty seconds . . . a minute . . . two minutes. No one breathed as the clock ticked in the desperate silence.

Doc took a deep breath, removed the stethoscope, and shook his head. "He's gone."

"No!" Luisa cried. "Help him. Do something!"

Marcello stared at Doc in disbelief. "He can't be gone." The walls of the room closed in on him. He couldn't breathe.

Angelo started to shake. "Doc wasn't home." He ran

trembling fingers through his hair. "Maybe if I'd found Doc sooner . . ."

Doc gripped Angelo's arm and spoke quietly. "That wouldn't have made a difference. He was shot at such close range, he had no chance. Even with surgery, we might not have been able to save him." He looked at their agonized faces, the blood-soaked cloths and towels strewn about the table, the bloody footprints on the floor. He shook his head, dismayed. "What the hell happened?"

"An accident . . . a terrible accident." Angelo's voice was barely audible.

Marcello stared at Jim. "This can't be happening." His knees weakened. He choked back a sob as Angelo's arm went around his shoulders.

Doc closed his medical bag. "I'm sorry. There was nothing I could do." He paused. "Tell the undertaker I'll have the death certificate for him." He made his way to the door and turned to the family. "My condolences." The latch clicked as he gently closed the door.

Tears slid down Luisa's cheeks. She pulled the blanket up under Jim's chin and sank into a chair beside the table. Leaning close, she gently smoothed Jim's curls from his forehead.

"I'll call on the priest tomorrow." Angelo's words were a thin whisper. He fought tears and sat beside Luisa.

Marcello stood immobile, his eyes on his brother. Luisa pressed Marcello's rosary into his hand and began to whisper prayers. He looked at his beads absently, then balled them in his fist and threw them to the floor. "What good does prayer do now? Where was God when Jim needed him?" The beads of the broken rosary rolled across the planking and came to rest at their feet.

"Marcello!" Luisa's eyes flashed with anger, and she held Marcello in her anguished gaze until he looked away. He lowered himself into a chair and leaned forward, his elbows on his knees. Luisa took off her blood-stained apron. She caressed Jim's injured hand and held it to her cheek before tenderly brushing it with her lips. She bowed her head, fresh tears falling, and finished the rosary while Marcello stared at the traces of their footprints on the floor.

They kept vigil over Jim into the early morning. It was still dark outside when Marcello finally broke the silence. "Before we call the undertaker . . ." He removed everything from Jim's pockets—a book of matches, coins, a wallet, and a pocketknife. He held the four-inch knife in his palm and remembered when Jim bought it at the company store. The double-bladed knife was high-quality steel. On one side of the handle was the engraving *Giacomo Corsi, Cumberland, Wyoming.*

Marcello turned the knife over. Beneath the transparent horn cover on the handle were the faded images of Mama and Papa. The third photo was Jim, taken in Italy before he left for America, a nineteen-year-old wearing a new shirt and bow tie, a shock of auburn hair falling over his forehead.

Jim had come all this way to Wyoming and survived freezing winters, summer storms, brawling cowboys, and backbreaking work. He survived the mine that could have taken his life any one of a hundred times. He survived it all, but in the end, it was his friends. He didn't survive his friends.

Marcello wrapped his fingers around the knife with the images of loved ones he'd never see again and slumped in the chair. His chin fell to his chest, and his body shook with sobs.

Marcello buttoned his coat against the blustery November night and grasped Luisa's hand as they leaned into the wind. She clutched her black bonnet while they walked with the Corsi families to Jim's wake. Marcello's mind churned as he thought about the events surrounding Jim's death. In the early morning hours while Jim lay dying, word of the shooting tore through the Italian community. Outraged, people blamed Vito for the shooting but found the greater guilt in Frank, the instigator, the outsider. A band of miners forced their way into Vito's house and left him bruised and unconscious.

Their real target was Frank. When the sheriff went to question him about the shooting, he found signs of a struggle—a broken lamp, an overturned chair, and Frank's coat still hanging on a hook. Frank had vanished without a trace. When asked about his whereabouts, the answer was the same from all of Jim's friends—a blank look, a shrug of the shoulders.

When the Corsis stepped inside the clapboard building that served as the Catholic church, they watched mourners file past Jim's open casket and find seats on the rows of benches. The parishioners had whitewashed the plank walls last year, brightening the large room, and dressed the altar with a white cloth edged in lace, the Bible, a crucifix, and tapered candles. A handmade wreath of evergreens and berries from the women of the church stood on a pedestal beside the casket. Marcello gazed around the room as the benches filled and the line stretched out the door. He nodded to familiar faces, grateful for their presence.

"Excuse me."

Marcello turned to the voice behind him. He'd never met the stout, gray-haired man before. Beside him stood a young woman not more than twenty, petite with golden brown hair. Dark lashes framed her deep green eyes.

"Are you one of Mr. Corsi's brothers?"

"I'm Marcello Corsi."

"My condolences, Mr. Corsi. I'm Evan Murphy, and this is my daughter, Ailene."

Marcello nodded and asked Mr. Murphy, "You knew Jim?"

"My daughter did."

Puzzled, Marcello shifted his gaze to the daughter. He searched his memory and suddenly spoke with recognition. "*You're* Ailene."

She nodded. "Jim and I . . ." She struggled to compose herself, and tears welled in her eyes. In a wavering voice she said, "I wanted to pay my respects."

Her pain left Marcello speechless. After a moment he replied, "Thank you for coming. You should know . . ." He paused. Ailene waited, hanging on his every word. "Jim spoke of you before he died."

Ailene sagged against her father, who put a comforting arm around her. "Thank you," she murmured. "That means everything." She bent her head and wiped away tears.

The mourners moved past a stand of votives beside the casket. Marcello anticipated seeing Jim's face one last time and would treasure that to its fullest. He looked into the casket and sucked in his breath.

It wasn't Jim's face he saw; it was his own.

A jolt went through him. With hesitant steps, he found where Luisa sat and dropped into a seat beside her. He stared into space, unable to rid himself of the image. He hadn't slept through the night since Jim's death three days ago. That would be reason enough to see things that weren't there, he told himself. Nonetheless, he was so shaken by the vision, he didn't hear a word of the priest's homily or prayers, and wasn't aware the service was over until Luisa nudged him when she stood to leave.

"I want to stay," Marcello whispered.

Luisa gave him a gentle smile and squeezed his hand before she left with the children.

The church emptied, and the priest told Marcello when he was through with prayers to latch the door when he left. The conversations of the mourners disappeared into the night as they walked home, leaving the church silent.

"You don't need to stay with me, Marcello."

Marcello froze.

Jim sat up and looked at Marcello. "Go home, be with your family."

Fear took hold, then faded, as sadness washed over Marcello. "I don't want to leave."

"You always had a soft touch about you." Jim's tease was tender.

"You bled to death in front of me. You died, and I couldn't stop it." Tears filled Marcello's eyes.

"Never thought something like this would happen," Jim said.

"You were playing cards. You weren't supposed to die!" Tears spilled down his cheeks.

"Things happen we don't expect."

"But a stupid argument? The slip of a finger?" Marcello's voice broke. "You were killed for no reason." He swiped away tears with a rough hand. "When I looked at you in the coffin just now, I saw myself. I could die as easily as you—at the mine, out hunting, another angry drunk."

"Don't live in fear, Marcello."

"I'm supposed to protect the family. Death shouldn't happen this way."

"It's done, Marcello. You can't change it."

"I know, but by God, I'll do everything I can to keep it from happening again." Marcello bent over and wept into his hands.

"Life is short, brother. I thought I had all the time in the world."

Marcello held his head in his hands. "I promised Luisa a good life here. I have to know she and the children can survive—with or without me."

"You'll do right by your family."

"How much time do I have?"

"I can't know that, Marcello. What I know is you tried to save me. I can be at peace with that. So should you."

Peace? Marcello thought he'd never find peace again. He wiped his face and raised his head. Jim lay in his coffin, a placid look on his face, the votives glowing like a halo above the altar.

"Jim?"

The wind howled outside the church.

Marcello bowed his head and, when he raised it again, the candles had flickered out. "Goodbye, Jim." He stood and left the church.

Chapter 33

The following Saturday, the early morning sun shone brilliantly in the crisp air while Angelo's family waited in their buckboard in front of Marcello's house. Angelo's horse whinnied and sent a cloud of frozen breath into the air.

"What's taking so long?" Marcello glanced repeatedly at the front door.

"No hurry," Angelo said. "The stores won't run out of wares before we get there." Rosa sat beside him, a wool blanket draped over their laps.

Marcello shifted his weight from side to side, impatient for his family to leave for Kemmerer. They had to be gone before Lucas arrived to help dig a new dugout, one with access from inside the house. It was crucial the children not know Marcello was storing moonshine. An innocent whisper about a secret storage space could bring disaster if moonshine was discovered.

Tony, Roberto, and Tomas tumbled out the door followed by Sophia and Luisa. The children settled into the back of the buckboard and bundled up in blankets with their cousins. Marcello helped Luisa into the front seat beside Rosa. "Price a coat for Tony, and I'll see if we have enough in savings." He tucked a lap rug around Luisa as she placed her feet on the heated brick covered with scraps of rug.

"I'll speak to that nice Mr. Penney," Luisa said. "His store sells coats." J. C. Penney's one-room store, founded in Kemmerer, was a favorite with the miners' families. His dry goods were of high quality and priced to compete with the company store. Reared a teetotaling Baptist, Mr. Penney owned a Main Street store that was surrounded by saloons.

Luisa leaned to Rosa. "Tony's cuffs will be at his elbows if we don't buy him a coat soon."

"Sure you won't come with us?" Rosa asked Marcello.

"Chores," said Marcello. "Back door needs repair." He and Angelo glanced at each other.

Angelo flicked the reins, and Marcello waved as they pulled away. "We'll bring back a surprise for you, Papa," Sophia hollered.

Marcello took his tools from the back porch into the bedroom and rolled up the rag rug beside their bed. There was no way to keep Luisa from discovering the dugout. Her daily cleaning included shaking every rug in the house. She'd discover it concealed under the bedroom rug the day after he built it.

He measured a square on the planking beside the bed and sawed the four sides. When he lifted the square, cold musty odors floated up into the room.

The front door opened. "Marcello?"

"In here, Lucas."

Lucas brought a short-handled shovel under his coat and a coil of rope into the bedroom and set them on the floor. "Don't think anyone saw me. Be back in a minute." He returned moments later with a cargo net stuffed into a large bucket. He eyed the opening in the floor and dropped to his knees. "If we dig down a good two feet, it should hold four kegs."

They set to work. The sound of their shovels breaking the dirt and the damp scent of fresh earth hit Marcello with a wave of heartache. It was only a week since his brother's death, and he found himself reliving Jim's service at the cemetery. He looked at Lucas. "I can't believe he's gone."

Lucas returned his gaze. "It doesn't seem real."

"I expect him to show up and crack a joke," Marcello said.

"Or tell some farfetched story." Lucas managed a sad smile.

The air was heavy with Jim's memory as they returned to work. When both buckets were full, Marcello carried them out back. He made sure no neighbors were about and dumped the dirt down the outhouse hole. When he returned to the house, he made note of the back door he'd fix when the dugout was finished.

When they resumed digging, Lucas asked, "Luisa still upset about the moonshine?"

"Nothing's changed, even though I told her there wouldn't be any trouble." Marcello gave Lucas a sideways glance. "That's right, isn't it?"

Lucas turned to Marcello. "Silverton was raided last night."

"What?" Marcello gaped at his brother.

"The revenuers have been hanging around town a couple of weeks, trying to find out where the bootleg is." Lucas paused. "They searched every house in Silverton and found some of Dan Lincoln's bootleg in his barn. They went through the saloon, but I'd moved my stash to a dugout along Silver Creek."

Marcello felt his stomach lurch. "Why are they snooping around Silverton?"

"Somebody must have tipped them off. I've been sending bootleg to Denver in Union Pacific coal cars. Dan didn't bribe the right people. I do."

"Denver? In coal cars!" Marcello was incredulous. "How long've you been doing that?"

"About two months. Blue Moon is my top-shelf recipe. It's selling so well, they're *asking* for it." Lucas couldn't hide his pride. "Can you believe that?"

"I had no idea . . ." Marcello realized he knew very little about Lucas's business. "Why Denver?"

"Shipping to Chicago is too dangerous. Another bootlegger

in Silverton—Ben Simpson—caught the attention of the revenuers, and they followed his trail from Chicago back to his front door."

"Did the feds catch him?"

"Simpson's competition in Chicago got to him first. Came to a bad end in Compton County."

"What do you mean, bad end?"

"Shot in the head."

A shudder ran down Marcello's back.

"Shipping out of Cumberland will be safer. The train comes every day for coal, and you're only two blocks from the tracks. It makes sense to find places in town for quick transfer."

"Who else is holding moonshine?"

"Besides Angelo? The Kaucheks and Delgatos."

"Don't tell them I'm storing it."

"I won't."

"Swear to me." Marcello's voice rose.

"I swear, Marcello."

"How do you load it on the train without getting caught?"

"I have people at the railroad."

"I should have guessed." Marcello bristled. Luisa was opposed to hiding moonshine *before* the raid. It was only a matter of time before word of it spread to Cumberland. She would be furious, and he could hardly blame her.

They worked alongside each other in an awkward silence. An hour later, the dugout was large enough to hold four kegs, ten gallons each. They rigged the cargo net with a rope to lower and lift the kegs. Adding hinges and a handle on the trap door finished their work. Lucas swept up the dirt, and Marcello unrolled the rug over the trap door.

"Finito," said Lucas as he brushed his hands together. He pulled a flask from the pocket of his jacket and took a swig before offering it to Marcello. "Have some Blue Moon."

Marcello took a gulp. "Wow, strong stuff." His eyes watered.

Lucas smiled. "I'll bring your whiskey kegs the next time Cheap John comes peddling his wares in town. It's a good distraction."

Marcello didn't answer.

Lucas sensed Marcello's uneasiness. "Having doubts?"

"I don't want trouble."

Lucas put a hand on Marcello's shoulder. "If you want out, just say the word, but if you're in, you're in all the way. Some of my buyers in Denver have mob connections. These guys fight for control. Even the locals in Silverton and Cumberland don't give an inch. More than anything, you must be tight-lipped. If word leaks out about our operation, the whole thing comes crashing down."

Marcello looked at his brother with mixed emotions. Lucas had climbed to the top of the bootlegging business. He led two lives—as a strong family man with ties to his community and as a player in the shady world of bootlegging. Lucas did things Marcello would never consider.

"It's hard to argue with your success." Marcello reached for the flask and tipped back his head.

"You have to stay one step ahead of your competition," Lucas said. "A little luck doesn't hurt, either."

"But the risks—"

"Prohibition's a stupid law. You'd be surprised the number of bootleggers in our county alone. Silverton's getting quite a reputation. It's known as Little Chicago." Lucas went on. "Things will quiet down now. Revenuers have a pattern—stake out a town, raid it, and move on."

"How do you know that?"

"I've been in this business close to five years now. I have people who watch the feds. They took us by surprise last night, but that won't happen again. I'll fix the problem."

"You've always put family first. That's not changed?" Lucas's answer was important to Marcello.

"I'll look out for you and your family. That's a promise." Lucas extended his hand, and they shook.

Still holding Lucas's hand, Marcello gave his older brother a somber look. "I'll count on that, but if any trouble comes to my family, you'll have to answer to me."

Lucas gave Marcello a decisive nod.

Sunday morning Marcello rose before dawn and dressed quickly in the cold bedroom. He poked the embers in the kitchen stove and coaxed life into the firebox, adding kindling and chunks of coal until warmth spread throughout the room. He rubbed his hands together and waited impatiently for Luisa to rise. He had to tell her about the dugout this morning. If she wouldn't change her mind about bootlegging, he had to convince her to tolerate it.

"You're up early." Luisa pulled her wool cardigan close as she came into the kitchen. She hummed while filling the coffee pot and set out the cast iron skillet. "You sleep all right?"

"Well enough," Marcello answered. Moments later the aroma of coffee filled the room, a pleasing antidote to the tension that churned inside him. "Luisa, I have something to tell you."

"Yes?"

"Lucas and I built a dugout yesterday while you were in town."

Luisa stiffened. She spun around, the color rising in her cheeks, and exclaimed, "After everything I said, you've gone ahead with this? You know how I feel—"

"Luisa," Marcello broke in, "I want to put your mind at ease." He waited for another wave of anger.

Instead, she turned her back on him and laid strips of bacon in the skillet. In an even tone she asked, "Where is it?"

"In our bedroom, under the rug."

Marcello heard her intake of breath. "You expect me to sleep in a bed above illegal goods?" Her rebuke hung in the air while the bacon sizzled. Finally, she said, "And the children?"

"They can't know. They'd never keep the secret."

Luisa set her fork aside, turned to Marcello, and crossed her arms. "How do you expect to put my mind at ease?" Her voice was icy.

"Lucas knows his business. He's been selling for nearly five years. He's smart, he's capable. He has a network—neighbors, miners, railroaders—people all over the county are involved with this. And he's cautious. He swears everything will be all right. I trust him."

"How will he bring it here?" Luisa arched her eyebrows.

"Horse and wagon. He plans to come when Cheap John is in town. The men will be at work, the women will be shopping with their young ones, and the older children will be at school."

"So, I won't be here?"

"Better if you aren't."

"What happens when Cheap John stops coming in the winter?" she challenged.

"Lucas will deliver in the dark—early morning or late at night."

"If deliveries are made when the children are awake, I'm taking them to Angelo's. Rosa and I agree on this, and you can't talk me out of it." Luisa's gaze never wavered.

"Angelo told me."

Luisa parted the gingham curtains at the window. Marcello rose from the table and stood behind her. He put his hands on her shoulders. They watched the cold fingers of a gray dawn creep over Oyster Ridge. She shivered, and Marcello wrapped his arms around her.

"Lucas and I will look out for the family," he whispered. He bent his head and nuzzled his cheek against hers.

Luisa pulled away and turned to face him. "Our plan was to come here and work hard, not to break the law and throw it all away."

"Luisa, I don't want to fight."

"You give me no choice."

He grasped one of her hands and held it against his chest. "I'm your husband. Respect my choice."

Luisa fixed her anxious gaze on Marcello. "When I see you so determined to do this, I feel like . . ."

"What?"

The crease in her brow deepened. "I don't know you anymore. I'm losing the Marcello I fell in love with." Her voice broke. "You take chances my Marcello never would."

Marcello looked lovingly into her eyes. "You'll never lose me." He kissed her tenderly. He wrapped his arms around her and whispered into her hair, "If I'm changing at all, I'm becoming a better provider. I'll give us a better future."

"I have to protect the children. The first sign of trouble—"

"I know." Marcello leaned back and tipped his head to one side. He smoothed her dark hair away from her troubled face. "How can you doubt my love for you?"

"I don't doubt your love." She opened her mouth to say more but Marcello put his finger to her lips, pulled her close, and kissed her again.

Chapter 34

Whiskey delivery began the next week, during Cheap John's last visit to Cumberland before winter set in. Marcello's dugout now hid four kegs of moonshine. For the next two months, the exchanges took place quietly and efficiently while Cumberland slept. Lucas paid Marcello for two months' storage, and the ten dollars bought Tony a new winter coat for seven dollars and eighty-five cents, with two dollars and fifteen cents left for savings. True to her word, Luisa bundled up the children and slogged through snowdrifts with them to Angelo's during daytime deliveries. When they slept and risk seemed minimal, Luisa's rosary was not far from her fingers.

Marcello hunched his shoulders against the biting cold on his walk to the mine. His breath hung like frozen crystals in the frigid February air. It had been three months since Jim's death. With the loss of his brother, Marcello had also lost his partner in the mine. The crew chief paired him with Angelo, whose even temper and skill were a reassuring presence for Marcello. Working side-by-side helped the brothers cope with Jim's death.

At lunch Angelo asked, "Have you heard about Lucas's farm?"

Marcello stopped chewing his bacon sandwich. "What?"

"It's in Utah, about a hundred miles from here, outside Clearfield." Angelo tipped his water container and drank.

"He bought a farm? Why Utah?" Marcello wondered.

"He said the soil is good for crops, and he raved about the

mountains. Reminds him of Italy. For now, he has renters working the farm."

Marcello sighed. "I have to hand it to him. He keeps cashing in on the American dream."

"Everything he touches—" began Angelo.

"—turns to gold?" Marcello finished. "I'd be happy just to own a house." He turned to Angelo. "Someday, I will."

Marcello stood on his porch at the end of the day and shook the coal dust out of his coat and cap before he went inside. He pulled back his shirtsleeve and checked his forearm, bruised and swollen from a heavy chunk of falling coal. He didn't notice Luisa until she was standing in front of him.

Tears brimmed in her eyes. "Marcello, I don't know what to do." Tony and Sophia hung in the background and avoided eye contact with their papa while they set the table. Luisa wrung her hands as the words tumbled out. "Roberto and Tomas were playing with the Abramov boys this afternoon. I went to the outhouse and when I came back, I found them in our bedroom."

"Don't tell me." Marcello slapped his hand to his forehead as if he knew what was coming.

"The trap door was open. They found the moonshine!"

Marcello clenched his jaw and felt the color rise in his neck. "Where are they?"

"In their room." She ran her hands nervously over her apron. "Should we say something to Oleg and Elsa?"

"I'll take care of the boys first." Marcello turned to the closed bedroom door and thundered, "Roberto, Tomas, come here!"

Roberto came first, his eyes wide as he approached his father and stood before him. His lower lip trembled. Tomas followed, stood beside his brother, and stared at his shoes.

"You were in our bedroom?"

"Yes," the boys mumbled together.

"Why?"

Roberto swallowed. "We were playing marbles."

"One of mine rolled under the door," Tomas said, "so we went in to get it."

"I told him not to," Roberto offered in defense.

"You came in, too," Tomas shot back at his brother. "You always blame—"

"Basta!" The veins on Marcello's neck bulged. "How did you find the dugout?"

The boys stared at each other. Finally, Tomas said, "I crawled under the bed to look for my marble and the rug moved, and that's when I saw it."

"You shouldn't have opened the trap door." The boys' heads drooped. "Look at me when I'm talking to you." Their heads shot up. "Did Leon and Dimitri look inside the dugout?"

The boys nodded. Roberto fought back tears.

"From now on, don't talk about the dugout to anyone, and don't go near our bedroom." He leaned into their faces. *"Lei capisce?"*

The boys nodded silently.

Marcello turned to Tony and Sophia. "The same goes for you two. Go to your room, all of you. *Scapa via.*" The children hurried away and shut the door behind them. Marcello slumped into a chair. "No trouble for two months, and now this happens."

"What should we do?"

Marcello raked his fingers through his gritty hair. "I'll think about it after supper."

Luisa caught sight of Marcello's arm and frowned at the bruise. "What happened?"

"It's nothing."

She gave it a closer look. "The skin's broken. I'll get the salve." Their gazes locked, and Marcello saw fear in Luisa's face. He knew it had nothing to do with his arm. He needed to reassure her, but the knot in his stomach forced him to face the truth: their secret had been discovered, and the consequences could be devastating.

That night Marcello and Luisa huddled under their quilts while wind howled outside the window.

"I knew this would happen." Luisa sounded desperate.

Marcello rolled onto his side and faced her. He was silent for a moment. "Maybe this isn't as bad as I thought. The neighbor boys saw kegs in our dugout. Everybody knows I make my own wine, so why *wouldn't* we have kegs in our dugout?"

Luisa was silent.

"It's possible Leon and Dimitri will think nothing of it."

"So, we do nothing?"

"For now." The wind swelled around the corners of the house. Luisa pulled the quilt tighter under her chin, chilled by the cold night and the lingering fear of the dugout's discovery. She closed her eyes, but sleep wouldn't come.

"Marcello?"

"Yes?"

"Get rid of it."

Marcello reached for her hand, but she pulled it away. "I'll tell Lucas what happened. He'll know if we should move the whiskey," Marcello said, trying to reassure her.

Luisa stared at the ceiling. When the first streaks of dawn penetrated the bedroom window, she knew fear had won the battle of the night, and neither of them had slept.

As a precaution, Lucas removed the whiskey from Marcello's house and waited. Nothing happened. After two weeks, Lucas restocked Marcello's dugout and deliveries resumed without incident. The winter snow melted into spring, gossip about impending raids ceased, and revenuers disappeared to faraway towns in other counties. Luisa embraced the calm that returned to their home.

Sophia spied a meadowlark perched on the clothesline post while she helped Luisa put away the breakfast dishes. "Look, Mama." Sophia pointed out the window and the yellow-breasted bird began its seven-note melody to the cloudless April sky.

"A sure sign of spring." Luisa sighed happily with the departure of frigid wind and drifts of snow, humming while she gathered the rugs to air on the clothesline.

Roberto and Tomas stood watch on the porch for Dominic, who had promised to show the children a surprise this morning. A horn sounded. "There he is!" shouted Roberto. The family spilled into the street as a shiny Studebaker touring car came to a stop in front of them.

"What do you think?" Dominic beamed from behind the steering wheel. "It's the 1924 touring car from the dealer in Kemmerer."

"Wow!" Tony gushed. He stared at the circular Studebaker hood ornament perched on the chrome-edged radiator between the headlights.

"It's really yours?" Tomas asked, wide-eyed.

Marcello gave a low whistle. "It's a beauty, Dominic." He circled the car and viewed the dark green finish, the four doors with chrome handles, and the shiny black fenders that curved over the whitewall tires. "If your papa could see you now."

"He wouldn't believe his eyes. I can hardly believe it myself." Dominic waved them into the car. "We're going for a ride." The children squealed with excitement and piled into the open-air automobile, Marcello in front with Tomas on his lap and Luisa sharing the backseat with Tony, Roberto, and Sophia.

Luisa ran her hand over the brass fittings on the door and the tufted leather seats. "It's beautiful. Oh, look—there's carpet on the floor."

"Are you rich, Uncle Dominic?" Roberto asked.

"No," he chuckled, "but I *am* a bachelor."

"What does that mean?" Tomas frowned.

"I think you must be rich to have such a fancy car," Sophia chimed in.

Dominic started the engine and let out the clutch, and the car lurched forward, bumping down the rutted street.

"Honk your horn," Tomas said. Dominic laid on the horn as they passed the Delgatos and Broskis who lived at the end of the street, which brought gaping stares from them and peals of laughter from the Corsi children.

"The horn sounds like a goose," Sophia giggled.

Luisa leaned over the front street. "Drive to Angelo's. He and Rosa have to see your new car."

"First, I want to take you out on the Kemmerer road, so I can show you how fast this baby goes."

Once they were on the open road, Dominic accelerated, and the wind hit them full in the face. Luisa gulped the air and grinned.

Tony hollered from the back, "How fast are we going?"

"Forty-five miles an hour," Dominic called over his shoulder.

"Ooowee!" shouted Marcello over the wind. "Reminds me of our train ride from Lanzo. Remember hanging out the windows?" He grinned at Dominic.

Dominic sped down the road, low hills unwinding around them, hitting an occasional bump that sent everyone out of their seats, shrieking with laughter. Dominic turned the car around, and when they returned to Cumberland, the Corsis waved wildly to their neighbors—Abramovs, McGregors, Constantines—and the slew of strangers gawking with envy and curiosity until Dominic had driven down every street in town twice.

"Have you seen this?" Angelo tapped the flyer posted on the

bulletin board in the mine office. He and Marcello had just picked up their paychecks and were heading home. Marcello leaned over Angelo's shoulder and read the notice:

All employees of Cumberland Mine
Meeting with Union Pacific Coal Company
Representative
Friday, April 30 at 7 o'clock PM
Town Hall

"Wonder what that's about," Marcello asked. "Must be important if they're having it after supper."

"Yeah, and somebody from the company's coming."

"Guess we'll find out Friday." Marcello slipped his paycheck into his shirt pocket. "Come on. I'm ready to call it a day."

The night of the meeting, Marcello walked to the town hall with Oleg and Angelo. They wound their way through the crowded hall and found seats beside Mick.

"Heard anything?" Marcello asked.

"Nothing," Mick said, "and that's odd. We usually have some idea why they call these meetings."

"Don't know if that's good or bad," said Angelo.

The miners quickly filled the chairs, and the overflow stood along the walls. Three men approached the lectern at the front of the hall, and the room quieted. Mr. Hopkins, the mine supervisor, called the meeting to order. "Lyman Fields is vice president of operations in southwest Wyoming for Union Pacific Coal. He has some remarks to make, so I'll turn the meeting over to him."

Mr. Fields stepped forward. "Good evening, gentlemen." There was a smattering of laughter from the miners, unaccustomed to such a formal greeting. "For the past two months we've been meeting with Mr. Hopkins and your union representative, Mr. Phillips, along with the board of directors from

Union Pacific Coal. Our talks involved changes in operations. We wanted to have a plan in place when we announced these changes."

A murmur rippled through the room, and the men shifted in their chairs. Mr. Fields looked out over the miners. "The seams of coal in Cumberland are nearly mined out. We're estimating that within six months we'll have no choice but to close the mine."

Chapter 35

The air went out of the room. Marcello sat stunned.

"Let me assure you," Mr. Fields said to a stone-silent room, "no one working in Cumberland Mine will lose his job due to the closure." There was an audible release of tension among the miners. "Production at Cumberland Mine the past three years has been among the best in Wyoming, thanks to the workforce here, so the company is rewarding you with transfers. I don't need to tell you how unusual this is. The sooner you choose a mine at either Spring Hill or Elk River, the better your chance of getting your first choice. We'll assign those who don't indicate a preference."

Marcello whispered to Angelo, "Can you believe this?"

Angelo shook his head, a dazed expression on his face.

Mr. Fields spoke. "We have contracted with a company in Salt Lake to move the houses from Cumberland to Spring Hill—"

Move the houses? Marcello's heart raced. The whiskey!

". . . in addition, we've talked with the school board and will move the schoolhouse to Spring Hill. We'll transport the children to and from school in coal wagons fitted with seats. These changes will take place over several months." He paused and drew a deep breath. "I'm sure you have questions. Mr. Hopkins, Mr. Phillips, and I will try to answer them the best we can."

Hands shot up, and questions rained down on Mr. Fields.

"How long's the company known about this?" a voice shouted.

"You sure there's enough jobs for everyone?" a miner hollered from the back.

"Will we work half shifts?" Ian McGregor asked. "How can you employ all of us full time?"

"What kind of jobs—night shifts? Shooters? I ain't gonna set off no explosives in the mine," an agitated miner said, which prompted a round of questions that ricocheted around the hall like volleys from rifles. Tempers flared, and the mood changed from shock to anger. Mr. Fields pulled a large handkerchief from his pocket and wiped beads of sweat from his balding head.

"Quiet, please." He raised both arms in an appeal for calm. "I know this comes as a shock, but let's keep order." He dabbed his forehead again, and the room quieted.

Marcello rose from his chair. "Will our wages be the same?"

"Yes, you'll be paid the same salary." The miners mumbled approval.

Angelo raised his hand. "How soon do we have to decide where we want to work?"

"Tell us your preference as soon as possible. We'll start phasing out mining here two months from now, in June. We'll put workers on new shifts at Spring Hill and Elk River in the order that we move houses, starting on the south side of Cumberland.

The meeting wore on. The air in the hall was stifling with the sweat of bodies and the heat of emotion. A trickle of sweat slid down Marcello's back. When the questions were exhausted, the hall fell silent. Mr. Field concluded, "Mr. Phillips has represented you and your interests throughout this process. Union Pacific has as much riding on this as you. We'll do the right thing for everyone involved."

Afterward, Marcello and his brothers stood outside the meeting hall in the twilight. Ian McGregor crossed his thick arms and rocked back on his heels. "This is a fine kettle of fish."

"I didn't think this would happen for years," Marcello said.

Angelo spoke with uncharacteristic urgency. "What'll we do now?"

"Choose between Spring Hill and Elk River," Marcello said.

"Suppose there aren't enough jobs for everyone?" Oleg Abramov asked.

"I wondered the same thing," Marcello said. "Maybe they expect some of us to quit the mine."

"I'm quitting," said Mick.

"What?" Angelo and Marcello spoke in unison as their heads swiveled toward Mick.

"I'm ready to farm full-time."

"You'd give up your salary?" Dominic asked.

"I've been thinking about it for a while. I can manage with income from the farm." He added, "Theresa would just as soon I quit the mine anyway."

"If I know my Elsa, she'll want to move wherever the Corsis move," Oleg said.

"That goes for me, too," Dominic said.

"The mine's closing, the houses and school will be moved—this place will be a ghost town," Angelo said.

The tension in Marcello's shoulders burned like a hot knife jabbed in his muscles. He rolled his head side to side, trying to ease the tightness. "Remember what Papa used to say: 'When you have a big decision to make, sleep on it.' "

"Dormiresuesso," Mick said.

"I'll need at least one night for this." Marcello's laugh rang hollow.

The brothers said good night, and Marcello headed home with Angelo through streets that were soon to stand empty, not knowing where he'd work or how to rid his house of moonshine. He doubted he'd sleep at all.

During May and June, every conversation in Cumberland centered on the closure of the mine. Marcello and Luisa caught up on the latest gossip every Sunday after Mass and lingered with parishioners outside church.

"We're moving to Elk River," Stanley Kauchek said. "My brother lives there. Seems like the obvious place for us." His wife nodded in agreement.

"Angelo and I have decided on Spring Hill," Marcello said.

"That's where we're moving," Mrs. Broski gushed, "unless my second cousin in Idaho finds work for my husband."

"There's a coal mine south of Boise—" Mr. Broski began.

"But we're not sure about the work yet," Mrs. Broski interrupted. She smoothed the folds of her skirt over her ample figure. "But I always tell Mr. Broski—"

Jakub Broski cleared his throat. "Like I was saying, there's a coal mine near Boise."

"I hope it works out," Marcello said. "We—"

"—'course my cousin's not the most reliable person—" Mrs. Broski took a breath, ready with more details.

Marcello gave Luisa a wink. "We should be going—Sunday dinner and all." They smiled with a nod and took their leave.

Marcello loosened his tie, and Luisa slipped her arm through his. The brilliant sun lit up her sapphire blue dress, a reflection of the June sky. Their footsteps thumped on the wooden walkway as they followed the children through the peaceful streets of Cumberland. Roberto and Tomas ran ahead, stretching the seams of their knickers to near splitting. Sophia chased after them in her new white eyelet dress, her long curls and hair ribbons flying behind her.

Marcello had approached Lucas about an increase in storage

payment from five to ten dollars a month. If Lucas could afford a farm, Marcello thought, this was a reasonable request. To his surprise, Lucas agreed without a counteroffer. The extra income of the past six months had given Marcello a nice cushion between monthly expenses and his paycheck. As they walked through the streets of town, Marcello noted with pride how fine his family looked in their Sunday best.

After learning the plan to relocate houses from Cumberland, Lucas searched for a place to hide Marcello's moonshine. He scouted a branch of the Hamsfork River and found a dense growth of brush and willow trees along the banks farther out in the county. Union Pacific wouldn't move employees for another two months, in August, ample time to move his stash from Marcello's dugout.

Marcello, Angelo, Dominic, and neighbor Oleg agreed to move to Spring Hill, only three miles down the road, but doubts needled Marcello. If he moved to Spring Hill, and it closed in a year or two, what then? Move his family to the next mine? And the next?

"Papa, I want to ask you something." Tony's words interrupted Marcello's thoughts.

He turned to his son. "What is it?"

"I talked to Mr. Hopkins last week."

"The mine foreman? Why?" Marcello gave Tony a sideways glance.

"I asked if there was a job for me during the summer at the mine."

Marcello and Luisa stopped in their tracks. Marcello looked at Luisa, who stared back in shock. He turned to Tony. "What did Mr. Hopkins say?"

"He said he would give me a job on one condition."

"What was it?"

"I'd be your apprentice."

Marcello saw the eagerness in Tony's face. "Since when have you wanted to work in the mine?"

"Always seemed like what I'd do, just like you."

Marcello was astonished. His son had witnessed the worst of mining in the death of his uncle Roberto. Two years ago, a gas explosion in nearby Flatbush killed twenty-nine men. Tony had attended funerals and watched families weep over their dead loved ones. In spite of it all, he wanted to be a miner.

Marcello cleared his throat. "No."

Tony looked at his father, puzzled. "What?"

"My answer is no."

"But Jakub and Bert are getting jobs—"

"I don't care what your friends do. *You* will go to high school and graduate. I won't apprentice you or your brothers in the mine." Marcello started to walk at a brisk pace, and Tony ran to catch up.

"But, Papa, in a few years, I could earn good money like you."

"You're only twelve. You'll finish high school and find a job that pays *better* than a miner."

"That's your answer? 'No'?"

"That's my answer."

When they reached the house, Tony hesitated and waited for his papa to speak further. Marcello stood on the porch, his lips pressed firmly together. Disappointed, Tony went inside without another word. Marcello stood with Luisa until the children were inside and let out the breath he'd been holding. Luisa laid her hand on his arm.

"Thank you," she whispered, her face flooded with relief, "for saying no."

"When did he decide to be a miner? Did he tell you?"

Luisa shook her head.

Marcello stared past her into the distance. "This changes

everything."

"What do you mean?"

Marcello began to pace their small porch. "Mining was my choice, but it's not for Tony. He's a good student, and he does well in school."

"His teacher told me he should graduate high school," Luisa added.

"I want him to dream big, just like we did before we came here, but I want him to see there's more to life than what Cumberland offers," Marcello went on, his voice rising with passion. "And not just Tony, but Roberto and Tomas. I'll not allow our boys to be miners. It's too dangerous. Besides, the mine's closing, the town's moving. What kind of future is that? Instead of deciding which mine to work at, I should take our family away, leave mining behind, and show the boys other ways to earn a living."

"What? Quit your job?" A line formed between Luisa's eyebrows. "Where would we go? How would you support us?"

"I'd find something . . ."

"But—"

His face lit up. "I could work for Lucas. I'll bet I could start tomorrow. Full-time."

Luisa's jaw dropped.

Chapter 36

Neither of them spoke.

Marcello's announcement was so unexpected, Luisa was at a loss for words. At length she swallowed her amazement and found her voice. "Work for Lucas? Doing what—or do I want to know?"

"He offered me work years ago when he first bought the saloon. Now, with his big operation, he needs help distilling whiskey, he needs drivers—there are any number of things I could do."

Luisa put both hands on her hips. "You'd make as much money as you do now in the mine?"

"Eventually, yes." Marcello spoke confidently.

"Stop and think what this means," Luisa pressed.

"I know exactly what it means. Providing for you and the children is my responsibility. But now, there's a bigger problem—keeping our boys out of the mine. Tony will do as I say for now, but not when he's older. If we left Cumberland and moved to Silverton—"

"So, you want him to watch you take part in something illegal? To my mind, that's worse."

"Nothing's worse than losing someone you love in the mine. Nothing. Have you forgotten Roberto—"

"How dare you suggest I've forgotten my own brother!" Tears stung her eyes. She shouted at Marcello. "I remember the pain every day. I don't want our boys to die in the mine like he did.

What do you take me for?" Angry tears spilled down her cheeks. "It's bad enough to have those illegal goods in our house. But work for Lucas? I don't want any part of it. I have a say in this, Marcello. I have a say!" She turned on her heel and stormed into the house, banging the door in his face.

She had disrespected Marcello, shouted at him on their front porch for all to hear, but she didn't care. Bootlegging! The thought of it rose like bile in her throat. Marcello was so stubborn in support of Lucas, he'd lost sight of everything else. When he talked like this, he became a stranger, and that chilled her to the bone. Luisa went straight to the bedroom and took off her Sunday dress. At the basin she wiped her face with a damp washcloth, put on a cotton blouse and skirt, and headed for the kitchen. She pulled an apron over her head and opened a bag of cornmeal to make polenta, ignoring everyone in the house.

They didn't mention the argument the rest of the day. Or the next. They spoke to each other with icy politeness and only when necessary, and they lay in bed at night with their backs to each other. By midweek, the tension had frayed Luisa's nerves to the point of exhaustion. She had to do something.

The next evening, Luisa carried dishwater from supper dishes outside and watered the scarlet geraniums potted in large tobacco cans on the front steps. She rationed the water for the vegetables Marcello tended in the small garden beside the porch.

"Need some water?" she asked.

Marcello nodded as he turned over the dirt around the pole beans climbing wooden stakes. "Maybe I'll have better luck with them this year." He finished working the soil and leaned the hoe against the porch. They sat beside each other on the front steps.

Luisa turned to Marcello and cleared her throat. "Are we to stay angry forever?"

Marcello avoided her gaze and brushed the dirt off his pant leg.

"When you said you'd quit the mine, I didn't know what to think." She drew a breath. "I'm afraid."

"I'm serious about keeping the boys from mining." Marcello leaned forward, resting his forearms on his knees. "I've never regretted being a miner, even in the sad days after Roberto died. But it taught me a lesson: I swore my sons would never be miners."

"If you quit the mine . . ." Luisa paused and chose her words carefully. "I can help out and take in laundry or cook meals for the bachelors—"

"I'll not have my wife support us." Marcello's voice was brusque.

"That's not what I meant. I *want* to help. Other wives take in laundry or do mending. Things are different in America—"

"Some things should stay the same. I'll take care of us, Luisa. Dominic will drive me to see Lucas on Saturday."

Luisa held her ground. "After you see Lucas, tell me his offer *before* you give him an answer."

Marcello pulled his pipe from the front pocket of his overalls. Luisa watched him chew on the stem as he thought over her request. "I'll let you know," he said. "But if it's a good offer, I'm taking it."

The sun peeked over Oyster Ridge when Marcello finished milking his three cows housed in the company barn. "Oh, good," said Luisa as she eyed the overflowing pail he set on the kitchen counter. "Just finished the last of the milk."

Marcello leaned over Luisa's shoulder and watched her dip thick slices of homemade bread in a mixture of milk and eggs. The bread sizzled when it landed in the buttery skillet and released a sweet aroma of cinnamon and vanilla. "Smells mighty good," he said.

"When's breakfast ready, Mama?" Tomas scooted his chair close to the table, picked up his fork, and danced it around the edge of his plate.

"In a minute. Sophia, set the butter out, please." Luisa brought a platter of French toast to the table and put two slices on Marcello's plate before the children helped themselves. *"Mangia."*

Marcello smothered his breakfast with cherry jelly and butter. "I'm so hungry, I could eat a bear."

Roberto swallowed a mouthful. "You couldn't eat a bear, Papa," he giggled.

"Oh, yes, I—"

The door flew open, and Tony came in, breathless, carrying the water bucket. "Papa, something's wrong. Dominic's running toward the house, but I couldn't tell what he was saying."

At that moment, Dominic burst into the kitchen in a state of panic.

"We've got trouble, Marcello. They're in town right now, and they're coming this way."

"Who's in town?"

"The revenuers! Two cars and a truck. I saw them drive in from the main road. They're raiding the houses! They're on the next block!"

Marcello leaped to his feet and sent his fork clattering to the floor. "The whiskey!"

"This can't be happening." Luisa brought her hands to her mouth. The children stopped eating and looked at their papa and mama, frowns on their faces.

"We can't wait for a truck, we have to move it now." Dominic looked desperate.

Marcello hesitated for a split second. "Your car—we'll put it in your car." He went to the front window and peered out.

"Where are they now?"

"They just left Constantine's house. When they're done with that street, ours will be next."

"If they've already gone through Constantine's," Marcello said, turning to Dominic, "then that's the direction to take it. Pull your car up to the side of our house. If we keep an eye out, I don't think they'll see us."

Dominic was out the door.

"I'm taking the children to Angelo's," Luisa declared.

"It's not safe. Revenuers will go through his house, too," Marcello said.

Luisa twisted her hands together. "Where, then?"

"In the car with Dominic." Marcello didn't wait for her response. "Luisa, go to the porch and watch for the revenuers. Tony, help me with the kegs." Marcello strode to the bedroom with Tony close behind. They unlatched the trap door and hoisted the first keg out of the dugout. After Dominic moved the car, he joined Marcello in the bedroom and helped lift the remaining kegs from the dugout. They carried the first one to the kitchen and stopped at the front door.

"Any sign of revenuers?" Marcello called through the closed door.

"No." Luisa's voice trembled.

"The car's right beside the house, facing the street," said Dominic.

"Good," said Marcello. "You ready?"

Dominic nodded. They carried the keg to the car and set in on the floor of the backseat. Marcello glanced down the street but saw no activity. Tony, Roberto, and Tomas rolled the second keg onto the porch. "Dominic and I'll get the rest," he told Tony. "Go to your bedroom, roll up your rug, and bring it out here."

"Our rug?" Tony asked.

"Yes. Hurry!"

They fitted four kegs on the floor of the backseat. The boys brought the braided rug from their bedroom, and Marcello spread it over the kegs.

"Marcello, look!" Luisa leaned over the porch and pointed to the street behind their house. "There they are!"

Two cars and a flatbed truck were parked in front of Kauchek's house. A crowd of neighbors gathered in the street and watched the revenuers carry kegs from the house and stack them on the truck. Marcello counted eight men, three in work shirts and overalls, the rest in jackets and ties. All of them wore fedoras.

"We don't have much time." Dominic looked anxiously at Marcello.

"Tony, Roberto, Sophia, climb in the backseat," Marcello ordered. "Luisa, sit in front. Tomas, squeeze in beside Mama."

"What about you?" Luisa asked.

"I'm staying here," Marcello answered.

"What? No!" Luisa's eyes widened with fear.

"If no one's here, they might lie about finding whiskey. They might destroy our house—who knows what else."

"But—"

"I'll be fine. Now, go!"

Dominic pulled the car out onto their street, drove to the end of the block and disappeared around the corner.

Marcello hurried back inside the house and carried sacks of potatoes and carrots from the shed to the dugout. He lugged a crate with bottles of homemade wine from the cellar and lowered it into the dugout beside the vegetables, latched the trapdoor and pulled the rug over it. Plates of uneaten food sat on the kitchen table. He cleared away all the dishes except his and sat. He took a deep breath, picked up his fork, and ate his cold breakfast.

Moments later, the approaching sound of vehicles brought Marcello to the porch. Two cars pulled up at Delgato's house at the end of their street, followed by the flatbed now loaded with kegs of moonshine. The truck sat with its engine running.

Marcello knew the Delgatos hid moonshine. Neighboring families, the McGregors, Broskis, and Abramovs, huddled together in the street, nervously watching the revenuers. Marcello's pulse pounded, his eyes on the Delgatos' front door. Ten minutes later the revenuers left empty-handed, split into two groups, and walked to the next houses.

Three more houses, and they'd be at Marcello's door.

He went inside and paced between the front window and the covered trap door in the bedroom. He noticed the coffeepot on the stove, wiped his sweaty palms on his pants, and poured coffee, milk, and sugar into his cup. The familiar flavors swirled in his mouth and calmed his nerves, helping him pretend this was a Saturday morning like any other. He took another swallow of coffee, pushed open the front door, and collided with a revenuer.

"Oh!" Marcello's heart pounded so violently, he was sure the revenuer could hear it. Coffee dribbled down the man's vest. Marcello struggled to keep his voice even. "Sorry. Didn't see you."

The round-faced man with a pasty complexion chomped down on the cigar butt between his teeth and held his badge up to Marcello's face. He pushed his way into the house, knocking Marcello's shoulder as he passed. A second man, stocky, with rolled-up shirtsleeves and hat, came onto the porch, gave Marcello a cold stare, and went inside. Marcello followed them and leaned against the doorjamb, acting uninterested, while they began their search.

In the shed off the kitchen, they turned over crates of turnips and onions, dumped a box of tools onto the floor, jerked sacks of flour from the cupboard, and felt the floor for loose boards.

"Do you have to—" Marcello began and stopped mid-sentence at the first man's piercing stare.

"You here alone? Where's your family?" the second man demanded.

"They're out of town," Marcello answered.

The two men split up to search the bedrooms. Marcello fought the impulse to grab them by their necks and heave them out of his house, but watched from his position in the doorway.

Moments later the first man hollered from Marcello's bedroom, "In here!" Marcello followed the partner into his bedroom where the revenuer knelt beside the exposed trap door.

"What we got here?" he sneered at Marcello and lifted the door. The smirks on the revenuers' faces turned to disgust as they stared at potatoes, carrots, and bottles of wine. "What the—" The first man glared at Marcello. "Nobody keeps vegetables in a bedroom dugout covered with a rug." He leaned into the dugout for a second look, then straightened up. "We know what you kept in here. We're not stupid."

Marcello shrugged his shoulders. "You've looked at all our storage."

The revenuer dropped the trap door with a bang. "We're gonna keep a sharp eye on you," he spat out. He leaned into Marcello's face and narrowed his eyes. "We'll git the whiskey, and we'll git you," he said, thumping Marcello's chest with a stubby finger. The two men stormed out of the house. "Nothin' here!" they shouted to the other revenuers in the street.

Marcello watched from the porch as they started their cars and drove around the corner to the next street. He steadied his coffee cup with both hands to keep it from shaking.

Chapter 37

Dominic gripped the steering wheel and drove slowly down the street, hoping to avoid unwanted attention. Luisa sat rigid, eyes on the street, her heart thudding in her chest.

"Mama, what's happening—"

"Be quiet, Roberto," Tony shushed. "Don't bother Mama."

Luisa glanced at Dominic and saw his eyes sweep from one side of the street to the other. It was Saturday, and most of the miners and their families were home. They stood on their porches, straining to glimpse the cars and truck that had just wheeled into town. Neighbors cut through the yards hurrying toward the commotion.

The Corsis rode in silence. Whenever they passed the open space between the houses, Dominic looked to his right for the revenuers one block over. He waited until the raid moved to the next street, then drove to Constantine's house, pulled up in the yard beside it, and turned off the motor. Luisa said nothing, her hands clenched in her lap. Dominic gave her a sideways glance. "You all right?"

"No." Her voice trembled with controlled anger. "We never should have hid . . ." She sucked in her breath and turned away.

From Constantine's yard, Dominic and Luisa had a clear view of the road leading out of town. The day was damp and windy. Yesterday's downpour left the creek on the west side of town spilling over its banks onto the road. Leaden clouds pressed down on the brow of the hills to the west, threatening more rain.

They waited.

"How long's it been?" Luisa kept her eyes on the road.

"An hour, maybe less," Dominic said.

"Mama, how long are we going sit here?" Tomas wiggled in the seat beside Luisa and looked up at her.

"I don't know."

"I'm hungry." His normally cheerful face was solemn.

"We can eat when we go home."

"When's that?" Sophia asked.

"When we see the men leave town." Luisa turned in her seat and looked into the anxious faces of her children. Tony's forehead creased with worry. Roberto fidgeted impatiently. Tears pooled in Sophia's eyes, and Luisa reached over the seat. "It'll be all right, dear." She patted Sophia's knee as a chilly breeze gusted from the north. "Warm enough?" she asked, moving her gaze from face to face. They all nodded silently. Luisa turned around, drew her shawl tighter, and hugged Tomas to her side.

"Mama, can we get out?" Roberto asked.

"No. Stay put."

The raid moved from street to street, away from them toward the other side of town, until they no longer saw the revenuers' cars or heard the grinding gears of the truck. The crowd noises grew faint.

"I think I see them leaving." Dominic strained his neck. "Yes, there they go." He pointed at the cars and truck heading out of town. The truck went a short distance and pulled off to the side of the road, while the two cars drove on and disappeared over the hill. Three men jumped out of the truck, climbed onto the flatbed, and pushed kegs off the back. They picked up sledgehammers and brought them down on the kegs with splintering crashes, until there was nothing left but a mountain of rubble.

Their job finished, the men climbed into the truck and drove away, the smell of whiskey trailing on the wind.

Marcello was waiting on the porch when Dominic pulled up in front of their house. "Go inside and wait in your room," he told the children. He turned to Luisa. "Are they all right?"

"They're upset," she managed.

Marcello led Luisa inside and held her hand as she sank into a chair. "And you?"

Luisa gave a tight nod, then froze at the sight of the overturned crates, the furniture askew, the vegetables dumped on the floor. She clutched her husband's arm. Her breathing quickened, and she turned fearful eyes to Marcello.

"They found the dugout," Marcello said.

Dominic fell into a chair. "Thank God we moved the kegs when we did."

"They were angry they didn't find any whiskey." Marcello drew a sharp breath. "They suspect we've been hiding moonshine and said they'd be watching us from now on."

Luisa felt the hair on the back of her neck stand up.

Marcello looked from Luisa to Dominic. "Did you have any trouble?"

"I parked beside Constantine's house. Leo never came outside—must have been afraid. We came back as soon as the revenuers left town."

"Marcello." Luisa felt her face flush. "It's too dangerous to keep the whiskey here." She slowed her breathing before she continued. "If they're watching us, we're not safe. This has to end."

Marcello met Luisa's gaze, his face empty of emotion. Dominic lowered his eyes and stared at the table.

Luisa raised her chin. "Don't bring it back in the house." There was a quiet resolve in her voice. "Take it away."

Marcello walked to the window that looked out on the rolling prairie. Luisa stared at his rigid silhouette and tried to read his thoughts. After the raid and the fear that gripped their family, she thought this should be an easy decision: protect the family whatever the cost.

She waited.

Dominic broke the silence. "Where would we take it?"

Without moving, Marcello said, "The new place along the river."

"When?"

Marcello set his jaw and turned to Dominic and Luisa. "Now."

"But it's broad daylight," Dominic protested. "The revenuers could be anywhere."

"Let's hope they went to Spring Hill or Silverton and aren't driving through the west county. Come on."

Luisa stood on the porch and watched the car speed off down the street. They couldn't drive the wretched moonshine away fast enough. But her relief to be rid of the bootleg was riddled with fear. The revenuers could be anywhere in the county. Now that Marcello was in their sights, the feds would follow him. She was certain they would chase after Dominic and Marcello and arrest them with the carload of moonshine. She was dangerously close to losing Marcello.

Luisa fought back the frightening scenarios and thought of Tony, Sophia, and the twins waiting inside, hungry, cold, and bewildered. Her courage was in tatters, frayed and useless as an old pair of britches. She doubted she had the strength to put on a brave face and reassure the children. Pulling her shawl tight around her shoulders, Luisa prayed for Marcello and walked back into the house.

"Come help with dinner," she called the children and tied the strings of her apron around her waist. Wide-eyed and silent, the children went about their tasks. Sophia helped pick up the vegetables from the floor, and Luisa placed a pot of water on the stove. Roberto and Tomas set the table while Tony left to refill the water bucket at the hydrant. Luisa forced herself to hum the old folk tune about the cuckoo bird she had sung to the children since they were babies. She sang the words in a whisper while she chopped carrots and plunked them into the pot. She repeated the verse, her voice stronger, and fear fell away from the children's faces.

Thunder rumbled in the distance. Dominic pressed on the accelerator and drove west on the county road, checking his rearview mirror every few seconds. Marcello swiveled in his seat, his eyes riveted on the road as it unwound behind them.

"I can see in the mirror if anyone's following us," Dominic said.

"Keep your eyes on the road," said Marcello. "I'll watch behind."

How it had come to this? Marcello planned to ask Lucas today about a full-time job. He was even prepared to ask about a partnership, although he hadn't told Luisa that part of his plan. Instead, his family had been forced to flee their home, and he and Dominic were scrambling to ditch the moonshine before the feds caught them. Marcello's mind raced with the speed of Dominic's Studebaker as he worked out their next move.

They drove to the Hamsfork River and followed a seldom-used road beside one of the tributaries that narrowed into a shallow creek dotted with trees along the banks. Dominic slowed the car to a crawl, until they came to a spot thick with underbrush. Marcello noted a gnarled cottonwood tree by the stream, which marked the place to hide the moonshine.

"This is it," said Marcello.

They got out of the car and scanned the surrounding hills. To their immense relief, they were alone. No one had followed them, and no one was lying in wait to arrest them. Thunder rumbled again, closer than before, followed by an eerie stillness.

Marcello smelled the dampness of the approaching rain. He tilted his head and strained to hear the usual sounds of the countryside. There were none. "I don't like this—"

"Stop, Marcello, you're spooking me," Dominic said. "Let's get this done."

They hefted the first keg from the car and carried it down the sloping embankment to the creek side. They glanced up and down the road for any sign of trouble before they ran back to the car for the next keg. By the time they carried the last keg to the creek, large drops of rain splattered their jackets. They slipped on the muddy embankment and lost their grip, sending the keg into the stream. Marcello and Dominic waded into the freezing water and hauled the keg back, struggling to keep their footing on the shifting bottom of the stream. The rain grew heavy and soaked their clothes. In their last effort, they dragged fallen tree limbs, dead branches, and brush to cover the kegs.

By the time they turned onto their street in Cumberland, the rain came down in torrents. Luisa threw open the front door and met them on the porch. Water trickled down their faces, their clothes clung to their bodies, and mud coated their pants and boots.

"It's done," Marcello said.

Relief washed over Luisa.

When Luisa heard the horn at the mine blare at five o'clock the next Monday, it signaled more than the end of the workday, it signified life returning to normal. She hummed happily as she prepared supper, sprinkling flour on the counter before rolling out dough for biscuits. It was good to have their life back. She smiled when Marcello walked through the door until she saw the look on his face and knew immediately something was terribly wrong.

"It's Lucas." Marcello blurted.

"What's happened?"

"He's been arrested." Marcello threw his jacket on a chair, his dirty face blotched with anger.

"What? No!" Luisa's hands went to her mouth.

"Julia left a message for me at the mine office. I called her back from the office phone when I got off work."

"What did she say?"

"She was so upset, I could hardly understand her. She said the revenuers showed up this afternoon and were searching the house. They must have been watching Lucas after the raid on Saturday."

"What will happen to him?"

"She said Mick is getting money for bail."

"This is horrible." Luisa crumpled into a chair. "Marcello, you promised this wouldn't happen."

"*Lucas* promised it wouldn't happen." Marcello ran his blackened fingers through his hair.

"What are you going to do?"

"Julia said there was nothing we could do right now. She's waiting for Lucas to get out of jail. I told her to call back if she wanted us to come."

Luisa nodded, numb with fear.

Julia hung up the phone in the Silverton mercantile after talking to Marcello and ran back down Main Street to her house. Revenuers swarmed the yard. The boys stood off to one side, their faces taut with fear, Frank and Peter with protective arms around their little brother, Marco. Two men laid a tape measure along the foundation. After determining the length, a man the others referred to as Brewster pushed his way into the house and down to the basement.

Julia rushed after him. "What are you doing?"

Ignoring her, he chomped on his cigar stub and paced off the length of the basement. When he reached the opposite wall, he stopped and frowned. "Not right," he muttered and strode the length of the basement a second time.

Julia clutched her chest, her heart pounding as though it would burst.

The man's puzzled look suddenly disappeared. "If the basement is smaller than the foundation . . ." He raced upstairs and returned with two men wielding sledgehammers. They tossed their suit coats aside, loosened their ties, and pushed up shirtsleeves. "It has to be behind that wall!" shouted Brewster. They walked to the far wall and swung.

"Stop!" Julia begged. "Please!" Tears filled her eyes.

The slam of hammers echoed off the basement walls as the men pounded, raising dust and sending chips of brick through the air. They hammered along the wall, higher and lower, their necks straining, but they couldn't find an opening. Brewster wheeled around and confronted Julia. "Where's the door?"

She shrank from him. "I—I don't know what you're talking about," she stammered.

"What do you mean, you don't know? You live here." He reeked of sweat and tobacco.

"I don't know anything about a door," she insisted, her voice trembling.

"Get something straight, lady. We've been watching your husband a long time. We know all about his operation. It's the biggest one west of Chicago. He bribes officials. He hides moonshine along the Hamsfork River and sends it to Denver on Union Pacific. We have orders from high up to close him down, whatever it takes, and that's what we're going to do!"

"I already told you—"

"If we have to come back tomorrow, you'll be sorry," he

snarled and stormed up the basement stairs.

Julia grabbed her skirt and ran upstairs behind him. "What do you mean?"

Without answering, Brewster strode out of the house into the yard. He conferred with two other revenuers, climbed into a truck, and drove off. By evening, the rest of the revenuers were gone, but Lucas was still in jail. Julia received word Mick couldn't raise the bail money until tomorrow.

After a restless night, Julia awoke the next morning to the sound of engines and grinding gears. She grabbed her shawl and hurried to the bedroom window. Two large cranes outfitted with metal booms, guy wires, and hoist ropes crawled down Main Street. She watched, frozen in place, as the cranes clipped limbs off the spindly trees on the narrow, dusty street. Heads appeared from neighbors' doors and windows, in fearful curiosity to see the advancing machines.

Heavy pounding on the front door sent her running downstairs. She threw open the front door and stared into the face of Brewster.

"Get out of the house. Now!" he ordered.

The cranes slowed as they neared the house. Julia's heart raced. "What are those? What are you going to do?" she cried, looking wildly from the machines to the revenuer.

"You had your chance," he said, his face set hard as stone.

"No!" Julia gasped a breath. "You can't come here and—"

"Yes, we can, and nobody can stop us." He spat on the ground and walked away.

CHAPTER 38

Dominic's car churned up the dusty road as it sped toward Silverton. Angelo leaned forward from the backseat. "What exactly did Julia say?" he asked.

Marcello's voice was strained with worry. "She was crying. She said Lucas was still in jail and the revenuers had come back."

"She must be terrified," Angelo said.

Marcello nodded. "She said they brought big machines and told her to get out of the house."

"Big machines? What does that mean?" Dominic asked.

"Damned if I know." Marcello shook his head. "*Questo è terribile.* None of this was supposed to happen."

Long before they turned down Main Street, they could see the tops of the cranes from a distance, spiking into the cloudless sky above the rooftops. Dominic pulled up next to the crowd in front of Lucas's house. Marcello's breath caught in his chest, and he tipped his head back, not believing the sight before him. "Dear God," he whispered.

"I didn't know such a thing was possible . . ." Angelo's voice trailed off.

Dominic's jaw dropped, and he made the sign of the cross.

Suspended above its foundation, secured by giant hooks on two large cranes with supporting timbers underneath, hung Lucas's house. A crowd of neighbors gaped at the spectacle in stunned silence. Marcello, Angelo, and Dominic climbed out of the car, unable to take their eyes off the white clapboard house hanging absurdly in the air.

They wove through the crowd to a cordoned-off area a few feet from the foundation and leaned over. It was the first time Marcello had seen the still, fully assembled. It was massive. It stood on the other side of the newly built basement wall, accessible through what looked like a heavy, spring-driven door. The space was vented to the outside through a tangle of wild rose bushes. Marcello marveled at the lengths Lucas had gone to conceal his still. A team of revenuers swarmed around it, congratulating themselves and shouting to another group of federal agents who peered into the basement from above.

Marcello stared at the exposed basement, then at the house suspended overhead, and feared the house would break apart, sending lumber crashing down on everything below. *"Non credo-questo!"* He was transfixed by the sight, even as he felt Angelo tugging on his arm.

"There's Julia." Angelo pointed the way, and they pressed through the crowd.

"Marcello, Angelo!" Julia burst into tears when they reached her. "I don't know what to do," she sobbed. "How can they do this?"

Marcello put his arm around her shoulder. He stared at the house, his disbelief turning to anger.

"Any word from Lucas?" Angelo asked anxiously.

She shook her head and wiped away tears. "We're still waiting."

The pain in her eyes stabbed Marcello's heart. He had seen that look every time Luisa had pleaded with him to stop bootlegging, and every time he had dismissed her objection as an unfounded overreaction. Now he saw Luisa's fears for what they were—the direct result of his actions, no matter how well-intentioned.

Lucas's boys huddled next to Julia. Marco clung to his mother's hand, tears in his eyes. Frank and Peter stared vacantly at their house, then looked at their mother with such sadness, Marcello had to turn away. In their faces, he saw Tony, Sophia, Roberto, and Tomas.

Marcello struggled to speak. "Do you want us to talk to the agents?"

"Would you? I tried, but they ignored me."

Marcello followed Angelo to the area near the basement. The scene swam before him like a bizarre nightmare. A supporting timber under the house groaned, and the house tilted like a toy suspended by a puppet master. The dining room table slid across the floor into the sideboard of dishes in an explosion of glass. The crowd gasped. The crane operator worked the levers to balance the house and sent the table scraping over broken dishes in the opposite direction. The table smashed through the picture window and crashed into the yard, spraying glass that sent neighbors running for cover. It was the only picture window in Silverton, Julia's pride and joy, and had set their house far above any other in town.

In the basement, sledgehammers slammed against wood and metal as revenuers smashed the six-foot-tall vats, splintering the wood and sending whiskey mash oozing over the floor. The neighbors returned to peer over the foundation, the sour smell of mash rising in the air. They gawked in disbelief at the size of the still, even as it was hacked to pieces. Revenuers hoisted gunnysacks of sugar onto their shoulders, climbed the stairway out of the basement, and tossed them onto the truck parked in the street.

Marcello suddenly sucked in his breath.

"What's wrong?" Angelo asked.

"That man over there," Marcello pointed to a revenuer chomping on a cigar. "He raided my house. Told me they were watching me." Marcello backed away from the foundation. "I can't let him see me here." Marcello slipped through the crowd, his head down, using the neighbors for cover until he reached Julia and Dominic in the back of the crowd. "I just saw one of the revenuers who raided my house—"

"Lucas!" A cry escaped Julia's lips as she stared past Marcello. Lucas and Mick approached from the street, Lucas lengthening his stride as he opened his arms to embrace Julia.

"Are you all right?" She sobbed into his chest.

"I'm fine," he murmured. He reached for his sons to include them in his embrace.

Marcello was flooded with relief at the sight of his brother. "Thank God you're out." He looked from Lucas to Mick. "Any trouble getting bail?"

"Lucas had it covered. It cost a hundred," said Mick.

Lucas drew Julia close to his side and spoke quietly to his brothers. "Thank you. It means everything that you . . ." He couldn't finish. He stood tall, his chin out, but for the first time in his life, Marcello saw fear in the eyes of Lucas Corsi. Lucas viewed the chaotic scene around him and raised his eyes to his house. "How the hell are they going to make this right?"

Loud voices drew their attention to the basement. "How're we supposed to get this thing out of here?" one of the men hollered. "This is the biggest still I've ever seen."

"Take it apart," barked a man leaning over the foundation.

Lucas's face flushed with anger as he watched the destruction, cringing with the blows of the sledgehammers. "This is insane!"

A moment later, Angelo joined them. "Spoke to one of the revenuers," he said. "They'll put the house on the foundation when they're through in the basement."

"When's that?" asked Lucas. "Whenever they feel like it?" His voice was brittle with contempt.

"He thought they'd be done before dark." Angelo tried to sound convincing.

"What about tonight?" Marcello asked. "Where will you stay?"

"There's room at the farm," Mick offered.

Julia managed a smile of gratitude. "Thank you."

"What else can we do?" asked Angelo.

Lucas shook his head. "Nothing. This could go on for hours. You might as well go home."

"Sure you'll be all right?" asked Marcello.

"Go," said Lucas. He embraced his brothers and Dominic.

"I'll drive Angelo and Marcello over tomorrow after work," Dominic said.

"Leave a message at the mining office if you need anything, anything at all." Marcello held Lucas in his gaze for a moment before he walked to the car.

They were silent on the ride back to Cumberland. The sun dipped behind the hills, streaking the sky orange and red, but Marcello didn't notice. His head throbbed with pain. He closed his eyes and saw his children's faces instead of Lucas's children, staring back, helpless and confused. He saw Luisa's face filled with torment, pleading with him to rid their lives of moonshine, a mother plagued with fear for her family, all because of him. If he continued to follow this course, he would drive her away, or worse, destroy their lives.

"Drive faster, Dominic. I have to get home."

Marcello burst into the kitchen and pulled Luisa from the rocking chair into his arms. He buried his head against her shoulder and held her tight. Luisa put her arms around him but said nothing.

"You tried to warn me, but I didn't listen. I didn't think it would come to this." He raised his head and looked into her eyes, overwhelmed by her devotion, and felt utterly worthless. He didn't deserve her. He turned away, trying to hide the shame he felt. "I'm sorry."

Luisa grabbed his hand and held it to her cheek until he turned back to her. His eyes brimmed with tears. Luisa's lips turned up in a trembling smile. "My dear husband." She pulled him to her and cried softly while they held on to each other.

Finally, she spoke. "What happened?"

They dried their eyes and sank into chairs at the table. "It was horrible." He shook his head, trying to rid himself of the images. "If I hadn't seen it myself, I'd never believe it." He recounted every detail from the moment they'd arrived in Silverton. He was done with half-truths.

Luisa's jaw dropped. "They did that to their house?" She shook her head in stunned disbelief. "Julia must have been terrified!"

"It wasn't until I saw her and the boys so scared that I knew how close our family was to disaster. It was like looking in a mirror and knowing it could happen to us."

Luisa reached for Marcello's hand and pressed it between both of hers.

"All I've ever wanted is to make a good life for us—you know that." Marcello searched her face.

"Of course." Luisa inhaled deeply. "But you never understood what *I* wanted."

"Didn't we want the same thing—to leave the poor life behind for a better life in America? That's been our dream. That was my promise to you."

"That dream belonged to both of us, but it costs too much if it puts your life in danger. Nothing matters if you're not at my side. I can live without shoes or a big house, but I can't live without you, Marcello."

All she wanted was him, their children, and a home. He

looked into her eyes and saw the girl he fell in love with. He saw that starry night on a hillside back home when all that mattered was their love for each other. They sat without speaking, holding each other's hands, the clock marking time in the silent room.

After a while, Luisa spoke, her voice hesitant. "What happens now?"

"I'll stay with the mine until I figure out something else. The possibilities—the dreams—are still there, but whatever I do, I won't put our family in danger." He stood and pulled Luisa into his arms again. He held her tight, treasuring her forgiveness. Whatever happened next, they would find a better way forward together.

Luisa fell asleep as soon as her head hit the pillow. Marcello was not so fortunate. Although exhausted from the trauma of the day, his mind would not rest. The sight of little Marco crying and the house suspended in the air played in a never-ending loop until he sat up in bed, his chest heaving. He looked over at Luisa sleeping peacefully and felt a rush of relief that her demons were gone. That's how it should be.

He slid under the covers and rolled onto his side. The Cumberland mine would close soon, and he had to find a job good enough to support his family. Every time he turned around, the children had outgrown their clothes or worn holes in their shoes. Wyoming youngsters needed heavy boots for winter or they could fall ill with croup, or worse. He recalled the horrible coughing of a neighbor's two-year-old dying of whooping cough. The burial at the edge of town in the children's cemetery with its tiny, precious grave was more than Marcello could bear to remember.

In the early dawn, Marcello dressed for work, pulling on his work pants and treading quietly to the dresser for a clean flannel shirt. Across the top of the dresser, a dim shaft of morning light illuminated the family picture Luisa had sent him from Italy. His eyes went to his parents—first Mama, then Papa. The longer he stared at Papa, the more his shame burned. What would Papa think of him, coming so close to disaster?

He had failed. He had broken the promise to make his father proud and had nearly destroyed the dream he'd promised Luisa. He was hanging by a thread, like Lucas's house suspended above its foundation.

Marcello had chased his dream since coming to America, with a determination that forced him to the mine every day even when his back screamed in pain and his knuckles bled. The kind of determination that ignored the grit in his mouth and settled deep in his lungs. But his family needed to build their lives on something more than his determination.

His thoughts traveled back to Italy. From his earliest memories, he'd helped feed and milk the cows, walk them to pasture every day, and bed them down every night. As soon as he could hold a spade, he tilled the rocky hillside next to his papa and brothers. He remembered digging holes and planting pear trees in the early morning when the earth smelled damp with dew. He tended crops as the sun warmed his shirtless back or drenched him in rain. He helped Papa scrape out a living from their small plot of earth—planting, tending, harvesting.

Suddenly, Marcello had his answer

CHAPTER 39

Early the next Saturday, Marcello hitched up the wagon for the two-mile ride to Mick's farm. A stiff breeze pushed wispy clouds across the bright July sky. Marcello took in the gentle slopes of the sandy hills and welcomed the peaceful scene after their week of chaos.

After the revenuers destroyed his bootlegging operation, Lucas had arranged with carpenters and brick layers to repair his house while he and his family stayed at Mick's farm. Marcello's wagon creaked as he turned down the rutted lane to the farm. When he pulled up in the yard, he saw Theresa and Julia through the kitchen window. In the backyard, children ran between the house and the barn in what looked like a game of hide and seek. Lucas opened the front door and waved from the porch.

"Morning, Lucas," Marcello called and tied his horse to a post beside the front steps.

"Morning. Come, sit." Lucas gestured to the chairs on the porch. He handed Marcello a ripe plum and kept one for himself. "Couldn't resist—Julia and Theresa are baking pies."

Marcello bit into the sweet flesh of the purple fruit and sighed. "Reminds me of back home."

"You know what I miss?" Lucas mused. "Mama's fresh-baked bread. Nothing better."

Marcello finished his plum and wiped his hands on his pants. He studied Lucas with sidelong glances to gauge his mood and found him composed, the way he often appeared when he faced problems. "How are things?"

"In a hell of a mess." Lucas leaned back in his chair.

Marcello shook his head. "And the family?"

"The boys are out of sorts. Julia's had nightmares."

Marcello locked eyes with Lucas. "It's been hard on all of us. Especially the wives."

Lucas folded his arms over his chest and gave Marcello a blistering look followed by a long silence. Shouts of the children echoed from the backyard.

Marcello brushed imaginary dirt off his pant leg and cleared his throat. "I have a proposal about your farm in Utah."

Lucas cocked an eye at Marcello. "What kind of proposal?"

"I'm ready to quit the mine, and I need a job. I want to rent your farm."

Lucas looked quizzically at Marcello.

Marcello tried to read his brother. Everything Lucas had built over the past six years was now destroyed, yet he showed no sign of defeat. He had been disgraced, but showed no trace of humiliation or regret. Even in failure, Lucas commanded respect.

"If I worked the farm," Marcello continued, "it would give me a new start."

"I'm facing court, maybe even jail." Lucas paused for the briefest moment. "What kind of deal you thinking about?"

"I buy the seed and equipment and rent the land from you at a fair rate. I reap the harvest—good or bad."

"And the farmhouse?" Lucas asked.

"Rent free." Marcello kept his gaze steady. He didn't know what Lucas was worth, but his cash reserves appeared endless. Lucas had already promised Angelo and Mick payment for their troubles with the feds. Both brothers had scrambled, just like Marcello, to move their moonshine ahead of the feds' raid.

Renting the Utah farm was Marcello's bargaining chip.

Lucas rose and stepped to the porch railing. He pushed his hands deep into his pockets and gazed at the prairie. Finally, Lucas straightened his shoulders and spoke. "There's an old tractor in the barn at the Utah farm. Not sure how well it runs." He turned and extended his hand. "We have a deal."

Marcello grasped Lucas's hand firmly. "Deal."

"I don't have a lot of choices right now," Lucas said, his hazel eyes unflinching, "but that will change."

"What do you mean?" Marcello frowned.

"We'll see what happens in court, but I'm not finished. Far from it."

Marcello inhaled sharply. "You're not thinking of bootlegging again, are you?" he asked, challenging his older brother.

"I'm not saying that—"

"Don't do it, Lucas." Marcello's face flushed hot, and he exploded, "Don't even think about it. You've put this family through enough!"

"Whoa, Marcello, calm down," Lucas said, surprised at his brother's outburst. "I have some unfinished business to take care of, that's all."

Marcello unclenched his fists and took a breath.

Lucas continued. "When the feds searched Mick's farm for moonshine, they overlooked something."

"What?" Marcello asked, dreading the answer.

"Ten barrels hidden under the barn floor."

Snow-covered peaks glistened in the August morning sun as Dominic drove Marcello through the Wasatch Mountains in Utah. The Studebaker's motor strained on the one-lane road in its climb to the summit. Patches of melting snow dotted the roadside. Marcello turned up his collar against the rush of cool air on their descent to Salt Lake City. From there, they turned north on a gravel road to Clearfield to see Lucas's farm.

"Mighty nice-looking country," Dominic said, admiring the mountain range.

Marcello nodded and gazed across the valley. A sparkling stream meandered through the surrounding pastures; lush grass spread from its banks to the edges of hay fields. "Luisa will love it here."

Marcello pulled a paper from his jacket with directions to the farm. Dominic turned off the road north of Clearfield and followed a dirt road west for one mile. He turned onto a lane that led to a white frame house with a wide front porch. Paint peeled around the door frame. A red barn stood to the side of the property farther up the driveway.

"This has to be it," said Dominic and turned off the motor. "Looks like nobody's home."

"Lucas said his tenant was moving. Maybe he's already left."

They climbed out of the car and walked to the edge of the field. "Have you ever seen so much farmland?" Marcello said, his arms spread wide. "In Italy you'd be lucky to own a little piece of land flat enough to till."

"No rocks in the soil, either," Dominic added.

Marcello crouched and scooped up a handful of dirt. In a good year, the fields on this farm would produce enough crops to support his family. He was sure of it.

They walked toward the house. "Know what I'm thinking?" Marcello asked.

"That you like the place?" Dominic grinned.

"I'll sell my cows and replace them when we move here. I'm going to teach the boys to be dairy farmers."

"What do they think about that?"

"Haven't told them yet." He pictured their resentment at rising before dawn to milk the cows and remembered his own grumbling as a youngster. It would be good for them, he thought with a smile. "I'll plant grapes, and Luisa can show Sophia how to make preserves."

"Aren't you getting ahead of yourself? What if Lucas wants to move out here some day?"

"He might, but he has jail time ahead of him. He wants Julia and the boys to stay with Mick until he's out. I think they'll stay where they are for a while."

They climbed the steps to the porch that wrapped the front of the house, and Marcello stopped to take in the view. The rugged range of snow-capped mountains rose in the distance beyond the farm fields. The porch was the perfect spot to sit with Luisa in the evening and reflect on the day. He took a deep breath of sweet mountain air. This farm was a new beginning, and his thoughts circled back to Lucas. Marcello had paid a price for choosing to follow his oldest brother without questioning the consequences. Funny how this chance for a new beginning had come from that same brother.

The children played outside in the fading summer light when Marcello and Dominic arrived home two evenings later. The aroma of roast beef and vegetables filled the kitchen when they walked through the door.

"Tell me everything," Luisa insisted as she ladled stew into their bowls while Marcello and Dominic washed up.

Marcello pulled his chair to the table, grabbed a warm biscuit, and spread it with butter. He took a bite and licked the drippings on his fingers. "The mountains look like the ones back home, the tops covered with snow. The farm's in the middle of a valley with natural springs." He blew on his steaming bowl and picked up his spoon.

"We figured it's about a hundred miles from here, give or take," Dominic said.

Luisa furrowed her brow. "That far?" She turned to Marcello, then Dominic. "You'd come to visit us, wouldn't you, Dominic?"

"Sure. And I'd bring your family—as many as can fit in the car."

"Promise?" Luisa barely contained her excitement.

"Anything for your beef stew." Dominic winked before shoveling in a spoonful.

Marcello continued. "The house has a sitting room and three bedrooms—"

"Three bedrooms?" Luisa sat up in her chair, the idea taking hold. "That means Sophia could move out of the boys' room and have her own."

"It's wired, too," said Dominic. "Lucas told us they got electricity out there last year."

"Three bedrooms, *and* electricity." Luisa pressed her hands to her chest and glowed at the prospect of a larger, modern house.

Marcello chuckled. "I knew you'd like it. The only drawback—we won't have neighbors next door like we do here."

"But there's a town?"

"Clearfield's two miles away. That's where the school is. There's a farm down the road from Lucas's, but we didn't stop in." Marcello paused and looked at her. "I know leaving the family will be hard."

"Just as long as we can visit each other. That will make it bearable."

Marcello finished his stew. He leaned toward Luisa and took her hand, his brown eyes bright with excitement. "The land looks good. The house needs new shingles and a few repairs, but the barn is well built. We could start out with two or three cows, get a few chickens—"

"It would be like back home." Luisa hadn't thought of renting Lucas's farm as a return to their past and was surprised when she realized that's exactly what it was. Mountains. Cows. Living off the land.

An idea came to her. "Could we plant grapes?"

Marcello strode confidently into the First National Bank of Kemmerer with a black Gladstone bag and stood in line at the teller's window. Bathed in heat and dust during the wagon ride from Cumberland, he ignored the sweat dotting his forehead and the shirt sticking to his back.

The line moved quickly, and Marcello was greeted at the teller's window by a young man wearing a suit and wire spectacles. "Good morning, Mr. Corsi," the teller said. "Nice to see you again. How may I help you today?"

Marcello reached into his shirt pocket and pulled out a worn passbook. "I'd like to withdraw my savings and close my account." Marcello pushed the passbook under the bars of the window toward the teller.

"All right." The teller opened the passbook. "Are you leaving town? We've had a number of families move away, what with the mine closing."

"We're moving to Utah."

The teller turned the pages of the passbook and nodded. "That will be a big change for—oh, my." He read the last entry and looked up at Marcello.

"Something wrong?" Marcello frowned.

"No, but your last deposit brings your account total to five hundred and twenty dollars and seventy-four cents."

A smile spread across Marcello's face. "That's right."

"And you want to withdraw all of it right now?"

"Yes, sir. We're leaving day after tomorrow."

"Mr. Corsi, would you step over here please?" The teller motioned for Marcello to step out of line.

"Something wrong?" Marcello asked for the second time.

"I'll only be a moment," said the teller and disappeared into a room behind the teller's window.

Marcello waited nervously and shifted his bag from one hand to the other with a growing sense of worry. He was sure his passbook was accurate. He always double-checked each deposit and added the numbers himself, then compared them to the bank statement.

When the teller returned, he whispered to Marcello, "It's best to take care of this in the manager's office." Marcello swiped perspiration from his forehead and followed the teller to the office, where he was greeted by a middle-aged gentleman in a dark suit and tie.

"How do you do, Mr. Corsi. I'm Mr. Bradley, bank manager." He shook Marcello's hand and gestured toward a table next to an oak rolltop desk cluttered with papers. A large black safe stood in the corner of the small room. "Mr. Johnson explained you're closing your account."

"Is everything all right?" Marcello asked.

"Everything is in order. We have a policy to transfer large amounts of money to our customers in private." He leaned toward Marcello. "Safer that way."

Marcello's shoulders relaxed. Mr. Bradley took the twenty-dollar bills stacked on the table and counted aloud, five hundred and twenty dollars, finishing with seventy-four cents in coin.

With a bounce in his step, Marcello walked out of the bank minutes later with neatly banded twenty-dollar bills in the bottom of his bag. He crossed the street where Tony waited with the wagon in the shade near the dry goods store. Marcello placed the bag onto the seat, and they climbed aboard.

Tony slapped the reins, and the horse lumbered forward. "How much money do we have, Papa?"

Marcello leaned over and whispered, "Five hundred and twenty dollars."

Tony's head whipped around. "Really?" He stared incredulously at Papa and then at the bag beside him as though it were a treasure chest.

"That's every penny I've earned since I came to Wyoming," Marcello said with pride, "and don't tell your sister and brothers how much money we have."

Tony nodded, his eyes big. "Are we rich, Papa?"

Marcello smiled. "No, but it's enough money to buy ten acres of land."

"Is ten acres a lot?" Tony asked.

"It's a good start. Someday I'll have enough money to own a farm," he nodded decisively.

Tony looked at the bag once more and guided the horse down Main Street with a grin on his face. He turned to Papa and mouthed "five hundred dollars."

They burst into laughter.

Chapter 40

Tomas and Roberto bolted into the kitchen. "The truck's here!" Tomas grabbed Luisa's hand and pulled her to the window. "See?"

Luisa peered out at the Reynolds Moving Company truck pulling up in front of their house.

Roberto ran to Marcello, who hefted a box of crockery from the floor. "They're here, Papa."

"I heard," said Marcello. "Hold the door." Roberto scampered ahead and pushed it wide. Marcello set the box on the porch beside crates filled with skillets, buckets, work boots, and tools. "Good afternoon." Marcello nodded to two muscular young men who hopped out of the truck.

Luisa propped open the front door and eyed the twins. "Stay out of the way, you two."

"Yes, Mama," the boys chimed and positioned themselves in a prime spot beside the truck as the movers opened the rear door.

"And don't get dirty," she called over her shoulder. Last night everyone had taken a turn bathing in the galvanized tub in preparation for their trip. The twins were so excited about riding on a train, it was past ten o'clock before they fell asleep. This morning they had put on freshly laundered shirts and combed their hair in place. Luisa had pinned two oversized white bows in Sophia's hair after brushing out the tangles in her blond curls.

"Tony, can you get the tub onto the porch?" Luisa asked.

"Sure, Mama," Tony answered and swiped at his mop of dark hair falling over his forehead. He grabbed the handle of the tub and dragged it from the kitchen out the front door.

"When you're through helping Papa, there are clean clothes on the dresser."

A warm breeze stirred through the open windows, now without curtains, while Luisa and Sophia packed food for the train ride to Utah. "We'd better hurry or they'll take the table out from under us," Luisa said. Sophia giggled and sliced the loaf of crusty wheat bread. Luisa wrapped cold polenta in a cheese cloth and placed it in a tin. She looked up and caught her breath. The movers carried her trunk out of the house.

They were leaving Cumberland.

Competing emotions tugged at her heart. She was eager for their new life on the farm where her daily fears for Marcello's safety would be over. A gentler climate would replace the harsh Wyoming winters, and towering mountains would fill that tiny fissure in her heart that longed for home. In spite of fear and heartache from Marcello's bootlegging, Luisa now found herself grateful to Lucas. He'd provided a new opportunity for their entire family, and Marcello was himself again, happier than he had been in ages.

But sadness tinged her joy. Marcello's family was her family now, and she felt as close to Rosa, Julia, and Theresa as if they were sisters born under the same roof. She had relied on them while she grew into her new home. With the death of her dear brother, the only link to her own family in America was gone. All the more reason to hold Marcello's family close. Luisa blinked away tears

"What's wrong, Mama?" Sophia's blue eyes clouded with concern.

"It's nothing, dear. Let's finish up."

Marcello stepped into the kitchen, a grin on his face. "Look who's here."

Ian MacGregor followed Marcello inside. "Wanted to say goodbye before you left."

Luisa wiped her hands on her apron and smiled at the burly Scotsman with bushy red hair whom she would forever think of as her savior. Jones's attack six years ago had shattered her world. The first time Luisa saw Jones after the attack was as he left the company store while she was shopping for shoes with Tony. The sight of him sent her heart shuddering. It took her months to walk past the boardinghouse without reliving that horrible day. The few times she saw Jones around town, he never looked in her direction, and over time, her confidence had returned. One day the next summer, a friend told Marcello that Jones had moved from Cumberland. They never saw him again.

"We're going to miss you," Ian said to Marcello. "Hard to replace a worker like you."

Marcello shook Ian's hand warmly and replied, "There's no finer man than you anywhere." There was a catch in Marcello's voice.

Luisa stood in front of Ian, searching for words as she looked into the face of this extraordinary man. He thought himself nothing but ordinary, just a neighbor who lived down the street, but she and Marcello knew otherwise. She steadied her voice. "You have a special place in my heart," she whispered. "Thank you." She leaned forward and kissed him on both cheeks.

Marcello and Luisa stood in front of their house and watched the moving truck disappear on the road out of Cumberland.

"There goes everything we own," Luisa said, a trace of worry in her voice.

"Not everything," Marcello whispered. "Don't forget about the Gladstone bag." He wrapped his arm around Luisa's waist and smiled into her dark eyes. She looked beautiful in her new navy dress, her thick black hair swept back in a loose coil, her cheeks flushed with the afternoon warmth. She smiled at him. The loss of Roberto and Jim no longer haunted them. They were ready for the future and the dreams waiting for them. Life burst with goodness.

The children waited impatiently beside Dominic's car, their clothes still relatively clean except for Tomas's smudged trousers. "Look, Papa," shouted Roberto. "There's Uncle Mick." Down the street rumbled Mick's wagon with Theresa, their daughters, and Julia with her three sons.

"All packed up?" Mick called as he pulled the wagon to a stop.

"The truck just left. Can't even offer you a glass of dago red."

Mick laughed. "No need." He unwound his long legs and climbed out of the wagon.

"We brought a little something for the trip," Theresa said and handed Luisa a round of creamy white cheese. "I know how the children gobble it up."

"And my chokecherry jam," Julia said, offering two jars.

"The children will have enough to eat all the way to the farm," Luisa said. "Thank you."

"Come sit on the porch while I change," Marcello said. He walked through the empty house to the bedroom and changed into a clean shirt and trousers Luisa had left for him. He raked his fingers through his hair and took one last look at the room. It was barren without furnishings, but rich with memories. This was where Roberto and Tomas were born. Marcello smiled, remembering his astonishment at their birth and the pride he felt. His mind shifted to another time when the room was a place of unbearable sadness, where Luisa wept for Roberto, and he mourned for Jim.

Marcello's eyes settled on the trap door, and he thought of Lucas, the only brother who wouldn't be here today to see him off to Utah. He was serving a nine-month sentence in the county jail in Kemmerer. Marcello remembered every detail of his visit to see Lucas yesterday. He had walked through the small brick building that served as a jail, an office in front and two cells in the rear. The sight of Lucas behind bars had shaken Marcello, but he'd forced cheerfulness into his voice.

"Good to see you, Lucas."

"Good to see you, little brother," Lucas replied.

Lucas wore a plain cotton shirt and trousers, his auburn hair rumpled, stubble on his jaw. Behind Lucas's brave face, Marcello saw a crushing sadness. He reached through the bars, and Lucas gripped his hand tightly. "I'm glad you came, Marcello."

"Of course I came." Marcello's voice broke. He stared at the floor, then raised his eyes. "I'd never leave without saying goodbye."

"You'll do well on the farm. I know it." Lucas managed a smile. "When I get out of here, I'll come check up on you."

"Promise?"

"I'll bring the family, too."

They held their gaze, their hands clasped. Marcello wanted to say so many things, but he couldn't find the words. He wanted Lucas to know he was sorry about the way things had turned out. He hoped Lucas could pick up the pieces of his life when he was released from jail, but Marcello was worried. He had heard troubling rumors that Lucas's former network of employees was building a new still in preparation for his release from jail. He and Lucas hadn't spoken about bootlegging since the day at Mick's farm, and that was the way Marcello wanted it.

Marcello shook off the memory of the visit and turned to

leave the bedroom. His eyes caught a glint of metal on the floor where the chest of drawers had stood. He picked up a coin and turned it over in his palm. It was the lira his father had given him the day he left Italy. By any measure, it was a small gift, a coin to fall through the planks of a bare floor and be lost forever. In Marcello's eyes, however, it was a legacy of his father's love and selflessness. He placed the rescued treasure in his shirt pocket, picked up the black bag, and left the house.

When Marcello stepped onto the porch, the five o'clock shift was over, and the crowd in his yard had grown. Angelo, Rosa, and their children were there with Oleg and Elsa from next door, along with their four sons, plus the Delgatos, Constantines, and Kaucheks from down the street. Isaac Johnson and Sullivan, still wearing pit clothes, stood nearby. Even Mrs. Broski and her husband were there with five children in tow.

Dominic brought two cardboard suitcases to the car and set them on the floor of the backseat. He turned to Marcello and Luisa. "Ready whenever you are."

Luisa clutched her hankie. She stood, looking into the faces of the people she loved, and tears slid down her cheeks. Rosa, Julia, and Theresa went to her, and the four women wrapped their arms around each other, their tears falling silently on each other's shoulders. *"Mia familia, mie sorelle,"* Luisa whispered.

"I will miss you," Rosa cried softly.

"Come see us?" Luisa asked them.

"We'll come," Theresa whispered.

Julia nodded, unable to speak.

The aunts turned to Tony, Sophia, Roberto, and Tomas, kissed them on both cheeks, and made them promise to be good and help their mama and papa.

Luisa reached for Elsa and the two hugged, fresh tears brimming in Luisa's eyes. *"Chi trova un amicotrova un tesora."*

Elsa leaned back and smiled. "I never could understand Italian." They burst into laughter while they wiped away their tears.

"It means 'He who finds a friend, finds a treasure.' " Luisa hugged Elsa again and whispered, "I never understood Russian, either."

Mick and Angelo stood beside the car, and Marcello pulled them into a hug. He looked up at Mick and said simply, "Thank you."

"For what?" Mick asked, puzzled.

"You helped me start over when I came here. I'll never forget that."

"You worked hard, Marcello. You did it yourself." Mick kissed him on both cheeks. "Safe journey, brother."

Marcello turned to Angelo. "I don't know what I would have done without you after Jim died."

"Me, either." Angelo's voice choked with emotion. He took a deep breath. "Do me a favor when you get to Utah."

"Anything," said Marcello.

"Keep your eye open for good farmland. I might be interested in buying."

"Only if you come and see it for yourself."

Angelo nodded, his eyes misting over. "Godspeed, Marcello." They embraced once more.

Marcello's family climbed into the car, and Dominic pulled away from the house as Marcello raised his arm in a final farewell. The children strained in their seats and waved wildly to their cousins and friends, who chased the car down the street.

Dominic drove past the company store, which was now boarded shut. Luisa leaned from the backseat toward Marcello. "Remember the first time I shopped there? So many languages, it made my head spin." Across the street, the American flag fluttered on the pole in front of the town hall, but the monthly meetings had ceased. The doctor's office stood empty now that Doc Chapman worked in Spring Hill full-time.

Tony, Sophia, Roberto, and Tomas waved until the car turned on the road out of town, and everyone disappeared from view. Marcello stared as they passed the dark entrance of the mine that operated with a crew half its original size. The coal train came every other day to fill their cars from the tipple above the track. There was no train today, and the mine was strangely quiet.

Marcello remembered again his grand plan to become the best miner ever to dig coal and work his way through the ranks to crew chief. He hadn't known mining was filthy, backbreaking, deadly. He hadn't known surviving the mine was its own reward. But survive he had, and that made him proud.

Proud he overcame the danger he faced every day and proud of every dollar in the bag he held in his lap. Proud he belonged to a brotherhood of miners, the toughest men he'd ever known, who conquered their differences—even hatred—through the punishing work of the mine. Before the movers had finished packing their belongings, Marcello insisted they make room for his pickax and four-foot drill in the truck. He never wanted to forget this place and these men.

He turned around in his seat and looked at the eager faces of his children. Luisa smiled, her eyes bright, and touched his shoulder. White, billowy clouds gathered in the hazy blue sky, and the warm August breeze brushed across their faces. Marcello took in the air and gazed ahead as they rumbled down the dusty road toward their new life.

FACT OR FICTION IN *MARCELLO'S PROMISE*

Sailing to America. At the turn of the century, many male immigrants settled in America and sent for their wives and sweethearts once they were established. Like Marcello and Luisa, my grandparents sailed to America three years apart. I used their actual sailing vessels for Marcello and Luisa. My grandfather arrived on *La Provence,* on October 23, 1909, my grandmother and father on *La Savoie* on December 2, 1912.

Marcello in the Kansas coal mines. In the late nineteenth century, coal mining was a major industry in southeast Kansas. The area became known as the "Little Balkans" from the influx of immigrants. The miners' strike Marcello experienced in 1916 was fictional, but in 1921 the United Mine Workers of America went on strike to improve wages and working conditions. The state took over operation of the mines and hired volunteers to replace the striking miners. From December 12 to 14, 1921, a group of wives, mothers, and sisters drew national attention when they marched on the coal camps to protest the hiring of "scab" labor. They became known as the Amazon Army and numbered nearly six thousand at one point. The women blocked the entrances to coal mines and used buckets of red pepper flakes to encourage the workers to stay away. While supporting the strike, they sang patriotic songs and carried American flags to show they were true Americans. Some women were arrested for what was considered shocking behavior at the time. Within the coal camps, these women were heroes.

Cumberland. There were two Cumberlands—No. 1 and No. 2, where my grandparents lived—that opened in 1901 and closed in 1930 and 1927 respectively. They were located a mile and a half apart, with a Catholic church standing halfway between. Three hundred and fifty people lived in each town, young immigrants from Italy, Russia, Austria, Poland, Finland, Wales, and Scotland. Both towns had a company store, an LDS church, and a school with grades kindergarten through twelve.

Most of the sons went to work in the mines before they finished high school, to help support their families. In the early years, the camp foreman acted as doctor. Eventually, one company doctor served both towns, usually a young man beginning his practice. The nearest hospital was twelve miles away in Kemmerer, impossible to reach in winter except with horses. Years ago, I walked the deserted hills where Cumberland once stood with my sister and cousins. Pieces of metal and broken crockery poked through the sandy soil, ghostly remnants of a vibrant community. I retrieved a square piece of iron, possibly the damper from an old kitchen range, that sits on my kitchen hearth today, a reminder of my father's childhood home.

Montgomery Ward Catalog. Montgomery Ward and Sears catalogs were more than wish books for families living in the mining towns. For rural Americans in the early twentieth century, they provided contact with the outside world and gave the folks purchasing power, much as the Internet serves today's shoppers. Remember Roberto's mail-order bride? That happened to a young bachelor who had just arrived in Cumberland from the old country. His friends convinced him to order a "bride" from the catalog. Like Roberto, he received a dress in the mail, much to the amusement of his friends.

Roberto's death. Many men like Roberto died in mine accidents in southwest Wyoming at the turn of the century. One of the worst disasters was at Frontier No. 1 mine at Kemmerer on August 14, 1923, when ninety-nine men were entombed with a raging fire in a shaft following an explosion. Investigations later concluded the accident was caused when a fire boss tried to relight the flame in his safety lamp with a match that ignited accumulated gas. Whenever someone was killed in the mines, work halted for a day of mourning. The bereaved family dressed in black and hung a black ribbon on the front door. My grandfather's brother-in-law and my grandmother's brother were both killed in mine accidents.

Ludlow Massacre. In chapter 26 Marcello refers to the Ludlow Massacre, which occurred on April 20, 1914. It was part of a larger conflict, the Colorado Coalfields War, which lasted from September 1913 to December 1914 and was the deadliest strike in the country's history. The findings of a congressional investigation into this tragedy were influential in promoting child labor laws and the eight-hour day.

Winemaking. Every fall, a carload of grapes from California provided fresh fruit for the coal camps and grapes for the large number of Italians to make wine. When fermentation was finished, the pulp was discarded by each winemaker, sometimes carefully buried, sometimes dumped in the alleys behind the houses. The scent of grape pulp attracted the cows that grazed on the surrounding prairie. They loved the pulp and ate it with relish. More than once my father watched their cows stagger home, intoxicated, which necessitated a reminder to careless neighbors and a good night's rest for the cows.

Holidays. Easter, Halloween, Labor Day, Thanksgiving, and Christmas were holidays celebrated in Cumberland. The biggest celebration of the year, however, was Independence Day, the Fourth of July. The day began with a cannon blast and was filled with festivities like those described in chapter 27, a tribute from a community of immigrants to their new country, America.

Dear Reader,

I love family stories.

I read somewhere that in each family there is one who seems called to be the storyteller, who shows the way forward by shedding light on the past. Families are a treasure trove of stories, and I feel privileged to share Marcello and Luisa's journey with you. I urge you to look to your own family and explore its past, dream its future, honor its goodness. We discover ourselves in the process; it is who we are.

Wherever you are on life's path, tell your story, and keep the dreams alive.

Jane

ABOUT THE AUTHOR

Jane Coletti Perry grew up in a small midwestern college town. With a degree in English and a love of history, she has written a memoir, "Finding Sarah Jane," published in *Patchwork Path: Treasure Box,* and her articles have appeared in *The Best Times,* a suburban Kansas City periodical. Jane and her husband have two children and five grandchildren. They have lived throughout the United States and England, where she has sung in church choirs, symphony choruses, and women's ensembles. She loves celebrating anything with the family and kayaking at their summer lake house. Her fantasy is to be on *Dancing with the Stars for Grandmas.* This is her first novel. Visit her website at www.janecolettiperry.com.

The employees of Five Star Publishing hope you have enjoyed this book.

Our Five Star novels explore little-known chapters from America's history, stories told from unique perspectives that will entertain a broad range of readers.

Other Five Star books are available at your local library, bookstore, all major book distributors, and directly from Five Star/Gale.

Connect with Five Star Publishing

Visit us on Facebook:
https://www.facebook.com/FiveStarCengage

Email:
FiveStar@cengage.com

For information about titles and placing orders:
(800) 223-1244
gale.orders@cengage.com

To share your comments, write to us:
Five Star Publishing
Attn: Publisher
10 Water St., Suite 310
Waterville, ME 04901